VICE AND VIRTUE

Books by Libby Klein

Poppy McAllister Mysteries

CLASS REUNIONS ARE MURDER

MIDNIGHT SNACKS ARE MURDER

RESTAURANT WEEKS ARE MURDER

THEATER WEEKS ARE MURDER

WINE TASTINGS ARE MURDER

BEAUTY EXPOS ARE MURDER

ANTIQUES AUCTIONS ARE MURDER

MISCHIEF NIGHTS ARE MURDER

SILENT NIGHTS ARE MURDER

Published by Kensington Publishing Corp

LIBBY KLEIN

VICE AND VIRTUE

KENSINGTON
PUBLISHING CORP.

kensingtonbooks.com

KENSINGTON BOOKS are published by

Kensington Publishing Corp.
900 Third Avenue
New York, NY 10022

All Kensington titles, imprints and distributed lines are available at special quantity discounts for bulk purchases for sales promotion, premiums, fund-raising, educational or institutional use. Special book excerpts or customized printings can also be created to fit specific needs. For details, write or phone the office of the Kensington Special Sales Manager: Kensington Publishing Corp., 900 Third Avenue, New York, NY, 10022. Attn. Special Sales Department. Phone: 1-800-221-2647.

KENSINGTON and the K with book logo Reg. US Pat & TM Off.

Library of Congress Control Number: 2024951043

ISBN: 978-1-4967-4855-3

First Kensington Hardcover Edition: May 2025

ISBN: 978-1-4967-4857-7 (ebook)

10 9 8 7 6 5 4 3 2 1

Printed in the United States of America

The authorized representative in the EU for product safety and compliance is eucomply OU, Parnu mnt 139b-14, Apt 123
Tallinn, Berlin 11317, hello@eucompliancepartner.com

For Dad, who gave me my love of music.

Acknowledgments

Special thanks to my beta readers who really knocked it out of the park this time.

Please follow me on all my social media, sign up for my newsletter, and listen to Layla's Playlist at libbykleinbooks.com.

VICE AND VIRTUE

Chapter 1

NOTHING SAYS YOU'VE MADE A WRONG TURN IN LIFE LIKE PLAYING "The Hokey Pokey" on electric guitar for an old couple's fiftieth wedding anniversary. My whole life has been about sex, drugs, and rock and roll—but the wrong kind of each.

The cinder block and plywood event stage at the Seahorse Lounge creaked under my hundred and thirty pounds, making me nervous that I'd crash through it as I rocked my hips in time to "The Chicken Dance" that I wailed on my guitar like Jimi Hendrix playing the national anthem.

Okay fine, a hundred and thirty-eight pounds.

The problem with being on this side of the action was my front row seat to tomorrow's regrets. The couple who would fight later because the wife's best friend was drunk and getting handsy with the husband. The teenagers sneaking champagne that had been abandoned on the banquet tables by their over-trusting elders, who in lieu of guarding the liquor, were flapping their arms like drugged birds on the dance floor. All drunk and disorderlies in the making. Today's happy family celebration would be tonight's domestic disturbance. Alcohol was always an accelerant.

It was no use saying anything. I'd learned long ago that you can't save people from their destructive behaviors. I couldn't even save myself.

I watched two boys empty leftover cocktails into a water bottle. I closed my eyes. *It's not my problem—I'm just the entertainment. I can't get involved. When I get involved people get hurt.*

I turned up the volume to drown out my nagging conscience. My father had bought me the teal-and-gold Les Paul when I'd turned sixteen many years ago. Other kids got cars. I got a custom guitar that up until six months ago had mostly collected dust in the corner. This was not how he'd intended me to use it.

I slowed the music down and started an instrumental version of "Unchained Melody." I didn't need one of the guests of honor to stroke out. Very few referrals came from dead clients.

Watching the happy couple so in love sent a stab of pain and loss through my heart. I tried to find another point of focus to distract me when a hand tapped my knee and I cast my eyes downward to a chubby face smeared with raspberry frosting.

I'd been joined on stage by a little boy with bright blue eyes and hair like a sticker bush. "Are your pants made of trash bags?"

I turned off my voice mike. "What? No. This is Italian leather." *At least it's Chinese vinyl made to look like Italian leather.*

"Why is your hair blue?"

"My hair is black. It just has blue streaks through it. Now go away."

"My mom says your name isn't really Layla. What's a gimmick?"

"It's something horrible that happens to little boys who won't let me finish my set." I looked around the ballroom for the kid's mother.

"Why do you have airplanes drawn on your arm?"

"They're hummingbirds, and they're called tattoos." Seriously. *Is no one looking for this sticky child?* I quietly made up a little ditty that matched the Righteous Brothers tune. "The Boogeyman is hiding uh-uhunder your bed. Are you afrai-aaaaaaa-ayaid?"

Unfortunately, it seemed to have the opposite effect I was going for. His eyeballs swelled to the size of the deviled eggs on the buffet table, some of which were currently stashed in a tin foil pouch in my guitar case in the restaurant kitchen. "And then what?"

"What do you mean 'and then what'? Good Lord, what are you watching on TV?"

"*Cosmic Fury Rangers.*"

"Okay, well quit it. That stuff will rot your brain."

"Ooooh." He reached up to touch one of the hummingbirds on my forearm.

"Come on, kid, I'm working." I tried to nudge him away with my foot and he sidled closer to me. I would take any kid's mother at this point.

"Are you a spinster?"

"No! Why? Did someone say I was old? I'm only thirty-seven. Go wash your face."

"My dad said I don't have to as long as I leave my sister alone."

I adulterated another verse to shoo him away. "Spi-iya-ders lay eggs in your braa-aya-ain when you go to-oo slee-eee-eep." *Ugh. He's hugging my leg now. Somebody kill me.*

I faded out the final chords as a woman in a gold sequined cocktail dress approached the stage with her hand out. "Come, Jeremy. It's time for Grannie and Pop Pop to cut their cake."

"Bye, Jeremy." *Wait till they get a load of Jeremy's handiwork with the raspberry frosting on the bottom layer there.*

Jeremy's mom gave me a nod. "We're going to do the toasts now. When we come back, maybe you can play something everyone can dance to. Do you know anything by Taylor Swift?" I shook my head and she sighed. "We could have had my boss's grandson's group, but they were booked until Christmas. I bet they would have been Swifties."

"Your mom and dad seem to be having a good time with the classics." I gave her the start of an encouraging smile.

She frowned. "You have a few minutes if you need the bathroom or anything."

I flipped the amp to standby and slipped my guitar strap off my shoulder. What I needed was a steady paycheck and some vegetables, but I would take something from the bar. I crossed the shabby orange sherbet dining room, grabbed the Deer Park cocktail from the tween thieves giggling in the corner, and marched up to the bartender. "Hey, George. Club soda and lime."

He poured my drink, nodding toward the anniversary party room. "How's it goin' in there?"

"It's not halftime at the Super Bowl but it's a living."

The Seahorse was an old dive-y kind of place that really wanted to be a fancy wedding reception destination but couldn't quite make it out of the low-budget prom zone. Because the people who booked events here were used to lowering their standards, I hoped those sentiments would be passed to me as well. I leaned my guitar against an empty barstool and chucked the offending water bottle into the trash before I could decide to chug it just to dull the pain of this night.

A snicker to my right caught my ear and I turned to see the most stunning man I'd ever laid eyes on. Skin a warm russet brown, eyes the color of the Caribbean Sea, eyelashes that Smashbox would bankrupt themselves to replicate in a tube. He was relaxed in that way that said he was comfortable in his own skin. Something I hadn't been—well, ever. "Something amuse you?"

He smiled and little crinkles formed in the corner of his eyes. "I just never heard a heavy metal rendition of 'The Bunny Hop' before."

Is he flirting with me? His shirt color matches his eyes to make them pop. He knew he was gorgeous and that made him trouble. No wedding ring or wedding ring tan line made him convenient. Sitting alone at the cash bar just outside a big happy family event where the alcohol was free on the other side of the door, made him a loner—and that made him perfect. I took the seat next to him. "You should hear my 'Alley Cat' on the electric violin."

He chuckled and his eyes sparkled as if on command. "I won't be able to get that thought out of my head all night." He ran a finger around the rim of his long-neck bottle, and I noticed he didn't have a cell phone attached to his hand like a normal person sitting alone would. "How long have you been playing?"

"My whole life."

"And what is that? Thirty years?"

"Give or take." I nodded toward the banquet room. "You could ask little Jeremy. He's got loose lips."

He laughed. "I take it Jeremy doesn't have a career with Homeland Security ahead of him?"

"God, let's hope not. Are you a guest of the anniversary couple or just trolling for single seniors?"

His smile flashed a playful spark. He was having fun teasing me. "Don't knock the three P.M. early bird special until you've tried it."

"I'll have to take your word for that. Unless you want to call it breakfast. Then I'm all in."

He swiveled toward me with a lazy smile and his eyes burned into mine with an intensity I hadn't seen from a man in a long time. "I'm always up for spending the day in bed."

An electric current shot through my body. "Now you're just bragging."

"It's not bragging if you can do it."

I wasn't thinking about my bad choices while my back was pressed up against the brick wall in the alley. Or of his T-shirt that was currently dangling from my free hand. I was only aware of his mouth pressed against mine and the tingle working its way down my neck. It had been a long time. *I don't remember it being this hot. Maybe it's because of those eyes.*

An ominous crackle of police radio in the distance jerked the slack out of my senses. *No no no no. Come on.*

A car door slammed, followed by a second. *Anyplace else.*

Mr. Gorgeous pulled away from me, concern playing across his face. "What's wrong?"

"What? Nothing. Why would you think something's wrong?"

His breath was hot on my ear and made a shiver dance across my collarbone. "For one thing, your lips stopped moving."

Another police radio crackle could not be ignored. I pushed against his chest. "Hold that thought."

"Now?"

"I just have to check something." I went back through the emergency exit into the kitchen and peeked around at the bar. Two uniformed officers were taking their hats off and settling in.

Why does someone up there hate me? I said I was sorry.

The cook, a chubby Mexican named Carlos who made sure to send me home with banquet leftovers whenever I played here—which was often, seeing as how I lived across the street—joined me and peered around the corner. "How's the gig going tonight, Layla?"

"Fair to middling. Better than the Everett wedding a month ago but not as good as that bar mitzvah where they thought I was related to Katy Perry."

Carlos snickered. "As if. Whatchu gonna do now? You want me to go distract the cops so you can sneak back in there?"

"Too risky. I'm gonna bounce."

"You gotta get over this fear, Layla. Cops have started coming in here from the station around the corner."

"Raise prices and you'll put a stop to that." I grabbed a napkin and a pen and scrawled a note to the woman who would be signing my check.

Family Emergency. Venmo half payment to my account. I'll return for my amp later.

I paid Carlos my last ten dollars to deliver it. "She's the one in the gold sequins with the little boy covered in pink frosting."

I snatched a chicken wing and my guitar case and dove out the back door into the night.

Mr. Gorgeous was patiently waiting, leaning against the brick wall of the alley with amusement playing across his face. He smiled seductively. "Everything okay?"

Ugh. He's so beautiful. This is the kind of guy they carve statues of. Maybe the cops won't come out here. No. Too risky. Why did this dive have to be a cop hangout? I grabbed my guitar that I'd leaned against the brick wall and stashed it in the case. "I'm really sorry to do this. You have no idea."

He stepped toward me, searching my face. He ran his hand down my arm. "Are you alright? Did I do something wrong?"

I started backing away. "You were great. Really. As far as distractions go, this one would have been epic."

I turned and took off running down the alley for the back lot.

He called after me. "Wait! I didn't even get your name!"

"Trust me, it's better this way."

Chapter 2

*T*HREE MINUTES LATER, I TURNED MY ANCIENT MUSTANG AT THE pink Airstream with the window boxes of fall mums, into Lake Pinecrest Mobile Homes where I'd lived for the past six months. We had an array of class here, from the Tudor cottage on the lake to the fancy double-wides, to the rust bucket on cinder blocks that looked like a meth lab someone had rolled up and deserted before entering witness protection. My little brown trailer was somewhere in between. Closer to the meth side. Meth adjacent. I didn't ask a lot of questions before I bought it.

It had a cute stone patio and a screened porch with one brave little rosebush by the front door. It would have been charming if it weren't the place where dreams go to die. Even my garden gnome looked sad to be here, and he was wearing a jaunty hat and holding a duck.

I pulled under the carport and the Mustang ground out a cough then passed out. A pink slip of paper was taped to my front door. It had curled up on the ends from flapping in the breeze coming off the Northern Virginia highway that cut through Potomac County, but I could clearly make out the words *Late Notice* scrawled in red ink. My monthly threat to pay lot fees or get kicked out. I looked down the street and saw pink slips were attached to just about every door in my row. Agnes Harcourt, the late notice queen and trash bin Nazi, had been having an especially festive day.

I ripped the paper off my door and balled it up. Agnes needed to get a life. No one lived here because they *won* the lottery. *And seriously, consider a different paper. It's hard to be intimidated by any color used to paint a baby's room, and this one has a kitten in the corner.*

I threw my keys on the TV stand inside the door and leaned my guitar case against the gray flagstone coffee table. I'd bought this single-wide when I cashed out my pension after being formally escorted from my old job. I didn't have the energy to be choosy with the décor, but at least it was clean.

I had a small gray kitchen off to the right, with a little stove that I'd never used and a fancy microwave that I was a master at operating. The 1950s-era silver Formica table and chairs came with the trailer. I bought the gray couch and chair set in the living room when I moved in. I didn't realize they would blend in quite so well with the gray walls and aluminum blinds. If I ever lost my depth perception, the room would look totally empty except for a floating TV.

One day I was going to get around to decorating, but that's a hard sell when you're deciding between throw pillows and heat. I was pushing forty with no job, no retirement plan, and pink frosting on my leather-ish pants.

I went to the fridge and grabbed the last grape soda and my leftover corn dog from Chauncy's Grill across the highway. Then I extracted the foil-wrapped deviled eggs from my guitar case. While I nuked the corn dog, I checked the voice mails on my cell phone. Capital One reminding me that my minimum payment was due three days ago. The electric company kindly threatening me to pay my bill or face electrocution. Adam Beasley wanting to grab a coffee and catch up. *Who the heck is Adam Beasley?* I thought the days of mystery men trying to make contact were behind me. Then there was one terse reminder from Agnes about the upcoming community meeting and potluck Sunday night.

"Layla, I'm bringing my famous rhubarb pie and I want you to bring napkins. Judging from the amount of Styrofoam take-out containers you keep errantly shoving into your recycling bin, I'm sure you don't know the first thing about cooking. Let's not chance everyone getting salmonella just so you can save face."

How exactly am I supposed to bring napkins if I've been kicked out for not paying my lot fees, Agnes, you dumb twit? Getting dragged through the woods by Bigfoot would be less painful than attending this meeting. I moved here to disappear, not make friends with the cast from *America's Most Wanted*. I should have found a cabin in the woods next to some doomsday preppers. At least they'd leave me alone.

I peeled off my leather pants and tossed them over the chair in my bedroom which was—you guessed it—also gray. I hated those pants. When I got too hot under the stage lights, they creaked like a rope swing. I changed into nylon track pants just in case miracles still happened and I worked up enough motivation to go for a run around the lake after dinner.

The microwave beeped in the kitchen, and I shoved the last deviled egg in my mouth. Then I took my corn dog and soda out to the little screened porch, pulled out one of the warped chairs around my plastic table, and logged into the banking app on my phone. I jumped through a lot of security hoops to confirm that I couldn't afford a Happy Meal. If I got hacked, I hoped they'd feel sorry for me and maybe make a deposit. A better gig needed to come along soon, or I'd be busking down at the Crystal City Metro Station. I was afraid I'd be stuck competing for tips next to Afu, a Polynesian banjo player with one leg who complained incessantly about the renaming of the Washington Redskins football team, and I just did not need that kind of negativity in my life.

I needed a break. If I could get a couple of decent gigs, maybe I'd be discovered. I was definitely coming late to the party having spent the first half of my adult life working in a *very* different field. But I'd told myself I was gathering inspiration for songs or therapy sessions—whichever came first. And Debbie Harry didn't make it big until she was in her thirties. Of course, she had a whole band, and I just had a guitar, fake leather pants, and the low self-esteem to play any venue for two hundred dollars.

When I was in high school and the guidance counselor asked me where I wanted my life to be in twenty years, I'm pretty sure this was not my answer.

Careerwise I was starting at the bottom, picking up the pieces. I had been happy with my choices. Mostly. More happy than miserable. I'd been cooking along pretty good, living life on my own terms. I finally felt like I was making a difference.

Relationshipwise . . . That was another story. I'd been in love. Once. Then one day, my whole world came crashing down around me, and when the dust settled, I was alone, I had gaps in my memory, and there was no one to blame but myself.

My only silver lining was that I wasn't the nightmare cover story on a gossip magazine.

Three times was enough.

Chapter 3

I WOKE UP HOSTILE AND MURDEROUS. IT WAS 7:48 A.M., AND MY "neighbor" was at it again. Marguerite Molina lived in the blindingly pink single-wide behind me and she had a demonic rooster, which she insisted did not exist. He was on the far side of demented, and just begging to be made into buffalo wings.

Every morning, he strutted right up under my bedroom window and gave two-thirds of a crow. I was pretty sure it was the rooster equivalent of the middle finger. I needed an electric fence. Or a chicken prod. I threw open the bedroom window and yelled, "Marguerite! Get this obnoxious bird out from under my trailer! You ever heard of the noise ordinance!"

She answered from inside her mobile home. "*No hablo ingles.*"

That game won't work with me, lady. "*No me hagas matar a este gallo!* I swear I will kill this rooster as soon as I get my hands on it!"

Marguerite called back, "I don't have no rooster, you *loca!*"

I pulled on a pair of sweatpants and a tank top and slid into my flip-flops. I grabbed the broom, prepared to whack a rooster to kingdom come. Every morning, "*Erka Erka*"—then nothing. *Stupid bird never finishes on purpose.*

I threw the door open and hit the brakes. A beautiful black Lab was sitting at the bottom of my steps. His tail saluted as he turned soulful brown eyes on me.

"Hey. Where did you come from?"

His tail started to wag and thumped against my recycling bin like a bass drum. He crept up the steps to nuzzle my hand and gave me a lick.

I stroked his muzzle and checked for a collar and tags. He had none. "You are a beautiful boy. Are you lost? Do you need some water?"

He lay down at my feet and rolled onto his back. I rubbed his belly while looking around for someone who might be looking for him. "How did you get here, buddy?"

An ill wind began to blow, and I overheard voices coming down the street. "Layla Virtue needs to cut her grass. It's almost a full inch over the acceptable length." Agnes Harcourt was coming down the street with her complaint posse and their grievance clipboards.

Great. "You need to stay away from the sour old cranksters, buddy. They think they're better than the rest of us because they own the row of fancy double-wides at the back of the lake."

"I heard that, Layla. And we do not."

"Agnes. What can I do for the grass length mafia boss today? Do you really have so few problems of your own that you have to fixate on mine?"

Agnes was a prickly woman of retirement age whose hobbies appeared to be telling other people what was wrong with them and sucking on lemons. She was thin as a reed with a hawklike nose, and her mouse-brown hair was pulled into a tight bun giving her eyes the look of a botched facelift.

Her partners in nuisance today were Myrtle Jean Maud—short and plump with twisted silver hair resembling a head full of gray cinnamon buns—and Clifford Bagstrodt, who appeared to have accidentally sat on a metal rod in his youth and had never gotten around to having it removed. I suspected Myrtle was just happy to be included in something for a change because she wore a celebratory sweater covered in appliquéd squirrels.

Agnes pointed to the Lab at my feet. "Is that your dog? You know you have to submit a request for occupancy approval before you can keep a pet, Layla."

I pointed in the direction of the trailer behind me. "Tell that to Marguerite and her psychotic rooster."

"I don't got a rooster!" Marguerite called from inside her trailer.

"Shut up, Marguerite. Watch your *Telemundo*!"

Kelvin, the nine-year-old who lived across the street, came out of his grandmother Donna's trailer bouncing a basketball that was one bounce away from being totally flat.

"Kelvin. Is this my dog?"

The dog looked across the street expectantly and wagged his tail.

Kelvin shot the ball at a makeshift hoop made out of a bottomless bucket duct taped to a light pole. "Nope."

I gave Agnes a pointed look. "There you have it."

Clifford wheezed out a crackly "Disgraceful," and made a note on his clipboard.

A shadow cast over me from behind. "I am so sorry, ladies. That's my dog. He's still being trained, and he got out of his collar while I was putting out the recyclables. I didn't know about the occupancy form."

I knew that voice. I turned to match it to the face and . . . *Oh crap.*

My eyes found themselves looking at Mr. Gorgeous from the bar last night.

I knew the exact moment he recognized me because our eyes locked, and he froze with a red collar midair reaching for the dog. "You."

I felt heat rush to my face and wished I'd at least put on my nicer sweatpants that didn't have *Bodacious* written across the butt.

The dog acted like they'd been separated for ages. He hopped around in a circle while whimpering and licking the man's face.

The man broke his attention from me and hugged the dog, rubbing his ears. "Who's a good boy? Should we go play Frisbee?"

The dog barked a resounding yes to the Frisbee word.

Agnes beamed an angelic smile. "Hello again, Mr. Hayes. I hope you're settling in."

He straightened to his full height and snapped for the dog to sit. "Yes, ma'am. And thank you for the casserole."

Agnes purred. "You are most welcome. We like to be neighborly here." She cut her eyes to mine and scowled. "Most of us."

"I didn't get a casserole when I moved in."

Myrtle Jean giggled.

I ignored the clipboard trio. "I take it you're the new neighbor on my left?"

He crossed his arms over his chest and narrowed his eyes in a way that said he was not going to just be cool and let this go. "Moved in two nights ago. Funny we haven't run into each other before with me being so close and everything."

Uh-huh. Okay, Mister Overdramatic. "Yeah, funny. Well, I usually work nights."

"Sure, sure, that explains it." He touched his chest. "I'm Nick, by the way. Do you want to tell me *your* name, or wait until you get to know me better? Some people are skittish about introductions." He quirked an eyebrow to punctuate his snark.

The dog stood between us following the conversation back and forth like we were playing keep-away with a tennis ball.

I sighed. "Since we're neighbors . . . and we're bound to run into each other . . . across the street and all."

He gave me a dramatic nod. "Naturally."

"My name is Layla."

He threw his hands up. "Whoa. Too fast. At least buy me dinner before you trust me with such intimate information."

Okay, someone's gonna be a grudge holder. I tried, and failed, not to roll my eyes.

His lips quirked into an evil little grin. "I can go get in line at Denny's right after I get the dog registered if you like."

We stared into one another's eyes for a beat, willing the other to cave first. The moment was broken when Agnes put her hand on Nick's pec. "That's okay, sugar. You didn't know any better. You can come over to the office and get the occupancy form this afternoon."

Nick glanced at Agnes's hand then gave her a polite nod. "Thank you, ma'am. I will do that."

"And be more careful. Especially with whom you choose to hang out with. It doesn't take much to ruin a reputation with the management."

Myrtle Jean snickered. "Just ask your new neighbor."

Clifford reached for the dog's head and the Lab leaned away from him against my leg.

Agnes took two bright green forms from her clipboard and handed one to each of us. "We have a mandatory monthly community meeting."

Nick gave me a quizzical look.

I made a don't-pay-attention-to-Agnes-she's-crazy face and shook my head. "Didn't you know you signed a deal with Satan when you bought your trailer here? We all have to chant the by-laws under a full moon, or the water gets cut off."

Clifford wheezed again. "A pack of lies."

The dog shoved his snout into my hand for me to pet him.

Agnes didn't seem to hear me. She was busy checking her clipboard for death threats. "We meet the last Sunday of every month in the clubhouse."

I gave Nick an eye roll. "The clubhouse is that double-wide over by the office for the residents of Lake Pinecrest Mobile Homes to use for special occasions—subject to management approval. The management only ever approves Agnes's community meetings and events. Agnes is the management."

Clifford wheezed out another complaint that got lost under Myrtle Jean's squeal of hysteria. Agnes smacked her lips and shrugged, unapologetically.

Nick bit his lip to keep from laughing and gave Agnes and her dream team a nod. "Understood."

Agnes consulted her clipboard again. "Layla, I have you down for napkins. And not the salty leftover napkins from your Five Guys order either. I want nice, new napkins."

"What am I, royalty? Agnes, no one is going to eat your sour pie even if the napkins are Irish linen."

Agnes's hands flew down to her hips. "And don't pretend you're out of town this time. I saw your light on last month. Ignoring my messages is one thing. Lying to my face is a whole 'nother level of rudeness and I don't appreciate it."

Myrtle Jean gave me a sharp nod. "Rude!"

Followed by Clifford's wheeze. "Disgraceful."

I was about to launch into a stream of something inappropriate that I could regret later, but Marguerite's rooster crowed. I threw my arm out and pointed at her trailer with a sharp look to Agnes.

Marguerite called from her trailer, "It's the TV!"

Nick snorted. He saw the look I gave him and forced a straight face. "Sorry." He put his hand on the dog's back. "Come on, boy. Let's leave the nice lady to it."

Agnes, apparently, only heard Agnes's thoughts. "Recyclables go out Monday, sugar. Napkins, Layla."

I went back to my trailer and looked over my shoulder. I caught Nick looking back at me over his. In addition to being gorgeous, Nick was also wickedly funny. Not a combination I was ready for. Why did that bar have to be across the street? This distraction just became dangerous.

I opened the door and grabbed my keys. "I need a drink."

Chapter 4

"MY NAME IS MIRANDA, AND I'M AN ALCOHOLIC."

I tried to slip into the Tenth Street Saturday morning meeting without making a big scene. But like so many other things in my life, this was a crash and burn. There were twenty people whose punctuality mocked me. The Alexandria-based Second Chance Church operated a soup kitchen every other afternoon, so the room smelled of burnt coffee and taco seasoning. There was a poster hanging on the back wall that said JESUS ALREADY KNOWS EVERYTHING YOU DON'T WANT YOUR MOMMA TO FIND OUT. Next to it was a sign that said NO SMOKING, NO CUSSING. THIS IS GOD'S HOUSE.

I lowered myself onto one of the metal folding chairs in the back by the coffeepot and it screamed like a crypt being opened by Indiana Jones. Everyone turned around.

Miranda, the meeting organizer, stopped sharing and frowned in my direction. She patted awkwardly at her French twist then reached for her neck. Miranda was perpetually uptight about most things. Punctuality was just a lone grain of sand on the seashore of her pet peeves.

I mouthed, "Sorry," and moved over a row closer to the wall listing the soup kitchen times of operation and outreach programs.

Miranda cleared her throat and tapped her fingers on the podium at the front of the community room. "Lord, give me the serenity to accept . . ."

I deep sighed. Miranda's serenity prayer was on speed dial.

A small Asian woman in designer jeans and a one-shoulder red flowy top slid into the seat next to me and whispered, "Can you imagine playing a drinking game for every time Miranda has a meltdown during a meeting?"

"I'd have to Uber home."

The woman laughed under her breath. "At least she finally lost that stupid serenity scarf she wears all the time. We've never officially met. I'm Scarlett."

She held out a hand sporting a glitzy manicure and a two-carat diamond. I offered my hand of calluses and jagged bitten nails in return. "Layla."

Scarlett continued whispering even though someone in the row ahead of us had shushed her. "I love your hair."

"Thank you."

"Not everyone can carry off the shoulder-length blue-black bob, but it looks amazing on you."

I was pretty sure that was a compliment, and I wondered if I should say something about her hair. "Yours is very . . . straight . . . In a nice way."

She nodded and the crystals in her eyeglass frames twinkled under the fluorescent lights above. "I've seen you around. I've been trying to introduce myself after the meetings, but you leave really fast. That's why I thought I'd better grab you now."

I felt a familiar force of fear wind out of my chest and shroud me with invisible body armor. I'd tried to have women friends in the past, but it never worked out. This woman talking to me now was a ticking time bomb of disappointment. I braved a smile that I intended to appear sincere, while relaying the message that I didn't want to talk further. "I usually work nights."

"Oh, where do you work?"

"All over."

Her head bobbed as she waited for more of an answer.

I looked around for an empty seat to move to because of my sudden allergies to . . . being back here. "I'm a musician."

"Very cool. What do you play? Are you playing anywhere to-night?"

Miranda banged the podium with the heel of her hand. She

pursed her lips and looked from me to Scarlett. "Who would like to go next?"

I did not want to go next. I did not want to go at all. I much preferred to lurk quietly in the shadows. But seeing as how this annoying little woman was determined to bond over our mutual misfortune of being in AA together, I figured sharing about last night's disaster was better than letting her braid my hair. I saw this as my lifeline and raised my hand.

I made my way to the front and gripped the sides of the podium so it couldn't sprout wings and fly away. "Hi, I'm Layla. I'm an alcoholic. I know I don't share often, but I've been sober for six months. Some of you might know that I'm a musician. Last night I had a gig at the Seahorse Lounge."

Heads bobbed around the room. Of course, this crowd would be familiar with the Seahorse. Any place that valued budget over quality was right up our alley. I mean, they advertised my services, for crying out loud. If you wanted to fly under the radar as a binge drinker, the Seahorse was exactly the kind of place you'd go.

"I started out fine. Centered myself for the temptation ahead. Then the more stressful the night got, and the more liquor I saw just sitting at arm's length from me, the harder it was to say no. I really wanted a drink, but I ordered a club soda and found . . . a distraction." *No one needs to know about my reckless choices out in the alley. Just keep it to addiction issues.* "Then two cops I thought I recognized arrived and I got spooked."

There was a lot of murmuring and commiserating over my aversion to cops, as usual. It both horrified and amused me.

"I made a bad call and ran out on the gig before I got paid. Alcohol ruined my last career and I'm trying to build a new one for myself. Music was my first love even though I went another way with my life. I figured it could be my fallback career, but I fell back further than I expected. It's been a lot harder to get started than I expected. I've paid my dues in other areas, but the credit doesn't carry over to competing with high school garage bands who work for tacos." *Polite laughter. Always good. That Asian lady is still there. I can only stall for so long.*

"I know I need to get over this fear of the uniform, but it brings up a lot of stuff I still need to deal with. One day at a time—right?"

I dragged myself back to Little Mary Sunshine who looked like she wanted to join hands and jump around squealing girly stuff together, reclaimed my seat, and took a deep cleansing breath.

Scarlett nudged me. "That was really good."

I'm pretty sure it was moments like this that started my drinking in the first place. I kept my eyes straight ahead. "Thank you."

Miranda closed us out with the Serenity Prayer while Scarlett caught my eye and mimicked taking a shot. I held in a snort and had to look away. The minute the meeting was over I made a beeline for the door and a fast escape. Scarlett had attached to my hip like a conjoined twin. Then I was blocked by a supermodel with waves of honey colored hair and deep green eyes. She jumped in front of me and linked her arm with Scarlett's. "Did you notice she finally lost that passive-aggressive scarf?"

Scarlett gushed. "Good Lord, yes! I was afraid I'd have to choke her out with it one day. She prays it like rosary beads whenever she wants you to know she's annoyed."

The girl laughed a great deep honk of a laugh. "We totally need to find her a twelve-step plan for accessories."

Oh no. Now there's two of them. I reached for the door handle. "Well, it was nice meeting you both." I tried to sidestep them to break free, but Scarlett grabbed my hand. "I want you to meet Bree. Bree, this is Layla. You have to catch her quick before she escapes."

Bree had the effortless beauty of a girl in her early twenties. Her flawless alabaster face was professionally made up in a stark contrast to her raggedy nails as if she was a frequent viewer of makeup instructional videos. I'd almost bought the same long-sleeved peasant blouse and chinos from Walmart, but my lust for Funyuns blew the budget once again. I gave her a smile. "Hi."

She pulled at a section of hair that flowed past her shoulder. "I loved your share. Like, so real."

I looked longingly at the door. "That's me. Keeping it real."

Scarlett shook my wrist. "Hey. Bree and I go out for coffee

and donuts with Charisse after the meetings. You know Charisse, don't you?"

She called across the room. "Charisse! Say hi to Layla!"

I'd heard Charisse share many times. She had the most elaborate hairstyle of braids and twists that I'd ever seen. She flashed me a smile and waved.

Now there's three. It's going to be my college dorm all over again, and I only lasted three months before dropping out. I'm pretty sure you're not supposed to leave AA wanting a drink more than when you got here.

Scarlett nudged me. "We've been meaning to ask you if you want to come with. Just a fun time to chill with people who understand you."

Bree nodded heartily. "There are so few cool girls here to hang out with and the coffee here tastes like butt."

Coffee and donuts. That's like catnip for cops. Absolutely not. "I'm sorry, I can't. I have a . . . thing."

Their faces fell. Bree shrugged it off. "Okay, whatev."

Scarlett slid into narrowed eyes. "You have a thing?"

"Sorry."

"Fine. More for us. Maybe we'll see you around."

Well, that relationship ended smoother than most. I gotta get outta here.

"Oh, Layla."

Crap. It's Miranda. Don't look at her neck. "Hey there, Miranda. Sorry about earlier with the chair."

"I have a favor to ask that I think can help both of us."

"A favor?" I tried to avert my eyes to her white pantsuit or her fancy high heels with the giant pearl buckles over the toes, but my gaze kept rising to her throat. *Thanks a lot, Scarlett. Now I can't stop staring at her neck.* "What's the favor?"

I switched my gaze to the top of her head but that made her take an awkward step back and touch her French twist again. "I know. My roots need doing."

"What? No, I was just . . . I assumed your hair grew like that naturally." *Really Layla. Nice save.*

Miranda cleared her throat. "Yes, well . . . My friend, Janice, needs some entertainment for her eight-year-old's birthday party tomorrow afternoon. Do you do kids' events?"

Memories of Jeremy flooded my mind with two words and the second was *no*. Realities of my bank account pushed back with the concept of being evicted. "Sorry. I'm not really a kids' musician."

Miranda reached for her neck, patted her collarbone, and sighed. "Are you sure? She's really in a bind."

A day with kids? *Let me check the temperature of Hell and get back to you.* "I'm sorry."

It's not that I don't like kids. They just terrify me. They seem very breakable and yet somehow always sticky. Their movements are erratic, like moths. They can fly at you without warning, and I don't like any scenario where I can't predict an exit strategy.

Miranda pulled a notebook and pen from her well-worn Coach bag and wrote down a phone number. "If you change your mind, call Janice. She's rich and she pays well."

I stuffed the slip of paper into my pocket. There were limits to my desperation.

I just hadn't found them yet.

Chapter 5

I DUG OUT ENOUGH CHANGE FROM VARIOUS CREVICES IN MY CAR FOR a blue raspberry Slurpee on the way home. That would be my breakfast and lunch for the day. When I opened the front door of my trailer, an older man was sitting on my couch. He had long wavy more salt than pepper hair past his shoulders, and he was wearing very expensive ripped jeans and a vintage Zeppelin concert T-shirt. The black Lab was snuggled next to him.

"Hey, girlie."

"Dad. What are you doing here?"

"I was just in the neighborhood."

"In this neighborhood?"

He shrugged. "Sure. Why not?"

"I find that completely unlikely. It's not my birthday. Or a holiday." My father had a way of dropping in for random visits without warning, then disappearing just as suddenly.

He flashed me a charming smile. "I wanted to see my baby girl. When did you get a dog?"

"That's not my dog."

Dad leaned away from the puppy like he suspected the Lab might secretly be a magician. "Whoa. He was waiting on the front step when I got here."

The dog looked at me and thumped his tail against the sofa like a metronome. I patted my leg and the dog jumped off the couch and came to me. "It's the next-door neighbor's and he must be the world's dumbest dog if he can't remember where he lives."

The dog dropped to his belly with a grumble. He laid his head on his front paws and turned his eyes up to mine.

"That won't work with me, buddy. Big scary men have tried to get my sympathy and failed. Come on, I'll take you home."

My father crossed one leg over the other and gave me a cryptic grin. He looked older than I remembered. Tired around the eyes. He was still tall and fit with broad shoulders and a mostly-flat stomach from good genes and a pretty active lifestyle for a man who had just turned seventy. Still, something was different.

He also looked like he was up to something sneaky, and that wasn't different at all.

"I'll be right back." The dog followed me over to the blue-and-white trailer next door. I knocked and waited.

After a few seconds, Nick answered the door wearing a canvas apron and holding a wooden spoon. The aroma of tomato and basil hung heavy in the air. He looked from me to the dog. Shock registered and he spun around to check for a duplicate of the dog somewhere in his trailer. "How did you get out again?"

The dog wagged his tail and gave me a goofy smile.

"You have a Houdini here."

Nick put his hand on the dog's ruff and nudged him inside. "I'm so sorry. Where did you find him?"

"Inside my trailer."

Nick's head tilted a bit to the side as he considered the believability of my words.

"My father brought him in. He said he was hanging out around my door. He thought the dog was mine."

His brow furrowed as he looked at the dog. "Interesting."

"So, does this dog have a name, or what?"

"Not yet. Right now, he's just called Boy. Sometimes he's Fella."

The dog grumbled his displeasure with either option.

"That's a terrible name. No wonder he wants asylum."

Nick laughed. Just like last night, it made me feel like warm honey was poured over my neck and shoulders. "He's still a puppy. We're working on a name."

The dog stood next to me and shoved his head into the palm of my hand. I rubbed his ears and bent to face him. "You are a good boy. You don't want to be called Fella, do you?" He licked me on the nose.

Nick watched the dog for a long moment. His lip quirked like he was holding in a laugh. "Just out of curiosity, what would you name him?"

I looked into the black Lab's chocolate eyes. His tail started to beat against the door like a drum. "Ringo."

The dog jumped in a circle and barked, his tail flying back and forth.

Nick's eyes flew open wide as he stepped back. "Okay. We'll try it out for a while."

I bent down to face the pup again. "Goodbye, Ringo."

Ringo licked my chin.

I stood and raised my hand to Nick, trying to escape those gorgeous blue eyes before I got sucked in and agreed to do things I'd later regret. "See ya later."

Nick stepped outside and shut the door keeping the dog inside. "Layla, wait."

"What?"

He flashed a sexy smile. "Would you like to get dinner sometime? A proper date."

Danger. Danger. An image of Jacob flashed in my mind and with it came a knot of shame that threatened to bring on a full-blown panic attack. There was no way I was ready to get dinner with any man. Definitely not one that I was willing to make out with in a back alley less than twenty-four hours ago. That one-night stand would have been great. And the self-loathing the morning after the fitting penance that I deserved. But actually, *dating* was off the table. "Oh, I don't think so."

"A drink then. That's hardly a date. A mini date. We can go to the Seahorse Lounge if you want."

"Nick, trust me when I say this, you can't handle me."

"How do you know what I can handle?"

"Consider this a public service announcement."

Nick held his hands up in surrender. He grinned at me, but his eyes held a touch of sadness. "Okay then. I'll give you some space."

"Thanks."

I could feel him watching me as I crossed the tiny patch of grass from his trailer to mine. I refused to look back this time. But every cell in my body wanted to. I opened the door and Dad was holding my guitar. "Do you still play?"

"Only idiot songs."

He cradled the guitar like a child before he gently placed it back by the couch. "Those are the ones that make the most money."

"The ones that make the most money end up in Disney movies and commercials."

Dad chuckled. "I wouldn't say no to some Disney money. Hey, have you talked to your mom lately?"

"No."

His face clouded over, and he stared at the ceiling. "Which one was she again?"

"The yellow bikini from Akron."

"Oh yeah. I liked her."

I fanned my hands the length of my body through the air. "Well, yeah. Obviously."

His expression went soft, and he looked far away. "You have her gray eyes."

"Thanks." I took a seat on the couch and faced him, determined to get to the bottom of the reason for this impromptu visit. "How long are you here?"

Dad dropped into the chair. His eyes wide, and innocent. "Here on the planet?"

"I was thinking more local. Like here in my trailer."

He laughed and gave me a shrug, trying to keep things light and breezy. I was familiar with his routine. This usually came before bad news. "I thought I would stay for a few days."

"What happened to Germany?"

"Germany fell through."

"Was it Simon again?"

Dad wouldn't look at me. He was hyperfocused on the aluminum mini blinds hanging in front of my window. "Not this time."

I took a long look at him. A history of drama followed Don Virtue wherever he went. It wasn't always his fault. It was just the way of life he'd chosen. A lot of drugs had been involved. A *lot* of drugs. I was used to his spaciness, having dealt with it my whole life, and I'd learned to roll with it. That was just Dad. "I'm sorry. I know you were looking forward to the reunion."

"Your trailer is really bland, baby girl."

I looked around. "Yeah."

"I haven't been to a store in a while, but do things still come in colors other than gray?"

"As far as I know."

"Well, you've got a spectacular security system for something you can break into using a can opener."

"I have to protect the guitar."

Dad nodded. "Where's the amp?"

"Had to leave it at a gig last night. The manager's holding it for me." *Probably for ransom.*

"You've got a manager?" He looked hopeful.

"No. The manager of the Seahorse Lounge."

His voice flattened. "Oh." He picked up the remote and powered on the TV but there was only the black screen with the *Call your Cable Provider* message. "I've seen this one." He switched it back off.

"Are you hungry?"

He grinned. "Yeah. I could eat. Do you have any nachos?"

"I wish. But no. I have a corn dog." I opened the fridge then remembered I'd already eaten the corn dog. "Nope. Forget that."

Dad opened the kitchen cabinet and found a ceramic lucky cat waving at him. He jumped like it had a gun. Then he looked at me. "I keep mine in the same place."

"That is yours."

"I thought I recognized it. It's got that creepy grin like it's judging me."

"I know what you mean."

"Why don't we just order a pizza? You got takeout menus?" He pulled open the drawer on the end where I kept the ketchup and soy sauce packets. It was full of late notices and past due threats. He slid his eyes to mine. "I'm paying."

Good. 'Cause that's the only way it's happening. I called in a pizza from Giovanni's down the street while Dad took out a wad of cash and tried to shove some into my hand. I kept pushing it back at him.

"Baby girl, what are you doing in this place? Are you hiding from the IRS? Because trust me, those suckers will find you."

"I like it here. It's quiet and people leave me alone." *Mostly.*

"Why don't you let me give you some money until you pull some better gigs?"

I put my hand on his shoulder. "Dad. I'm okay. Really. Now how long do you plan to stay?"

He shrugged. "Couple weeks maybe?"

"Are you sure you don't want to go to the Ritz? Or the Willard downtown?"

He shook his head, his expression a little confused as he searched the recesses of his mind. "I'm not allowed back at the Willard. Or maybe that was the White House. I don't remember. It was somewhere in DC. Besides, I want to be with you. I came to see my little girl."

"Okay. Good. A couple weeks." *I'm gonna need some groceries. And to avoid eviction.* I pulled out the slip of paper with Miranda's friend's phone number on it. Apparently, I was wrong. I hadn't reached the bottom of my desperation yet. I swallowed my pride and texted Janice telling her who I was and that I'd take the birthday party job. Maybe I could windex my pants.

Dad sat back on the couch and looked around the room, his eyebrows knit together. "Didn't you have a dog?"

"No."

He bit his lip and blinked. "I could have sworn there was a dog in here."

"That was the neighbor's dog."

"Oh right. What's his name?"

"The neighbor or the dog?"

Dad considered the question for a few seconds. "The dog."

"We're going with Ringo."

Dad threw his head back and laughed. "That totally fits."

"The neighbor is Nick."

He got very serious. "It's not Nick Jonas, is it? 'Cause that guy's a punk."

"Why would Nick Jonas be living in a trailer park?"

Dad shrugged. "Why is Layla Virtue living in a trailer park?"

"That's definitely not the same thing."

"It could be if you'd let me make a call."

"Absolutely not."

There was a hollow knock on the thin metal door and Dad handed me five Benjamins for the pizza. "It's twenty-two dollars, Dad. Relax."

"Tell him to keep the change."

"Absolutely not." I grabbed some smaller bills from his wallet and opened the door. I gave the kid thirty dollars, which he was stoked about, then handed Dad the rest of his pocket change after closing the door.

I took the pizza to the kitchen table and got down some plates. We sat across from each other like we'd done this a million times and not just the odd weekend whenever he was in town.

Dad took a slice and held it up. "You know what would go good with pizza? Beer."

"I can't Dad. I'm recovering."

He sighed and frowned at the pizza. "Yeah. Me too."

Chapter 6

*T*HE SUN HAD JUST DIPPED TO THE EDGE OF THE WAREHOUSE ROOFTOP, *and I shielded my eyes from the glare. My brain was foggy, but I knew something was wrong. My heart slammed against my rib cage. My hands were clammy, and I felt like a fifty-pound amp was sitting on my chest. I looked around the concrete and cinder blocks for Jacob to tell me what was going on, but he wasn't there. And I had the eerie feeling that I was being watched. I slipped into the shadows, but I could still feel eyes on me until my skin crawled with a thousand pinpricks. Then I spotted him across the parking lot on the warehouse loading dock. That wasn't where he was supposed to be. Jacob threw his arm out violently warning me to back away. I yelled to him—What are you doing? He couldn't answer me because an explosion split our world in half. He flew backward from the force and large flakes like gray snow drifted to the ground at my feet.*

I screamed, but no sound came out other than the half crow of a deranged rooster.

I woke up panting, my heart drumming a solo in my ears. I'd sweat through the sheets again. I tried to kick the damp cocoon off my legs, but they were weighted down around my knees. I lifted onto my elbows and stared into the face of my next-door neighbor—the four-legged one. His tail started to thump against the mattress as he lifted his head and gave me the dog version of a smile.

I called out, "Dad!"

The only response came from under my window. *"Erka Erka."*

The dog looked at the window and gave a sharp bark.

"What are you doing in here, Ringo?"

The Lab wagged his tail playfully.

I fluttered my fingers under his nose. "Okay. Shoo. Shoo."

Ringo jumped off the bed with a grumble.

I threw a blue hoodie over my tank top and shorts and went into the living room.

Dad was sound asleep on the couch with his hat over his eyes. "Dad!"

Ringo licked his face and he started to giggle. "Stop it, darling. I gotta go back to work now."

"Dad!"

His head came up sharp and the hat fell to the floor. "Is that you, baby girl? What's wrong?"

"Did you let this in here?"

Dad looked at Ringo, who thumped his tail against the chair. "Hey. When did you get a dog?"

"This is the neighbor's dog. Remember?"

"Then why is it in your house?"

I sighed. "Did you hear that rooster?"

Dad scrunched his eyebrows together. "No. Did you maybe imagine it? 'Cause I do that sometimes."

I went to the bedroom and pulled the cord to my mini blinds. Marguerite was sitting at a wooden table under a watermelon-patterned umbrella. The rooster was strutting around the grass at her feet like the trailer park ambassador.

I dropped the cord. "Come on, Ringo."

I threw on a black ball cap with the initials *PCNU* sewn in gold across the front and banged through the trailer door. I marched around to the back to give Marguerite a piece of my mind. "I told you to keep that demon away from my trailer!"

Marguerite was a plus-sized Latina with wide eyes that always looked just a little surprised. "I dunno whatchu talking about. I don't got no rooster."

I pointed to the red-and-black bird with the Phyllis Diller feather hairdo that was currently strutting around the legs of

Marguerite's rusty kettle drum barbecue. "What's that right there?"

Ringo barked at the bird and wagged his tail.

Marguerite shrugged. "Not mine."

"Then why do you have a bowl of dried corn?"

She took a relaxed sip of her iced coffee. "It's my breakfast."

I gave her a hard stare. "Then eat some."

Marguerite took a dainty handful and tossed it back. The corn bounced off her cheek and flew over her shoulder. The rooster ran for it.

"That didn't even go in your mouth."

She smoothed her hands down her purple dress. "You need to get a life, *chica*. Quit worrying about what I'm doing."

"You need to keep your noisy pet from waking me up at the crack of dawn every day."

"It's ten o'clock. You just lazy."

"I swear to God, Marguerite. If that bird wasn't in the next yard over scratching at Benny's trash can right now, I'd strangle it."

Ringo was down in pounce position, about to snoot the rooster like a soccer ball. Marguerite threw a handful of corn on her patio. The bird came running at the sound of the clatter with Ringo right behind him.

The woman was impossible. *I can't deal with this first thing in the morning.* "Lock up the bird." I whistled for the dog and started back to my trailer.

Marguerite called after me, "It's not my rooster. I think he's wild."

A figure crossed the edge of my sight sending the hair on my neck to full alert. I was already stressed out and now someone was banging on my front door. How did they find me? This was my house. No one other than my father was supposed to know I was here.

In one motion, I dropped to the ground and rolled behind a lawn chair. I could just see past my awning to the edge of my steps. Some guy was casing the place. *Brown work pants, shirt a half size too small in the gut, slack jaw, no visible weapon.*

Ringo ran up to the man with his tail wagging like the park's official welcoming committee. *That dog needs to be taught not to trust so easily.*

The man bent to pet the Lab. I crouched lower behind the rusty aluminum to disappear into the green-and-white weave. The front door opened, and the man handed something to Dad.

It's just a delivery. I waited until he got into the passenger side of a white sedan and drove off, then extracted myself from my squat and brushed the dry leaves from my shorts as I moved closer to the front door. A classic, cream-colored Aston Martin DB5 was sitting at the curb and Dad was dangling a ring of keys from his index finger.

"I thought you were just in the neighborhood."

Dad's expression was the model of innocence. "I was."

"So how did you manage to schedule a car delivery if this is an impromptu visit?"

Dad looked at the keys in wonder. "It must be that Wanda at the Psychic Network again. Wow, she's good."

I looked at the gorgeous antique sports car James Bond favored, then noticed the faces peeking through various shades, curtains, and mini blinds from trailers all around me. "What happened to the Porsche?"

He handed me the keys and shrugged. His cheeks puffed. "I don't remember where I left it."

"How can you . . . why are you giving me these?"

I tried to give them back and he pushed my hand away. "It's for you."

"Dad. I can't afford to change the oil in that car."

He tried to shove the keys in my hand again. "I'll change it for you."

I gave him a bemused look.

His face split into a grin. "Well, I can pay someone to do it." He tossed the keys at me.

I tossed them back. "Would you stop being ridiculous?"

Ringo sat at my feet watching us play hot potato. He nipped at the keys to get in on the action.

Dad held my wrist and placed the keys on my palm. "Just keep these while I'm here so you can drive me around."

"You want me to drive you?"

He laughed like this should have been obvious. "I don't have a license."

"Since when?"

Dad rolled his eyes skyward. After scanning his brain for a minute, he smiled. "April. I think I might have pushed a casino minibus into the harbor."

Sigh. "Go back inside before the neighbors come out here and start asking questions." I climbed in behind the wheel to move the car out of the road and melted into the buttery leather. *I could live in this car. I would have this car's baby.*

I pulled in the yard next to my Mustang for the time being. Then I gave a curt wave to three nosy neighbors and went back inside.

Dad was on the couch, snuggling with the dog. He was holding the flyer for the park meeting that Agnes had forced on me like a ransom note. "Hey! We should go to this."

"No way."

His eyes widened in surprise. "Why not? I want to meet your friends."

My cell phone buzzed, and I checked the screen. "Then the community meeting is the last place we'd go." The text was a reminder from Janice about the birthday party with a link to her address. *Crap. Is that today? Why does that street sound familiar?*

Dad continued to make his case while I headed to my room to change. "If I'm going to be here a while we might as well do some things together."

I shut the door and grabbed a pair of intentionally ripped jeans out of my dresser and a red leather halter top from my closet. "Like you haven't been to DC before. We went to the Linkin Park concert my senior year. When most people come to town they go to museums. Or the Kennedy Center. Or a Caps game. No one wastes their time with a gripe session about whose plastic flowers need to be updated in their window box."

"I want to see where my daughter lives. Meet your friends."

I fluffed my hair and applied enough hair spray to survive a hurricane. "I don't have any friends, Dad. Remember?"

"Baby girl, you need friends. Who is your support network?"

"I get plenty of support."

Dad started to sing. "When you're through with your life and all hope is lost, just hold out your hand . . ."

I opened the door and cut him off. "Don't misquote Queen to me. The answer is still no."

He smacked his lips and gave me a tired expression. "I'll put us down as a maybe."

I grabbed my guitar. "Look. I have to pick up my amp at the dive I played the other night, try to collect from the gig I ran out on, and then do a horrible set for an eight-year-old spawn of some rich lady. I want you to stay here."

Dad's face lit with joy and maybe a little relief. "You have a gig. That's great." He reached for his wallet to give me some cash—his reflex to any problem or reward.

"Put that away. This isn't a gig. It's a birthday party. I might as well be opening for Yoko Ono."

"The only shame in small gigs is cheap after-parties. Let me come with you."

"Do you want to get me arrested? No. I'll be back soon. Stay here and keep out of sight."

Chapter 7

I PULLED THROUGH THE IRON SECURITY GATE AND CHECKED THE ADdress, wishing it would magically change from Grand View Estates to someplace less terrifying. Maybe Anacostia in Southeast DC at two A.M.? Nope. Still a McMansion on Wonderbread Lane. And one that I'd driven by many times in my former life.

Miranda's friend, Janice, lived in a tan brick modern mansion surrounded by other tan brick modern mansions. All with perfectly landscaped yards containing the exact same plants in the exact same formations. The only interesting thing of note was the blatant rebellion happening across the street where the occupant—in what I could only assume was some kind of protest against the powers that be—had placed a pink flamingo in their boxwood hedge. Those were the neighbors I wanted to meet.

A security guard in a red coat fought his way through the birthday balloon wall toward me and I rolled down my window. "I'm the musician."

He gave a sniff and eyed my car like he was concerned I would affect his Yelp review.

"Janice hired me."

He spoke into a walkie-talkie and gave my name and license plate number in case there'd be a police report later. Once he had confirmation from the other side that I wasn't a party crasher looking for handouts he said, "Drive around the back to the service entrance. Past the duck pond and around the medi-

tation garden. If you leave oil in the driveway, you'll be sent a
bill."

"I'll have you know my Mustang is a classic." The Mustang
gave a death rattle that signaled it was about to stall, and I had to
throw her in neutral and rev the engine. *Don't embarrass me now.*

The attendant waved me forward with a smirk. I followed the
winding flagstone driveway past the tan brick castle, keeping an
eye out for hidden Mickeys, and pulled up next to a lemon-yellow
van whose license plate read CHUKLZ and had a larger-than-life
photo on the side of a happy clown being shot out of a cannon.
The custom paint was faded and peeling in several places, making the clown look like he was missing a few teeth.

Getting my gear, I looked around the property. A resort pool
sat in the center of the backyard surrounded by cabanas and
wooden lounge chairs. A waterfall ran along the back of the
patio next to a sauna and a hot tub. On the side of the house was
a two-story tree house with a higher tax rate than my trailer, and
farther back in the yard, the kids surrounded a life-sized
wooden pirate ship. Three boys perched at the top of the crow's
nest pelting the girls below with water balloons. *What am I doing
here? I said I'd never come to this bougie neighborhood again.*

A shapely fortyish redhead in a floral maxi dress and designer
sunglasses came out of a large pool house carrying a glass of
wine. She shielded her eyes. "Are you Miranda's friend? The
singer?"

"Layla. Guitar player really. I sing a little, but I'm no Mariah
Carey."

"I don't care. Come with me." She sipped her wine until I
caught up with her. "I'm Janice, Trilbee's mom. Thank you so
much for doing this on short notice. Your greenroom will be the
pool house. I've had a stage set up around back. A word of warning . . . Stay away from the clown."

"Why?"

She started moving toward the pool house. "He's vile." Janice
threw one of the double doors open and I stepped inside. "One
more thing. Absolutely no 'Baby Shark.' You go on in fifteen. I'll
be at the bar if you need me."

A chubby man in a color patch nylon suit was sitting on the edge of a rattan sofa talking on his cell phone. He had a wild ring of blond hair running around his bald head from ear to ear that I mistakenly assumed was his clown wig. Then he pulled out a bright blue afro and yanked it down to his ears one-handed. "Two G's on High Society in the fifth. You know I'm good for it. You can trust me, Butchie. I'm at some Richie Rich's house doing another gig." The clown farted, looked my way, and mouthed *Sorry.*

Everything about this day already sucked. I set my amp and guitar down and eyed the wet bar. A half-empty bottle of Glenlivet sat next to three crystal tumblers. An invisible force pulled at me. I reached into my front pocket and ran my finger around the rough edge of my six-month sobriety chip.

The clown wedged his cell phone under his chin and took a giant pair of shoes out of a black case and pulled them on his bare Fred Flintstone feet. He farted again and took a swig from his whiskey glass. "It's a sure thing, Butchie. I'll try to be there with cash in hand before the bell." He set his phone down and gave me a cheesy grin. "Sorry about that." He scratched his butt, then shoved the hand in my direction. "Whoa, where are my manners? Chuckles McCracken, King of Kiddie Soirées and Professional Bouncy House Coin-a-sewer."

I stared at the hand but didn't reach for it. "Layla Virtue. Musician."

Chuckles's eyes roved over me a little too long. He reached into his trunk again and took out a pink tackle box and a makeup mirror. "You must be new to the circuit. I've never seen you before."

I pulled out my cell phone and Googled songs to play for a kids' birthday party. "Last-minute addition."

He sponged white makeup over his razor stubble. "Don't let the moms scare you. They don't all bite. But you can get contact-drunk from the fumes if you stand too close to them. I wouldn't even be here today, but my alimony is due. I got a bit of a dicky tummy from some bad clams casino."

I glanced again at the Scotch.

He pulled out a bright pink business card from his volumi-
nous pocket and handed it to me. It said *Chuck McCracken—
Concierge Life Coach Masseuse.* On the back it had a picture of a
clown giving a massage.

I laughed at what I thought was an obvious joke, realized I was
the only one laughing, and cleared my throat in an attempt to
swallow my discomfort.

"Clowning is my side gig. I only get the birthday parties on
weekends. The rest of the week I rub your troubles away while
offering life-changing advice. I'm running a startup promo if
you're interested." He colored in giant eyebrows with a blue
greasepaint pencil and wiggled them for me.

*There is no way life coach masseuse is a real thing. And that whiskey
is screaming my name.* "I'm pretty sure a masseuse is a woman.
Wouldn't you be a masseur?"

"Are you serious?" He dropped his head and groaned. "Man,
I just bought these cards. I invested a fortune. Not to mention
the massage table. Well, I'll just have to send away for some new
ones."

I handed the card back to him. "At least you have a plan."

It disappeared into the folds of his nylon. "I'm always looking
for new investors."

"Sure. A concierge life coach masseur is obviously in high de-
mand."

He clearly did not pick up on my sarcasm. He finished his
whiskey and poured himself another round. "Hey, let's just keep
this between us for now, okay?"

"Uh-huh."

Janice banged on the window. I couldn't hear her, but by the
way she was waving her arms and pointing at her wrist, I suspected my fifteen minutes was up. The pool house door flew
open and an older blonde in white slacks and a ruffled blouse
yelled, "Chuck! Why aren't you dressed? You go on two minutes ago!"

Chuckles nodded toward the formidable lady. "Layla, meet
my agent, Paula."

Paula had the look of a woman whose last nerve was plucked like an E string. She waved me off. "Nice to meet you, Laura. Chuck, move it!"

Janice tapped the window again.

"Break a leg out there, Chuckles."

He took a long drag on a pineapple-scented vape pen. "You too, Layla. Rock on."

I took my amp out to the stage and looked for a place to plug it in. Kids were running riot all over the yard. A boomerang flew past my head, and I almost reconsidered Dad's offer to bankroll me. A group of trophy moms were huddled around a tiki bar, each with her own fishbowl of sangria. Not their first of the day from the looks of it.

I asked Janice if I could unplug the blender to use the outlet for my set. The women stared at me like I'd just asked to punch a baby. Then one of them in a white miniskirt suggested that they could make the margaritas inside the pool house in a pinch and they all relaxed.

A little towhead terror in stripes flew past us and a new mom stumbled around the corner in a tight blue dress. "Hey, sweetums. Don't hit anyone today or your Xbox goes in the microwave."

Janice pulled a blue bottle from an ice bucket and misted her chest and neck. "My God, Tina. Are you drunk already? It's only half past one."

The brunette misjudged how to walk in her ridiculous stilt shoes and fell into the tiki torch, setting the edge of the grass roof on fire. "Oops. I may have had a couple mimosas while I waited for Baron to get out of karate."

I grabbed the ice bucket and tossed the water at the roof before the fire could spread. Tina had also come pre-lit, and I worried that she'd driven little sweetums in that state. *None of my business.* I plugged in my amp and took to the stage.

I played a few chords to check my tuning, set my amp, then started "Twist and Shout." The kids came flying at the stage to jump around in the grass. When the song ended, I transitioned into "Wooly Bully" but I made up most of the words because I'd never learned them and most likely no one would know the difference. The whole while my eyes kept wandering to the smoldering tiki bar where the moms were tossing sangria back like sailors on shore leave. Tina struggled to stay upright and spilled wine down the front of her plunge neckline.

A small child wearing a gold crown loudly complained, "I don't want you. I asked for Melvin the Magnificent. I want him to make my sister disappear."

"You must be Trilbee."

He crossed his arms and wouldn't look at me.

I tried to come up with age-appropriate material, but the smell of wine and peach schnapps filled my mind and all I could remember were songs about booze. No one said anything when I played "Tequila" and substituted the name "Sheila." Then it became obvious the moms weren't paying attention when no one realized that I'd slipped into an AC/DC drinking song I changed to "Have a Stink on Me."

Chuckles emerged from the pool house and caught Janice on her way toward the mansion. He said something in her ear, and she slapped him. Then Tina came out of the pool house with a whiskey tumbler and threw the liquid in his face.

The moms didn't notice, and the kids didn't care. They danced around to everything I played. I thought I might be okay after all.

Then the requests started coming in.

Trilbee requested "Baby Shark" right out of the chute. I suspected he was still punishing me for not being a magician. I made eye contact with Janice who shook her head and sliced a finger across her throat.

"I don't know that one. How about 'Stairway to Heaven'?"

Then a little girl with blond pigtails said, "Hey, lady, can you play 'The Gummybear Song'?"

"I have no idea what that is."

The little girl started to bounce around singing it and I instantly regretted my honesty.

"Stop that." *I gotta get control here. What did my dad sing to me when I was little?* I started the intro to "Sweet Child of Mine."

"No! Gum-ee-bear! Gum-ee-bear!"

Now all the kids were chanting it like a wild pack of cartoon squirrels. Where was the respect for Guns N' Roses?

Pigtails was the clear rebel leader of the pack. She seemed like the kind to have a new pet hamster every month after the one before met an unfortunate demise. She climbed on the stage and yanked my microphone cord. "Do you know 'Let It Go'?"

I started playing "Let's Go" by Def Leppard and the kid went and narc'd on me. I could see her pointing her little finger and stomping her foot at a Pilates Mom in a red halter dress. I tried to focus on my finger placement and the paycheck at the end of the gig.

The Pilates Mom stormed the stage with two of her friends ready to drag me out to the road and back over me with their Lexus SUVs. The one in a white miniskirt shook her finger. "Jusssst what do you think you're doing?"

"Entertaining the kids."

She slurred, "Kidsh are impreshhhhinable. Play something approooo-priate."

"What did you have in mind?"

The woman tried to shrug and threw herself off balance. "Hey, what's a good song for kidsh?"

Pilates Mom—mother to the demon in pigtails, stumbled into her friend and said, "How about that 'Baby Shhhark' song?"

Of all the careers to fall back on, why didn't I learn something more marketable? Something that doesn't involve using words like waddle *and* quack. *Like accounting. Or cattle rustling.*

Twenty-six kids had created a mosh pit, demanding "Baby Shark," and Chuckles jumped on the stage and took over. You know your life hits an all-time low when the vaping, farting, whiskey-slugging clown feels sorry for you.

"Hey, kid. You got this." I thought maybe I'd misjudged Chuckles. Then he patted my butt.

I was not used to people being so forward with me. In my last career, reaching for any part of my body could get you shot. I jerked away from him, and the kids all gasped like I was attack-

ing Santa, so I flashed them a smile and patted him on the head
instead.

I turned off my amp and handed the mic to a shamefaced
Chuckles and left the stage. I passed manager Paula, who avoided
making eye contact, and headed toward the pool house for ten
minutes without the little hellions just as Tina pulled a row of
grass off the roof of the tiki bar. "I can't be here. I have to go
pick up Fanta from swim lesshons before her coach calls the
nanny again." Then she fell over a marble urn of ornamental
grass and landed in the inset hot tub.

Janice cussed at her. "Tina, I told you. No polyester in the
Jacuzzi."

Tina pulled herself out using the urn. "Who moved the
pool?"

I knew the moms would handle it.

I hoped the moms would handle it.

The moms weren't handling it. They were too busy gossiping
about Tina's husband's affair and her botched nose job which I
thought looked fine.

I had my hand on the pool house door when a dripping Tina
squelched past me with her keys dangling from her index finger.
*Now would be a good time to practice my boundaries. Like letting people
make their own mistakes.*

Tina stumbled.

Maybe I should start with mistakes that don't kill bystanders.

I grabbed Tina's wrist. "Do you really think you should be
driving?"

She shrugged out of my grasp. "Get off me!"

I snatched her keys and pulled out my cell phone while walking her to the front of the mansion. "Give me your address. I'm
calling you an Uber. If you've sobered up, you can get your car
when you come back for your kid."

Tina whined all the way around the meditation garden, then
fell in a heap down by the security station aka balloon wall. She
whined until the Uber arrived but did as she was told and got in
when she saw the look on my face.

Is it too late to go to manicure school?

When I got back to the party, the pool house door was wide open. A goon in a gold track suit was rifling through the clown's bags. He had the dim-witted look of being someone smarter's muscle for hire. "What are you doing?"

He glanced at me, unfazed. "Where's Chuck?"

I looked through the window. "On stage making balloon animals. His manager, Paula, is on her cell phone by the pirate ship."

The goon dumped the contents of Chuckles's duffel bag onto the rattan sofa. "I'll wait."

I glanced at the whiskey bottle. Still there. I'd missed my chance at a break and headed back to the stage.

Janice and the moms were busy bad-mouthing me. "Who wears jeans that tight to a kids' party?"

"Where'd you get that singer anyway? She doesn't even know 'Bananaphone.'"

Janice rimmed another glass in salt. "This was the only entertainment I could get on short notice. Trilbee's mom was supposed to take him and his sister to SeaWorld but canceled because her dog is sick. So now suddenly I have to throw Trilbee a birthday party. More like she's recovering from the facelift she just got. Being the stepmother is a thankless job."

Pigtail's mom drained her glass. "Divorce can make you insane, ladies."

I passed them and swapped places with Chuckles on stage to start another set. The demon in pigtails appeared at my side. "Can I use your microphone to sing 'Let It Go'?"

"No."

She screeched something only dogs could hear then capped it off with a head-splitting "Mo-oom!" Every mom in the yard shot me full of hot leaded irritation for interrupting their wine time.

My first career ended in a literal explosion, and it was still better than this one.

I quickly started Stevie Wonder's "Isn't She Lovely" with some side glare at Pigtails until everyone drifted back to their oblivion. As I played, I watched the muscle in the gold track suit twisting Chuckles's arm around his back. Chuckles was pleading with the man and twisting to get away as the thug was forcing him into the pool house. Chuckles eventually came back out, but I never saw the guy in the track suit again.

I played a Jackson Five medley until Janice asked me to play "cake music." I didn't think she meant "Cake by the Ocean" since that was rather dirty, so I played a few bars of "Alley Cat" while the cake was brought out and presented to Trilbee who I thought should make a wish for a different name.

Chuckles and I were told to take a break until the presents were opened.

"Oof. My dogs are barking." He bent double and farted. "Outta my way. I gotta use the toilet and get these shoes off."

His manager grabbed his arm. "Not so fast, Chuck. We need to talk this out."

Chuck hopped on one foot. "For the love of all that is holy, Paula. Not now!"

"I told you this was the last straw, Chuck. How could you do this to me?" Paula dragged the clown past the pool house for a not-so-private argument.

I was starving. I should have ordered two pizzas last night so at least Dad and I'd have had breakfast today. And maybe if I ate something I could stop thinking about that whiskey I could hear singing sea shanties to me from inside the pool house. I hovered around the cake table planning to swipe some of the birthday boy's icing while the kid opened his presents. I was just reaching for a one-eyed yellow blob in blue overalls . . .

"Layla!"

Janice again. I grabbed a napkin and pretended to wipe something off my guitar. "Yes?"

"Trilbee's finished opening his presents and I can't find the clown. You're on. Try to play something that came out in this decade."

Great. I don't know anything from this decade. My last job didn't give me a lot of time to listen to the radio, so I never learned anything that released past my high school graduation.

I filled the time with a few retro covers they would think were new until Chuckles stumbled on stage with a duffel bag of juggling balls and bowling pins. We swapped places and I played background music to his act. He wasn't great. In fact, he was terrible.

He stumbled around missing pins and breathing heavily. His greasepaint was starting to run. One of the moms floated a rumor that he was drunk, which seemed plausible under the present circumstances.

He called out to the sugar-fueled mob, "Hey, kibbies, who wants to learn how to jubble?"

The only appropriate circus music I knew was from Three Dog Night—"The Show Must Go On"—so that's what I played while the kids rushed the stage like juggling was the new Hunger Games and grabbed at the pins.

Chuckles stumbled and fell to one knee and the kids piled on top of him. He started flopping around like a live wire and they laughed maniacally.

Something about the way his body jerked around set the hair on the back of my neck to full attention. My hand hovered over my strings waiting to see if my hair was right.

Chuckles stopped moving and the kids grew quiet. One by one they moved off him and stepped back to reassess the situation. Pigtails poked him with the toe of her boot.

Trilbee whined, "This is why I wanted a magician. This clown's no fun."

I fought against my nature to take control. I started to head to the stage to check the body, but Chuckles's manager beat me to it. She rushed the stage and bent over him.

She dropped to her knees and put her ear to his chest. "Call an ambulance." She started chest compressions and the kids picked up the juggling tools and tried to teach themselves.

I reached for my phone, but my hand froze. I can't be the one. Surely someone else . . .

The moms were moving in slow motion. Janice was the first to react. She grabbed her cell phone. "Bernie. The birthday party clown just died in my backyard. Please tell me I have liability coverage for dead clowns."

He must have told her to cover her butt and call an ambulance right away because she hung up immediately and dialed 911.

Pigtails's mom was on stage trying mouth to mouth. Her daughter was poking Chuckles in the belly with a juggling pin. It wasn't looking good.

I told myself to chill, but instinct kicked in and I laid my guitar against the pool house. Jumping on the stage, I shooed Pigtails away. She stuck her tongue out at me. I checked for Chuckles's pulse. Nada. Neither was his chest moving.

I gave the women a word of encouragement. "You're both doing great. Keep up the compressions until the paramedics arrive."

I looked around the yard. *Oh no, no, no, no. This is not good. I gotta get out of here. I know what happens next. First the ambulance, then the fire truck, then the squad car.*

"I don't know what I'm doing," Paula cried.

"You've got this. To the beat of the Bee Gees's 'Stayin' Alive.' " I reached out and grabbed my amp. Miniskirt Mom narrowed her eyes my way, but I didn't care. This called for a quick retreat. I could not be here when the police arrived. Not in this precinct.

I jumped off the stage and approached Janice as soon as she disconnected. "Do you think I could get paid now? I have to go."

Janice had a wild look in her eye. "Why me? I need a Xanax."

I wrapped up my cords and craned my neck checking to see if my car was blocked in. "Stay with me, Janice. Can you Venmo me? PayPal? Cash App?" Janice had left reality. I had to run for it before the police arrived while I had plausible deniability. It's not illegal to flee a heart attack. And these ladies had things under control. Mostly. An invisible force held me back. That force was called unemployment. *I am flat broke.* "So, Janice. What if you just give me half now and I can come back tomorrow for the rest?"

Sirens sounded nearby.

"I'll take restaurant gift cards."

They had breached the front gate. I was sure of it. Red lights bounced off the pool house. First came rescue, then the black-and-whites, just like I'd called it.

I considered hiding out in the pirate ship but there was no time. I tried to disappear and inched my way behind the tiki bar blenders.

The EMTs rushed the stage with their cases and took over for Paula who immediately began to weep.

Dear God, please let things go my way for a change.

"Layla Virtue, is that you?"

I slowly turned to face a chiseled jaw and eyes of dark scorn from Detective Dayton Castinetto, Potomac County Police. *Darn it.*

He sneered. "I should have known I'd find you around a bar."

Chapter 8

"WHAT ARE YOU DOING HERE, VIRTUE?"

"Just moving on with my life, trying to make ends meet like everyone else."

Dayton's lip curled. His near-black eyebrows digging into each other. "You think you deserve to move on?"

"Everyone deserves a second chance."

"Everyone isn't responsible for that cluster down at Stratton Park."

My mouth went dry. I'd known he'd go there, but shame doesn't take a day off. "Just take my statement and let me go, Castinetto."

I could feel all six feet of disgust rolling off his broad shoulders. It used to be said around the station that if the Potomac County Police had a sexy calendar, Dayton Castinetto would be the centerfold. Frankly, I didn't see it. Women threw themselves in his path, both on and off the force. They'd go all quivery for his green eyes and square jaw. As far as I was concerned, he loved himself enough for the both of us. And I couldn't get past my memory of who he was in high school.

"We both know I can't trust a word that comes out of your mouth. Not then, not now. Not until you disclose the truth about that day and make things right."

"I put everything I remember in my report."

"Temporary amnesia. How convenient. I'm sure that eases

the mind of Jacob's family and all the others. You're the epic screwup of the decade. I wouldn't even be talking to you now if I wasn't the officer in charge of the scene."

I flicked my eyes to his. "Then take charge of the scene and quit trying to bully me into telling you something I don't know."

He took a step back and sighed like he was considering arresting me just for breathing. I used to give suspects that same look. "What are you really doing here with a bunch of second wives and trust fund kids?"

"Don't forget the clown. He's the dead guy under the red nose."

One of the paramedics came over to brief him that the patient was deceased from an apparent heart attack and the medical examiner had been called.

Dayton reached for the radio on his shoulder to call the update into dispatch. Then he pulled out a small notebook and smirked. "You know how to give a statement, don't you? Let's get this over with so I can get back to work and you can get back to getting wasted on the job."

I have never in my life been wasted on the job. At least not until Stratton Park. Breathe in . . . breathe out . . . you're not the one being investigated this time. "I know nothing. I saw nothing."

Dayton rolled his eyes. "Really. You're gonna be a hostile witness now too?"

"Witness to what?" I threw my arm out in the direction of the stage where the paramedics were treating Janice for hyperventilating next to the prone body of Chuckles. "The dude was pushing sixty, more than fifty pounds overweight, covered in greasepaint and nylon, and halfway through a bottle of Scotch on a warm Sunday afternoon. I'm surprised he made it past the Pin the Tail on the Donkey."

"So, you didn't see anything suspicious?"

I so did not want to be involved with this, but Cop Layla butted in again. "No . . . Other than the heavy in a track suit looking to shake him down for money and his manager ripping him a new one during the birthday cake—nothing."

He glared at me for a solid beat then jotted down some notes. "How long have you known Chuck McCracken?"

I pulled out my phone and checked the time. "Almost two and a half hours."

His pen hovered over the notebook, and he raised his eyebrows.

"I've never seen him before today. We were both hired to entertain at this kid's birthday party. Chuckles—or Chuck—has racing forms for Charles Town Raceway in his box of greasepaint. I heard him placing a bet before I went on. The goon probably has something to do with that."

"What was the altercation with his manager about?"

"From what I can tell, he was working her last nerve. And he did something to creep out the lady who hired him and possibly one of the guests who left already. That's all I know."

"Which one is his manager?"

I scanned the yard and nodded toward the petite blonde lying on a lounge by the pool. Her eyes covered with a washcloth, an empty margarita glass dangling from her fingers.

Dayton nodded and checked his notebook. "I see you've moved to Lake Pinecrest. That's quite a drop in status for you, isn't it?" When I didn't comment, he looked away and snickered. "You're free to go since I know how to find you. We'll be in touch if anything comes up."

I stashed my guitar in the case and grabbed my amp. I just wanted to get the heck away from Castinetto and his Mount Everest–sized ego. He couldn't do his job without throwing a few potshots my way. I didn't blame him entirely. One thing he said was true. Stratton Park was a career-ending, life-altering disaster.

Chapter 9

I STOPPED AT A 7-ELEVEN ON MY WAY HOME AND BOUGHT TWO FRO-
zen burritos and a pack of napkins—the price of keeping Agnes
Harcourt off my back tonight. I parked my Mustang in front of
Donna's butter-yellow single-wide.

Okay, that's a lie.

The Mustang stalled out in front of Donna's little porch with
her jungle of potted plants, and I didn't have the patience to
coax it back to life just for twenty feet.

Ringo called hello from inside Nick's trailer. Nick opened his
front door and the black Lab galloped out with reckless abandon like I was returning from war.

I set my guitar case behind me, out of paw's reach. "Hey,
buddy. Who's a good boy?"

Ringo jumped around a bit then flopped on his back, doing
wiggles in the few fallen leaves, for me to rub his tummy, which
I obliged.

Nick stood by silently watching with a bemused look playing
across his face. "Is that your dinner? Two convenience store
bean burritos?"

I adjusted the pack of napkins under my arm while I tried not
to squish the wrapped burritos in my hand. "Technically one is
beef and cheese."

He half rolled his eyes. "Well, you gotta have options."

"If you're gonna heckle me, I want you to get your facts straight.
And maybe you haven't noticed, but this ain't the Taj Mahal."

Nick looked from Kelvin's basketball bucket to my D.O.A. Mustang to Benny's sun-bleached plastic window box flowers and grinned. "Taj Mahal wishes they had it this good."

Marguerite's rooster crowed.

Ringo gave me a surprise snout punch on the cheek. Apparently, that was the Labrador version of a kiss.

I snorted and gave Ringo one final pat. "Did you work up a good excuse for later or will you be serving time at the community meeting?"

Nick went stone-faced. "Um . . . mandatory."

"That's because Agnes has no real friends to hang out with and Myrtle Jean Maud loves the rush of adrenaline she gets from wielding her two-cookie-per-person mandate."

Nick ran his hands up his arms. "Ooh, so much power. I just got the shivers."

"Yeah, well, pace yourself. You haven't been interrogated about your toilet-flushing habits yet. But you can be sure Clifford Bagstrodt—water patrol—will hit you up for all the details."

His eyes twinkled with excitement. "I'll get ready for the inquisition."

"You do that." I gave him a wave of my burritos as I crossed to my door. "I'll see you down there."

Dad was sitting on the couch watching the stock market report. "Hey, baby girl. How was work?"

I set my guitar case on the kitchen table. "A clown died."

He clucked his tongue. "Boy, if I had dollar for every time that's happened to me." Dad flipped the channel to CNN.

"When did we get Internet?"

"I ordered a pizza earlier and gave the delivery boy a hundred dollars to hook you up."

"Hook me up to what?"

Dad shrugged. "I dunno. The main line?"

How long before Verizon discovers that? I held up the burritos. "Beef and cheese or bean and cheese?"

"Surprise me."

By the time I had nuked the burritos and brought them to the living room, Dad had flipped through all the channels twice. He paused on a Walmart commercial set to "Dirty Deeds Done Dirt Cheap" and laughed so hard he had to wipe tears from his eyes. I handed him his plate and he turned the TV off.

"What'd you do while I was gone?"

He held up his burrito and looked around the living room. "This."

I nodded, and we ate together in silence for a couple of minutes.

His eyes widened like he just remembered where I'd been all day. "How was the set? Did you play 'Hot Girls'?"

"It was a little kids' party, Dad."

He stared at me for a beat. "That's not a no."

I swallowed a bite of burrito. "I changed it to 'Hot Potatoes.'"

He laughed, then grunted like he just remembered something. He put his plate on the table and rubbed his hands together, then pulled the green flyer out of his pocket. "I found this. I think we should go."

"That's the same flyer you showed me this morning."

He cocked his head and looked at the flyer like it had tricked him on purpose. "Is it?"

"I told you I don't have any friends there for you to meet."

He examined the flyer like it was a legal contract and he was looking for the loophole. "This one says you owe late fees. I could pay them for you."

"I can pay my own late fees." *Eventually.*

"Baby girl, I missed most of your life. I wasn't there like I should have been. I just want to know that you're settled and happy."

Oof. Then this is going to be a rough visit. "Dad. You were working. I get it. And you weren't there a lot, but you made up for it with the memories we made when you were. Besides, you called all the time. You lacked a working grasp of time zones, but I didn't mind. We don't have to go to a lame community meeting for me to know that you love me."

"I do love you. And I want you to have as many happy memories of me as possible." Dad's face deflated to a pout. "We've never done a small town before."

"What does that have to do with anything?"

"It could be fun. Think of the stories you can tell your children." He gave me a cheesy grin just like that time he convinced me to ride the Rebel Yell at King's Dominion and said it would be ironic.

Sigh. "Fine. On one condition."

Dad's look of glee let me know right off that I'd regret this.

"You have to wear a disguise."

"Why?"

"Because I still have to live here after you leave."

His eyes rolled up in thought. "What? Like a business suit?"

"I have something else in mind."

Two hours and one trip to the clothesline around the lake later, I had Dad outfitted in one of Myrtle Jean Maud's pink dresses with an all-over pattern of cats wearing glasses. He tried to protest her forty-two double D bra filled with Kleenex, but I told him the dress wouldn't lay right without it. I'd also grabbed the purple scarf Marguerite had left out on her picnic table next to her bowl of "breakfast corn." Then I found a curly red wig in my closet from last Halloween where I went as Winifred from *Hocus Pocus.* "We'll use the scarf to smash down your hair points."

"I like the hair points where they are." Dad fussed with his Kleenex boobs to make them even. "What about shoes? I'm thinking . . . with this hemline . . . three-inch pumps?"

"Do you have a pair of size eleven three-inch pumps?"

"No. Wait . . . No."

"Then your Gucci sneakers will have to do. No one will be looking at your shoes anyway."

Dad's nose screwed up as he puckered and applied a layer of pink passion lipstick. "That's not true. That's just a lie parents say to kids when they're running late. Everyone looks at your shoes."

"Uh, that's what you said to me when I was eleven and we were going to that big corporate fundraiser."

"See. That proves it." He smacked his lips and grinned.

"You look gorgeous."

"What's my name?"

"Hmm. Who do you feel like?"

He appraised himself in the mirror. "I hear a lot of people named Karen these days. How about that?"

"That's not what you think it is. How about Linda? We can tell everyone you're my aunt."

"Sure. Sounds good. Do I get a pocketbook?"

"I didn't realize you were going to be so high-maintenance. Maybe we should revisit the Karen idea." I pulled a leather bag from my boho phase out of the closet and handed it to Dad. "What are you going to put in it?"

He clutched the bag to his bosom. "A lady doesn't tell."

"Okay then."

A few minutes later we were out the door and walking down to the clubhouse. This was not my first unconventional outing with Dad. My whole life he'd had a way of opening doors that should have been closed. Like our private Mall of America shopping spree at two A.M. A phenomenon that had a direct link to his American Express Black Card.

Dad committed to the part of Aunt Linda very convincingly— strutting and swinging his hips. "Where'd you get this walk?"

"Freddie Mercury."

"Maybe don't mention that at the meeting."

The monthly community torture was in a blue double-wide around the lake by the main office. A hand-carved sign with the word CLUBHOUSE was plunged into a wooden bucket of mums by the front door. Many of the more easily controlled park residents were already inside mingling.

The door swung open, and Agnes Harcourt gave me her usual welcome scowl. "Layla. Did you remember the napkins?"

Oh crap.

Agnes smirked. "I knew you'd forget." She called over her

shoulder, "Myrtle Jean, put out the backup napkins we brought. She wiffed just like you said she would. And Layla, who is this you've brought with you?"

It was on the tip of my tongue to say my aunt Linda. But Dad thrust his hand out and said, "Trixie. Trixie Hamm—two m's. Pleasure."

I narrowed my eyes and mugged him with more than a little annoyance.

Dad passed me and winked as he sashayed into the white-wood paneled room sounding a lot like Robin Williams doing Mrs. Doubtfire. "Helloooo, everyone. It's so goood to be with you."

This is gonna be a disaster. At least I won't have to break my lease when I'm kicked out.

My other next-door neighbor was piling a paper plate high with chicken wings. He was a short man with a deep tan and a smile that made you happy. He stopped piling long enough to take Dad's offered hand. "How you doing? I'm Benny. I'm a used-car salesman over in Vienna. If you ask me to cut your grass, I'm gonna let all the air out of your tires while you sleep. Savvy?"

Dad's eyes lit up and a grin split his face. "Righteous. Hey, man, are those chicken wings for everyone?"

I nudged my foot on top of Dad's and Mrs. Doubtfire returned.

"Oooh, what a lovely spread. Just look at that pink pie."

Benny grinned and passed Dad a paper plate. "That pie is toxic. Eat it at your own risk."

Donna from across the street sidled next to me with her grandson in tow. "Hey, lady. Where'd you get that fancy new car?"

I grabbed a red Solo cup and poured myself some iced tea. "It's my Da . . . aaamaged Aunt Trixie's." *Sigh.*

Behind me I heard Myrtle Jean say, "I love your dress. I have one just like it."

Trixie responded, "Me too. Cats in glasses are so sophisticated, don't you think, doll?"

Donna's eyes popped a little. She leaned her forehead next to mine and whispered, "Why is she damaged? What happened?"

I rolled my lips in and shook my head. "She's had it rough. Identity theft. We don't like to talk about it."

Donna *tsk*'d and shook her shiny black bob while keeping her eyes on Dad. She sensed Kelvin was about to take another piece of cake behind her back and snapped her fingers. "Uh-uh." Her long burgundy fingernails clicked against each other. "Boy, I know you're not about to take more dessert before you eat some of that chicken."

I looked around her ample body at her husky grandson in his Sponge Bob T-shirt.

Kelvin cut his eyes to mine and slid the cake slice back into the pan. "No, ma'am."

Donna pursed her lips. "I didn't think so." We moved around the table, and she reached for one of Myrtle Jean's cookies.

Myrtle Jean snapped a spatula against a paper plate. "Two cookies per person."

Donna rolled her eyes. "Yeah. I know the drill, Myrtle Jean." She glanced at me. "Cookie fascist."

I held in a snicker. Donna was the first friendly face I'd met when I moved in. She'd brought me a chicken noodle casserole and invited me to her wine drinking club for whine and cheese night where they choose a different book to pretend to read each month. I had yet to attend on account that I didn't want someone who lived within egging distance of my house to turn against me. She didn't seem to take it personally or hold it against me, which was a nice change.

Dad had made himself a plate and was perched on a padded folding chair between Benny and Marguerite. He was surrounded by residents who were laughing and smiling, doing their best to talk his ears off. He shot me a big toothy smile—he was having a blast. His knees splayed open, showing knee-high stockings already shrugging down his hairy calves. He waved one of Myrtle Jean's cookies and I noticed that he had three more on his plate.

I sipped my iced tea. *That figures.*

The trailer door opened, and Nick was led in by Ringo on a

red leash. "I'm sorry I'm late, but I brought some coleslaw. My momma's recipe."

The ladies awed like he'd risked his life to save a kitten from a burning building. He shot me a satisfied grin. I rolled my eyes and took a seat near the back. Ringo broke free of his grip and ran to me, his tail thumping everyone he passed.

"Hey, buddy. Did Daddy drag you here to help him score points with the warden?"

Ringo laid his head in my lap, and I stroked his velvety ears.

Nick appeared at my side and made a sound of dissent. "I most certainly did not. That would be devious." He gave me a sly grin and took the seat next to mine. "What's going on with the famous rhubarb pie?"

"Same thing as every month. It just sits there looking sad."

"No one ever eats it?"

"I have a theory that Agnes has brought the same exact pie for six months running."

"What does she do with it in between meetings?"

"Probably keeps it in a shrine and prays to it." I watched Clifford approach Dad with his trusty clipboard and nudged Nick. "Pay attention, you'll be next."

Clifford cleared his throat. "Miss Hamm, water is a very precious commodity here at Lake Pinecrest and we share one community bill for it. How often would you say you flush the toilet over the course of a day?"

Dad fluttered his eyelashes. "Why, I don't rightly know. I guess it all depends on how bored I am."

I choked on my tea a little.

Nick asked me, "Is there a penalty if the number's too high?"

"There's a penalty for everything, Nick."

Agnes tapped a fork against a plastic cup. "Let's get the meeting started. Clifford, not now."

Clifford murmured something then made his way to the front of the room and dragged over a rickety wooden podium for Agnes to use. He took his position on the barstool at her left and Myrtle Jean sat in the folding chair on her right.

Dad excused himself from his admirers and said he was going to go sit with his niece. He fluttered his skirt and side-stepped down the row to the aisle. I gave him a little wave.

He threw his plate away and pranced back to the vacant chair on my other side. "I don't know what you're talking about, Layla. These people aren't stink butts. The one who looks like someone sucked all the air out of her face said she'd give me her recipe for that pink pie. Hey, I know that dog."

Nick stared at Dad then cut his eyes to mine. His eyes narrowed slightly.

I gave him a lopsided grin. "Nick, this is my *aunt Trixie.*"

He gave Dad a friendly smile. "Nice to meet you."

Dad fluttered his eyelashes and giggled.

Is his frame of reference for how girls act from Gone with the Wind?

Agnes opened a spiral notebook on the podium. "We have a lot to cover tonight. Thank you, Myrtle Jean, for bringing your delicious cookies and the much-needed and *strongly predicted* backup napkins."

Agnes glanced my way and Marguerite turned her head and gave me a smug look.

Nick chuckled under his breath. "You had one job."

"That's not true. I had to get Aunt Trixie ready, and she was obsessed with her purse matching her shoes."

Agnes droned on. "If you haven't done so already, please sign up for what to bring to next Friday's fall bonfire. We don't want a repeat of last year's chips and salsa nightmare. Now, it has come to our attention that someone on Fontainebleau still has a Fourth of July flag displayed."

I whispered, "And by 'come to our attention' she means they canvass the neighborhood like the Gestapo."

"According to the bylaws, all holiday decorations must be taken down and stored until next season within seventy-two hours of the holiday end."

Nick whispered back, "Isn't a Fourth of July flag just a regular American flag?"

Agnes leaned against the lectern and looked around the

room. "Now listen up, people. Is it really worth three weeks of community service for breaking the laws?"

Clifford gave a stern bristle to each of the residents in attendance.

Dad patted his hair points. "Oh my. Is this your jurisdiction, Layla?"

"These laws are only in Agnes's mind, Aunt Trixie."

Clifford shot me a scowl and wheezed. "Disgraceful."

Myrtle Jean *tsk*'d and gave her spatula a menacing shake in my direction.

Donna raised her hand. "I think you're talking about Jeanette Winthrop's trailer."

Agnes checked her clipboard and narrowed her eyes. "Hmm. That's right, yes. She'll need to see me about her assignment. I've ordered her an orange vest to wear while she picks up the trash around the lake."

Donna continued. "Well, I don't think she's gonna be able to take that flag in anytime soon."

Clifford bristled. "Whyever not? Those are the bylaws and consequences that we put into place to keep Lake Pinecrest orderly."

I tried to mind my business. It wasn't going well. "I don't remember voting on these bylaws."

Nick hummed. "You're trying to get kicked out my first meeting, aren't you?"

Donna tilted her head. "Jeanette died a month ago. Don't you remember the ambulance?"

Myrtle Jean looked as though she might pass out. She crossed herself and fanned her spatula.

Agnes did a double take on her notebook and scratched through the entry with her pen. "I'll make a note to cancel the vest. Let's move on. Any community issues?"

A young man about thirty, a bit on the pudgy side, stood to his feet. He searched through six pockets in his cargo pants before pulling a folded paper out of his top pocket. In a squeaky voice he said, "Hello everyone. My name is Foster."

Agnes leaned against the lectern, tiredly. "Foster. Everyone here knows who you are. You grew up here with your gran, may she rest in peace, and you bring the same issue every month."

He nodded, then started over. "Hello, everyone. My name is Foster. I live on Versailles, and I want the management to designate part of the common ground as a playground for Pippi. Pippi is a good girl, and she deserves a seesaw."

Nick nudged me. "Who is Pippi?"

I chuckled. "That's the wrong question. But I'm not going to spoil the surprise."

Agnes nodded at Foster. "We'll put that issue on the docket for next month."

Foster would not be denied. "Yes, but you said that at the last five community meetings. In April, after you said not everyone appreciates Jesus, and Easter decorations should be limited to rabbits and eggs. In May, after the warnings not to feed the squirrels leftover rhubarb pie. In June, after you yelled at Layla about painting sunflowers on her trash cans."

Nick snickered. "You what?"

I shrugged. "I got a warning that they were looking shabby."

Agnes raised her palm. "Thank you, Foster. I remember. Fine. We'll discuss it at the next management meeting."

I supplied, "The next time they crawl the park looking for malfeasance."

Agnes shot me a look. "I heard that, Layla. If your lovely aunt weren't here, I'd let you know what I think of your smart-aleck comments."

Myrtle Jean smacked a paper plate with her spatula and Nick snickered. "I think she just cussed you out in old white lady."

Marguerite raised her hand. "I'm being harassed by one of my neighbors who shall remain nameless."

Everyone turned in their seats to look my way.

Dad breathed out an uh-oh.

Agnes's lips flattened. "What have you done now?"

I held my arms up. "She has a rooster who crows under my window first thing in the morning on purpose."

Marguerite shrugged. "I dunno what she talkin' about."

"Back me up here, Benny."

Benny smacked his lips. "Sorry, Layla. You know normally I'd have your back, but she's about to put a down payment on a twenty-eighteen Audi."

Agnes shook her head. "Layla Virtue, you have the most active imagination of anyone I've ever met." She turned to Clifford. "Make a note to exchange that orange vest for a medium. It's just a matter of time."

Chapter 10

*D*AD CLUTCHED THE PAINTED CERAMIC FROG TO HIS CHEST AS WE headed toward the door after the two-hour meeting that could have been an email. "I will treasure this for the rest of my life."

Agnes patted his shoulder. "It's just a shame we have to bribe folks with door prizes to attend."

Clifford muttered to whoever was listening, "No civic duty this generation."

Myrtle Jean wrapped the remaining cookies in foil and handed them to her new bestie, Trixie. "It was so nice meeting you, dear. How long will you be staying with Layla?"

Dad pulled at the side of his bra and winced. "Oooh, I think just for tonight. She has her own obligations and doesn't need her old aunt Trixie hanging around."

Clifford squared his shoulders and bristled. "Nonsense. A lovely lady like yourself should be welcome anytime."

I muttered under my breath, "Clifford needs to get his eyes checked."

Nick snickered and adjusted Ringo's harness. "Behave, or you'll be wearing that orange vest home."

Myrtle Jean patted Dad on the shoulder. She giggled. "Absolutely, hon. Come back and see us soon."

Agnes handed me a white slip, apparently after sniffing a dead fish if the look on her face relayed anything. She said my name with a pinch of judgment too. It was a receipt for late fees paid in full. I cast a sour look to Aunt Trixie who backed toward the door.

"Well, it's been a lovely time. Must be going. Toodle-oo."

As I was shutting the door behind us, I heard Clifford wheeze again. "Handsome woman that Trixie."

We walked down the street toward our trailers, Ringo walking between Nick and me. Dad pulled at his bra straps again. "I can't wait to get this thing off. I've never taken one off myself before. Maybe you can show me that trick where you gals pull it through your sleeve."

Nick snorted.

I rolled my eyes. "Let's talk about this when we're *alone*, Aunt Trixie."

Dad gave a big clueless smile to Nick then passed the smile to me. He put his hand out for the leash. "Why don't I take . . . this fella?"

Nick passed it to Dad and Ringo trotted jauntily ahead.

Dad followed the pup forward. "I hope you know where we're going because I have no idea."

They were a few paces in front of us when Nick slowed so we could talk. "Your . . . aunt . . . is interesting."

I felt guilty lying to him. Especially when it was so obvious that he could see right through it. "Uh-huh."

"You said yesterday your dad was visiting. Did he go home? Or is he . . . usually Trixie Hamm?"

"Dad is not for public consumption. He'll be back tomorrow. And no, he isn't . . ."

Nick nodded. "Not that it matters."

I shook my head. "Trust me, it would be an easier alternative."

Nick slowed his pace to a stroll. "How long have you lived here?"

"In the last chance resort? About six months."

"What brought you here?"

"Bad life choices. You?"

"It seemed like a good place to start over."

"Here?"

He waved his arm around. "Why not? You got the lake, the trees . . ."

"Geriatric enforcers on a power trip."

"Cool neighbors." Nick gave me a warm smile, followed by a long look like he was considering whether or not he should say something.

"What is it?"

He laughed under his breath. "I came here because I'm looking for a less complicated life."

I pointed to myself. "Well, you are really barking up the wrong tree here, my friend. Because my life is about as complicated as they get."

He flinched like he'd been slapped. Nick's tone changed immediately to defensive. "I wasn't suggesting anything . . ."

"Good. Because I told you yesterday. I'm not in a place to start a relationship right now."

His lips flattened and his eyes turned dark and hard. "Layla. I'm not hitting on you. I'm just trying to get to know you better."

That was always the beginning of the end. "Why?"

Nick stopped walking and faced me. His jaw tight with controlled emotion, his tone sharp. "What do you mean, 'Why'?"

"Everyone has an agenda. What's yours? Is it my dad?"

His eyebrows shot up. "Have you always been this cynical or is it just with me?"

"I'm an equal opportunity cynic. It saves time."

Nick stared into my eyes for a moment like he was trying to read me. When I gave him nothing to go on, anger and hurt shone back at me. He started toward home at a normal pace. "I don't have an ulterior motive. I thought we could be friends."

A wave of regret rolled over me. *I sound like such a jerk.*

I'd never been good with people. It wasn't entirely my fault. I'd learned very young that most people only wanted to use me. Until I knew for sure what their motives were, I had a tendency to say all the wrong things and push them away. Apparently, I wasn't getting any better at it.

We walked the rest of the way in silence and said good night at my mailbox where Dad was waiting with the dog. Dad handed Nick the leash without saying a word. He examined my expression but didn't pry.

Nick crossed the yard to his trailer and disappeared inside. Only Ringo looked back.

Dad opened the door for us. "I take it that did not go well."

"As well as it always does."

Chapter 11

*G*UNFIRE ERUPTED FROM INSIDE THE CONCRETE WAREHOUSE, AND *I dropped to the ground. Where was it coming from? And what went wrong? Everything was hazy and disjointed. Melissa Bayles, one of my officers, was yelling something to me but I couldn't make it out. I motioned for her to repeat it, but more gunfire peppered the air. I reached for my sidearm, but my holster was empty. I started to panic. Where's my gun? My heart thumped in my ears. Jacob appeared on the loading dock and yelled to me. A second later, an explosion rocked us, and Jacob was gone.*

Melissa was on the ground six feet in front of me, bleeding out. "I thought you had my back, Layla."

I skittered to her side. "I'm sorry. Stay with me." I put my hand on her thigh to try to stop the bleeding. It was no use. The light in her eyes was going out.

My heart pounded against my chest, this time louder like metal on metal and Melissa started to fade.

I woke on the floor under my bed, out of breath, my heart racing, my head foggy.

There was the pounding again. It was coming from the other side of the trailer.

I rolled out from under the bed and reached for the Glock on my nightstand out of habit. I got a handful of hairbrush. I threw it on the bed, frustrated.

I crept to the window and peeked through the blinds. There was definitely someone out there. The clock said four minutes to eight in the morning, so obviously not a social call from someone who actually knew me.

Silently moving through the living room, I grabbed Dad's ceramic frog from the TV stand and threw the door open, ready to strike.

My vision filled with a cached image of Melissa.

"Whoa! You wouldn't hit an un-frogged man, would you?"

I shook my head and the image vanished. A young cop with wheat-colored hair stood on my bottom step. "Do I know you?"

The man grinned. "It's me, Officer Virtue, Adam Beasley from the precinct. You were assigned to mentor me right before . . . you know . . ."

I placed the frog on the table by the door. "Before I was kicked off the force in shame?"

He gave me a little shrug. "I was going to say before Stratton Park."

I gave him a once-over. "Same thing. What are you doing here, Beasley?"

"I've been assigned to follow up on your statement."

"They're giving that job to rookies now?"

He made a sheepish grin. "Castinetto's my mentor these days. It was his idea."

"Of course it was." I turned to tell Dad I'd be going outside for a few minutes, but the couch was empty. "Dad?"

I got no answer from the living room, so I checked down the hall. I pulled a hoodie over my tank top and track pants and shoved my feet into my sneakers. "Dad? Are you in here?"

Adam had let himself in and was looking around the living room like he was examining a crime scene. Dad's blanket was neatly folded on top of his pillow. "Something wrong?"

I pushed past Adam and went down the steps. "My dad seems to have wandered off."

"Maybe he just went for a walk."

"Not at this time of day. He's usually just gone to bed." I looked around the courtyard. The Aston Martin was still in the carport. The Mustang was across the street with a ticket under the windshield wiper. Not a legal ticket, one of Clifford Bagstrodt's homemade unenforceable tickets. Three tickets and you lost your outdoor grilling privileges. Ten and you had to do post community meeting cleanup for a year. I had about thirteen in the menu drawer in the kitchen. One more and I'd have to wear the sash of shame at the next meeting.

"Do you want me to call in a silver alert?"

"No. My dad's not that old. And there's nothing wrong with his mind that the seventies didn't cause." I walked around the back of my trailer and found Dad, undisguised, sitting at the picnic table with Marguerite. An iced coffee condensating in front of him and the rooster in his lap. "What the . . . ?"

Dad gave me a smile and a wave. "Look, baby girl. A rooster."

"Yeah, we're acquainted."

Marguerite picked up her iced coffee and took a loud slurp, her eyes never leaving mine.

Dad grinned. "We're naming him Steppenwolf, aren't we, sugar?"

Adam took a step closer to the picnic table and pointed. "Hey, isn't that . . ."

I grabbed his arm and pulled. "Nope. Do you want my statement or what?"

As I dragged him behind me, he craned his neck to look at Dad and fired off a couple of questions. "Are you sure? Because I just saw him on the news. . . ."

"No, you didn't. Let's go down by the lake and get this over with."

Adam shoved his hands in his pockets and followed me across the street and through the woods to the picnic area by Pinecrest Lake, dragging his feet like a petulant teenager.

The leaves were changing to the autumn rainbow of yellow, orange, and red. The colors reflected on the lake like a mirror to another land. Several grills were set up for barbecuing, just waiting for a bag of charcoal. "Wow, this is nice. You don't usually see something like this in a dumpy trailer park."

I took a seat at one of the splintery picnic tables and reminded myself that smacking a cop was a class six felony. "First of all, it's a mobile home community, and it started out as a seasonal camp resort then went bankrupt in the fifties when they built the turnpike through here."

He stared at me slack-jawed, then scanned the lake, taking in the ring of mobile homes and cabins set into the woods.

"Second . . . What did you want, Beasley?"

He climbed onto the picnic table across from me and pulled out a little notebook. "I'm supposed to go over your statement from yesterday with you."

"Why? Is it standard procedure to follow up on witness statements from a heart attack now or did something turn up on the tox screen?"

"The tox screen. Apparently, the deceased, a Mr. Chuck McCracken, aka Chuckles the Clown, had enough nicotine in his system to kill a baby elephant."

"Really? So, he was murdered."

Adam's face scrunched up. "Why do you say murder?"

"Because it would be near impossible for a man of his size to accidentally vape himself to death."

Adam opened a little notebook and jotted something down. "Maybe it was suicide."

Suicide? Now I remember who this guy is. He's dumber than a box of rocks but he's related to the commissioner or the mayor or some muckety-muck. That's how I got stuck with mentoring him in the first place. "There are a dozen different ways to kill yourself that don't involve diarrhea and balloon animals. Nicotine poisoning at a child's birthday party would not be at the top of anyone's list. Besides, he placed a bet on a horse race before the party started and he thought it was a sure thing. He made plans to be there to collect. He wouldn't off himself before the race began when he expected to win."

Adam had that blank look on his face like everything I said

was a brilliant surprise to him. "They found nicotine patches shaped as shoe inserts in his clown shoes."

"That's . . . creative. Just in his clown shoes?"

Adam consulted his notes again. He sucked in a low hiss through gritted teeth. "I'm not really supposed to tell you anything."

"Fine. I don't want to know anything."

"But . . ." Adam glanced at me then his notebook again. "They do want me to re-question everyone who was there at the party. Not the kids, of course."

"I'd give that pushy one in pigtails another look. Don't write that down, Beasley. I was joking."

He put his pen back down. "Right. What do you know about the guy in the track suit who searched Chuck's belongings?"

"Probably a dead end."

Adam seemed confused, which as far as I remembered was status quo. "So, you don't think that guy killed him?"

I shrugged. "How would I know? It's none of my business."

His face slid into a pout. "You said in your statement that you saw that guy threaten the victim."

"It's still unlikely that he killed him."

"Why?"

"For one thing, Chuckles already had his shoes on before that guy arrived. And if he worked for Chuck's bookie or a loan shark, he was just there to scare him and shake him down for any cash he had on hand. It's bad business to kill people who owe you money."

"Then that just leaves the women. In her statement, Janice Kestle said the women all stayed together the entire afternoon except for the clown's manager, Paula Braithwaite."

"I didn't notice anyone going off alone with the clown. But poison is usually a woman's weapon, so I'd still look into the women closer. You're going to want to widen your search to women who had a problem with Chuck who weren't at the party when he died."

"Why?"

I sighed. *Come on, Beasley.* "Because the poisoner was probably long gone before the party started. When the weapon is poison, the killer doesn't have to be there when the victim dies. They usually aren't. They're somewhere else establishing an alibi. The killer could have planted the inserts then taken off. We were there almost three hours before Chuckles died. Find out how long it takes for that much nicotine to kill someone."

Adam made a note. "You don't think one of the ladies tampered with Chuck's shoes while he was getting ready to go on?"

"I saw him take his shoes out of the bag and put them on myself. He could have left his bag unattended and wandered around the property for a while before I got there. Follow up with the security team Janice hired as to when he arrived."

Adam wrote that down with his tongue sticking out of the side of his mouth. "That's a good idea. There are traffic cameras in the area too."

"See. Now you're thinking. If Chuckles and I got there around the same time, the inserts were planted in the shoes before he ever arrived at the party. That means you can't limit your suspect pool to the rich, drunk moms at the party. Figure out who hated Chuck McCracken enough to kill him. And get a rundown of his whereabouts for the twenty-four hours before he died."

Adam nodded like he got it, then his eyebrows scrunched together, and Mr. Clueless was back. "How do I do that?"

"It's called police work, Adam. Just keep me out of it. I'm off the force."

He closed his notebook. "Thanks, Officer Virtue. I want you to know that things haven't been the same without you."

I climbed off the bench to head home. "I'm sure most people would say that's an improvement. And it's just Layla now."

"You really don't remember anything?"

"Bits and pieces."

"I wasn't there the day stuff went down, but I know it wasn't your fault."

"Except it was, Adam. It was a hundred percent my fault."

He was quiet for a minute. "You were a great cop. Everyone says so. Well, *most* everyone. You got a whole bunch of awards before . . . You ever think about clearing your name and coming back?"

"Not interested." I gave the kid a wave of my hand and walked through the trees. Back to my trailer and the smoldering remains of my life.

Chapter 12

I FOUND DAD WITH HIS HEAD IN THE FRIDGE.

"I'm hungry. All you have is olives and a kiwi."

"When did I get a kiwi? Oh. I think that's a lemon."

Dad looked at me like I'd lost my mind. "How do you live like this?"

I shrugged. "I usually try to grab something when I'm playing a gig."

He shut the door. "We need to go shopping."

A war raged in my conscience. I knew he couldn't stay here with nothing to eat for two weeks. Still. It was risky going out. "I'm not taking you out in public."

"Why? That lady this morning didn't recognize me."

"No, but the cop did."

"I'll wear another disguise if you want."

"We still have the cat dress."

His lips puckered in a pout. "I wore that last night."

"So?"

"So, what if we run into someone we know? They'll know it's a repeat."

"When did you become such a princess? Hold on." I dug around my closet and found a floppy hat from that one day off I had where going to the beach seemed like a good idea. "Put this on."

"Is that going to be enough?"

"This is just to get you to the car."

He grabbed his boho purse and we ran to the Mustang where Dad scrunched down in the seat. I tried to start her up and the gas needle laughed in my face.

He jabbed his thumb at the fancy car sitting in the carport. "Why don't we take the Aston Martin?"

"To the grocery store?"

"James Bond had to eat sometime."

"Alright, fine." I looked out the window and checked the mirrors. "It's clear. Go go go."

Dad dove out of the Mustang, did a roll across the street, and popped up at the edge of my yard. I hit the unlock button and he launched himself inside the sports car. I climbed in and melted into the leather. When I started the engine, a little piece of me went to heaven.

Dad grinned and nodded. "Yeah?"

"I can't get used to this."

"Why not?"

"Because it's not my life anymore, Dad."

Dad shrugged. "Sure. Whatever. Now where?"

I drove around the lake to the back of the property, aware that everyone with eyes would be drawn to us as if we were throwing twenty-dollar bills out the window. We pulled up outside a brown shack that hailed back from when the community was a summer camp resort. The sign over the door said SHOWERS AND LAUNDRY. Judging from Clifford's complaints about water usage, I figured about half the residents in the park used these laundry facilities on the sly. "Come on."

I ran inside praying that it was someone's wash day. The dryers were running. *Jackpot.* I pulled one open and grabbed a red nightie.

Dad followed me in, his eyes growing to the size of that kiwi lemon in my fridge. "No way! I can live on pizza and Chinese if I have to. I've lived on a bus."

I shoved it back and pulled out a large yellow one-piece jumpsuit. It took me a moment to process what I was looking at. "I think this is Donna's laundry." I tossed it to Dad. "Here. I'll make it up to her later." I turned my back while he changed.

"I don't know how this goes on. Or what it is."

"I think it zips up the back. I'm pretty sure she wore that to the end-of-summer picnic last month."

After a minute of grumbling I heard, "How's this?"

I failed miserably trying not to laugh. He looked like the Chiquita banana lady with chest hair. I stuffed some socks into the shelf bra and hoisted up the neckline to cover a selection of tattoos.

Dad's face soured. "Are you sure I can't just wear my own clothes? No one even remembers who I was."

The dryer buzzed, signaling that the cycle was over and the owner would be here soon to pick it up. "You know that's not true. Now take this sweater, pull your hat down, and get in the Aston."

Dad snatched the pink sweater from me, muttering about the things we do for love. Then he started to sing "The Things We Do for Love."

I turned out of the trailer park and set course for Giant Food.

"Where are we going?"

I glanced at him to see if he was teasing me. "What do you mean 'Where are we going?' We're going to the store."

His eyes were wide and unblinking. "For what?"

"Food. We just talked about this. Are you that hungry that you blocked out the last thirty minutes?"

Dad looked away and chuckled. "You know the music takes me away."

"Okay then." *There's your warning against doing drugs, right there.*

"Hey, how's your mom?"

"I don't know. It's been nine months since she got out of rehab so it's about time for her to relapse."

"I'm sorry, baby girl. Which one was she again?"

"Yellow bikini from Akron."

"Oh yeah. We lived together for a while. She had gray eyes.

I've never seen anyone with gray eyes before. You have her eyes."

"I know."

"What about you? You still on the force?"

"What? Like part-time?"

He shrugged. "Yeah, I guess that wouldn't work if you had a gig, would it?"

"It would probably save time getting to some of the crime scenes." I pulled into the strip mall and parked at a cluster of empty spots away from the store. "I've got a hundred and twenty dollars."

"For dinner?"

"For the month."

Dad stared at me open-mouthed.

"I'm thinking ramen packets and macaroni and cheese."

Dad was still staring.

"Baby girl, I'm seventy years old. I'm not eating ramen unless Jet Tila makes it for me."

That war on my conscience came back around and stabbed me in the appendix. "Fine. You can buy. But just the stuff for while you're here."

Dad gave me the olive and kiwi-lemon look of bewilderment again.

"I got into this mess, and I'll work my own way out." I locked the Aston Martin and passed Dad my mirrored sunglasses. "Here. Put these on."

He slid the frames on his face, and we crossed the parking lot. He grabbed a cart and stashed his purse in the basket. "What? I've gone shopping before."

"I thought you had people to do this for you now."

He shrugged. "No one really bothers me in California. I'm boring."

"In your wildest dreams you could never be boring." He was not lying that he knew his way around a grocery store. He bagged potatoes and corn, some fresh strawberries, then went to the deli counter and basically bought a half pound of everything. Then the meat counter where I learned the butcher keeps the prime cuts in the back and brings them out if you flash some bills. We were loaded up with enough steaks and burgers for several block parties and a triple bypass. Then Dad turned us down the cookie aisle. He held his arm out and swept an entire row of Pepperidge Farm bags into the cart without slowing down.

One hour later, we had enough food to keep us alive for a year in an underground bunker. Then we hit the beer and wine section. We both stopped dead in our tracks. Just the sight of a bottle of champagne took me back to seventh grade, and the memory of sneaking it to school mixed in my 7 Up. That was a silent cry for help that never got answered. By the time I was in high school I was leaving the 7 Up at home.

After a moment of silence, Dad started singing Joe Walsh's "One Day at a Time."

Mostly.

I'd say eighty percent of the words were right. I was very nervous someone would recognize him.

I probably shouldn't have joined in on the chorus.

Dad veered the cart out of the danger zone and headed for the register.

I turned over a box of macaroni and cheese so I couldn't see the nutrition panel. "You've been sober for a while now."

"Nearly three years."

"You've got so much time behind you. That must make it easier."

"Don't be fooled, baby girl. The further you are away from your last drink, the closer you are to the next. Addiction is a cruel mistress. I'm so sorry it's something I passed on to you."

"You didn't, Dad. I made my own choices."

I reached for a pack of Hershey bars and Dad yanked me into a surprise hug. "I'm glad you stayed away from drugs, baby girl. You did, didn't you?"

"Dad, you're smothering me."

He eased up and wiped at his eyes.

"Yes, I stayed away from drugs. My homelife was a perpetual cautionary tale. It's the whole reason I dropped out of college and went to the police academy. I saw too many lives ruined by drug addiction."

Dad squeezed my shoulders. His eyes misted with tears.

I grabbed a bag of giant marshmallows from an endcap as we passed it. "I just didn't realize I was developing an addiction of another kind until it was too late."

Dad pushed the cart around the corner past the ice cream aisle. "Maybe I could join you at your AA meeting."

"Absolutely not."

"Why not?"

"Because they don't want anything from me. Once they know who my father is, that'll change."

Dad grew quiet and I felt remorse inch its way up my back. "Why don't you go to your usual meeting with Keith?"

Dad *tsk*'d. "AA's become a drag since Steven won't stop talking about that macrobiotic diet."

A squatty senior redhead was working the only open register. "Did you find everything okay?"

Dad read her name tag. "Why, yes, we did, Vi. Thank you so much."

Vi stopped dragging cookies across the scanner and stalled on Dad's face. "Your voice is so familiar."

Dad grinned. "Is that right?"

She gave him a beaming smile. "Have you ever been on television?"

I stepped on Dad's foot. "No, Nana just has one of those voices." I muttered under my breath, "That she forgot to disguise."

Vi swept through the belt of groceries with one eye on Dad and the occasional scowl for my benefit.

Dad stood there grinning under his floppy hat behind my mirrored sunglasses. He adjusted the Kleenex boobs inside his jumpsuit and tightened his sweater. When the checker was done, she gave us a bill total that would feed a kid through college graduation.

Dad pulled his wallet from the boho bag and released a wad of hundreds. Drug lords carried less. He passed a few bills over. "Keep the change, darlin'."

Vi practically swooned. "So familiar . . ."

I grabbed Dad's arm. "Come on, Nana. Time for your dialysis."

Chapter 13

I PULLED INTO THE CARPORT AND WAS MET BY A BLACK LAB ON MY front step. Ringo's tail started to swing like he was playing a snare drum.

"Hey, boy. What are you doing out here by yourself?"

He ran to greet me.

I bent to pet him and was rewarded with another snout punch. "You need to go home. Where *you* live."

Dad climbed out of the passenger seat burdened under the heavy load of his bakery bag. "I thought he lived here."

Ringo dropped to his belly and grunted.

"This is Nick's dog, Dad. The guy from last night." I ran my hand over his muzzle. "Your owner is probably looking for you right now. Why don't I take you to him? See if he's still mad at me."

Ringo rolled his sad eyes to mine.

Dad laughed. "I think he wants to stay."

Ringo's head came up and he gave a sharp bark and started to wag his tail again.

Nick's front door opened, and he called out. "Ringo! Are you out here?"

Ringo barked and looked in Nick's direction, but he stayed at my feet.

"He says he's trading up."

Nick came around the corner and looked at the dog. Then at

Dad in his sunglasses and yellow halter top pantsuit, a tuft of gray chest hair peeking out of the plunging neckline that had sagged in the car. Dad had thrown the sweater in the back seat and his arm and shoulder tattoos were on full display. "I don't blame him. Your house looks like a lot more fun. I just sit at a computer all day." He gave Dad a bemused look. He avoided looking at me.

"We went grocery shopping," I told him, as if that answered everything and smoothed over my rude behavior from last night.

Dad grinned and held out the wax paper bag. "Baby bear claw?"

Nick peeked in the bag and extracted a small pastry. "Nice. Why don't I help you take the groceries in? Then I can get this one out of your way."

Ringo gave me another playful bark.

It was uncomfortable with Nick. He was giving off a definite cold vibe, clearly not over what had happened between us. "That'd be great, thanks."

Dad had already disappeared into the trailer. He had always been more the *pay-for-someone-to-do-it-for-you* type than the hands-on, *do-it-yourself* kinda guy. A side effect of getting rich so young. I popped the trunk while Nick extracted the bags from the back seat and took them in. After several trips we had the car unloaded and the groceries put away. Dad ambled out of the bathroom in five-hundred-dollar jeans, a white Italian silk shirt, and a linen flat cap that I was sure was designer.

Nick's eyes were drawn to him instantly and they widened in surprise.

I cleared my throat. "We have company."

Dad was halfway to sitting on the couch, his hand reaching for the remote. He hovered over the seat. "Was I supposed to wait to change?"

Nick's eyebrows dipped. "Hey, isn't that . . . ?"

I grabbed his arm and two grape sodas. "Nope. People make

that mistake all the time. Let's go down to the lake. Come on, Ringo."

The dog barked and vaulted for the door.

Dragging Nick away was like pulling a feather through molasses. "But I'm sure . . ."

I pulled harder. "The dog's waiting."

Nick reluctantly followed me outside. He gave me some side-eye but kept his mouth shut.

I led them across the street behind Donna's trailer and through the woods where I'd taken Adam this morning. We passed the picnic tables where I'd given my debrief and went a little farther down the path around the lake to where a row of empty rental cabins with private boat launches circled the water's edge across from us. We moved toward a cluster of wooden Adirondack chairs near the old swimming dock.

Ringo headed straight for the dock and Nick gave him a stern command. "Ringo. No."

The Lab stopped moving forward and looked to see if I'd be on his side.

I swept some dried leaves off the seat of one of the Adirondack chairs, sat down, and popped the cap on my grape soda. "You better not jump in that lake, buddy."

He came back to my side and dropped down to my feet with a grumble. He laid his head on my foot.

Nick stared at the dog for a moment then sat in the chair next to mine. "What did you say your last name was?"

I sipped my soda and watched the dragonflies buzzing across the lake. "I didn't."

I could hear his wheels turning.

I reached over and touched his knee. "I'm sorry about last night. I didn't mean to offend you."

His voice was soft. "It's fine."

"I've been told I have trust issues."

"Is that right?"

I cast him a snarky glance to match his tone.

"And what do you attribute that to?"

"Teenage girls. I did not exactly grow up in a conventional home and my high school years were rough because of it. My mom moved us around a lot to *start over.* And by 'start over,' I mean find new bridges she hadn't burned yet."

He nodded and took a pull of his grape soda. "And why did you choose a career in music?"

"Musician is my backup career. I was a cop for the last eighteen."

"Did you retire?"

"Officially, I was suspended and subject to an Internal Affairs investigation where they wanted to demote me, but I saved them the trouble and resigned."

"Wow. What happened?"

"I made a critical error in judgment."

He tapped my knee with his. "I'm sorry. Did you like being a cop?"

"Most of the time. It's a lot harder now than it was when I was a rookie. Kids in the suburbs weren't overdosing on fentanyl-laced heroin eighteen years ago."

Ringo shifted his snout on my foot and let out a sigh.

Nick took another drink of his soda. "I can't imagine how hard that must have been. Are you happier here in the 'burbs?"

"Don't be fooled. The suburbs may have a better class of crime and more expensive drugs, but they're as corrupt as the inner city. Rich people just know how to dress it up better. How about you? What do you do when you're not hanging out at the Seahorse Lounge cruising for chicks?"

Nick snorted. "I loiter at the diabetic supply store looking for my next sugar momma."

"Of course you do." He grew quiet and the shift in the air played across my shoulders and made my breath freeze in my chest.

"I work as a government contractor in tech security."

I could feel that there was more he wasn't saying, but I didn't ask for details. We were on an unspoken, you-don't-pry, I-won't-pry agreement.

Ringo's head shot up and he stared down the shoreline to the woods.

I put my hand on him. "What's the matter, boy?"

His nose lifted and he growled quietly.

The sound of a bell tinkled and a voice carried softly on the wind. "I think there are folks down by the lake, Pippi. Let's go say hello."

I made sure I had a good handful of red leash before what I knew was coming around the lake finally appeared. "Okay, Ringo. Be calm."

Nick craned his neck to look around me. "What is it?"

Foster emerged from the woods walking a black pig the size of a fat little Pomeranian. It was wearing a pink tutu and had a crown of flowers and pink ribbons tied to its head.

I grinned so hard I felt my cheeks crack.

Nick breathed out and said, "Oh. My. God. Is that Pippi?"

I snickered with glee. "In all her glory."

"This was definitely worth the wait."

Ringo barked like he wanted to kill Pippi and her entire family, but his tail never stopped wagging.

Nick snapped his fingers and Ringo dropped to his butt in the sand.

Foster walked the pig closer to our chairs. "Oh, it's you, Layla. Hello. And you are the new neighbor who lives in the blue-and-white trailer. You were at the meeting last night. You had four chicken wings."

Nick held out his hand. "That's right. I'm Nick."

Foster stared at his hand, struggle playing across his face. He reached out and tapped the hand for a lightning second then wiped it on his cargo pants. "This is Pippi Snickelfritz. She's a miniature American Guinea Hog. She's very smart."

A wide grin played across Nick's face. "I'll bet she is."

Pippi snooted Ringo and ran a few feet away, then turned to see if he would chase her. Ringo glanced at me and then Nick. Nick nodded and I unclipped the leash.

"Go play."

The two of them chased each other in zigzags through the man-made beach like old friends instead of babies from two different species. I had never been able to make friends that fast in my entire life.

Foster sat on an empty chair next to mine and stared out at the lake.

"How are you today, Foster?"

"I'm doin' fine, Layla. How you?"

"Not bad. I like Pippi's flower crown."

Foster stared at his hands. "Yeah. She's a good girl. Gran says girls like flowers so I made Pippi flowers she could take with her. She likes marigolds and daisies. Roses are no good. Roses have thorns. Do you like roses, Layla?"

I nodded. "I love roses, but they wouldn't be any good to wear in a crown."

"Yeah. Roses have thorns. Thorns are not good for a crown. Do you like roses, Nick?"

Nick gave Foster a grin. "I think I really like daisies and marigolds."

Foster thought about that for a moment, then his lips curved upward. "Yeah. So does Pippi. Pippi's a good girl. She's my best friend. She keeps all my secrets. Pippi never tells anyone."

Nick glanced at me. "Absolutely. Keeping confidence is part of the pact. Good friends are hard to find. You have to treasure the ones you get."

I picked up my soda and took a drink, staring at the lake as if the Loch Ness Monster would emerge at any second.

Pippi came to a stop at Foster's feet, her flower crown now a necklace. Foster reached down and shifted it back to her head. "You're a good girl, Pippi. Let's go home. Gran's stories are on soon."

We said goodbye to Foster and Pippi, and Nick and I walked Ringo back through the woods to the trailers. Ringo was worn-out and ready for a snack and a nap. Another reason I felt we were kindred spirits.

We emerged alongside Donna's trailer by her little patio, and I could already see that problems were brewing at home. "Oh no."

Nick snorted. "I think your dad has forgotten he's supposed to be Aunt Trixie."

I sighed. Dad was outside, sans disguise, and he had attracted a crowd. "This never ends well."

Chapter 14

*D*AD WAS SITTING IN THE SCREENED PORCH WITH A FEW OF THE more shameless Lake Pinecrest ladies. From the looks of things, word had gotten around that a rich, eligible bachelor had moved in, because they'd come a-courting—and the heavy smell of apple pie hung in the air.

Agnes had dressed in a fuchsia bodycon dress with a slit up her thigh that wasn't fooling anyone as to her intentions. Marguerite's long dark hair looked like she'd had a Brazilian blowout, and her eyelashes had grown tarantula legs. Myrtle Jean was wearing so much rouge and lipstick, she looked like a kewpie doll. And Old Lady Henson, the ninety-year-old spinster with a thick patch of cannabis growing in her front flower bed, was wearing what looked an awful lot like a wedding gown, albeit yellowed with age. She batted her eyes and gave me a one-shoulder shrug—God love her.

Dad was surrounded by a banquet of baked goods, grinning for all he was worth. "Hey, baby girl. You're back. Look who came to visit."

The ladies tittered like thirteen-year-olds at a boy band concert.

Nick snickered under his breath. "Which one do you think will be your stepmother?"

I grunted. "Yes. How very neighborly of you ladies." I cast a glare at Dad who tried to hide behind a glass of lemonade.

Agnes patted her updo. "Well, your aunt Trixie was such a

lovely woman, when Marguerite said your father was in town, I wanted to come say hello and meet him too."

I threw a scornful glare at the Latina busybody, which she deflected with a toss of her hair like a Pantene shampoo model.

Dad peeled the paper off a homemade blueberry muffin. "You're welcome anytime, sugar."

Agnes purred. "Layla, I can't believe this is your father. He's so nice." Agnes purred again and touched Dad's chest then pulled her hand away like it was hot.

Oh good Lord.

Dad nudged the muffins Nick's way. "And you lovely ladies know my daughter's boyfriend, don't you?"

"Dad! He is not!" The heat in my face threatened to make me sweat.

Nick snickered. "Don't be like that, sugarplum."

Myrtle Jean giggled and scooted her chair closer to Dad. "Oh yes, we met Nick the other day when he moved in. How long will you be staying with Layla?"

Dad grinned at the silly old girl. "I haven't decided yet, doll."

I'm pretty sure we had. "You said two weeks."

He shrugged. "Thereabouts."

Marguerite picked up the pitcher of lemonade and topped off Dad's already full glass. "You'll have to let me make my enchiladas for you one night, Corbin."

Corbin?

Dad winked at me.

Nick murmured disbelief next to me. "Corbin? Mmm-mm. No way."

I jabbed him with my elbow.

Dad was king of the suck-ups. "I would love that, honey. I'm sure Layla has a gig or two where I'll be left to my own wicked devices."

Agnes fanned her face with a paper plate. "I'm sure I know that voice."

Myrtle gave Dad her best coy look. "Did you do TV commercials?"

Dad shook his head. "Not that I remember."

Agnes slapped his arm. "You were on the news."

Dad took a swig of his lemonade and gave her a flirty grin.

Marguerite ran her hand through her hair to be sure the breeze caught it just right. "No, *chica*. He has the silky voice like a radio man. Are you a DJ?"

Dad sat back in his chair and crossed his legs. He gave me a wink. "Now that you mention it, I did do a pretty famous commercial on the radio once."

The ladies clapped their hands like they'd won a prize and congratulated themselves for being so clever.

Dad got that *Did I leave the oven on?* look on his face. "Wait. I think I did a TV commercial in Germany once. No. Maybe that was someone else."

I couldn't listen to their prattling any longer. If they had any idea what that commercial was for, I'd be done here. It was just a matter of time. I left him with his fan club in the screened porch and dragged the lawn chair around to the front of the trailer out of their view. I plopped down and Ringo appeared by my side.

Nick followed us and looked from me to the dog and back. "Do you want company, or do you want to be alone?"

"Alone."

"Send Ringo home when you're done with him."

I put my hand on the Lab's back and nodded. Flirtatious laughter from the twittering idiots on the porch reminded me of why I don't get involved with people in the first place. An area of my butt ripped through the broken plastic strip reminding me I needed to score some gigs soon or I'd have to get a real job driving for Amazon. I also might want to cut back on the corn dogs.

Kelvin came out of his trailer and shot some bucketball while I played on my phone and stroked Ringo's ears. I was drifting into cute baby animal video oblivion when Ringo's tail started to thump against the lawn chair.

I looked up and Kelvin was standing over me watching the video of a raccoon nibble a vanilla wafer. "What up, Kelvin?"

Ringo stood and sniffed Kelvin's offered hand.

"Why don't you like kids?"

I flipped the phone over on my lap. "Who says I don't like kids?"

He shrugged. "The lady who wears those animal sweaters told Ms. Harcourt when they were writing up your trailer for your screens."

"Myrtle Jean Maud." *Nosy old busybody.*

Kelvin nodded. "She said that's why you never had any. You're not nocturnal."

"What does that have to do with—oh. Did she maybe say I'm not ma-ternal?"

Kelvin's eyes did a little fade. "Yeah. That might have been it. So why don't you like 'em?"

I ran my hand down Ringo's back. "I don't like the criers or the ones who go off without warning like car alarms. But you're pretty cool."

His trailer door opened, and Donna stuck her head out. "Kelvin! You best get your butt in here and do this homework."

I raised my eyebrows and Kelvin muttered, "School sucks."

I nodded. "I feel ya, friend."

He turned slowly and dragged his feet. "Coming."

Kelvin crossed the street and disappeared into the trailer. Donna gave me a wave. She pointed to the screened porch and shook her head in amusement. I made a finger gun and put it to my head. She laughed, then waved again and shut the door.

I tried to shake off what Myrtle Jean Maud had blabbed. Who was she to say I wasn't maternal? She didn't know me. And if she'd spent her career surrounded by drugs and gang violence in middle schools, she wouldn't be a huge fan of kids either.

It's not that I never wanted kids. The opportunity never presented itself. Plus, I had no idea what I would do with one if it came along. I didn't exactly have the best role models. Both of my parents were in and out of rehab my whole life. Mom fell apart each time she got a new man. And Dad could never leave his job long enough to stay clean. This was the longest he'd been clean and sober in my entire life.

I thought I'd broken the cycle when instead of following in their footsteps I'd joined the police force. Unfortunately, I'd underestimated the amount of pain that was out there every day and my ability to handle it. What could my life have been like if I'd been stronger?

I was trying really hard to turn it all around. I wasn't sure how long I'd be able to hide out in the Lake Pinecrest Trailer Park. With Agnes riding my tail about late fees, and Dad's new gang of Golden Girls, the situation here was a ticking time bomb. I ran my hand down Ringo's neck.

He turned and licked my elbow.

"Thank you."

Ringo put his head in my lap and sighed.

"You're right. I just have to keep going. One foot in front of the other. Just do the next thing."

The silly broads on the screened porch cackled, giving me the overwhelming urge for a drink.

"It looks like the next thing is going to a meeting."

Chapter 15

I PLANNED TO CREEP INTO THE MEETING AND SLIP UNDER SCARLETT and Bree's radar. While I was sure they were still mad that I'd dissed them the last time, I was hoping they were on the avoidance side of irritated and not the confrontational side. One problem with people working the program is they get too comfortable discussing their feelings and want to care-and-share slap you across the face with them without warning.

I was currently working on my own confrontational urges. Everything in me wanted to give that self-righteous Miranda a piece of my mind for sending me to a den of baby vipers for a gig. I'd been a cop for eighteen years, and I thought I'd seen it all. But never in my wildest dreams did I expect someone to murder the clown at a kid's birthday party.

I turned the doorknob as silently as possible to not disrupt the proceedings. Charisse was at the podium talking about her husband inviting clients to dinner who'd brought wine as a hostess gift and how she spent the night hiding in the kitchen so she didn't embarrass him.

Scarlett and Bree were sitting in the back row close to the coffeepot. Scarlett caught my eye and waved wildly, her beaded blouse clacking with every move. She pointed at the empty chair in between them.

Bree mouthed, "We saved you a seat."

The last thing I wanted was to piss them off more. No. Strike that. The last thing I wanted was to sit next to the creepy guy who smelled like old potatoes. And since the only other empty chairs were around him, I reluctantly joined the girls in the back. "Hey."

Bree gave me a wide grin and twirled her blond ponytail. "Hey, Layla."

Scarlett nudged me and her gold bracelets clacked together. "Why you late?"

"I've got drama at home."

Scarlett gave me a knowing look behind her designer glasses. "Man trouble?"

"You could say that. My dad is visiting and it's causing problems with the neighbors."

Bree twisted her ponytail around her finger. "Parents, am I right?"

Miranda loudly cleared her throat and threw us a glare on her way up to the podium in her black, high-necked designer suit. "Thank you, Charisse. I apologize for the chatter in the back."

Scarlett made a rude gesture in Miranda's direction.

Charisse took her seat and Miranda assumed the position at the podium, unwrapped a length of toilet paper from her purse, sniffled, and dabbed her eyes. The room gave a collective eye roll they could feel at the bus station across the street.

Miranda took a long penetrating look around the room. "My ex-husband was murdered."

Bree whispered. "Oh. That's very sad."

I nodded.

Scarlett chuckled under her breath. "I wonder if this is a confession."

Miranda sniffled again. "He was working with children when he died."

The hair on my neck stood at attention.

Scarlett grunted. "Children are tiny little ebola carrying viruses."

I snickered, but my focus was drilling down to a pinpoint on Miranda. I mean, what were the odds?

She daintily blew her nose. "I'm just shocked. I've been reeling ever since I got the news. And I don't want to sound heartless, but now I'll never get my alimony."

Scarlett said something that Bree giggled at, but I didn't hear what it was because I was hyperfocused on the fashionably dressed woman at the podium crying into a wad of Charmin.

"Chuck was six months behind. He never was good at managing his money, but I still can't help but miss him."

"Holy Mother of God." The words slipped out before I could stop them. Miranda glanced my way but went right on with her share about how much she loved her ex and felt lost without him and other nonsense I wasn't really listening to. *Good God. Chuckles the farting clown was Miss Perfect's ex?*

Scarlett leaned close to me and whispered, "Is she talking about that pudgy birthday party clown on the news?"

Bree gasped. "My mom was just talking about that this morning."

Scarlett shook her head. "There's no way."

I whispered, "I was at that horrible party. Miranda set me up with her friend Janice to play for the future inmates of America."

Bree grabbed my arm. "You were there?"

Scarlett had my shoulder in a Vulcan death grip. "Tell us everything."

I hissed at them, "Shh. After. She's watching."

Miranda was gearing up for the big finish on her monologue. She patted her heart as her voice shook with emotion. "I will always love you, Chuck. There was a time that you were the light of my life. My knight in shining armor. I always thought we'd get back together one day."

I shook my head. "This has to be some kind of misunderstanding. I mean this is Northern Virginia. More than one person can be murdered over the course of a week here."

Scarlett huffed. "I have So. Many. Questions. Is everything about Miranda a lie?"

Bree crossed her arms over her chest. "We have to ask her. I'll never be able to focus on my Jane Eyre essay with this burning in my brain."

Miranda heaved one last dramatic sigh and returned to her seat.

We suffered through two of AA's longest shares—including one from old-potato-smelling Varish about his stolen hedge clippers that turned out to be in his garage—before the meeting was finally adjourned.

I left my seat and headed straight for Miranda, Bree and Scarlett on my rear like we were riding a tandem bike.

Miranda grasped my hand. "Layla. I'm so glad you're here. I've been wanting to talk to you about that horrible day."

"You mean yesterday? The birthday party at Janice's?"

Her eyes flashed a moment of irritation. "What else would I be talking about?"

Scarlett inched closer. "So, the party clown was really your husband?"

Miranda let go of my hand and dabbed her eyes. "I was very young and foolish when we got married. Chuck was a serial cheater and a terrible businessman, but I still loved him. You can't possibly understand, ladies. I'm embarrassed to admit this, but it was like he had some kind of hold on me."

"Chuck McCracken?" I asked. "Chuckles the Clown? Bald, blue wig?"

Miranda nodded with a faraway look in her eyes. "He was my first love. We'd still be together if it weren't for his string of torrid affairs."

I let that wash over me and tried to picture the chubby version of Harpo Marx standing next to the stylish Miranda in a tuxedo and clown shoes.

Bree twirled her hair. "Eww."

Miranda grabbed my hand again. "Did you see anything strange happen at the party?"

"You'll have to be more specific."

"Any menacing characters hanging around? Chuck had been known to frequent some questionable establishments from time to time."

"I think those are questions for the police. I'm just a musician."

"But you were there, Layla. Was there anyone you saw who threatened Chuck?"

"He was surrounded by children and making balloon animals all afternoon."

A flash of anger passed Miranda's eyes and her prim and proper facade cracked around the edges. "He owes some pretty unsavory people money, and they tend to follow him when he works. I can't believe you didn't see anything at all the entire time. I'll have to ask his manager, Paula. She'd know. I'm pretty sure she's in love with him."

"Is there another Chuck McCracken who works as a clown?"

"What were you even doing there that you didn't see anyone threaten him?"

Okay, weird. "Uh . . . I was trying not to get stabbed in the face for playing 'Baby Shark' while your friend Janice and the other party moms had enough booze to drink Charlie Sheen under the table."

Scarlett poked the back of my arm. "Do you know something the police don't know, Miranda?"

Miranda looked down her nose at the tiny Asian American. "No. How could I? I wasn't there. But you were, Layla. Maybe you could have done something to help. Janice said you and Chuck disappeared for like twenty minutes. What were you doing, Layla? Did Chuck lure you off somewhere and seduce you?"

My mind went blank again. "The middle-aged clown with the beer gut? That Chuck McCracken?"

Bree stepped to Miranda. "Just what are you accusing her of?"

I put my hand gently on the young girl's arm. "Miranda, have you lost your mind? I wasn't doing anything with Chuckles the Clown. I was putting one of the drunk guests in an Uber instead of letting her drive home."

Miranda sighed and clutched at her bare neck. "Paula should have kept a better eye on him to make sure he was safe. She's a terrible manager. Chuck never got the national attention with Ringling Brothers he deserved because she was too busy trolling the Tuesday open mic nights at Dooley's Pub for her next break-out star. That's where we met, you know. He should have had so much better."

Behind me, I could hear whispering between Scarlett and Bree, and I knew what was coming.

Miranda was called to the front by Varish who was having an existential crisis with a folding chair. The moment she was gone, Bree grabbed my arm. "We have to go to that pub."

"Based on what?"

Scarlett tossed her head. "Because I want to ask the fat clown's manager if she was having an affair with him."

"What good will that do?"

"Don't you want to see what this guy's superpower was that he was the love of uptight Miranda's life?"

Bree held up her phone. "I just Googled him, and no way could this guy seduce anyone. Miranda must be a freak."

My mind went to Chuck's revelation about his life coaching masseur side hustle, but this wasn't my job anymore. "You want to stalk his manager? You don't think that's totally inappropriate?"

Scarlett dropped her chin and gave me a look. "Miranda got upset with me for not sending her a thank-you card after she gave me a Lifesaver. Bree?"

Bree stuffed her phone in her back pocket. "Miranda once gave me a twenty-minute lecture about crossing my legs to sit like a lady when wearing a dress."

Scarlett again. "She offered to give my seven-year-old son, who she's never met, lessons in etiquette and proper table setting. You better believe I want to find out what this guy's secret power over her was." Scarlett pulled her cell phone out. "Let's meet at Sundrop Roasters tomorrow right after the meeting then we'll head down to Dooley's. You can play something for open mic, and we'll try to catch this manager and trick her into telling us what was so special about a middle-aged bald clown."

Bree nodded, her blond hair bouncing around her wide innocent eyes. "My money is on Miranda's a freak."

Scarlett shook her phone at me. "Come on. What's your number?"

A gnawing fear rose up from my belly and gripped me around the throat. "I can't make it."

Scarlett's mouth slid to a frown. "What? Why not?"

"No offense, girls, but I'm really more of a loner."

They both stared at me for a beat, then they started talking over each other.

"What do you mean 'no offense'?"

"That's totally offensive."

"Why don't you want to hang out with us? Is it because I'm Asian?"

"You think I'm a kid, don't you? Like I can't hang with you because you're old. I have life experience."

"What, you think I live on egg rolls and tai chi? I mean I do eat egg rolls but so do white people."

"I'm twenty-three and I've been in rehab more times than you both put together."

"What do you have against the Chinese? I'll have you know I was born in Indiana."

I held up my hands. "Whoa! It's not personal. It's not because you're Asian and it's not your age. I just don't do the girlfriend thing. It doesn't work for me."

They were silent for half a minute and I thought it was dropped. Then Scarlett said, "What the hell is that supposed to mean?"

A dozen people freaked out and shushed her because of the no-cussing rule. Threat of the group losing meeting privileges in the church hung heavy in the air. Mostly because we all suspected Varish was a tattletale.

"It means I don't do coffee with other ladies. It always ends with hurt feelings and bad attitudes."

Bree's eyes searched mine. "Wait. Like, yours or theirs?"

"Both. Look I am never going to be the person who says the right thing, or cries over your Hallmark movies. You're better off looking elsewhere for a gal pal."

Scarlett scowled. "I think you're just afraid you might like us."

That wasn't all I was afraid of. I was also afraid of the Don Virtue phenomenon that would inevitably take over any relationship I tried to have and turn it into emotional blackmail. "Trust me, it wouldn't be mutual. Eventually, you'd be ducking my calls and pretending you moved away when I can't give you what you want."

Scarlett wouldn't let it go. "And I thought you were so cool. You haven't even given us a chance, you big chicken."

Bree shrugged and turned her face away. She pulled on the cuffs of her sleeves. "You might not want to be our friend now, but one day you'll have to trust someone. I don't know what your life was like before addiction, but you can't walk this path alone, Layla."

Chapter 16

I DROVE HOME IN A FUNK. ATE COOKIES IN A FUNK, SLEPT IN A FUNK, woke up and screamed obscenities at Marguerite's rooster—Steppenwolf apparently—in a funk. Why did I let those women make me feel so bad about myself? That usually happened after becoming friends with girls. I still wasn't over Philomena Potts putting all those embarrassing pictures of me in the school yearbook to punish me for not letting her have her birthday party at my dad's house. I was used to being judged not good enough, not cool enough, not pretty enough, all while being called a snob who thought I was better, cooler, and prettier than everyone else. All from women who didn't even know me. But this was the first time I was called too stuck up for AA. It was like a homeless shelter getting a one-star review.

One day you'll have to trust someone, Layla. The smug look they both gave me when they said I was just afraid to take off my mask. They haven't walked a day in my shoes.

Ringo was glued to my side as if I had pockets made of beef jerky. I tried to shoo him home hours ago, but he refused to leave. I'd sent Dad next door to let Nick know where his dog was. Dad said Nick just nodded and said, "Tell her to send him home when she's done with him."

I was scouring the kitchen floor for the third time today. Ringo was sitting on the chair pulled up to the table out of self-preservation. "Why can't people just leave me alone? Is it too much to ask for some privacy? We aren't in AA to make friends. I mean, neither of the A's stands for *Amigos*. Am I right, Ringo?"

Ringo barked and his tail thumped against the metal slats of the dining chair.

I sprayed another layer of lavender-scented floor cleaner on the linoleum and the Lab dropped his head to his paws on the table and grumbled.

Dad came through the front door and hovered just on the other side of the threshold. "I apologized to that gal next door for what you said."

I stopped scrubbing. "What did I say?"

"You threatened to call a Kenny Rogers Roasters to sell them Steppenwolf."

"I wouldn't really do that."

"I know you wouldn't, but whatshername don't know that."

I shrugged and tried to scour another daisy off the tile.

"You wanna talk about what happened to spin you out this way?"

"Nope."

Dad started to sing. "*Please, come talk to me. You have to unlock this misery.*"

"No matter how much you butcher Peter Gabriel, I've got nothing to say."

Dad sighed. "Let's go somewhere. Like Mexico. Or Walmart. Walmart's a real place, isn't it?"

"It is."

"There you go. We can buy you a vase."

"What would I do with a vase?"

I heard him click his cheeks. "I dunno. You get a vase and I'll get you some flowers. You like flowers, don't you?"

"Flowers die."

"Okay, bitter ray of sunshine. You still need to find someone to talk to. You need some friends."

"I have friends." I reached for the floor cleaner and Dad snatched it out of my hand. I nodded to the dog. "Ringo's my friend. Aren't you, buddy?"

Ringo barked and gave me a dog smile.

Dad shook his head. "You've got more issues to unpack than Britney. You can't put that much pressure on a dog."

Ringo whimpered.

"What pressure? He listens to me gripe in exchange for bacon."

Ringo's ears shot to attention at the b-word.

"Not once has he sent an unflattering picture of me to a tabloid for fifty bucks."

Dad pulled out the chair next to Ringo and fluffed the dog's ears. "How could he? He'd never get a cell signal here."

My hands were pink and pruney from hours of scrubbing and I was starting to see everything through a lavender haze. "I need some air. I'm going down to the lake. Can you behave if I leave you for a while?"

Ringo barked and jumped off the chair. He pranced in place excited that we were going somewhere.

Dad chuckled. "Of course he can behave. He's a good dog."

"I was talking to you."

"Oh. Then probably not."

"I'll be back soon. Your job is to fly under the radar while I'm gone. Not to sit on the screened porch and give false hope to the trailer park's desperate housewives. Come on, Ringo."

The black Lab followed me down to the lake. He picked up a random stick that was twice as long as he was and carried it along the shoreline by my side. A pile of green and blue canoes were stacked on the bank by the abandoned rental's hut. A rusty chain looped around them in case any trespassers got wild ideas about forbidden sails. I picked up a flat rock and skipped it across the face of the lake, making a quivery trail in the water. Ringo dropped the stick and synchronized his panting to his tail wags.

"You've got the life, buddy. No one expects you to be anyone other than who you are."

Ringo lay at my feet and put his chin on my shoe. He rolled his eyes to mine. I dropped into the sand and let him put his head in my lap. Running my hand over his velvety ears I felt calm wrap around me like a blanket.

"Life is much simpler without people, Ringo. No one to judge you. No harsh criticism. No one to examine you under a microscope and print that you're both privileged and abused all on the same day. Your heart can't be broken if you don't give anyone the chance."

I stopped petting him and he snooted my hand to keep going.

"Look how sweet you are. No one is watching you, waiting for you to fail. Judging you for your parents' mistakes. You don't even know who your parents are, do you, buddy? As far as you're concerned, your dad is Nick. And he's pretty cool. I did everything different from my parents only to end up following in their footsteps anyway. And every bad decision I make comes with dire consequences."

Ringo wiggled farther into my lap and heaved a contented sigh. We sat by the water's edge watching lazy dragonflies touch down on the lake and the fish trying to catch them. A heron migrating south struck at the water and sent a shock wave of ripples across the surface. Ringo raised his head and wagged his tail at the new sight.

"I bet your dad is wondering what happened to you." Just thinking about Nick made me feel weird. Nick was temptation in Levi's. The kind I normally avoided at all costs. The attraction when we first met was intense like the flash and crackle of a heat storm. I'm not normally alley trash who makes out with strange men in eyeline of a dumpster.

I'm also not *never* alley trash. I've made that bad call too many times. But I do have the tendency to pick guys I know I'll never have to see again. My heart was still broken from losing Jacob and I didn't think I would ever get over it. Plus, let's be honest. My personality does not improve with time. The first impression I make was always my best. Chalk it up to speaking my mind without reservation the more comfortable I get with someone. Just about the time I thought Mindy Farkle was going to stick around for a while, she wrote me a seven-page letter on how I'd hurt her when I said I thought her boyfriend was cheating on her and we couldn't be friends anymore. I was trying to help.

People who say they want me to be myself usually mean the

fantasy me they imagine me to be. The real me is lacking in diplomacy and is way more abrasive and opinionated. Not qualities most women jive with.

Ringo heaved another sigh.

Nick had turned out to be much kinder than the men I usually attracted. He must have something wrong with him. Maybe he was the rescuer type who was drawn to broken women he could be the knight in shining armor to. Jacob was one of those guys and it got him killed.

The unmistakable sound of eighties hair metal floated out to the water's edge.

"Ringo, we gotta go."

The Lab jumped up and wagged his tail expectantly.

I started back around the lake, moving a little faster this time, Ringo trotting to keep up. The music was getting louder with every beat of my heart. I knew that song. It's "On the Sharp Edge of Your Tongue." People criticized it when it was released, for being too dirty. They didn't look deep enough because it wasn't about sex at all. It was about the breakdown of a marriage when two people have so much bitterness, they can't talk to each other any longer without being harsh and hurtful. But once you think something's about sex you can't hear it any other way.

We emerged through the trees next to Donna's trailer just as she charged out of her front door, glaring across the street. "Layla, is that your house blasting Society's Castoffs?"

The windows of my trailer were vibrating. "I'm sorry. I'll go turn the speakers down."

"I love eighties rock as much as the next girl, but I've got my ladies over for our monthly whine and cheese and we can't hear each other's complaints. Not to mention Chantelle is having flashbacks to prom night and wants to call Bobby Dwyer. We had to hide her cell phone."

I crossed the street and yelled back, "I'll take care of it."

She held up the rocker salute. "Great taste though! This one's a classic!"

I smiled and saluted back, then flew into the trailer and pulled my electric guitar jack from the amp mid-chorus, the music squelching to a hum before I turned the amp off.

"What's the matter, baby girl?"

"What part of fly under the radar confused you?"

Dad shook his head, his face blank and clueless. "Whaddo-youmean?"

"I live in a tin can twenty feet away from a half dozen other tin cans. The whole neighborhood can hear you."

"Am I outta tune?"

I groaned and took my guitar from his hands. "I have to go."

"I thought we would watch that *Yellowstone* tonight. I just found the Paramount channel."

"Maybe when I get back."

"Where you goin'?"

"To wipe a smug look off some know-it-alls' faces and explain why I'm right and they're wrong so they'll stop judging me."

Chapter 17

*M*Y CAR WOULDN'T START. OBVIOUSLY BECAUSE I'M LAYLA VIR-tue and today was Tuesday and the universe hadn't punished me enough for being a screwup.

I had to stash my guitar and amp in the trunk of the Aston Martin and take the James Bond car to Sundrop Roasters. I tried to hide it in the back of the lot behind a bakery truck so Scarlett and Bree wouldn't see me get out of it.

I had a lot of experience with coffee shops for someone who was a non-coffee drinker. My partners were always big fans. Back in the day you could show up in uniform and your cuppa joe was on the house. That was before the days where viral videos and protests broadcast the worst of the badge. Now the bad cops were thrust into the public spotlight where the stench of their behavior tainted everyone wearing a uniform. Protect, serve, and be reviled. We were guilty by association; lucky they didn't throw that coffee in our faces. That was one thing I didn't miss from my old life.

This local roaster was new to me, having opened after I was ex-communicated. The large front window had SUNDROP painted in curvy orange script. A tiered shelf filled with trailing vines had a giant spikey yellow plant next to some hippy dippy sign about the sun's energy. I considered bailing, but Natalie Cole played overhead so I figured they couldn't be all bad.

A hundred paper stars in every size and color dripped from

the ceiling by strands of pink sparkle lights. Scarlett and Bree were sitting on a teal velvet couch, each with a giant purple mug and saucer resting on a table made out of a yellow surfboard and milk crates. Charisse was curled into a fuchsia leather club chair shaking a plastic cup of what could only be described as iced purple space juice.

Behind the girls was a ten-by-ten open bookshelf loaded with worn paperbacks and hardbound bestsellers cutting the room in half. A handwritten sign on the third shelf said TAKE ONE, LEAVE ONE—NO JAMES PATTERSON.

Separating the eclectic lounge from the espresso counter was a rear hub of long polished dorm-style tables where students and out-of-office workers lined up on violet leather barstools, head-to-head with ear buds firmly implanted. The wire spaghetti of their devices sprawling across a landscape of laptops, pastry bags, and to-go cups.

A to-go cup would be a good idea. That way I could fly out of here if they ganged up on me. There were two reasons I didn't hang out with women. They could turn vicious in a pack environment, and I had an aversion to drama. *Let me just get this over with so I can put the unpleasantness behind me.* I dropped into the fuchsia leather chair next to Charisse and kept my body angled so the door was in my sight.

Scarlett leaned against one of many orange beaded pillows strewn across the couch and crossed her arms defiantly over her chest. "What are you doin' here? Slummin' it?"

Bree kicked her. "Okay, stop. You came. We thought you wanted to be left alone. Do you want like, some coffee or something?"

"I told you I'm not a coffee drinker."

Scarlett leaned forward with one eyebrow cocked and loaded. "It's not about the coffee."

Charisse gave me a wide smile, tiny parentheses appearing around her mouth. "They have other things too, you know."

"What are you drinking?"

She held her cup out to me. "Iced ube latte. Girl, don't make that face. It's a purple potato. It doesn't taste like potato. It's just sweet."

"I'll have to take your word for it."

Bree placed her cappuccino bowl in the saucer with a clink. "Why don't you like, check out the menu? They have whipps. They're like milkshakes."

I begrudgingly headed toward the coffee counter to order while they talked about me behind my back.

The barista looked like a high school freshman held together by a series of oddly placed metal clips and pins. She navigated me through a dozen not-coffee options. I tried to focus, but my attention kept veering to the lounge area where I imagined Scarlett making a passionate plea for ditching before I returned.

They were still there when I took my double fudge whipp back to the table and they began their group interrogation, starting with Scarlett.

"So, what's your deal anyway? Why do you dislike us?"

"I don't know you well enough to dislike you."

Bree cocked an expertly trimmed eyebrow. "Then why don't you want to hang out after meetings?"

"I'm just here to work on my addiction, not make friends."

Scarlett narrowed her eyes. "How do you expect to do one without the other?"

Charisse lazily kicked her foot out. "What about your sponsor?"

"Gone." I sipped the chocolate overload and let my brain take a spin on the sugar hit. "A month after I entered the program she bailed."

Bree's face was full of pity. "Oh . . . Layla. I'm so sorry. Are you looking for a new one?"

No. "Yeah."

Scarlett nodded slowly, measuring my words like she was trying to figure out just what mental illness to ascribe to my issues. "I see. So, is it just women in recovery that you shy away from?"

"No. I don't get along with women in general."

Charisse's eyes widened. "No one? Like fifty percent of the planet? I mean, have you met us all?"

I sighed. I knew they wouldn't understand. "It was a mistake coming here."

I reached for my purse so I could go when Scarlett said, "Look,

I get it. I don't generally get along with women either. But at least I give them a chance first."

Bree shot her a look. "I thought you liked me."

Scarlett reached for the girl. "Of course I do. You're a sweetheart. I'm just saying I understand. There haven't been a lot of women I've been friends with in my life."

Hmm. That almost sounds like she agrees with me. I hope this isn't a setup that will come back to bite me in a minute. "Why do you think that is?"

Scarlett shrugged. "They can be catty, competitive, jealous, judgmental . . . What else you need?"

Finally someone was making sense. I put my drink on the surfboard table and turned myself to face her. "I would add *vindictive* to the list. When men get insulted, they usually just move on. But when you offend a woman, she wants to ruin you. She'll take you down with lies and gossip and steal your possessions to sell on eBay, destroying your reputation and everything you love."

Bree's eyes grew to the size of her cappuccino mug. "Wow. Who hurt you, Layla?"

"That list is long and bitter like your coffee. And I definitely don't want to get into it. Just take my word that I've learned it's safer to avoid the drama altogether. Women analyze every word that comes out of your mouth for secret meaning and hidden agendas. And if they're insecure, they'll assume one whether you've said it or not. Then they go after you with whatever they think will hurt you the most."

Bree absently fluffed her wavy locks and looked skyward. "That's true. I've had girls assume things about me my whole life. I have a lot of social anxiety and tend to be really quiet, so they figure I must be a snob."

Charisse hummed a trill of a laugh. "That right there. It's because you're beautiful, honey. When you're a homely girl they accept that you're shy, but when you're tall and shapely they call you stuck-up. I'm sure Layla knows all about that."

"I don't think I've ever qualified as shapely." I clutched my plastic cup and took a long sip of my fudge whipp.

Bree pulled on golden strands of her honey-colored hair for

further inspection. "I started doing drugs in high school to deal with crippling fear in social situations. I would just freeze whenever I entered a room with a lot of people. So, I'd lock myself in the bathroom and get high until I could face them. Then I'd come out and try to be friendly and the girls would accuse me of flirting and trying to steal their boyfriends. I just could not win."

Scarlett frowned. "And you're so sweet too. I wish I could smack every one of those girls who hurt you."

A cheesy grin snuck onto Bree's face and disappeared in a snap. "One day this mean girl called me Effie Trinket, the rich escort from *Hunger Games*, because I wore a blue dress with puffy sleeves to school, and it just made me so mad. I didn't even really get why. It was a beautiful dress and it cost me a fortune. I've never been rich. I had an after-school job, I had to do chores for allowance, I saved up for that dress. After that I was too ashamed to wear it out in public. And like . . . today . . . I am so beyond broke. Many of them went off to big universities and I still live at home with my parents taking online classes from a questionable school that might not even be real. I can't even afford a studio apartment around here and yet, I can't shake the nickname. They still call me Effie Trinket no matter if they run into me at Target or on the Metro." Bree tugged on her long sleeves and gave me a timid smile.

Charisse drained her space juice and placed the empty cup on the table. "It seems like once people make up their mind about you, nothing you do can alter their opinion. No matter how much you grow and change, they still have the old version of you cached in their head like a web page. I let it slip that I bought myself emerald earrings for my fiftieth birthday. Now I can't go to an office party without being sized up like I've been embezzling the firm's retirement fund for a jewelry addiction."

Bree tilted her head and looked at the paper stars overhead. "Aren't you upper management at some fancy investment firm?"

"Yeah, so?"

She shrugged. "I guess I thought people would stop judging you once you got . . ."

Charisse raised an eyebrow. "Old?"

Bree blushed. "Successful?"

Charisse snorted. "Honey, people never stop judging you. My looks are judged, my clothes, my hair, my voice. Women up the ladder fear that I'm coming for their job and women down the ladder accuse me of sleeping my way to the top. No one ever says *Wow, you must have worked real hard to get where you are. Respect.* I can't stand feeling like I'm under a microscope all the time."

The hair on the back of my neck tingled, reminding me that I'd had the same thought earlier.

Scarlett placed her cappuccino on the table and the cup rattled in the saucer. "I grew up in a white town with Chinese parents. You think I haven't been judged and criticized? No, I don't sound Chinese. And yes, I'm good at math—get over it! And I married a rich white guy, okay. Apparently, that makes me a gold digger or the trophy wife, even though I have a pharmacy degree. Women make assumptions about who I am all the time. And now that *Crazy Rich Asians* movie has people thinking I float around my mansion lighting candles with hundred-dollar bills."

A laugh bubbled out of me before I could lock it down. "Women are vicious. Just when you let your guard down and say what you really think, you find out they don't like you after all, and they've been mentally belittling you. It's not worth it to trust anyone. Just keep to yourself and be happy."

Bree frowned. "That makes me so sad for you."

Then you've never had your best friend film you while drunk so they could go viral on YouTube. "I've just learned to avoid potentially toxic relationships, so I never have to be hurt again."

Scarlett edged forward on the sofa. "Okay, but why hurt yourself in the process? Being choosey I understand. But choosing not to get close to *anyone* is only denying yourself happiness. People aren't made to be alone."

Her words were a kick in the chest. I was determined not to let her get to me. If I let my guard down now and got hurt, I could spiral, and my sobriety was still pretty new. I was barely hanging on after what happened with Jacob and the rest of my team. "I appreciate that, but there's a lot about me that you don't know. I tried telling you it wasn't personal. I'm sure you are a lovely person. All of you . . . But I'm a train wreck. I say what I'm thinking. I don't play games and that doesn't usually gel with women. I don't need the added pressure of massaging someone's hurt feelings while I'm trying to move on with my life."

Scarlett gave me a sad smile. "That's too bad because I think you sound awesome. And I get it. Women can be grudge holders, but you have to take a chance sometime. This life is hard. Do you really want to go through it alone?"

The answer that pushed against my rib cage was no. I shoved it aside. "I think alone works best for me."

The women sat quietly and watched me.

Scarlett sighed. "Then why did you come here today?"

"Because you were so sure I wouldn't."

The time flew by, and it was getting dark outside. I checked my phone and considered the commute to Alexandria ahead. I had to go to be at Dooley's for open mic night.

My time at the Sundrop had not been the torture I'd expected. Except for the unfortunate incident where someone changed the music to Adele, and all the women in the coffeehouse slipped immediately into post-breakup-depression phantom pain until it was replaced with Norah Jones, and they all relaxed.

The ladies didn't discover anything about my life, so whatever impression they walked in with they would take back out with them. Nothing learned, nothing to be disappointed in. My instincts told me they would be good friends. And I had learned the hard way that outside the police force, my instincts were always wrong.

I grabbed my keys and stood, looking for the trash can, waiting to deflect the inevitable "Where are you going?"

Scarlett glanced at me, checked her watch, glanced at me again, and drummed her fingers on the arm of the sofa. "Well, we gotta go. I don't want to be late, and rush hour should have slowed down by now."

Bree's shoulders drooped on a sigh, and she put her cup in the saucer.

They gathered their things, and each passed me, saying good-bye, and said they'd see me at the next meeting. They filed out the door as I stood there alone, stupidly with my keys dangling from my finger, expecting something but unsure of just what it was. This was exactly the kind of noncommittal aloofness that I normally appreciated.

So why did I feel like I was the kid eating lunch in the class-room while the others were having fun on the playground?

Chapter 18

WHAT JUST HAPPENED? DID THEY DIS ME? AND WHY DO I CARE? THIS is what I wanted.

I crossed the parking lot to the Aston Martin and climbed in. All the way to Dooley's Pub I couldn't shake the feeling of rejection. It was totally stupid. I didn't want to be friends with them. Even though they seemed a lot cooler than I'd expected. Charisse intimidated me a little bit. I suspected she was old enough to be my mother, but she had a toned body, great smile, and million-dollar hair. Literally. Possibly. Maybe. I don't know. Black hair was like a religion. I had a former partner who went to the salon to change her look so often it was like a part-time job. She did look fantastic though.

And Charisse was a real career woman. She was what was called a "functional" alcoholic—now in recovery.

I was not. I was "the screwup who let everyone down and people I loved died" alcoholic—now in recovery.

I slowed down for a yellow light and traffic flew past me. Three cars ran the red light. *Where are the traffic cops when you need them?*

Bree, God bless her, was the "should have been dead of an overdose but spared for some reason" addict. She seemed like a sweet, gentle kid who had done several tours through rehab. Maybe more than my mom—and that was saying something. I didn't know what her parents were like, but they probably deserved a medal and combat pay for what they'd been through.

The light turned green and the car behind me immediately laid on their horn. I went to flick on my siren and a crash of disappointment hit me that those days were over. I got back underway with a slight itch for a drink and my thoughts went right back to where I had left them. The annoying women.

Scarlett was the closest in age and edge to me. What she lacked in height she made up for in sass. She wore wit like a suit of armor. Scarlett was dangerous like Nick. Dangerous because she was so freakin' easy to like. She was obviously hurt by my attitude. I hated telling her I wasn't looking for friends because I could see that she was—and she'd be—a good one. For someone else.

I didn't want to get involved with any of them. And I was so frustrated that I couldn't stop thinking about them. It was better to get out now before I failed to live up to their expectations.

I pulled into the pub's back lot and the Porsche Cayenne that had been riding my tail all the way there pulled in behind me. I readied the Northern Virginia stare down meant to send a message that the other driver was pissing you off, and found myself looking into the square glasses of Scarlett the pharmacist-not-trophy-wife.

She got out of the car and threw her hands to her hips. "Whoa! First of all. What a gorgeous car. And second, what do you think you're doing here? I thought you were a loner."

Bree climbed out of the passenger side and gave me a tiny wave. "I thought you like, didn't want to do this or something."

I popped the trunk. "Do what? I'm here for open mic night." I pulled out my guitar and amp. "Musician—remember? I thought you all had changed your mind about coming."

Charisse climbed out of the back seat and snorted. "No way. We're hoping to spy on that dead clown's manager if we can figure out which one she is."

"You've met her though, haven't you, Layla?" Scarlett gave me a look of challenge that I returned right back to her. "I bet you could introduce us, and she'd not think twice about it."

I looked at all their expectant faces staring at me in anticipation. "Fine, since we're all here. But this is a one-time thing, okay? You're not going to suck me into your weird purple ube potato latte coffee club."

Charisse squeezed my arm as she passed me for the door. "That's the spirit."

Bree clapped her hands and made a cheesy grin. "Yay. I totally feel like Enola Holmes right now. This is so exciting."

Scarlett and I stared at each other and sighed at the same time before turning to follow the other two inside.

The floor was sticky. That was already a bad sign. Dooley's was part dive bar, part Irish pub. A large black stage was at the far end of the room with an upright piano off to one side. What looked like a twelve-year-old boy was center stage, playing an acoustic guitar under a baby spotlight. The room was packed for the Tuesday night half-price wings and beer. The large imposing four-sided bar sat front and center just inside the door where a tall bald man was pouring a shot.

He made eye contact with us and pointed at Scarlett. "No. No way." He tapped a photo over the tequila on the DO NOT SERVE wall. It was a Polaroid of a drunk Asian woman being hauled off the bar top. He pointed to the door. "Get out!"

Scarlett squinted at the photo. "What? Is that supposed to be me? That looks nothing like me, you racist. That woman is clearly Korean. I suppose you're gonna tell me all Asians look alike to you too."

The man's indignation slid into nervous panic. He looked at the photo then back at Scarlett. "That isn't you?"

Scarlett pulled out her cell phone. "Hold on, let me just get this on TikTok that you're denying service to Asians because you can't tell us apart."

The color drained from the bartender's face. "You don't have to do that, ma'am. I apologize. It was an honest mistake. Please, ladies. Whatever you want. First round is on the house."

Charisse raised her hand. "I'll have a Coke."

The rest of us nodded and said we'd all have the same, except for Bree who ordered a ginger ale with a cherry.

The bartender backed away through the little swinging half door. "Three Cokes and a Shirley Temple. Let me just get some more cherries. Please make yourselves comfortable out at one of the tables. I'll come to you."

He disappeared down the hall and Scarlett snickered at the photo. "Yeah, that's totally me. I forgot about this place."

I looked around the room at the fresh young faces. "Did they lower the drinking age?"

Bree pointed to a table of six rowdy guys. "I went to high school with some of them."

Charisse clucked her tongue. "They get younger every year."

"I'm gonna go put my name on the list. If I spot Paula, I'll give you a sign."

Scarlett squeezed her nose and honked.

"What is that?"

"That's the sign. It's a clown nose. Get it?"

I stared at her. "That's a terrible sign. People will think I'm weird."

"Look around. You're about twenty years older than everyone in here. They already think you're weird."

"So are you." I started toward the side stage muttering, "And I'm fifteen years older at best." I found a clipboard on a barstool and signed up for a ten-minute slot starting in forty minutes. I took a seat in the little offstage area by the back office and watched the acts that went on before me.

I didn't even recognize any of the songs. I took another look at the crowd on the floor. *Is this the right night? These aren't tryouts for a high school musical, are they?* Bree waved to me from the center table and held up my soda and grinned. I gave her a tight smile and a nod. Scarlett held her hand to her nose and mimicked honking it. Then she shrugged. I shook my head no and pretended I was swatting away a mosquito in case anyone had seen me.

A group of five took the stage with two acoustic guitars, two vi-
olins, and a clarinet. They reminded me of a flock of seagulls.
Not the eighties group. A literal flock of seagulls. I'd never heard
rage violin before, but I thought my ears might be bleeding.
They were obviously a crowd favorite since everyone was banging their tabletops in time to the music. Music? *I wonder how
much alcohol this group has had.*

A slam poet finished his set on being verbally abused by
cheese. He was followed by two girls who looked to be barely my
age if you combined theirs.

Then it was my turn to go on. I pulled out my amp and plugged
in my electric guitar, adjusted the microphone, and scanned the
room for potential scouts.

The crowd seemed to be whispering and pointing at me like a
rare dinosaur sighting.

I remembered I was also supposed to look for Paula and did a
second scan while I set my loop station pedal on the floor and
picked the preprogrammed drum beat that would fill in my
sound. No blonde in a power suit. I took a breath and started
playing the song that matched my current mood of lightly de-
pressed "Dream On." It had a long opener, which gave me time
to center myself. The AA girls sat a little taller and leaned toward the stage. They looked impressed and I was embarrassed
by how satisfying it was.

The rest of the room was tepid. Maybe they didn't appreciate
the classics. Maybe they didn't play Aerosmith on the Disney
Channel. Maybe it was the curse of never playing anything that's
beloved because it's hard to win over a crowd with an Aerosmith
song when you're not actually Steven Tyler. Haven't these kids at
least played Guitar Hero?

I was winding down the final chorus to the outro when the
late Chuckles McCracken's agent walked through the door and
up to the bartender who'd tried to throw us out when we first arrived.

I made eyes at the girls, but they were too busy swaying to the music. They may have forgotten why they were there in the first place. The song ended and I cranked up the gain and morphed into "Tears of a Clown" by Smokey Robinson. The crowd livened up and started to clap, but I got no reaction from Paula. I stared at Scarlett and nodded toward the bar in time to the music.

Scarlett and Bree were dancing in their seats. Charisse was singing along. Still—no realization. At least the audience was finally into something I was singing. The idea occurred to me that they may have thought it was an original number.

The girls were hopeless, and Paula was still chatting up the bartender, so I made another change into "Tears of a Clown"– heavy metal style.

Paula slowly turned to face the stage. I finally had her. Her eyes grew big in recognition. I was sure she remembered me from the birthday party. To her credit she didn't flee. She approached an empty table at the back by the bar and took a seat.

I finished my set to polite applause and a three-woman standing ovation. *I gotta give it to the ladies, they are pretty enthusiastic for being sober.* I moved my gear off stage and headed over to Paula's table to lightly schmooze.

The girls eyed me as I made my way through the crowd. When they saw where I was headed, they bolted to join me.

Scarlett grabbed an empty chair from the next table over as the occupants started to protest. "What? You don't need that."

Paula was a little stunned by my entourage, but I think I played it off well. "Hey, you remember me? Layla Virtue."

Scarlett reached out a hand for her. "We're her backup singers."

I cut her a look of surprise, but she deflected it like I wasn't even there.

Paula breathed out. "I caught the end of your act there. Quite a theme."

"What can I say, I was inspired."

Bree nodded vigorously and handed me my soda. "Doesn't she have a wide range?"

Paula blinked a few times. "That is one way to put it. Are you looking for an agent, Layla?"

Calm down. Don't seem too eager. "If the right person came along, sure."

Paula sat back and appraised me. "You're a lot older than who I'm signing today."

Bree squeeged up her nose. "Okay, but like, weren't you that old clown's manager?"

I kicked her under the table and gave Paula a smile. "Chuckles McCracken was easily twenty years older than me."

Paula glanced at Bree then away. "Chuck was my first client. I signed him back in the day when clowns were popular."

Charisse's perfectly sculpted eyebrows shot up to her braids. "I must have missed that trend."

Paula continued on like she hadn't heard her. "He'd gotten to be too high maintenance. Chronically offensive and always coming on to the moms at the birthday parties. Did he say something inappropriate to you, Layla? I apologize. He was a PR nightmare. You wouldn't be the first woman to slap him with a restraining order. Not to mention that I'm pretty sure he was setting up his own side gigs behind my back, the little weasel."

"What makes you say that?"

"He'd started giving me blackout dates. Saying he'd have to check his schedule and call me back. I used to be in charge of his schedule. He was suddenly very busy. Especially at night."

Bree twirled her hair around her finger. "Eww. Who hires a clown for a night party?"

Paula smirked. "Chuck was in debt up to his red nose, but he owed more money than he'd made in the past ten years if my ten percent is any indication. I'm pretty sure he was living out of his van. And I just loaned him ten thousand dollars to get the van repainted and loaded up on supplies. Alimony kept him below the poverty level."

We all looked at each other for a brief second. I knew we were thinking the same thing. *Miranda.*

"Then why keep him as a client?" I asked.

"I was getting ready to drop him. I only came to the birthday party to make sure he was sober and tell him I wasn't renewing his contract. He was lucky to get that gig. He'd already worked his way through that group of kids. And he was caught in flagrante with one of the moms at a birthday party a few weeks ago. I'm not allowed to tell you who it is, but her husband plays professional football. He threatened to kill Chuck if he ever saw him again. Word like that gets around and the calls to book parties dry up faster than day-old birthday cake."

Charisse held up a hand. "Wait. Are you saying a professional football player's wife was fooling around with that guy?"

Scarlett pulled out her cell phone and started tapping the screen like a court stenographer.

Paula took a sip of her wine. "According to the wife, Chuck forced her into the coat room."

"But you don't believe her?" I asked.

Paula shrugged. "Chuck may have been a creep, but that wasn't his style."

Bree made a face. "But like, could that guy have done it? The football player. Do you think he killed Chuckles the Clown like he said?"

"He was in Philadelphia playing a pre-season game. Thousands of people saw him."

Cop Layla showed up and started talking before I remembered I was here to be discovered. "Did you know Chuckles had a gambling problem? I'm pretty sure he was visited at Janice's party by someone looking to collect."

"Chuck had all the problems. It wasn't uncommon for his loan shark to send guys to threaten him at an event."

Scarlett crossed her arms and grilled the agent. "What about you? We heard you might have been in a romantic relationship with Chuckles the Clown."

Paula choked on her wine. "Gross. No. Who told you that?"

I handed her my cocktail napkin to wipe her chin. "His ex-wife, Miranda."

"Oh *her*. Well, she's wrong. Why are you all so interested? I thought you were looking for an agent."

"I am . . ."

Scarlett cut me off. "We don't want no agent who'd been sleeping with her clients."

I narrowed my eyes at Scarlett. "And how exactly would that affect *us*?"

She shrugged. "Morale. Keep up."

Paula took out her cell phone. "Look, I'm willing to try you out on a temporary basis. Do you do anything current?"

I shifted in my seat, aware of four sets of eyes on me. "I'm more familiar with the late seventies through the early two thousands."

Bree narrowed her eyes. "How old are you?"

I shifted my eyes to Paula. "I'm thirty. Ish. My former career didn't catch me a lot of radio time."

Bree doubled down. "Why didn't you just stream it?"

I gave her a pointed look to shush. "That wasn't an option."

Paula checked her phone. "Well, the Widder bar mitzvah is out. But I've got an eighties cover band booked for an engagement party this week and they just lost their female lead. If you don't mind filling in last minute, you could actually help me out. But you can't let me down. If you fail to show up, or don't stay for the whole gig, the deal is off."

I nodded casually while wondering who she'd been talking to. I didn't skip out early on that birthday party. Mostly because I couldn't get my amp packed fast enough—but she didn't know that. I put my hand out. "Deal."

Charisse smiled sweetly at Paula. "I'm sure Layla is a much better musician than Chuck was a party clown."

Paula gave me her business card and took my number. As she stood to go, she considered me for a moment before saying, "You know, Chuck was a terrible client, and I'm sad that he's dead. But I'd be lying if I didn't admit that it's a relief not to have his loan shark breathing down my neck anymore."

Scarlett waited until Paula had left then held up her phone. "So, guess what I just found out on Neighborhood dot com?"

I shook my head. "I don't know. What?"

"The football player's wife who was caught with Chuck while her kid was snarfing down cake and ice cream? Kelly Richardson."

"How'd you find that so fast?"

Scarlett waved her hand. "Please. There are a hundred different ways to gossip on social media. I'm proficient in all of them."

The door flew open and a miserable old prune in a black trench coat walked into the bar carrying what looked like a large black doctor's bag. She was heartily greeted by the bar set like she was a regular. I slumped down in my chair and tried to cover my face with my hand.

Bree followed my gaze. "What, is that like your grandmother or something?"

I hissed, "No, that isn't my grandmother. It's my landlord, Agnes Harcourt. What is that old bag doing here?"

Charisse grunted. "You owe her money?"

"Of course I owe her money. I owe everybody money." *Rats. I forgot they saw me drive in here.* I really didn't want to explain how someone with a car worth more than this entire bar would owe mobile home lot fees.

Agnes looked our way and Bree and Scarlett leaned toward each other, blocking me from view. Agnes threw back a shot then headed toward the stage. The boy playing guitar finished his set and Agnes shooed him away. She ripped off her trench coat revealing a shiny pink-and-green striped cabaret dress.

Bree let out a shuddering breath. "Oh no."

Agnes opened the case and removed an accordion.

Scarlett chuckled. "Awesome."

Charisse shook her head. "This isn't good. Accordions only count for music when you're in France."

Scarlett gave me an evil grin. "I bet she plays 'La Vie en Rose.'"

I peeked around them then ducked back. "I just noticed the feathers in her hair. You can't say she isn't committed to the theme."

Agnes launched into "Non, Je Ne Regrette Rien" and Scarlett smacked the table. "I was so close."

"She gets ten minutes so . . . there's still time." I reached for my guitar. "This is where I say goodbye, ladies. I need to get out of here before she spots me."

Charisse downed the rest of her soda. "We'll cover you."

I remembered my gear still on stage. "Oh no. I've got to get my amp and my loop station."

Bree pushed back from the table. "I'm on it." She headed to the side stage area while I cowered behind Scarlett and Charisse. Then they screened me as I shuffled to the door.

I was stashing my gear in the trunk of the car when Charisse handed me a flyer. "It's the open mic schedule in case you want to come back. They have it three times a week. Look, Saturday is Classic Rock night. That should be right up your alley."

Bree grinned and her shoulders rose with her smile. "I put our phone numbers on there. Let us know and we'll like, totally come to be your groupies."

"That's a really sweet offer."

Bree cooed. "I know, right? Make sure you call us."

Scarlett waved her cell phone and read the screen. "Just so you know, while you were lying about your age to the manager, I called my kid and asked him when the next birthday party is."

"Why?"

"All those rich kids go to school together so the odds that I would know at least one of their mothers is pretty good."

Charisse raised one eyebrow. "Who do you know, girl?"

"Her name is Heather. She's a friend of a friend of Miranda's. But don't tell Miranda because we don't want her coming along."

Bree's eyes grew big, and she shook her head. "Totally. I get enough judgment during my shares in the meeting." Bree pulled at her sleeves.

Scarlett continued. "Heather's son is having a birthday party on Saturday afternoon. Kelly Richardson's kid should be going. I scored us an invite."

I shut the trunk to the Aston Martin. "What is this *us?* And why would you do that?"

Scarlett looked at me like she wanted to ask if I'd been dropped on my head as a baby. Little did she know the answer was probably yes. "First of all, I'm bored. I used to work sixty hours a week. Now I watch daytime TV and eat cereal for lunch. Second, Miranda! And now Kelly Richardson! I want to know what the deal was with this guy that Kelly Richardson would fool around with him behind her football player husband's back. Don't worry." She pulled open the door to her Porsche and got in. "You don't have to come with us."

Chapter 19

I LAY IN BED AND LISTENED TO THE SILENCE. I KNEW IT WAS MORN-
ing because the sun had broken through my mini blinds, making light stripes on the gray walls of my bedroom. But why was it
so quiet? Maybe Agnes had finally caught the rooster and called
wildlife control. Farm life control? Barnyard control? Who
would you call to report a rogue chicken?

I peeked into the living room and saw the couch was empty.
The bathroom was empty too. Looking through the blinds I saw
the Aston Martin was still parked in the driveway. The Mustang
was now covered in Clifford's passive aggressive tickets. Dad
must be at Marguerite's again.

I took a shower and blow-dried my hair, then I dressed in
jeans and a Poison T-shirt. I went through to the living room
picking up socks and candy wrappers. Dad wasn't back but his
shoes were still here. That was weird. Did he go over to Marguerite's barefoot? I hope he's had a tetanus shot. Lake Pinecrest Mobile Home Park seemed like it would be ground zero
for at least ten kinds of viruses.

I went to the fridge to get a soda and found Dad's hat inside.
I took it out and stared at it. *Is he drinking again? He seems more
burned-out than usual.*

My phone rang and I grabbed it off the counter. "Hello?"

"Hello, Layla. It's Myrtle Jean Maude."

"Oh hello, Myrtle Jean." *I see the complaints are coming directly to me instead of waiting for the community meeting now. At least that will save time.*

"I got your number from Agnes. Um . . . your handsome father is at my house." Myrtle Jean's voice dropped lower. "He seems a bit confused."

Dad had fried a lot of brain cells in his time, so confused was his status quo. But Myrtle Jean was all the way around the other side of the lake. How could Dad get over there without his shoes? "I'll be right there."

I slid on a pair of Keds and headed out the door. Maybe I shouldn't have been so quick to tell Dad he couldn't come to a meeting with me. I could've at least recommended one for him across town. I bet Dupont Circle had a meeting he would feel right at home in.

I walked through the woods and around the dock to Myrtle Jean's soft blue double-wide. Hers had been the park model the original owners had used to lure seasonal buyers back in the day. She had a wide porch and a large purple butterfly bush in her front yard. Her door flew open before I could knock.

"He thought this was your house. He's in the formal parlor where I'm serving tea. Earl Grey. And biscuits."

I followed her through a tidy living room full of ceramic cats, through open French doors into an alcove probably intended to be a second bedroom. Myrtle Jean clearly thought she was living in a Jane Austen novel. The tiny space was dominated by a rose chintz patterned sofa and a coffee table laden with a hundred miniature crystal figurines. Dad was sitting on a pink velvet throne drinking tea from a china cup and saucer, his pinky sticking up like a flag. He gave me a wide grin. "Hey, baby girl. Have you tried this fancy Earl's tea? It tastes just like Fruity Pebbles."

"No, I can't say that I've had the pleasure."

Myrtle Jean flounced onto the end of the sofa closest to Dad and nudged a plate of Walker's Shortbread Scotties his way and giggled.

I gave the older woman a long look, not convinced she hadn't in fact lured my father into her home with the promise of "goodies." He would have been familiar with the premise but thrown off by the payout being packaged snacks. "What are you doing here, Dad?"

He placed his cup on the saucer. "It's the funniest thing. I thought I'd take a little walk around the lake, and when I got over here, I completely forgot where I was going."

"Did you also forget you were wearing your slippers?"

He looked at his feet and gasped. "Well, look at that." He gave a charming grin to Myrtle Jean. "I may have overdone it in the seventies and eighties."

Myrtle Jean shrugged and grinned. An enormous white puff the size of a beach ball jumped onto the couch and walked into her lap. It circled a couple of times then settled down and began to purr. "That's quite all right, Brad. I may have indulged a time or two myself."

The thought of Myrtle Jean Maud dropping acid was almost too much for me to handle at this time of the morning, and I was sure she thought Dad was talking about something very different. I cast a side glance at Dad. "I thought your name was Corbin."

He chuckled. "Was it?"

Myrtle Jean grinned so wide, her eyes turned to slits. "Brad is his nickname."

Dad pointed to the enormous cat and looked at me. "Do you see that too?"

Myrtle Jean put her hand on the cat's head and giggled. "You're so silly, Brad. This is my baby, Marshmallow."

Dad picked up his teacup, slid his eyes to mine, and mouthed, "Oh my God."

"Thank you, Myrtle Jean. I'll just walk Dad home now if you don't mind."

She patted Dad on the knee. "You're welcome to visit anytime."

Dad shotgunned whatever was left of his Earl Grey, then replaced his teacup in the saucer and stood. "You have a lovely home, sugar. Thank you so much for inviting me."

Myrtle Jean giggled, looked at me, and shrugged.

Once outside and heading for home, I couldn't hide my irritation. "What the heck was that all about?"

"That nice lady invited me in for tea."

"No, I mean how did you get over here?"

Dad shrugged. "I walked. I wanted to see the lake, baby girl."

"She said you thought that was my house."

"The poor thing exaggerates. I think she's lonely. Did you see that hairy baby of hers? Yikes."

"That was a cat, Dad."

"Then what was wrong with its face?"

"It was a Persian. That's just what they look like."

Dad shook his head as he probably pondered that as being one of the mysteries of the universe.

"And in the future, if you're going to wander around looking like—*you,* then you need to remember what you tell people your name is."

"Why can't I just tell them I'm Don Virtue?"

"Because they'll recognize your name, and they'll go from recognition to Google to TMZ before the cookies are on the plate."

Dad grunted. "Did you see that big house on the lake?"

"That's the owner's cottage."

"Is it for sale?"

"I don't think so. Why?"

"It's bigger than yours."

I narrowed my eyes at him. "Not everyone needs a mansion, Dad."

He chuckled. "Baby girl, I've been on back lots with dressing rooms bigger than your house."

"It's enough for me."

We passed the kayaks and the stack of weather-beaten lounge chairs while Dad told me all about Myrtle Jean's assortment of glass animals. "Who needs three kinds of crystal badgers? I thought I kept seeing the same one over and over until she told me their names."

"What were their names?"

"I don't know, but she told them to me. Maybe Peter, Paul, and Mary?"

"I seriously doubt that."

We were coming around the bend in the lake where the path through the woods to my trailer began when we noticed we were not alone. Foster had set up an easel by the water's edge and he was painting Pippi's portrait. Naturally, he was wearing white painter's overalls for the occasion. Pippi, in a show of solidarity, was also dressed in white painter's overalls as she sat in a red wagon eating a mango.

"Hi, Foster."

"Hi, Layla. How you?"

"I'm fine. How are you?"

Foster nodded. "Beautiful day for painting, isn't it?"

"If you're going for overcast then I would say so, yes."

Dad stared at Pippi for a second then looked at me. "I think I need to go to a meeting."

Foster paused with his brush over the palette. "Isn't this your aunt Trixie?"

Dad put his hand out. "Hellooo."

I nudged him and cleared my throat. "No. This is my dad, Trixie's brother." *Who is supposed to stay inside the trailer for reasons just like this one.*

Foster stared at Dad with a blank look. "You and your sister have exactly the same face."

Dad shoved his hands in his pockets. "We're identical twins."

"Hm." Foster went back to his painting. "You are very lucky to have your father, Layla. My dad left when I was little. He said I was too hard to be around."

I didn't know Foster very well, but I'd learned early on that the community kind of watched out for him. I suspected we were around the same age, but he seemed much younger. He'd grown up with his grandmother and she passed away before I moved in. "I'm sorry. I know that must have been hard for you."

Foster put another stroke of black snout on Pippi's portrait.

"Nana said it's not my fault, but I sometimes think if I hadn't been different, he'd still be here."

Dad gave Foster a tickle of a smile. "In my world 'different' is a good thing."

Foster nodded slowly. "That's what Nana says too. I talk to her sometimes when I'm lonely. She doesn't talk back, but I know she's listening."

My heart took a little swan dive and words of comfort seemed inadequate. Next to me, Dad breathed out a shaky sigh.

"Well, we'll let you finish your painting while Pippi is cooperating."

"Yeah, she's a good girl. She won't leave me."

Dad's voice trembled a bit. "She seems like a very good girl."

"Bye, Foster."

My irritation with Dad vanished in a moment and had been replaced with an icy grip of compassion around my heart and a lump in my throat the size of Pippi's mango. I knew Dad felt the same when he reached over and took my hand.

Chapter 20

"WHERE'S YOUR STASH, DAD?"

His eyes rolled skyward as he considered my question. "I'm almost sure I have no idea what you're talking about."

I leaned in and sniffed him. "You're acting weirder than usual. Are you using again? Let me see your eyes."

Dad opened his eyes wide and leaned in. "It was just a walk. I can't sleep all day like I used to." His voice lowered. "I can't sleep all night either, but I blame my prostate for that."

I made a close inspection for signs of dilated pupils then checked his face for white powder. "Myrtle Jean really scared me. Why didn't you just wait for me to get up?"

"Baby girl, I don't want to be stuck in this trailer all day. I feel like I'm in my shoe closet at home."

"I don't want you stuck in here either. But I also don't want paparazzi camped outside my front door because someone reports a sighting."

Dad chuckled. "I think you overestimate my newsworthiness these days."

A loud bang erupted from under my window followed by another. I dropped to the floor on all fours, my heart racing, bells ringing in my ears. "Get down!"

Dad squatted next to me. "Is it Cinco de Mayo?"

I was too breathless to speak. A vision of the concrete warehouse forced its way in my mind. I saw Jacob being blown back from the blast, his hand reaching for mine. Fire raged from the loading dock door. I tried hard to push the images away.

Dad reached down and tied his shoe. "No, that's ridiculous. I'd be craving tequila and guacamole."

I started to combat crawl away from the smoke.

Dad stood back up and parted the mini blinds just as another bang erupted farther away. "Oh, it's the trash collectors. Wow, look at them throw those cans back into your yard. Ha! That one's afraid of Steppenwolf. Look at him run."

His words barely cut through the falling flakes of gray. My T-shirt was damp against my skin. I rose to my knees and tried to steady myself, but I couldn't shake the image of Melissa bleeding out on the pavement. I clutched the arm of the couch. *Not now!*

I was struggling to catch my breath. "I'm going out for some air, Dad."

"Are you sure you're okay to be outside? You sound like you need to lie down."

I didn't give him an answer. I just had to get away before the walls closed in. The back door shut behind me. I took a deep breath and let it out. Steppenwolf strutted through the yard and gave me an "*Erka!*" It sounded a lot like *coward* and felt like an ice pick to the brain. I had to fight the urge to overreact and throw something at him.

I looked over at Nick's trailer wondering what was going on inside and whispered, "Ringo." Then I looked behind me to see if anyone had seen. Inching closer, trying to look like I was examining my grass, I cleared my throat and tried again a little louder. "Ringo."

Nothing. This feels stupid. Maybe I could just ask to take the dog for a walk. I'm sure Nick is busy doing . . . something.

I walked over to my kitchen window and flicked off a beetle. "Ringo!"

I held my breath and listened. Nick's trailer door opened,

and Ringo bounded out. "Oh hey, boy. What are you doing out here?"

Nick stuck his head out and scanned me through narrowed eyes. He cocked his head side to side like he was checking to see if I had a discrete cannonball wound. "Hey, Layla."

I squatted down and let Ringo cover my face in kisses while trying to keep my voice light and airy. "Hi, Nick. How's it going?"

He stepped out onto the porch and watched as the dog knocked me over. He shoved his hands in his pockets and nodded. "Good, good. He was just whimpering at the door to go out. I guess he heard you rambling around out here."

"Wow. He must have really good hearing if he heard me cleaning the windows."

He pursed his lips. "Uh-huh. Yeah. Yeah, he does. You want to borrow some glass cleaner or something?"

My heart rate was returning to normal and my head was beginning to clear. "No, why?"

Nick shrugged, a tiny smirk forming at his lips. "I dunno. It would probably clean your windows better than just flicking the bugs off by hand."

"Don't question my methods, new guy."

He grinned. "Can you keep an eye on him for a while? I've got a Zoom meeting to go into and I'll be a little bit."

I ran my hand down the Lab's sleek black fur. "I could if you want."

Nick chuckled. "I'd appreciate it. Just bring him back when you've had enough."

He disappeared into his trailer, and I smiled at the Lab. "It's just you and me, buddy."

Ringo's tongue shot out and caught me right on the mouth.

"Okay, I could do with less of that."

He smiled and his tail whirred around like helicopter blades.

Nick opened the door and threw a bean bag ball in our direction. Before he disappeared back inside, Ringo had leapt into the air, caught it, and dropped it at my feet.

I don't know how long I tossed that ball for him, but nothing would wear this guy out. I'd been slowly going to pot since I'd been off the force. I used to be able to chase a perp several blocks through back alleys and a construction zone in tactical gear. Now I was winded playing catch with a puppy.

Ringo dropped the ball about ten feet away from me and waited for me to stop panting. A door slammed across the way, and he temporarily shifted his attention toward Kelvin's trailer.

The unmistakable sound of a basketball low on air thumped out to greet us. "You want to go say hi?"

Ringo's tail wagged.

"Come on." I led him around the front of my trailer and across the street. Kelvin put his ball on the asphalt and offered his hand to Ringo, who slowed his approach with his ears soft and his eyes gentle to give it a sniff.

"You've got Hottie McMuscle's dog again?"

My grin slid into a blank expression as I raised my eyebrows to the kid.

He smiled. "That's what Gran calls him."

I chuckled. "Well, your gran is not wrong."

Kelvin grinned. Then the grin disappeared. "Please don't tell her I repeated that."

"Your secret is safe with me. You home from school already?"

"Yeah, it was a half day, so we came home after lunch. Today we had sloppy joes. My mom's favorite."

"Yum. I've never met your mom. Where is she?"

"She's dead."

"Oh. Kelvin, I'm so sorry." My heart felt like it moved two inches lower in my chest. I reached for Ringo and ran my hands over his back.

Kelvin shrugged and picked up the basketball. "Overdose."

The words got lost in my throat. Kids like Kelvin were why I'd joined the force. To get the drugs off the street. So many hearts broken. Lives that would never be the same. It all went horribly wrong. I failed Kelvin. I failed them all.

"Kelvin!" Donna opened the screen door and stuck her head outside. "Get in here and finish this homework before you play ball."

Kelvin rolled his eyes to mine. "Yes, ma'am."

He and Donna switched places as she walked over to greet Ringo. "You sure are getting cozy with the new neighbor's dog. One would think he belonged to you."

Ringo looked at me and smiled.

"He thinks he belongs to me."

She ran her hand over Ringo's muzzle. "Hey, gorgeous." She sighed. "I heard you ask about Kelvin's mom."

"I'm sorry, Donna. I didn't know."

Donna gave Ringo a pat on the head. "I know. I just don't like him dwelling on Jennifer. His mom's addiction was not his fault, and he can't change the past. He needs to focus on his own life."

"I understand. I wish there was something I could do to make it better."

Donna waved me off. "Jennifer was the only one who could have made it better and she chose to get high instead. We tried detox. We tried house arrest. We tried rehab, both voluntary and forced. She'd be clean for a while, then she'd go back. Her old ways, her old friends, her loser boyfriend . . . She just couldn't break free."

"Drugs put you in a stranglehold that never stops demanding obedience."

Donna gave me a smile that didn't reach her eyes. "So true. And a momma can only do so much."

My mom's face appeared in my mind. Both sadness and resentment rose in me like a tide. "You can't outrun the devil inside you."

Donna shook her head sadly. "And you can't help someone that doesn't want help. And Jennifer didn't want help. She was so afraid that people would judge her, she thought she could deal with her addiction on her own. In the end, that's probably the mistake that killed her."

* * *

I took Ringo home and kissed him goodbye. Nick did not invite me in. Things were still not back to normal between us after our walk home the other night. Nick was pleasant enough, but he wasn't his flirty jovial self anymore. Of course, I did smack down his advances pretty hard. I would be upset with me too.

I was jittery for the rest of the afternoon. Feelings were starting to get on top of me and my efforts to push them down were cracking around the edges. I didn't like feeling emotions. They were fleeting, untrustworthy things. Too influenced by other people's opinions of me. How quickly I doubted myself when someone said I wasn't good enough.

Everywhere I looked was a reminder of my failures. Scarlett, Bree, and Charisse had me second-guessing myself. Maybe I was the problem with all my relationships.

And something was wrong with my dad. I could sense it, but he wouldn't talk about it. He was acting extra dippy. And what was with that freak-out in the grocery store?

People were dead because of me. People I let down. People like Kelvin's mom. My team—Melissa, Oscar, Eddie.

And Jacob. I saw him everywhere. Out of the corner of my eye, I'd get a flash of someone and think it was him. Guilt playing tricks on me. Things did not end well between us. The morning of Stratton Park, if I'd known it would be the last time we'd talk, I would have said very different things.

I wanted to escape. I wanted a drink, and no distraction would shake the thought. It was pathetic how often it pinged my brain. Like a little kid who hits you with a constant barrage of please, please, please, please, until you give in. I started drinking way too young. And I probably had always drunk too much. But it was only in the last few years the booze started bossing me around and I found myself powerless to say no. Twice I pulled out my cell phone to call someone.

But there was no one.

I couldn't call my sponsor; she cut me out of her life when

she relapsed. I couldn't call the girls. I'd made it pretty clear that we weren't friends like that. How stupid would I look if I went back on that now? Donna had her hands full with her grandson and grief over losing her daughter. I'd repeatedly pushed Nick away.

I was alone.

Chapter 21

*G*UNFIRE *ERUPTED FROM DEEP WITHIN THE WAREHOUSE. I DIDN'T SEE Oscar or Eddie so they must have been inside. Melissa was across the parking lot by the loading dock door, crouched down beside a white pickup truck. She looked like a child in a police costume. She yelled something to me, but I couldn't understand her. Then she gave me the signal to stay back, but everything was wavy and distorted like I was looking through a pane of fun house glass.*

Jacob appeared on the loading dock shouting. His grimy face wild with panic, blood trickling down his temple. I cupped my ear to signal that I couldn't hear him, and he waved me away. What was he doing? Was he punishing me for what I said earlier?

Then the explosion.

Jacob was blown back by the force and part of the roof above him caved in. The second-story windows shattered and rained down shards of glass. I screamed as flakes of gray ash swirled around me like dirty snow. I ran for the pickup truck, but I was too late. Melissa lay half-buried under a chunk of concrete, a thick shard of glass like an icicle sticking out of her thigh. Her eyes empty, shouting silent accusations. You got me killed.

Feeling around, I became aware that I was lying in the damp grass, panting. *Where am I? Have I made a fool of myself?*

I received a lick on the cheek.

Oh, I really hope that's the dog.

Opening my eyes, I tried to focus in the dark. My head felt like I'd drunk a fifth of Jack on an empty stomach.

Ringo was lying in the grass in front of me, his nose to mine. His tail started wagging aggressively. Right next to him, Nick was kneeling, his hands on his knees. He gave me a gentle smile. "You're safe. Everything is fine."

"Where are we?"

He bobbed his head to the side. "Behind my trailer. You were yelling, 'Wait for backup!' "

I groaned. "Welcome to the neighborhood. Your neighbor is a nutjob. What time is it?"

"I dunno. Two A.M.? Do you want to talk about it?"

Ringo belly-inched closer to put his head on my shoulder and gave me another lick.

I reached out and buried my fingers in his soft fur. "Sorry. I don't remember anything."

His voice was soft and kind. "That's alright. Want to come inside for a drink?"

I pushed myself up onto all fours. "Look, I probably should have told you this sooner, but frankly, I didn't think you'd stick around this long. I'm an alcoholic."

He held his arms out like a salesman trying to sweeten the pot. "I have alcohol-free hot cocoa."

I looked across the grass at the bottom of my trailer, noticed my skirting was rusted and wondered how much more embarrassing this could get than lying in the neighbor's yard in the middle of the night? That's when I realized I wasn't wearing pants.

Nick followed my eyes. "Come on. I have sweats that will fit you." When I still hesitated, he lowered his voice like he was telling me a secret. "I grind the chocolate myself."

I rocked back to my heels. "Why would anyone do that?"

"Come try it and you'll see why." He flashed me that cheesy smile again and I wanted so badly to laugh.

Turmoil rolled inside me. This was me, literally at my worst other than being wasted. What I wanted was to crawl under my covers and hide until he'd forgotten all about tonight. But if history was any indication, I wouldn't be able to relax for hours. Dad was probably sound asleep on the couch. I didn't want to wake him. Plus, I didn't have cocoa, and now that the seed was planted, I really wanted some. "Okay. If you promise not to judge me for coming over half-naked."

Nick grinned. "How could I judge anyone who likes Lita Ford?"

I stood, self-consciously pulling my vintage concert T-shirt to try and cover some of my underwear. Also trying to remember what pair I had on without actually looking.

Nick had already started walking around the trailer to his front door. Ringo stood at my side, waiting expectantly to make sure I was coming with him. I took a few steps and stopped. *Maybe this is a bad idea. What message am I sending?* Ringo stopped with me. His brown eyes watching me without judgment. I smiled at him, and his tail gave a couple shakes. "Alright. One cup of cocoa and I'm outta there." His tail wagged faster and his whole butt wiggled in response.

Nick had left his door ajar, so I walked in without knocking. He was just returning to the living room with a pair of red sweatpants, the gold letters *USMC* running down one leg. He handed them to me and headed straight for the kitchen.

I quickly pulled them on and tightened the string. "I didn't know you were a Marine."

He took a saucepan out of a cabinet and nodded. "Mm-hmm."

Nick's trailer was very similar to mine—in setup. It was lacking that certain air of hopelessness that mine was dripping with. His beige living room was on one end, blue kitchen in the middle, and then presumably a bathroom and bedroom down the hall. My mouth went dry thinking about how close I was to Nick's bedroom, and I forced myself to examine his bookshelf full of tech manuals instead.

You don't want to screw this up, Layla. Nick's the first real friend you've made in years other than Jacob.

It's hard to make friends with cops when you're on the force. Not everyone subscribes to the partner camaraderie you see on TV. Some of the men can't get past thinking of you as a bimbo

with a badge. The ones who are happily married—their wives
see you as a relationship time bomb, ready to blow up their
happy home with infidelity. And a lot of the women you work
with don't have time for friends. Many of them are juggling the
pressures of the job with spouses and kids and society's disdain
all while putting their lives on the line every day. They're working twice as hard to be taken half as seriously in their career
and they won't tolerate another woman making their gender
look weak. If I'd made friends, I would surely have lost them all
by now.

Nick was busy doing something with what sounded like a buzz
saw. He wasn't kidding about grinding his own chocolate. Did
chocolate need to be ground? Doesn't it just come out of the little packet with the dehydrated marshmallows?

He glanced my way and gave me a crooked grin. I returned
an awkward thumbs-up.

"Why don't you make yourself at home. This will only take a
couple minutes."

Ringo showed me around the tidy living room. His dog bed
was next to a black leather sofa with recliners on both ends. A
red leash hung from a peg by the front door next to a desk that
had a computer and two huge monitors side by side. I sat on the
couch, and he systematically brought me every one of his toys
for inspection. There was a stuffed baby Yoda, followed by a
stuffed squirrel, then a raccoon, a duck, and a purple dragon
with wings. Every one of them had been ripped in the middle
with the stuffing pulled out.

I held up the disemboweled dragon. "What happened here?"

Ringo sniffed it and gave it a nudge with his snout.

"Did it sass off and you had to teach it a lesson?"

His tail started to wag.

Nick lit the gas stove. "No squeaker is safe. The minute he re-
alizes something is in there, he's relentless to extract it. He
would have been a good Marine."

Ringo brought me a bean bag ball and shoved it into my
hand.

"Am I allowed to toss this inside?"

Nick nodded. "That dog can play sixteen hours a day. I don't have that kind of time, so I toss him his ball while I work at my desk."

I tossed the bean bag, which Ringo caught and tossed back immediately. I nodded toward the computer station before tossing it again. "What exactly are you doing there? It looks like a setup from *The Matrix*."

Nick turned off the stove and poured thick dark cocoa into two mugs. "A lot of stuff I can't talk about." He crossed the small space and handed me a black mug with the New Orleans Saints logo on it and took a seat on the other side of the couch. "Let's just say that I ran secure ops in the Marines, and now I do it as a government contractor."

I nodded, not at all sure about what any of it meant. "I might be stealing Internet from you."

He paused with his cocoa to his lips and laughed. "You're not. But you'd better hope Marguerite pays her bill if you want to keep watching Netflix."

I wrapped my hands around the mug, trying to absorb its warmth.

Nick nudged his knee into mine. "So, what's going on with you? You give me a secret and I'll give you one."

Every instinct I had said, *Tamp it down.* I gave him a smile that even I knew didn't convey sincerity. "I'm fine."

"Come on. Lay it on me."

My heart felt like it had rocks weighing me down and they were slowly pulling me under waves of regret. Then Nick's eyes turned soft and pleading; they whispered that there was nothing I could say that he wouldn't understand. If my former therapist had had those eyes, I would have told her everything in our first session.

"It's my fault my entire team was killed in an op that went bad. Four people. Dead. Because of me."

Nick cradled his cup in his lap. "I'm so sorry."

The minute the words were out of my mouth I regretted saying them. "Do you want me to leave? I don't deserve this cocoa."

Nick reached out and squeezed my shoulder. "I'm not judging you. That's a heavy enough burden to carry; you don't need anyone adding to it."

I didn't know what to say.

"Do you want to talk about what happened?"

"Gross negligence. I was on the Potomac County Narcotics Unit investigating a drug ring we'd been watching for months."

He nodded, his face calm and understanding, waiting for me to continue.

I shrugged. "The day we were set to infiltrate their operation and take them down I was late getting to the drop site. I only know that I'd been drinking because of my tox report. I have flashes of memory but they're hazy and distorted. I see them die over and over."

His eyes were sad. "We're human. We make mistakes. Some are more devastating than others."

"Tell that to their families. Tell that to kids like Kelvin who I was supposed to protect."

Ringo jumped on the couch and curled down against me, his head in my lap.

Nick looked at a framed photo of his platoon next to a model of the *Enterprise*. "I bombed a school that was supposed to be a chemical factory. My hand literally launched the missile. No matter what excuse you want to give me—following orders, bad intel, a regime that uses kids as decoys—I will always carry the weight that I killed twenty-six children that day."

My mind went completely numb. I suspected that was the kind of thing a person never really got over. Human beings are capable of the most horrifying treatment of one another. I saw it all the time on the force, but nothing to the degree that soldiers and Marines see at war. How the man sitting next to me was able to get out of bed in the morning was a testament to his inner strength. I wanted to hold his hand, but I knew that would be crossing a line. "I don't know what to say. I'm so sorry."

The words turned to gravel in my mouth. They felt hollow. They were what you say in this situation, but you have no idea of the pain the person has endured for your meaningless platitude. I was usually on the receiving end of these, and no matter how sincerely I meant it, it still felt empty. "I can't imagine what you've been through."

He gave me a gentle look. "Likewise."

We clinked our mugs together and took long drinks to fill the space of awkwardness that pain and vulnerability had created.

Nick returned his mug to the table. "I just want you to know that you're not alone, Layla. If you ever need to talk, I'm here for you."

I was thrown by his compassion that I didn't deserve. After all he'd been through, and he was still so thoughtful. Life had not been fair to me and I chose to shut everyone out. All I had done since we'd met was lead him on and turn him away. And he kept reaching out to me. His kindness was an unusual sensation and I had to fight the urge to throw up. "And thank you for sharing with me what I'm sure was the worst day of your life."

Nick stared at the photo of his platoon. "Not even close."

Chapter 22

I'D RETURNED HOME JUST AS THE SKY WAS STARTING TO GLOW PINK and lavender. I was sure I'd spend hours staring at the ceiling, but to my surprise I fell right to sleep the moment I was horizontal. No nightmares. No regrets. I was so relaxed—my mattress was like a giant marshmallow.

I wasn't sure exactly what time it was when the sun sliced through my blinds. It felt like I'd slept for hours, but one thing was definitely missing. The unhinged *"Erka Erka"* of Steppenwolf, the strutting barnyard bird flu.

It was peacefully quiet.

Too quiet.

Maybe Marguerite had killed the rooster.

No. That's crazy. She loves that rooster. Although . . . Do I smell fried chicken? No. Maybe?

I lay there for a while trying to shift my mind, but I couldn't shake the sensation that I was smelling KFC. *I'm hallucinating smells.*

I rolled out of bed, still wearing Nick's Marine Corps sweats, and pulled on a hoodie. Voices murmured on the other side of my bedroom door. It sounded like Dad had the TV on so I knew it must be late. Hopefully, he was still in the house.

I opened the bedroom door and spotted Dad at the other end of the trailer sitting at the kitchen table. Ringo was sitting in a chair next to him like a human waiting to be served. Dad waved and held up an extra crispy chicken leg. "You want some lunch?"

Oh God! My stomach rose up to my throat. He didn't! He wouldn't know how. "What did you do?"

Dad cocked his head. "Hey, baby girl. One of the neighbors came over."

"And you killed him?"

He squinted and peered over his chicken leg. "What?"

I crept down the hall and the full kitchen came into view. Marguerite was sitting at the table on the other side of Ringo eating a chicken wing. She watched me through narrowed eyes while she chewed like she always knew this day would come. The day Layla Virtue totally unraveled.

"I can't believe you, Marguerite. I thought he was your emotional support rooster or something."

Marguerite stared at me then pointed the chicken wing to my floor. Steppenwolf strutted around the trash can pecking at the linoleum. "*You* a psycho. *You* know that?"

Dad held up a red-and-white striped box. He chuckled and pulled out a biscuit. "Don't tell Steppenwolf about the Colonel. We told him we're eating Tofurkey."

Marguerite cackled.

Well, I felt like an idiot. "That thing better not poop in my house."

"For your information, *chica,* he just did his *bizness* before *jour* father invited us in."

I glanced at Dad. He waved his biscuit and grinned.

Ringo, my loyal shadow, had completely abandoned me for the possibility of an extra crispy handout.

"*Dad,* how did the dog get in here?"

Dad slathered butter on half a biscuit. "I thought he came in with you this morning."

I crossed the tiny living room, stepping over the rooster, and pulled open the fridge. It was packed to the rafters, including a bottle of dish soap on the top shelf next to the TV remote. The guilt of being near forty and having my father pay for my groceries would have been crushing except now we had jelly donuts, so I was able to get over it. I grabbed a Dr. Pepper then got the box of Krispy Kremes off the top of the microwave and headed out to the couch.

Marguerite stood and shook out her pumpkin-colored sweater. "*Gracias* for the hospitality, Keanu."

I flipped open the donut box. "And who exactly is Keanu?"

Marguerite scowled in my direction. "Your father said I could use his nickname." She touched Dad on the shoulder. "Would you believe this is the first time I have seen the inside of this trailer?"

Dad gave her the shocked and horrified reaction she was hoping for. "What? No! I can't believe that, sugar. Well, you are welcome over anytime. And you don't have to bring lunch either. Layla loves company. Don't you, baby girl?"

I rolled my eyes and plucked a fat jelly donut from the box. "Layla does not."

Marguerite smirked at me and picked up Steppenwolf. "*Hasta luego*, Keanu."

"*Hasta luego*, sugar." As Dad boxed up the leftover chicken, Ringo jumped down from the table and moved the front line of his attack to the couch where eleven jelly donuts were still resting in formation.

"Baby girl, have you seen my hat?"

"Which one?"

"The gray flatcap."

"Is it still in the microwave?"

Dad pressed the button and the microwave popped open. "Nope."

"Where did you leave it?"

Dad chuckled. "That's the million-dollar question."

"Why is the dish soap in the fridge?"

He gave me a confused look over the sink. "I thought that was where *you* put it."

"I didn't put it there."

He pursed his lips then shrugged. "Must be bandits." Dad's eyes glazed over, and he broke into song. "I'm a cowboy. And still on this horse I ride. I'm wanted. *Want-e-ed* . . . Dead or all right."

"That is not even close, and Jon would be horrified."

"You can send him a fruit basket later." He washed and dried his hands and pulled out a folded yellow flyer from his back pocket. He came around the corner and presented it to me with a flourish and a toothy grin.

It was a good thing those donuts were glazed so they could keep on sliding past the lump in my throat. "Where did you get that?"

He blinked. "It was on the coffee table last night when you went to bed."

"You mean inside my purse on the coffee table?"

He shrugged. "Six of one . . . Hey, I have an idea."

"Uh-huh."

He dropped into the chair across from me and leaned in with his elbows on his knees like he was about to lay out a plan for a bank robbery. "I didn't know you were doing the open mic thing. Why don't I go with you to the next one? I could help you hype the crowd. Create some buzz. We could bring the house down."

"No way, Dad. You'd cause a riot in that little bar."

His hands flew over his head. "It could be epic. We could do that fun little duet you like so much."

"'Dancin' in the Street'?"

Dad snapped his fingers. "That's the one. I can start stretching my mouth out this afternoon."

"It's not worth the chaos. And you swore off Jagger, remember?"

Dad's eyes narrowed. "Oh right. Frickin' Jagger." He chuckled. "Are you sure you wanna be a rock star?"

I picked another donut from the box. "Depends on the day, Dad."

Dad stared through me. I thought maybe he was mad that I was rebuffing his attempts to bond under hot lights and spandex.

I'd spent the last twenty years trying to learn who I was without him. To create my own identity. One where every conversation didn't begin like a tabloid interview. What's it like to be Don Virtue's daughter? Did he really OD in Topeka? Is your mom still in rehab? I heard he's cheating on that actress from *Days of Our Lives* with a Victoria's Secret model. You're so lucky, you'll never have to work for anything in your life. How about taking us all to Vail and I'll tell my Instagram followers that you're really cool?

So, I'd crashed and burned here recently. That didn't mean I couldn't be someone, even without Don Virtue bankrolling me. I wasn't defined by my parents' successes or failures.

Dad had been staring into space for a really long time. "Hey! Are you okay? Dad!"

I snapped my fingers and his eyes focused. "What?"

"Is something going on with you?"

He cocked his head like he was thinking. "Now that you mention it, I think I'm losing my hair." He ran his hands through the silvery gray strands past his shoulders. "It feels thinner at the top."

I think you're losing your mind. "No, not that. And you're not. You seem more . . . burnt-out than usual."

He shrugged and shoved his hands in his pockets. "I'm getting old . . . baby girl. The mind is willing, but the flesh will stab you in the backside. You know how often I go in the bathroom to pee and only a trickle comes out? What a waste of time that is."

"Alright. If something was wrong you would tell me though, right?"

Dad looked around the trailer and snorted. He held his hands out to his sides and turned an astonished look my way.

"Yeah, I get it. I'm not exactly living the dream. This is what the bottom looks like when you're not rich and famous."

"Baby. You are rich."

"No, Dad. You're rich. I don't get six figures to walk across a stage. I'm lucky if I get deviled eggs and gas money."

Ringo groaned that the argument was interfering with his begging.

Dad's eyes were sad. He searched my face. "Honey, everything that's mine, is yours. I wasn't there for you when you needed me. You deserved more than a few hours between layovers and interviews. I want to make up for that now."

"You don't have anything to make up for. I thought my life was normal until I hit junior high. I didn't know everyone's Dad wasn't on TV. And to be fair, a lot of kids I grew up with had a parent with an addiction. At least you turned your life around. I'm still working on it."

"What can I do to help?"

I took the flyer from Dad and shoved it in my pocket. "Just stay here while I'm gone tonight. I have to work an engagement party and I don't know how late I'll be. How about tomorrow we grill those steaks and maybe watch a movie?"

He dropped to the couch. "Whatever you say, dear. Where's the remote?"

"In the fridge next to the dish soap."

"Frickin' bandits."

Chapter 23

SOME DAYS SEEM LIKE THEY'RE JUST OUT TO GET YOU. SOMETIMES the attack announces itself right out of the chute so you can begin damage control. Buy a couple gallons of ice cream, some chocolate syrup, sign into Netflix, and hunker down for the aftermath.

Today was not one of those days. Today snuck in like a stealth missile programmed to kill on contact. It blew up in my face before I could form an escape plan.

I had the engagement party gig tonight so my hair was teased up to a proper eighties altitude, my eyeliner was as thick as a Sonic milkshake, and my Mustang still wouldn't start so I had to take the James Bond car around the beltway into DC.

After parking in the underground garage of the LOFT, I carted my guitar and amp up the service elevator to the top floor and was ushered through the kitchen to the event stage. The rest of the band had arrived ahead of me and were setting up in what would surely pass as a palace to most of the world.

Three-story windows on all four sides of the immense room made a panoramic view of Washington, DC's monuments. Round banquet tables covered in white linen tablecloths were dotted with gold-rimmed china and crystal stemware. Suspended over each table was a gold ring centerpiece dripping with white roses and blue hydrangeas.

The room smelled of money. The kind where the interest

alone was more than most people would see in their lifetime. *I think I had a Sweet 16 party in a place just like this.*

The staff rushed about in swanky tuxedos, lighting candles and twisting napkin swans while I started to regret my choice of shocking-violet suede bustier over a black lace miniskirt.

Then I met the guys. They had taken the uniform of an eighties cover band to the next level. I'd never seen nylon parachute pants in the wild before. Garrett, the front man and keytar player, told me that Neon Dreams had lost their female lead vocalist when she went into labor two weeks early. "Paula said you could shred, but please tell me you know 'Walk Like an Egyptian'?"

"Yeah."

"'Like a Virgin'?"

"Definitely."

"'Take On Me'?"

"Of course." *Just don't ask me to do much from the past twenty years.*

He breathed out a *whew* and handed me a plastic baggie full of colorful rubber bracelets. "Cammie left these for you, but I see that you've already got the lace gloves."

I slid the neon rings over my wrist. "That's alright. The eighties was the decade of more is more."

Garrett removed a sheet of paper from a folder and handed it to me. "Let me know if there's anything on the set list that you can't do."

"I'm out for 'Ninety-nine Luftballons.'"

"You don't know it?"

"No, I know it. But it gives me a rash if I have to play it."

"Alright, but just so you know, we each only get one veto song. Mine is 'Walking on Sunshine.' If anyone requests it, you pretend you've got mic feedback and didn't hear them."

"I can do that."

We ran over the set list, then I plugged in my gear behind the curtain and went to the greenroom to wait for the party guests to arrive. The guys were nice enough. Dave on electric drums.

Barry on synthesizer. Mohinder on bass. They shared vocal duty depending on which eighties one-hit wonder was up, and there were a ton of them on the list.

After a two-minute warning, we were announced and headed for the stage. That's when the evening detonated and showered me with the shrapnel of shame. I grabbed my guitar and found myself staring at a sea of cops from my precinct. My hands went clammy and my suede bustier turned into a shocking-violet oven. My lungs were under the false impression that I'd just run a mile. I missed the first couple of bars of "Everybody Have Fun Tonight" and Mohinder gave me a dirty look and then nudged me hard in the back. Wang Chung was their big opener, and I was blowing it.

I started to play while my eyes darted around the room looking for an exit. My gaze landed on Dayton Castinetto during "Safety Dance," and I tried to fade back behind the drummer, but Dave jabbed me out to the front because "Sweet Dreams" was next on the set list and Barry was not about to have his big synthesizer moment ruined by my stage fright.

My voice went reedy thin when Castinetto moved to the front of the room and mouthed something to me. Suddenly the Cosmo tower in the middle of the room seemed like the Trevi Fountain beckoning me to dive in and do the vodka backstroke. I tried to make my mind focus on the words of the song and just stay in the moment.

A pretty little brunette draped in a BRIDE sash dragged her shy groom to the stage and requested "Girls Just Want to Have Fun." Garrett looked to me, and I nodded. The bride didn't pick up on the frostiness coming from half of her guests, but my fingers were icy as I tried to pluck out Cyndi Lauper.

The cops from my precinct were clumped together, jabbing at each other, and laughing. They had their heads together, staring at me—some of them not so subtle with their glares. That's when they started calling out requests of their own.

"'Tequila'! I bet you know that one, Virtue."

"How about 'Red Red Wine'!"

"Wasted away in 'Margaritaville.' Isn't that your theme song?"

My temp band mates were giving each other looks that said they were realizing they'd made a horrible mistake letting me play. The cops yelled out whatever song titles they thought would shame me, including a few that I didn't think were legit songs at all. Then a big bear of a man who I happened to know worked desk dispatch called out Taylor Swift's "Champagne Problems." He giggled at himself and his face pinked like Porky Pig.

Dayton Castinetto didn't try to drunk-shame me, but he stood by with a sneer sharp enough to cut through barbed wire.

We'd played through half the playlist when the father of the bride came up to give a toast to the happy couple. Fifty cops pressed against the stage for the big moment and my heart started to race. A slew of servers in uniform carrying bottles of prosecco crowded around me, and I had to fight against a strong urge to flee. When they shouted a whoop of congratulations and two dozen corks popped at once, everything went black.

I came to, flat on my stomach, with Dayton Castinetto's face in mine. He was crouched down at the foot of the stage staring at me. "Virtue. What the heck is wrong with you? Are you drunk right now?"

"No, I'm not drunk." I tried to catch my breath. "I have low blood sugar. Where am I? Oh right, the LOFT."

"Low blood sugar doesn't make you yell, 'Take cover!' before you dive on the ground."

"Sure it does." I pushed up to my knees and tried to steady my breathing like my court-ordered therapist had shown me. "I'm fine. It's all part of the act."

The father of the bride was pouting that I'd ruined his big moment. By the way Garrett was frowning, it was the last time I would be asked to sub in with Neon Dreams anyway. He announced, "The band is going to take fifteen while dinner is served. We'll be right back with more great hits from the eighties."

I wasn't sure that applied to all of us, but as the band left the stage, I crawled to my feet and checked my guitar. It was mercifully intact. Apparently, I fling it to safety and use my body as a shield when I black out.

Dayton Castinetto was still hovering over me with a frown of disapproval.

"What are you even doing here, Castinetto?"

He ran his eyes over me in the cop way of checking for something they can make a big deal out of later. I knew the routine. I was really good at it. "My sister is the bride."

"Give her my congratulations."

He put his hand out to help me off the stage. "You need to be checked out."

I pushed him away. "I'm fine."

His hands flew to his hips and his lip curled. He called back to the bartender. "Don't serve this one alcohol under any circumstance."

Many of the partygoers rubbernecked the argument, either curiosity or concern in their eyes. I was today's unnatural disaster. Heat rushed to my face. "You have no right . . ."

"I'm trying to help you."

"No, you're trying to embarrass me. Well, mission accomplished."

He hissed at me. "I'm trying to embarrass you? I'm not the one who took a stage dive in front of everyone."

"Just stay away from me, Castinetto."

His eyes flashed fire and brimstone as he backed away. "Get your act together, Virtue. You're a disgrace."

I hustled back toward the greenroom, mortified. Did my every mistake have to be on display for the whole world? I was ready to grovel to the band and beg them not to tell Paula about what just happened, but that Boy Scout, Adam Beasley, was waiting for me just outside the door. *Great.*

He held out a sparkling water. "Are you alright?"

I accepted his offering and popped the top. "I'm fine. What do you want, Beasley?"

"You're really good. Where'd you learn to play like that?"

"YouTube."

"Wow. That's amazing. I can't believe you were wasting your time with the police."

Adam clearly did not pick up on sarcasm. "Yeah, what was I thinking trying to keep people safe?"

"What a coincidence that I'd run into you here at Castinetto's sister's party."

"Why are there so many cops here, anyway?"

"She's marrying Jensen from the six twenty. Didn't you know?"

I took another swig of my water. "Poor girl."

Adam chuckled. "Yeah. If you're alright, can I ask you something?"

I gave him a look I hoped conveyed the right level of irritation but that I was still appreciative for the water.

"It's about the McCracken case."

I sighed. "What?"

"We checked into Chuck McCracken's gambling like you suggested. He frequently borrowed money from Sal Polaski. I called a few past birthday party clients, and they all reported a shady character hanging around their property during the party just like you did. Castinetto figures the shady character works for Polaski, and he was waiting for the right opportunity to kill Chuck McCracken."

"He was probably looking to collect the party payment as soon as it hit Chuck's gloved hands."

Adam's eyes widened. "That's a good theory."

"I told you, a loan shark would rather keep you alive so they can take your house, your car. Get you to take out a loan with a gullible family member. You can't collect from a dead man. Unless Sal Polaski took out a life insurance policy on Chuckles the Clown, it's not likely he's your killer."

"But his guy was there when McCracken died."

"Beasley, if a shark wanted you dead, he'd have his muscle shoot you or beat you to death with a crowbar. He wouldn't craft poisoned shoe inserts from nicotine patches. That sounds like a jealous lover. I'd look into possible girlfriends. Ask his manager who he had problems with. And don't let Castinetto see you talking to me, or you'll be on desk duty until you retire."

The greenroom door opened, and the band emerged. Garrett's lips flattened. "Are you going to be able to finish the set or do we have to have Mohinder sing the female lead?"

Mohinder growled at me.

"I'm fine. The popping took me by surprise, that's all." I cast a glance at Adam hoping he'd keep his mouth shut.

Beasley gushed, "I was just back here to get your autographs. She's great." He jabbed his thumb in my direction.

Garrett brightened. "Come see us after the show and we'd be glad to sell you a hoodie or some CDs."

I followed the band out to the stage, and we assumed the position behind our instruments.

Castinetto was back front and center to shower me with disapproval. He smirked, then cupped his hand to his mouth and shouted, "Play 'Crazy Train.'"

Little did he know this was my wheelhouse. I looked him right in his eyes and started the opening riff of the Randy Rhoads song and watched the smug look slide off his face. The rest of the band joined in without missing a beat, but I suspected a new veto song would be added tonight.

Chapter 24

My drive home from the Castinetto soirée was uneventful other than my bustier riding up to my throat. I pulled under the carport and the headlights shone on Dad and Agnes sitting on the screened porch, their look of surprise like two raccoons caught ransacking the trash cans. Agnes turned away from the light and touched Dad on the shoulder. He reached up and patted her hand like an old married couple who'd been having a heart to heart.

Oh. This can't be good. Where is his usual type of babe—B-list models and actresses? I needed to get him back on the road or at least back to L.A. before he grew attached to the trailer park Queen B.

I grabbed my guitar and went inside without a word. I'd used up all my energy on stage tonight. Not just fending off a roomful of scorn and malice, but I did a fantastic rendition of Bonnie Tyler's "Total Eclipse of the Heart" that brought a quarter of the house down.

I grabbed a cold chicken leg and a grape soda and ate standing up over the kitchen sink. Plates were for winners.

I tried to scrub off the shame of the day in the shower, but it was like an ex-lover's tattoo. I threw on Nick's sweatpants and a T-shirt and hopped into bed hoping I could actually fall asleep without incident. The instant replay of Dayton Castinetto's words stabbed me in the face over and over. *Get your act together, Virtue. You're a disgrace.*

I flip-flopped between anger and depression like a revolving door, eventually hurling myself out of bed in disgust. It was midnight. Insomnia was the price I'd pay for sleeping in earlier. I grabbed my purse and my keys and crept past Dad asleep on the couch. I scrawled a hasty note that said I was going out and not to worry.

Dad mumbled in his sleep, "You can't drive the tour bus, baby."

I smiled to myself as I gently shut the door.

There was a chill in the air along with the scent of molding leaves and Benny's famous smoked brisket he'd started for tomorrow night's community bonfire.

I got in the Aston Martin and coaxed the engine awake. I pulled onto the street, rolled down the windows, and cranked the radio. I cruised around aimlessly for a while, lost in dark thoughts, then drove into a data center to turn around and found myself facing a four-story concrete warehouse like the one where Jacob had died.

I could still smell the acrid stench from the bomb. My eyes stung from smoke that was never here—my team died across town. One wrong turn and I'd gone back in time. With icy hands, I reversed out of there as fast as I could, but nothing would slow the beat of my heart. Whitesnake's "Here I Go Again" coming through the radio sounded like it was fed through a tin can.

I could feel the darkness calling to me and I knew blacking out would come. I pulled over and turned off the car, then tried a Hail Mary—breathing exercises that I'd sworn didn't work.

I got my heart slow enough that the ringing in my ears quieted and I thought I was out of the danger zone. I started the car. *Put it in gear. Pull forward. Just drive. Don't think about Jacob. Don't think about Melissa or Oscar or Eddie.* Why did they go in without me? I told them to wait. Jacob always had something to prove. Why couldn't he follow orders for once? And I'd never be able to make it up to his family now.

Melissa was so young. She had a promising career in front of her. Not to mention boyfriends. Marriage. Kids. Grandkids.

Heck, even if all she wanted was a labradoodle it would have been better than what I gave her.

The rest of my team. I never even saw them, but the reports told me all I needed to know.

I'd been driving for a while and had lost my sense of where I was headed. I pulled into a parking lot to get my bearings and found myself outside a dive bar that Jacob and I used to frequent after our shift. As I recalled, the bar's best features were cheap beer and no cops. My throat burned with the memory of it.

A part of me started to drift out of my body and head inside. *It's been a bad day. I can handle just one drink. I'll start being sober again tomorrow.*

You're lying to yourself.

Normal people can have a drink after a bad day and stop at just one.

They haven't been through half of what you have.

I reached into my pocket to rub my sobriety chip, but it wasn't there. These were Nick's sweats.

The part of me that was grounded started to panic. I knew where this would lead if I didn't stop it now, and I was scared to death that the alcohol would win. I reached into my purse, grabbed my cell phone, and made another Hail Mary. I pulled out the open mic flyer and dialed the number written in the margin. *This is what hopeless feels like.*

"Hello?"

"It's Layla."

"What's wrong?"

"I'm outside Flanagan's on Braddock Road trying to convince myself not to go in."

"I'll be right there."

Scarlett pulled up next to me in her Porsche. I felt like a world-class idiot but that's what desperation does to you. Right behind her a white Toyota minivan pulled up followed by a gold BMW, and Bree and Charisse jumped out of their vehicles.

"You didn't all have to come."

Bree hopped into my back seat wearing Strawberry Shortcake pajamas. "Of course we did."

Charisse was dressed for a midnight sobriety check better than I'd be to go to a wedding. Linen did not wrinkle on her. She got in next to Bree and made her scoot across the seat. "Mm! It smells so good in here. That's not that vegan leather crap. That's the real thing, baby."

Scarlett opened the passenger door and climbed in next to me wearing jeans and a T-shirt that I knew for a fact cost more than Bree and Charisse's outfits combined. "Let's get out of here."

I started the James Bond car and backed out of the lot. "Where are we going?"

Bree was way too cheery for the middle of the night. "Anywhere you want."

Scarlett took her glasses off and cleaned them on the edge of her T-shirt. "I'm craving nachos."

I drove to the nearest convenience store in silence. The ladies chattered the whole way like this was a planned outing. I waited for them to complain about my inconveniencing them or the sacrifice of coming to rescue me. Maybe they were waiting for the end of the night like a teacher who wanted to scold you after class.

I parked in front of the door, and we ran inside like a fire drill, loading up on Big Gulps and snacks. Anything cheesy, deep fried, or covered in sugar. Nachos and hot dogs, and those pink snowballs that didn't resemble anything in nature. We went back to the car with a stack of napkins and my dignity on a tight thread.

Charisse ripped the wrapper off a Heath Bar. "My husband left me."

"What? Why!" We were all strongly outraged for being people who'd never met the man.

She shrugged. "Apparently my sobriety came too late. He's had someone on the side for months and they want to move in together."

I turned to the woman and gave her a look of sympathy. "Charisse, I'm so sorry."

She nodded. "Me too. He should have left me ages ago if I'm honest. I've embarrassed my husband so many times at those corporate dinners that he stopped going with me. But leaving me now when I've been sober for nearly a year is a gut punch."

"Of course it is."

Scarlett looked in the makeup mirror at the back seat. "Why do you think he's doing it now?"

"One of our CDs just matured."

Bree's eyebrows squeezed together. "Okay, but like, what does that even mean?"

Charisse gave her a sad smile. "It means he was waiting to cash out our money so he could start over in Vermont with *Dollie*."

Scarlett called him a few scandalous expletives that made us all giggle. Then she asked Charisse, "What do you need?"

Charisse shook her head and looked at each of us. "This."

We sat in the stillness of the night; the only sound was Bree loudly reaching the bottom of her Wild Cherry Slurpee.

A greasy-looking kid pulled up on his bike and moved to the side of the building under the light, a bevy of moths circling overhead. We watched as he waited a couple of minutes before a car parked on the side. A lanky guy got out and approached the kid and they swapped paper bags.

Scarlett snorted. "Amateurs."

We all chuckled as the lanky guy ran back to his car and peeled off like he was being chased by a SWAT team.

Bree shook her head. "At least pass the bags in the dark, idiots."

Scarlett pointed her Slurpee out the window. "I would have used the dumpster as the drop. No lights, no security camera, and you can make it look like you're throwing something away. If you're caught you can say it's someone else's trash. Plausible deniability."

We all nodded.

"Solid plan." I admitted.

Bree reached for one of Scarlett's nachos. "I used my job delivering pizza as a drop. People would call in and order the four-twenty special and I delivered a special topping on the side."

Scarlett turned to her. "Did you work for Jacamo's?"

Bree nodded.

"I think I ordered from you once."

Bree giggled. "You might have. All those mansions look alike to me."

Charisse laughed. "That is messed up, ladies. I have to admit, I've never done drugs. I'm just an old wino. I'd rather drink my drugs in crystal stemware."

"Me too." I confessed. "I only got high once in high school. This kid named Dayton Castinetto was the connection and he gave me my first joint in exchange for flashing him my boob. I was so freaked out that I threw up after smoking it. I've never touched the hard stuff. I spent most of my adult life trying to keep drugs off the streets after seeing my mom and dad single-handedly put Colombia on the map."

The ladies laughed.

Scarlett hoisted a chip laden with cheese from the paper carton. "I didn't smoke a lot of weed. My thing was Percocet. Being a pharmacist was like working in the candy store. You wouldn't believe how many people in this town are on painkillers. And apparently none of them count their pills when they get home."

I passed her half a snowball. "Do you still work as a pharmacist?"

"No. I lost my license. And I can never go back. Not if I want to stay clean. It's a miracle I'm not in prison." She offered me the nachos. "Do you want to talk about what happened tonight?"

I placed my Dr. Pepper in the cup holder and sighed. "I had to face a room full of cops at a gig and I crashed and burned. Full-on meltdown."

The ladies hummed understanding.

I filled them in on the engagement party and blacking out while skipping my history with the boys in blue. They didn't pry for more. No one judged. We were all too broken to throw stones. They did however clap when I told them the Neon Dreams asked me to fill in until their female lead can fit back into her miniskirt.

After a while I felt like I could handle going home on my own so we drove back to the bar, which was now closed, so they could get their cars. I'd had a nice time for someone about to throw away six months of sobriety a couple of hours ago. I'd say it went pretty well.

"Layla?" Bree asked as we pulled up next to the Porsche. "What did you mean when you said you spent your adult life trying to get drugs off the streets?"

The back of my neck started to tingle. I'd been down the road of unfortunate discovery many times. Sometimes the subject was my mother. Usually, it was my dad. This would be the first time it was my career. It never ended well, but they came to support me in the middle of the night without hesitation, so I owed them the truth. It would very likely be my final share, and that made me really sad. I kinda liked them, but I couldn't say I didn't know this moment was coming. "I have a strong aversion to cops . . ."

They watched me expectantly.

A voice in the back of my head warned, *Don't say it.* I ignored all common sense and plunged forward with my words—as per usual. "Because I *was* one. For almost twenty years. Part of why I'm off the force is because of alcohol."

Three sets of eyes stared me down with a mixture of shock and horror.

Charisse let out a low whistle.

Bree's face turned pink. "That's not something you keep from people, Layla." She pulled at the sleeves of her pajamas. "How could you think that wouldn't be a problem?"

"I'm sorry. I should have told you sooner."

"You got that right!" Bree grabbed the door handle and threw herself out of the car like it was on fire.

Charisse followed behind. "I'll talk to her."

I was left alone with Scarlett. The moment I'd been dreading had arrived, but I just felt an odd sense of peace that it was over. Somehow the threat of their rejection hanging over my head was more upsetting than their actual rejection. The hollow pain in my heart would fade in a few days—it always did, and I could find another AA meeting just like I found this one. I sighed. "I guess you want to go too. I did try to tell you all that there were things about me that you wouldn't like. Since this is the last time we'll hang out, let me say thank you. There aren't a lot of people in my life who would come out in the middle of the night to talk me down, and I'm sorry it ended this way. For the record, I regret saying anything almost as much as I regret not saying it sooner."

Scarlett's eyes flicked to mine. She rolled them away and shook her head. "Okay, drama queen, settle down. No one said anything about this being the last time. We've all had problems with the cops. Obviously, you included. Bree just has deeper issues with them, but that's her story. You're only responsible to be yourself and speak the truth. You aren't responsible for how people receive it. Don't let all that therapy wisdom fool you. Inside, Bree's just a hurt little kid. She'll come around."

Chapter 25

"*S*TEPPENWOLF! IT'S TEN IN THE MORNING. SHUT UP BEFORE I come over there and hit you on the head with a rock."

I waited a minute.

All was silent, so maybe the rooster could be reasoned with and that was the magic phrase.

Then there was a knock on my front door and Ringo barked from Nick's trailer. *So help me, Marguerite, if you're here to make a fuss about that rock on the head comment, I'll choke you out too.* I shut the window and rolled out of bed pulling on a sweatshirt on my way out of the door. Dad was sitting on the couch in his T-shirt and shorts staring into space trying to wake up. "This better not be another surprise visit by the trailer park bachelorettes."

He shrugged. "I've done worse."

"Oh, I know." I pulled the door open and found not Marguerite but Agnes on my doorstep. "What do you want?"

She blinked and tried to look past me. "I'm looking for your father."

A six-pack of Miller Lite was sitting at her feet. I stepped out into the smoky air and closed the door behind me. "Agnes, you can't bring alcohol to my house."

Agnes looked at the golden bottles. "They're not from me. That was here when I arrived."

I looked at the beer again. A piece of paper was sticking out from underneath. I reached down and shifted the six-pack.

Below was a copy of Melissa's obituary. *You killed her* was written across it in red ink. A piece of my heart chipped off and fell away.

"What's that?" Agnes craned her neck to read the fine print.

"Nothing." I crumpled the paper and shoved it in my pocket. "Just someone's idea of a joke. What did you want?"

"I told you. I'm here to see your father."

"What for?"

She reached up and patted her new fancy updo. She'd gotten red-and-gold highlights, and her hair was piled up in curls on top of her head like she'd be singing backup for the B-52s. "I wanted to bring him this."

She handed me a flyer for the bonfire and potluck tonight. It had "Hugh" written across the top in her red pen and Clifford's pickled beets was circled twice.

"What for?"

She chuckled—a sound that turned into a smoker's wheeze. "Why, so he can come of course—yeees. When we talked about it last night, he didn't know anything about Benny's brisket or the beets—so shame on you."

"Why were you here last night? What were you two jawing about on my screened porch?"

She lazily crossed her bony arms over her hoisted boobs that likely hadn't been at that altitude in two decades. "Nothing."

"It didn't look like nothing."

She gave me a one-shoulder shrug. "We were just getting to know each other."

"Uh-huh."

"Besides, anything your dad says to me is kept in the strictest of confidence."

"What the heck is that supposed to mean?"

"Don't worry about it."

"I am worried about it."

"Well, it's not my secret to tell. You'll have to ask him."

"My dad is not on the market, Agnes."

Her eyes glinted the irritation that I was used to seeing and she was back to her sour old self. "You just worry about your, Layla Virtue. And you need to bring something to the potluck. Don't try to use that excuse that you've got more important things to do, because I already know that you spend most of your time sitting in your trailer in the dark feeling sorry for yourself."

"You don't know the first thing about me. Or what I'm doing in there."

Agnes grinned in an evil way that said she thought she had some intel that gave her the upper hand. "I happen to know that your father loves brownies. Why don't I put you down to make some for the bonfire?"

"How about you let me decide what to bring?"

Agnes sighed. "I just think it would be a nice gesture. You need to treat your dad well, Layla. You don't know how much longer he'll be around."

Irritation snapped in my head like a rubber band to the brain. "What is that supposed to mean?"

She turned and flounced down my steps. "I'm just saying, you need to enjoy the time with your loved ones while you can before it slips through your fingers."

What kind of nutjob speech was that?

I went in the house and found Dad pouring himself some pineapple juice.

"Who was at the door?"

I shoved the flyer in his hand. "That was Agnes. She brought this for you."

He grinned. "Nice gal. She the one with the rooster or the giggly one with the sweaters?"

"The skinny one with the superiority complex and the proclivity for leopard print."

He nodded. "Ah. Nice gal." He looked at the flyer. "Who's Hugh?"

I took a Dr. Pepper from the fridge. "Apparently, that's you, Dad. You've also been Brad, Keanu, and Corbin. If you're gonna make up names for these women, you need to remember what you've told them."

Dad chuckled. "Keanu. That's a good one."

I leaned against the counter and took a long look at him. He looked good for someone who dropped acid more times than he could count before Reagan was shot. There was a roadmap of lines around his face from years of hard living, but his blue eyes were clear and bright. He still had all his hair even if it was only past his shoulders now. He'd started cutting the lion's mane years ago when it got too wild.

"What are you looking at, baby girl?"

"I'm just looking at you. What did you tell Agnes last night?"

Dad sipped his juice. "Was she here last night?"

"Yes. You were both on the porch when I came home."

His eyes brightened. "Oh right. We were talking about the good old days. At least the ones we remember. We were at Woodstock at the same time. Can you believe that?"

Hmm. "You don't think she remembers you, do you?"

Dad laughed. "Baby, that was a lifetime ago. I hardly remember being there except Simon says we went together."

"That can't be good. Still, she thinks your name is Hugh. Alright. Well, I hear you want brownies."

Dad gave me a funny look. "You know I can't have that anymore."

"I mean the chocolate things, Dad. Just brownies."

His eyes lit up. "Oh! Yeah, I freakin' love those!"

"Okay. I'll be back."

I grabbed the six-pack and headed next door. I knocked on Nick's trailer and was greeted with a cacophony of barking. A moment later I heard Nick gently say, "Quiet," and all went silent. The door opened and Ringo launched at me like I'd been missing for weeks.

Nick ran his hand over his hair and sighed. "We're still working on that."

I rubbed Ringo's ears and let him kiss me. "He's doing a good job. Aren't you, buddy?"

Nick grinned. "What's up?"

I straightened and offered him the Miller Lite. "Someone left this on my doorstep, and I thought you could use it. Plus, I was hoping I could borrow something."

He took the beer, giving me a funny look. "Oh-kay."

"Agnes signed me up to bring brownies tonight to the bonfire."

He stepped aside and motioned for me to come in. "What do you need?"

"Weren't you listening? I need brownies."

He threw his head back and laughed. It was a lovely sound that warmed me like a shot of whiskey. "Do you not know how to make brownies? Even with a box?"

"No, smarty pants. I don't. Baking isn't exactly a course in police basic training."

Nick shut the door and moved toward the kitchen, placing the beer in the fridge. Ringo stayed glued to my side as I followed him in. "You want some coffee?"

"Why would I want coffee?"

"What do you mean 'why'? I thought the police force ran on this stuff."

"Maybe in Barney Miller's day. Today's cop's drink of choice includes Red Bull and Mountain Dew. My sophisticated palate, however, prefers Grape Nehi or Strawberry Quik."

Nick stared at me, and his lip quirked for the briefest moment. "I see. What about donuts?"

"Who doesn't like donuts? We're not Neanderthals. Just don't ask me to eat them in public."

"Okay. I'll keep that in mind for your future visits."

My stomach quivered and I rebuked it sharply. Maybe the ice had thawed between us.

He opened the cabinet and pulled down a brown container of Hershey's Cocoa and turned it around for me to read the back. "The recipe is right on the can."

Upon seeing my skepticism, he removed the lid and handed me a spoon. "Taste it."

I got a heaping spoonful of brown cocoa powder, and it was heading for my mouth. Nick's eyes went wide. "Not that much."

Too late. It was like bitter chocolate–flavored dirt. It hit me at the back of the throat, and I coughed out a brown cloud of dust. I wheezed, "That's disgusting. Why would you make me do that?"

Ringo pressed against my leg and nosed my arm.

Nick laughed and covered his mouth with his hand. "I didn't think you would take that much. You have to add sugar, you weirdo."

He handed me his cup of coffee and I took a swig to keep from choking to death. Then I grabbed my throat and made an involuntary *kkkk* sound.

Nick placed the lid back on the cocoa and handed me a tea towel. "When you're done trying to strangle yourself, you can tell me what else you need."

I wiped my mouth, replaced my hand on top of Ringo's head, and read the ingredients. "All of them."

"All of them?"

I nodded. "And a pan."

He laughed. "And a pan? Have you never baked anything before?"

"Why would I take a perfectly good job away from Hostess?"

Nick shook his head in mock disdain. "How about I help you this time and we make them together?"

I tried to play it off that I wasn't excited about his offer, so I cocked my head and shrugged. "Sure. If you want to. I guess we could do that."

Nick rolled his eyes and laughed again. "My grandmother would beat me with her shoe if I made brownies before breakfast. Sit down. Do you know how to make an Egg McMuffin?"

"Roll up to the speaker box and order it."

He took eggs, cheese, and Canadian bacon out of the refrigerator and put them on the counter next to the stove. Then he took a bag of English muffins from a box next to the microwave. He cut his eyes to mine and *tsk*'d. "Philistine."

I sat on the barstool on the opposite side of the counter while Ringo tried to shove a stuffed squirrel into my hand. "I'm all about keeping the fast-food economy going."

Nick split an English muffin and dropped it in the toaster. "Well, they don't have Mickey Dee's in the desert, so you learn to improvise."

"I thought you had those little dehydrated dinners."

He started the stove, then cracked an egg into a small frying pan next to a slice of Canadian bacon. "MREs are for while you're in the field. On base we have a cook, and we share duties. My gran taught me to cook in case I never got married, so that was one of my duties."

"So you've never been married, I guess?"

He shook his head. "Never found anyone who'd want to put up with all this long term."

"Yes, I can see that you're a handful what with the blue eyes and the cooking and the abs and all."

Nick grinned and flipped the egg and bacon with a flick of his wrist.

"You're showing off for me, aren't you?"

"Yeah, I am. Is it working?"

I snickered. "It might be."

"Good. How about you? Have you ever been married?"

"No. Being a cop is a relationship Hiroshima."

The English muffin popped out of the toaster and Nick put it on a plate. "I thought lots of cops got married."

"They do. And then divorced. And then remarried. And then divorced again."

Nick frowned and placed a slice of American cheese on the toasted muffin.

"It takes a special person to stay married to a cop. You need to put up with bad hours, secrecy, random threats, undefined anger and depression, in my case alcohol addiction."

"That all sounds like normal life to me." Nick gently tipped the frying pan and nestled the fried egg and the bacon on the cheese, then placed the other muffin half on top. He slid the plate across the counter and our hands touched. I looked up and felt the same draw that had pulled at me the night we first met at the Seahorse Lounge.

Ringo barked and I nearly jumped out of my skin. He looked to the front door. A moment later there was a knock.

Nick came around the counter while Ringo went crazy. His bark threatening to rip off the head of whoever was out there, his tail threatening to wag him down the street. Nick snapped his fingers. "Quiet." Ringo dropped to sit, and Nick held out a treat for him.

Nick opened the door and Dad was standing on the step. "Hey there . . . I'm looking for my daughter. Little thing. Yea high, blue hair. Is she here?"

Nick stepped aside. "Yeah, come in."

I hopped off the barstool. "Is everything okay, Dad?"

Dad smiled and ran his hands over Ringo's ears. "Super. I smell fried eggs. And since we're up at this ridiculous hour, I thought maybe we should have a proper breakfast."

Nick and I passed a look to each other.

"You did?"

"Do you have a McDonald's around here?"

Nick chuckled under his breath. "You never had a chance, did you?"

Dad sniffed and wandered over to the counter. He took the empty barstool and pulled my Egg McMuffin over. "This looks great." He flashed a smile at Nick.

Nick grinned back. "Why don't you join us? I can make more."

Dad would have agreed, but his mouth was full of my Egg Mc-Muffin, so he nodded and gave him a thumbs-up.

Nick bit his lip and wouldn't look right at me. He moved the frying pan back onto the heat and cracked another egg. He kept staring at Dad. "Are you having a good visit with your daughter, Mr. Virtue?"

Dad blurted out, "Dude, call me Leo."

I covered my mouth and coughed, "Hugh."

Dad's eyebrows took a plunge. "What?"

I spoke low, through gritted teeth. "Your name is Hugh."

"The guy the bonfire invitation is addressed to?"

I rolled my eyes.

Nick let a giggle escape his lips. "Leo. Like DiCaprio?"

Dad pointed at him with finger guns. "You got it. Are you going to the bonfire tonight . . . dude?"

Nick flipped the egg in the pan. "I wouldn't miss it. You?"

I muttered, "All six of us."

Nick's lip twitched. "In the dress? Or no?"

Dad threw me a look of panic. "I don't have to go dressed like a chick, do I?"

I narrowed my eyes at Nick. "No, Dad. We can probably find you something else."

He breathed out. "Alright. But if we're going out in drag again, I'm gonna need to get my platform heels back from Gene."

Chapter 26

DAD AND I SPENT THE MORNING AT NICK'S. DAD PLAYED WITH
Ringo while Nick and I made a batch of one-bowl brownies—the
title of which was a total lie. It took two bowls, a pan, some measuring cups and spoons, and a big rubber thingy Nick called a
scraper. I tried to crack an egg and it exploded like a chicken
grenade. Nick had to dig the shells out with his hands, and he
revoked my right to touch the eggs after that. That was probably
fair.

Let's be honest—I wasn't bringing much to the baking effort
here. Nick did most of the work.

Ringo forgot I existed once Dad brought the Frisbee out—
story of my life. When Nick suggested we should sit together at
the bonfire later, it was the least I could do to say yes after he'd
made us breakfast and brownies and some fancy hot cocoa.
After being so close to Nick all morning, my nerves were tingly.
I told myself it was seasonal anxiety from the days getting
shorter.

I ran home and gathered supplies for the bonfire later, thinking I'd take in an AA meeting before the potluck. I was having
naughty thoughts about Nick that I needed to put the kibosh
on, and an hour around Potato Varish would kibosh anyone's li-
bido.

I was rifling through the bottom of the linen closet where all the things I'd never use but couldn't throw away were shoved. An old set of lace curtains, or maybe it was a tablecloth. I think it had been my grandmother's. A beach towel from summer camp when I was fifteen. That was the worst thirty-six hours of my life. An old quilt that was rumored to have been made by my great-grandmother. A leather bag of prescription meds. Wait.

Prescription meds? My heart started to race. I pulled out a bottle and read one of the labels. *Oh no. Dad. You said you weren't using. I trusted you.*

I dumped the contents out on the bathroom floor. These were party drugs I'd never heard of. I pulled out my phone to Google them. A pop-up informed me that my data plan was used up for the month, and I could pay to upgrade it now if I wanted to live a normal twenty-first century life.

I didn't want Dad to catch me going through his stash. Fortunately, I knew someone who used to be a pharmacist and would know all the addictive narcotics in order of personal preference. I didn't want to send the wrong signal about my interest in taking our relationship further—nor did I want to use anyone for ulterior motives—but I was desperate. This was my father. I looked in my call log and hit Scarlett's number.

"Hello?"

"Hey. It's Layla."

"Yeah. I got that when my screen flashed *Layla who doesn't want to be friends* across it. What's up?"

"I'm sorry to call again. I was hoping you could tell me about a couple drugs."

"I thought you didn't do drugs."

"I don't. I found these."

"Hold on." She put her hand over the mouthpiece. "Stop teasing the cat and let her have it! Sorry. I think the nanny is hiding again. He's trying to see if he can make the cat run up the wall after one of those laser lights. What are the drugs?"

"Flomax?"

"Helps you pee."

"Huh, okay. At-or-va-sta-tin?"

"Lipitor. High cholesterol medicine."

"Losartan?"

"High blood pressure. All useless if you're trying to get high."

"What about all these over-the-counter meds? Prevagen, Lion's Mane, gingko."

"Whose drugs are you looking at?"

"My father's."

"Is he having memory issues?"

"Who can tell? Why?"

"Those are all over-the-counter memory and cognitive aids."

I thanked her and said goodbye and put the drugs on the coffee table. I grabbed a grape soda and a glass of ice then sat on the couch facing the door and waited for Dad to come in so I could interrogate him. Was he sick? Why was he keeping it from me? And what did I need to know about it so I could help him?

After ten minutes Dad hadn't come home, and I was getting nervous. What if he was wandering around the lake and got lost again? Oh no, was that because he was sick? I thought it was because he'd done drugs before there were after-school specials warning you not to.

I checked the time and determined I would wait another ten minutes. Maybe he was still playing with Ringo. After four minutes I couldn't take it anymore and I headed for the door. I threw it open and smacked right into Dad who was returning home with the dog. "Where have you been?"

Dad looked at Ringo then back at me. "Which one of us are you asking?"

"The one who speaks Human, Dad. You!"

His eyes had that half-confused, half-terrified look I'd seen on many perps who were too high to come up with credible alibis. "I was next door with that dude who made us breakfast. I kept waiting for him to leave, but when he started the dishes, I realized you didn't live there. So I left and brought the dog home."

Ringo gave me a grin and fanned his tail to the beat of "Should I Stay or Should I Go."

"Dad. That's not my dog." I stepped aside and Ringo came in. He jumped on the couch, spun around twice, and lay down in a tight ball with one of his front paws out at a weird angle. He rolled his eyes to mine with a challenge to evict him.

Dad snickered. His gaze shifted to the drugs on the table. He swallowed hard. "Oh."

I pushed the door closed. "*Oh* is right. What do you have to say for yourself?"

Dad shrugged. "I'm old." He crossed the room and joined Ringo on the couch, his eyes going back to the amber containers. "The doctor said it's a miracle I'm still alive after all I've done. I should be thankful my biggest problem is an enlarged prostate."

I took the chair facing him and sat on the edge. "Are you sure? This seems like a lot of medicine all at once."

Dad laughed and waved his hand, resting it on Ringo's head. "That's nothing. You know how doctors are. I had one little appointment where they ran a bunch of tests and they put me on that stuff. Don't worry about it."

A puff of air left my chest as the stress went down a notch. Then it ratcheted back up two notches as my cop suspicion joined the party and shouted that Dad was lying. "How long have you been on it? Because I found your Speed Stick in the freezer and I'm pretty sure that just happened today."

Dad's eyes rolled to the far recesses of his mind. "Sometimes a man likes to feel like he's in the Alps."

Of all the—"What men, Dad? Have you even been to the Alps?"

He shrugged. "I'm pretty sure I have. I've been to some mountains that were snowy. Unless that was a video."

"You're talking nonsense."

"It's no big deal, honey. Those hospital doctors just want to get you out of the emergency room fast so they can give your bed to someone else."

"Hospital! Why were you in the hospital?"

There was a tight rap on the front door. Ringo launched off the couch and went into save-the-villagers mode.

Dad grinned. "Company."

"This isn't over."

Dad reached for his hat on the back of the couch and plopped it on top of his head, indicating his portion of the discussion had concluded.

I snapped my fingers at Ringo and said "Quiet" like Nick had done, and the Lab dropped to his butt. "Who is it?"

Through the door came the voice of an annoying rookie cop, determined to provoke me to move to that cabin in the woods. I opened the door and stared him down while nudging Ringo behind me. "What do you want, Beasley?"

He grinned and lifted his hand. "I just wanted to check on you after that nasty business at Castinetto's sister's engagement party. They had no right to treat you that way."

Dad's voice floated across the room. "Who treated you what way?"

Adam tried to follow the sound and look around me into the room. I stepped to block his view. "You didn't have to do that. I'm fine. Really."

I started to close the door and Adam pushed against it. "It's not fine. You lost your partner and they're acting like it's your fault."

"They're saying what's your fault?" Dad again.

"Nothing." I told Ringo to stay, and stepped outside to the porch, shutting the door behind me. "It *was* my fault. I should have been there with my team, and I let them down."

Adam shook his head. "Maybe there's more to it. I could look at your file to see if something doesn't sound right. See what the crime scene techs found. Maybe I could find something to spark your memory."

That was a sweet offer, but absolutely ridiculous. This guy couldn't find a hidden agenda if I drew him a map. And the last thing I needed was for the higher-ups to think I'm out here whining that I was unfairly suspended. "Stay out of my file, Beasley. If you ever want a promotion, just mind your business, and focus on your current cases."

He sighed. "I'm not just here about the other night. I did what you said and checked with Chuck McCracken's manager, Paula Braithwaite. She said that her client took care of his own costume. She just lined up the jobs and tried to keep him out of lawsuits. But Detective Castinetto says the manager is still a person of interest because Chuck was setting up side work and cutting her out of her ten percent."

I reached over and plucked a dead leaf off my little rosebush. "He's not wrong. That could be motive."

"Then why don't you look convinced?"

My shoulders twitched and I tried to stretch my neck to cover it. "For one thing, he owed her ten thousand dollars. If it was me, I'd like to collect first. Besides, he was a weekend birthday party clown, not opening for Van Halen. How much could her ten percent possibly be worth? She sure couldn't retire to Martha's Vineyard on that. She probably couldn't vacation in Martha's Vineyard on that."

Adam was wearing his customary blank look of bewilderment. "Yeah, but what he was doing was wrong."

"It's doubtful that she would kill him for being an unethical creep. She knew what he was up to. She was still making money off him. If Paula was tired of being screwed over for a few dollars, she'd sue him or drop his representation, which was likely coming soon anyway."

Adam grunted. "But we don't have anyone else. The ex-wife has an alibi for the time of death. She was at an AA meeting across town."

"Across town where? You need to be more specific in your reports, Beasley."

Adam pulled out a notebook and consulted it. "McLean."

"Are you sure you don't mean Alexandria?"

"No. It says right here. The John Adams in McLean. Do you know it?"

"Of course I know it. I just didn't know there was an AA meeting there. Besides, Miranda leads the meeting in Alexandria. Why would she go all the way to McLean? Something doesn't sound right."

He shook his head. "Not Miranda. Tina, the ex-wife. Tina Crumm."

"Are we talking the same Tina who came to the birthday party pre-drunk? That Tina?"

"Uhh . . . Tina who was at the party to drop off her stepson, Baron."

"I thought Miranda was his ex-wife."

Adam consulted his notes again. "Chuck McCracken had four ex-wives."

"Get out! That guy's been married four times?" *I can't even commit to a phone provider.* "Does he have a current wife?"

Adam shook his head. "Nope. Tina said he was between marriages."

My scalp started to tingle. "Do you know when Chuck's last gig before Janice Kestle's was?"

He checked his notes. "Uh . . . no. Not yet."

"Well, you need to find out. Because nicotine patches don't last forever. They had to be planted in between parties."

Adam wrote something in his book. "I'll check the guest list."

I started to inch back through the door. "You do that."

He waved goodbye and followed the patch of dead grass back to his patrol car.

I waited until he shut his door to shut mine and continue my interrogation of Don Virtue, the shifty and squirmy. Dad was sound asleep on the couch. His hat over his eyes and Ringo's head lying in his lap. They were both snoring. Great.

I grabbed my cell phone and went to Google the times for the McLean meeting where I was smacked down again by the *you don't pay us enough to let you use the Internet* pop-up.

I didn't want to call Scarlett again. I couldn't have her thinking we were going to start palling around getting pedicures together. But Bree was over me, and Charisse had enough troubles with her husband leaving her. I didn't want to pile on.

I deliberated for a few minutes and considered calling Reena, my old sponsor, but she'd had enough of me months ago and told me not to contact her again. I resigned myself to humiliation and hit the contact for a tiny Asian ball of sass.

Chapter 27

"*D*ID YOU FIND MORE PILLS?"

"No."

"Talk to your father?"

"Yes."

"How'd it go?"

"He gave me a confusing runaround, which isn't that different from all our conversations so it's hard to tell how it went."

"I like him already. What else is going on?"

I considered bailing on the plan, but I did want to go to a meeting. Checking on Tina would be a twofer. "I'm sorry to ask you for something else, but I don't have any data left on my phone."

"It's no problem. I'm just sitting here watching my Turkish soap opera."

"I didn't know that was a thing."

"Every culture has a soap opera. People love drama."

"Do you speak Turkish?"

"No."

"Then how do you know what's going on? Are there subtitles?"

"Nope. There's a lot of yelling and arm waving, and I figure people are pretty much the same all over the world, so I know what's happening just by who's doing the yelling. I make the rest of it up."

"Okay."

"Quit stalling and spill it, Layla. We're going to be friends whether you like it or not."

I knew arguing wouldn't get me where I wanted to be, so I ignored her nonsense. "Do you want to check out an AA meeting at the John Adams to spy on one of Chuck McCracken's ex-wives with me?"

"More than anything."

"Can you Google it and see when they meet?"

"Way ahead of you. The next meeting's in an hour. Should I come pick you up?"

I looked around the bland trailer that I actually called home on purpose and considered Scarlett's Porsche Cayenne. "Maybe I should come get you."

She gave me the address and said she'd let the security gate know to expect me. I left Dad a note that I'd be back in time for the bonfire and grabbed the keys to his car.

I knew Scarlett lived in a ritzy neighborhood because she'd mentioned a security gate, but I had no idea. We lived in a neighborhood like this when I was little. That lasted until the house was seized by the IRS. Dad loved the highlife, just not as much as the gettin'-high life. Paying taxes was not at the top of his priorities.

I showed my ID to the security guard and he waved me through. "Mrs. Weatherspoon is waiting for you."

I wove around acres of spotless golf course and pulled up in front of a gleaming gray brick colonial. A team of landscapers were updating the expansive winding beds with feathery orange plants around the burning bushes.

I rang the bell expecting a butler, but Scarlett threw it open herself. Behind her was a polished marble foyer with twelve-foot ceilings and double winding staircases. Something blue and glittery was oozing off the curvy banister to the right. It landed on the marble floor with a plop. "I have a surprise for you."

I hoped it wasn't that pile of jelly goo. "Oh yeah?"

Scarlett moved the door to fully open and a very timid Bree gave me a finger wave. "Hi."

I was taken aback after the way we left things the other night and my poker face made a momentary slip. "I didn't expect to see you today . . . or ever again."

"I know. I hope it's okay. I need to apologize to you for the way I acted. You were supposed to be in a safe space, and you needed us. I shouldn't have telegraphed my issues onto you."

"I get it. You don't like cops and you felt betrayed that I hadn't told you."

She looked like she wanted to say more, but another plop of blue goo hit the floor with a splat.

Scarlett smiled broadly and nodded. "See. See. Now we're getting somewhere." Then she tipped her head back and yelled at the ceiling, "Ambrose, get your little butt down here and clean up this slime or so help me you won't see your tablet for a month!"

A three-foot-tall Asian kid in a tiny business suit pouted all the way down the stairs in slow motion, each step getting more forced. He caught my eye and didn't let go for the last five steps which he came down on his butt.

Scarlett said something to him in Chinese. He petulantly stomped his foot and shouted, "You know I don't speak Chinese!"

Then she said something else in Chinese much louder and he jumped up, yelled, "I do not!" and ran from the foyer.

She rolled her eyes at me. "Whatever. He's the nanny's problem for the next couple of hours. Let's go."

We settled into Dad's car, and I continued around the circular driveway back toward the security booth. "This is a nice neighborhood."

Scarlett shrugged. "Yeah. Expensive as heck though. My husband loves it. We still eat tacos for dinner and spend the night watching Netflix like everyone else."

Her attitude about her wealth was as relaxed as her words. I'd been in her situation, and I found myself mortified. I told the girls in my seventh-grade class that I was the housekeeper's kid. Then my dad came home in one of his "work outfits" and the jig was up.

I looked in the rearview mirror at Bree, twisting the hem of her turtleneck.

She gave me a tight smile.

"You're awfully quiet."

She sighed. "I owe you an amends, but it's hard for me to talk about."

"Didn't we already do that?"

Scarlett turned in her seat and looked through the headrest. "Go ahead. We're here to support you, whatever you need. Besides, Layla has to keep her eyes on the road, so she won't be able to look at you when you tell her. Easy."

I muttered. "Geez, how bad can it be that you don't want me looking at her?"

Scarlett jabbed me. "Shut up. Watch the road."

Bree let out a long breath. "My brother was killed by a cop during a routine traffic stop."

I lost focus for a moment and didn't notice the car in front of me was slowing for a red light and had to pound the brakes. "Bree, I'm sorry."

"He was stopped for reckless driving, and the cop said he pulled out a gun from under the seat. The cop claims my brother was dressed like a gangbanger and he fired in self-defense, but my brother was coming home from a party and he didn't have a gun."

It was every cop's nightmare. I kept my eyes on the road and let her continue.

"My dad got a copy of the police report. The scene investigator didn't find a gun. They found a cell phone that my brother had started to dial. He was probably going to call my dad and ask him what to do. He died before the ambulance could get him to the hospital."

"How old was he?"

"Eighteen."

My mouth went dry as all the energy left my body. I pulled into the John Adams parking lot and started to veer toward the guest parking. Scarlett nudged me and pointed to the sign saying VALET. She held out a twenty. I glanced in the mirror at Bree. Her eyes were wet with tears.

"I swore I'd never forgive the police, then here you come. You're so young and cool and you understand what we've been through. I thought, *She would be fun to hang out with.* I didn't know . . ."

"You didn't know I'd bring all this up for you."

She shook her head. "I thought you were just a musician. I'm sorry I freaked out."

We pulled up to the door and I put the car in park. A sharply dressed valet rushed out to open the door for Scarlett. A moment of confusion crossed the expression of the valet, probably because the driver of the Aston Martin was wearing worn Levi's and an Outer Banks hoodie with a tear in the kangaroo pouch, but he covered it as soon as I passed him the keys.

I went right to Bree. "You don't owe me an apology. What happened was traumatic. I understand why you feel the way you do. It's okay."

Bree threw her arms around my neck, and I was momentarily off balance. "Thank you, Layla. I don't want this to keep us from becoming great friends."

I cut my eyes to Scarlett who gave me a cocky grin that said, *Just try to shake us now.*

Chapter 28

*T*HE POLISHED GRAY AND GOLD LOBBY OF THE JOHN ADAMS HOTEL was a relative ghost town. Two uniformed hosts busied themselves with tapping on their computer keyboards and avoiding eye contact while a lone couple stood by waiting to check in. A sign next to the desk listed FRIENDS OF BILL W. meeting and gave the room's location down the hall.

We breezed by the check-in desk like we'd been there a thousand times before and found the room just past the elevators. A dozen or so people had already arrived and were munching on decorated autumn-themed cookies from a circle of plush gold velvet chairs.

Scarlett pushed into the room past me and headed for the snack table. "Oooh, swanky. Is that Starbucks coffee?"

She was followed by Bree, who grabbed my arm before making a beeline for the baked goods. "Those cookies are frosted, Layla. Frosted!"

I was right behind them clutching my own paper plate. "Dude. All our meeting has is knockoff Chips Ahoy and that two-liter bottle of Food Lion iced tea."

A thin man with a pencil mustache placed a bowl of half-and-half creamers next to the Starbucks coffee boxes. "What meeting do you ladies normally attend?"

Bree grabbed a scarecrow cookie and added it to her pile. "Second Chance Church in Alexandria."

He nodded. "I've not been over there. My boss lets me hold this meeting twice a week in the hotel for free. Our in-house bakery lets us have the day-old cookies."

I poured myself a cup of Arizona Sweet Tea. "That's very generous."

He handed me a lemon wedge with silver tongs. "My boss is also my sponsor so . . . This benefits us all."

The room was filling up, so we excused ourselves to get seats before they were all claimed.

Bree wiggled down in the velvet. "I don't think I can go back to Miranda's meeting. Not after this."

Scarlett nibbled the stem off a pumpkin cookie and looked around. "It does make me wonder though, if the meeting organizer provides the refreshments, maybe Miranda isn't doing as well as she wants us to believe. That, or she's suuuuper cheap."

I scanned the room for Tina. "No, you're right. Something's off there. And she's always complaining about money."

Scarlett nodded. "She wears designer clothes, but always from several seasons ago. And her jewelry is costume."

Bree leaned in and whispered, "Her hair has been out of a bottle for a few months now too. That's not a salon job."

"How can you tell?" I asked.

She tilted her head and gave me a knowing look. "Brassy. And her ends are fried."

I had no experience with that. My hair had always been black like my dad's before he started to go gray. Come to think of it, his hair is pretty white now. But then he is much older. And he has done more than his fair share of partying. My mood deflated just thinking about my father getting older and on all that medication, his mortality slapping me into a funk.

Scarlett nudged me in the side. "You're gonna tell us which one is Tina, right? 'Cause we weren't at the murder party."

I nodded toward the door. "Speak of the high-class devil." Tina walked into the room and pulled up the seat closest to the exit. I was very familiar with that strategy. She was planning to bolt as soon as the meeting was over. "That's her in the green plaid blanket."

Bree leaned in closer. "That's a wool cape, and they're very in right now."

Scarlett added, "And that one is Burberry. Designer."

Bree and Scarlett focused on Tina with laser eyes. She was lucky the velvet under her butt didn't start to smoke from their intensity.

I hissed at them, "Don't stare at her!"

Bree hissed back, "I don't get it. She looks normal. I thought she'd have a unibrow or something."

Scarlett nodded. "She's not dumpy or pock marked at all."

I had to keep myself from laughing. "Why would she be pock-marked?"

Scarlett's lip curled. "Do I need to pull up the picture of her ex-husband for you?"

"Pudgy bald men need love too."

Scarlett snorted. "Have you forgotten about the clown suit and the farting?"

The image of Chuckles farting and waving his hand behind his butt flooded my mind. "Yeah. That's a hard pass."

The meeting was called to order, and we sat quietly listening as many of the regulars shared about their struggles with the steps since their last meeting. Clearly the John Adams catered to a wealthier class of alcoholic. They had the exact same problems as the rest of us, but with higher price tags. I wondered why Scarlett didn't attend this meeting to start with, and for a moment found myself worried that she might switch over now that she knew this one was available. I didn't like that feeling. Worried that someone else would leave me.

Why do I care? Wouldn't that solve my problem?

We had almost given up hope that Tina would share, but our patience was rewarded when she raised her hand at the end.

"Hi, I'm Tina. I'm an alcoholic. I've been sober for four days. I threw away two years of sobriety after having the worst week of my life where I made a huge mistake."

Bree whispered, "I wonder if by *mistake* she means killing Chuckles?"

Tina's lip started to tremble. "I've done so many things that I regret. Things I'm ashamed of. If only I could take it all back . . ." Tina started to cry and the woman next to her put her hand on her shoulder. That was the end of her share. I'm not gonna lie. Even for AA it was suspicious. The hair on the back of my neck agreed. I told my hair to shut up because I wasn't going to get involved seeing as how I was no longer a cop. I was just here to observe.

Tina stared at me like she was trying to place where she knew me from and my hair tingled that it still had cop tendencies.

After the meeting, Scarlett started to bolt for the petite brunette, but I grabbed her arm. "Whoa. Slow your roll, Ali Wong. Give her some space."

"She's gonna get away."

"She's trapped by mustache there who brought in the cookies. Let's just scoot over and make it look casual. Right, Bree? Bree?"

Bree had gotten past me and was across the room wrapping Tina in a hug.

Scarlett pointed at them and gave me a grunt.

"Oh, for Pete's sake. Okay, let's go."

We crossed the room in time to hear Bree say, "This is our first. We usually go to the Tenth Street meeting in Old Town Alexandria."

A slight pink crept up Tina's neck. "I know the one." She caught my eye. "Didn't I see you at the birthday party?"

"If you mean the one at Janice's, then yes, you did."

She cocked her head to the side and searched her memory. "I'm so embarrassed that you saw me like that."

"Hey, it happens to the best of us. I'm glad you got home okay. You missed all the excitement with the clown dying and the police questioning everyone."

Tina's eyes grew very shiny. "Yeah, that was lucky."

I didn't want anything to do with this alternate reality investigation that Scarlett and Bree were setting up. When I was on the force I would have slapped them with a warning about obstruction so fast, their heads would spin. But Tina's story was nagging the cop instincts at the corner of my brain and I couldn't shut them up. I couldn't exactly haul Tina in for questioning, so I hoped to get her to offer the information on her own. "I heard in your share that you must have gone off the rails right around that time. If you don't mind my asking, what worked you up like that?"

She bit her lip and looked away. "Just a bad investment."

Scarlett nodded. "Financial problems. I hear ya." She looked at me with flat lips and narrowed eyes and shook her head no.

Tina fidgeted with the fringe on her fancy cape. "My husband will kill me if he finds out."

Scarlett licked her lips and nodded slowly. "Did you by chance *know* Chuck McCracken? In a personal way?"

Tina's eyes grew to the size of the acorn cookies on the refreshments table. "Why are you asking?"

I hedged. "I thought everyone knew Chuck. He was quite the fixture on the birthday party circuit."

Bree tried to play along, and it immediately became clear she was out of her depth. "I just loved the way Chuck . . . did that thing . . . that he did. You know. With his . . ."

"Balloon animals," I threw out there.

Scarlett and Bree both gave me horrified looks and Bree said, "Eww."

Tina's shoulders drooped. "Chuck was an expert in balloon animals. Did you ever see his Roger Rabbit?"

Scarlett muttered, "Is that what he called it?"

Bree was scanning for an exit. "I need a minute."

Tina was clearly hiding something, and I was not known for letting a suspect slide, so I pressed forward. "Are you sure that what you went through before your bender had nothing to do with Chuck McCracken? I heard he was known for being a bit handsy."

Tina's face blanched. She wrapped her Burberry cape around

her and stepped to me. "Don't you ever say that name to me again. If he wasn't already dead, I'd kill him myself. I made one mistake and I just want to put it behind me. And if you know something and you're trying to blackmail me, that's too bad. Because I'm not paying you a dime for you to keep quiet!"

She flew through the door in a huff.

Scarlett and I passed a silent message between us. *What the heck was that all about?*

Bree flitted back with another stack of cookies. "Aww, she left. I asked the director when the next meeting was and told him we've heard so much about his group from Tina." Bree looked us each in the eye in turn. "He said that was surprising since this was her first time here in months."

Well, there goes her alibi.

Chapter 29

"*B*ABY GIRL, WHAT TIME IS THE BONFIRE? WHAT? WHY ARE YOU looking at me like that? Is that not tonight?"

I was sure Dad was punking me since I gave him a five-minute warning four minutes ago. "It's now, Dad. That's why you have that jacket on."

Dad looked at the plaid barn coat we borrowed from Benny's sun porch that he was wearing. "Oh. I thought it was just hot in here." He reached behind the couch and pulled out his acoustic guitar.

Panic started rising in my chest. "Where did that come from?"

"I told Jimmy I was staying with you for a few days, and he had a courier bring them over. My Pearl's in the shower. Maybe we can play together later."

"What do you need them for?"

"The lady with the bird nose asked me to play 'Kumbaya' or something. Come on. Don't be like that. It'll be fun. I thought we could do a duet like in the old days."

"If I remember correctly, security had to rescue you from a stampede more than once in the old days."

Dad rolled his eyes and stuffed a couple picks into his breast pocket. "No one knows I'm here, and my fans lost the ability to stampede more than a decade ago. I promise to only play songs of mediocre grandeur. So nothing I wrote. Okay?"

"I still think it's too risky. Even with Foster's overalls, and those ginormous bedazzled sunglasses, I'm afraid someone will recognize you."

I grabbed the quilt and pan of brownies Nick was generously letting me be the front man on and pulled the door open.

Nick and Ringo were waiting on the sidewalk to head down to the lake with us. Ringo tried to jump forward to lick me, but Nick held him tightly on the leash. "Whoa! Elton John called, and he wants his sunglasses back."

Dad stopped in the doorway and touched the blinged-out blue shades. "He said I could keep them. Dude! Stick to a decision!"

Nick was too busy catching flies with his giant mouth open, so I tried to cover the moment with an awkward chuckle. "He's kidding. Dad—behave!"

I passed Dad the blanket and reached my hand for Ringo's velvet ears. "Hey, buddy. Are you my plus-one?"

Nick's smile almost made me forget what a crappy week I'd been having. "I like to take him with me as often as I can, so he gets accustomed to crowds. It will help him learn to be calm when he meets new people."

Dad laughed. "I should have tried that with you, honey. Maybe you wouldn't have freaked out in ninety-six at the Weenie Roast."

Apparently, hypocrisy makes my spine go ramrod straight because I flew upright. "Are you kidding me? You lost me at the Amphitheatre."

"I did not. I left you with Ozzy."

I cut my eyes to Nick, regretting going down this line of discussion. "Well, he was a terrible babysitter, and he never did bring me that hot dog."

Dad chuckled. "Sweet guy. Little scatterbrained." He reached for the leash and passed Nick the quilt we were going to share. "Hey, man. Let's trade."

Ringo followed his nose toward smoked brisket and Clifford Bagstrodt's much-advertised pickled beets, and led the way across the street, and down the path by Donna's trailer.

Nick smacked his lips, his eyes narrowed. His bemused look

burned into my soul. He was way past just being suspicious about Dad's identity.

"What?" I poked him.

His lip quirked and he shrugged. "Nothing."

"Uh-huh."

We emerged through the woods and found most of the trailer park people were already there. Agnes had set up two long tables with orange plastic tablecloths and Clifford was staged as sentry at one end to make sure no riffraff fast food was snuck in with the homemade vittles. I kind of had a feeling that was for my benefit.

Foster was blowing bubbles, and Pippi, wearing a straw hat covered in sunflowers, was trying to bounce them with her snout.

Myrtle Jean Maud bum rushed Dad as soon as we emerged through the trees. "Hi, Brad. Can I take your brownies over to the dessert table for you?"

Nick said, "Leo."

And I said, "Corbin."

Dad smiled broadly at the silly woman. "Sure thing, sugar. The girl has them."

Myrtle Jean glanced at me and took Dad's arm. "She can probably find it herself." She started to drag him toward a cluster of camp chairs ringing a stack of wood that Benny was struggling to light. She'd only gone a few paces when Marguerite spotted her and launched out of her own lawn chair for an interception. She barreled head down shoulders back toward Dad like a linebacker with a grudge. "I saved you a seat with me, Keanu."

Nick said a breathy "*Oh no.* She's gonna sack that old lady."

Marguerite didn't have a chance against Agnes, who was surprisingly willowy and limber for a woman of her age, in her leopard print turtleneck and a belt the size of a radial tire.

Agnes stepped into the Latina's path and waved. "Yoo-hoo. Hugh darling. I brought my accordion. I'll take it from here ladies. Hugh is my special guest, and he has the prime saved seat by the fire where he can play for us. Isn't that right, Hugh?"

Dad grinned at the ladies. "Now now, there is plenty of me to go around."

Clifford watched the hens clucking—eyes green with jealousy—and grunted. I suspected that he'd been the Lake Pinecrest's most eligible bachelor up until now. He'd even come dressed in his best holiday church wear but a flashier peacock had arrived. I handed Clifford the brownies.

He gave them a long inspection and a sniff, then smacked his lips. "You made these yourself?"

"Nick helped."

Clifford cast a questioning look at Nick who stood his ground. "That's right."

The retired military man was not persuaded. "You sure she didn't mash together a bunch of brownies she bought from Boston Market again."

I *tsk*'d. "Like I would waste Boston Market brownies on this crowd."

"Down at the end there." Clifford handed Nick the pan of brownies then switched his attention back to the Lake Pinecrest bachelorettes and Old Lady Henson—who was pushing her way through Foster's perfectly laid blanket toward Dad, using an aluminum lawn chair for a walker. She got snagged on Foster's picnic basket and started to swing the lawn chair like a claymore. Pippi ducked like a champ.

Nick gasped. "Not today, Satan." He passed me the brownies and took off to stop Old Lady Henson from breaking a hip, sprinting across the field of blankets. Ringo stayed put by my side while Nick gently wrestled the chair from the frail woman's vice grip.

Someone tapped me on the shoulder. "Hey, lady."

Behind me, Donna was holding a bowl of potato salad for Clifford to approve. Kelvin stood behind her cradling a two-liter bottle of Mountain Dew like Frances carrying a watermelon. "I'm surprised to see you here. I thought you didn't like these forced community socials."

I took a deep breath and ripped the Band-Aid off. "My father is in town visiting and he wanted to come, so . . ."

Dad started to play the opening notes to one of Society's Castoff's ballads, despite our nothing recognizable agreement.

Donna turned to follow my gaze and her mouth dropped open. She looked like she was screaming but no sound came out.

Kelvin tugged the hem of her gold baby doll blouse. "What's a-matter, Gran? Why is Hottie McMuscles tryin' to take Old Lady Henson's chair away?"

Donna lifted a finger and started to point at Dad like the Ghost of Christmas Future.

I grabbed her hand and covered it with my own. Then I dragged her to the other end of the table where Clifford couldn't eavesdrop. He had his plate full of spying on his women anyway. I dropped the pan of brownies in between an apple pie and a bowl of something green with marshmallows. "Shh! Stop it."

"But that's . . . That's . . . Here . . ."

"Donna. Look at me. Can you please keep this a secret? No one else here knows."

She didn't take her eyes off Dad. "How could they not? Have they been living under a rock? He was just inducted into the Rock and Roll Hall of Fame."

Ringo was glued to my side, watching me intently, his tail stone still. "Look around, Donna. Do these people look like they follow *Rolling Stone*?"

She looked me in the eye. "Ohmigawd, I cannot believe he's your father and you didn't say anything. That was him playing the other day and not the radio, wasn't it? He's been right across the street this whole time? That explains the fancy car."

Ringo groaned, expressing my feelings exactly.

Donna was just gearing up. "I am such a fangirl. Can I meet him? Is your mom still in rehab? Isn't he supposed to be on a world tour? Oh my gawd—that commercial he did! Is he still dating that dancer from Argentina? You know . . ."

Oh no. Here it comes.

Ringo shifted on his feet and leaned his head against my leg.

"Kelvin's school has a fundraiser coming up for the science

lab. Do you think your father would be willing to perform—for the kids."

"He doesn't really do that."

Her eyes narrowed. "Why not? He's rich enough. I mean, you like Kelvin, don't you? And you know he lost his mother to a drug overdose. I heard your dad just finished rehab. He would be sympathetic."

Not the Make-A-Wish card. "There's more than a hundred thousand public schools in America and they all have fundraisers. He can't say yes to them all, so he doesn't say yes to any." *He discreetly gives away a fortune in his mother's name, but no one knows about that.*

Ringo shoved his snout into my hand and gave me a lick.

Donna's eyes widened. "Yeah, but I could ask him. Right? I mean he's right there."

I sighed. "You could, yeah. But he'll tell you to call his agent who'll never return your call."

She put her hand on my arm. "I bet he'd say yes to you."

"Donna, I learned a long time ago not to do that. Can you trust me on this?"

Kelvin whined. "This is gettin' heavy, Gran."

Ringo whined right along with him.

Her eyebrows knit together. "How about you then? You're a musician. We could tell everyone who your dad is. That should at least double the attendance to see Don Virtue's daughter."

"Donna, couldn't you please keep this to yourself? I don't want it getting around the park that my father is Don Virtue. People will never leave us alone."

Donna's face flushed, and her lips flattened. "You think you're too good to play at a kids' school so they can get some microscopes? No wonder you don't want to come to my whine and cheese. I should have realized you'd think you were too good for us too. What are you doing living here, anyway?"

"That's not fair, Donna. I've never said I was better than anyone. Nor have I ever treated you like I thought that. I can't come to your whine and cheese because I'm a recovering alcoholic."

I also couldn't come because of this pressure right here, right now—but I kept that to myself too.

Nick limped over, rubbing his shoulder where Old Lady Henson had whacked him with the chair, and passed a quizzical look between Donna and me. Ringo snooted him and grunted. Nick took the Mountain Dew from Kelvin and placed it on the table with the other drinks. "Layla, your dad's looking for you."

"I'm sorry, Donna. I have to go." I walked away from the table, "Another One Bites the Dust" playing in my head.

Nick caught up to me with Ringo on my heels. "What was that all about?"

"Same story, different day."

"It looked quite intense."

"Does my dad really want me?"

"I'm sure he does. He asked Myrtle Jean if you were coming to the bonfire."

I snorted and shook my head.

Nick was quiet for a minute. "Just so you know, I think Benny might have figured out who your dad is, even with the disguise. He's been looking at him funny since he started singing."

I stopped walking. "How long have you known?"

"Since he asked if he offended me backstage at the Grammys when he said 'Uptown Funk' was a rip-off and I should apologize to the Gap Band."

"He thought you were Bruno Mars?"

Nick grinned and nodded.

"When was that?"

"The day we put away the groceries."

I counted back. Five days. "I'm sorry I didn't tell you sooner."

"Hey, I get it. If my mom was Janet Jackson, I wouldn't tell another soul. People would be constantly asking me personal questions about growing up with Michael, have I been to Neverland Ranch, and asking me to pay them to be in my entourage. Forget that."

I felt my heart lift higher in my chest. "Yes. Exactly."

"What I don't get, is why are you living here if you're *that* Layla Virtue?"

"I like it here."

"No, you don't."

"Yeah, I don't. But I like that no one bothers me. At least not in the celebrity way." I glanced at Donna who was glaring at me by the pickled beets. "Not until now, anyway. Besides, it's easy to disappear here. As long as your recycling bin goes out on time."

"But why the struggle? Surely your father has connections. He could at least get you a demo track in front of some record companies."

I watched Dad and Agnes jamming by the bonfire. I had never heard "Rock You Like A Hurricane" on the accordion before, and I hoped I never would again. "I want to make it on my own. If I let Dad have his way, he'd have me opening for Society's Castoffs on tour. I'd be judged harsher because I'm Don Virtue's daughter. I might get a single on the charts out of it just because of the notoriety. But the band would resent me, no one serious would want to work with me, success would disappear overnight, and I'd be a *where are they now* story within a year. The music industry is harsh."

We started moving forward slowly. "Not to mention my dad's got a reputation. Not everyone wants to work with him."

Nick chuckled. "I've read the stories. I don't see it personally. He seems very laid-back to me."

"You haven't seen him coked up."

"Except backstage at the Grammys."

"Obviously there. It would hurt *his* career too. No one respects nepotism. I don't want to see Dad reviled at the end of his career for trying to make my life easier. Besides. What if I don't have what it takes? Talent isn't always passed in DNA. When I go onstage as Layla Virtue I live and die by my own name. If I go out as Don Virtue's daughter, Dad will get the credit or the condemnation for my performance. I don't want either of those things."

"I hear you, but I still think you could go your own way in a proper house that's not on cinder blocks and has decent water pressure."

I laughed and Ringo looked at me and smiled. "I had those

things, and I let alcohol steal them from me. Now I live here because if I mess up, I don't have as far to fall."

"If you're trying so hard for anonymity, why didn't you change your name? When I met you, you were playing as Layla Virtue."

"Dude, my name is all I have left. And I was very happy to be Layla Virtue long before I knew there was a price to pay for it."

"What about your mom? Wasn't she a musician too?"

Dad was beckoning to me to join him. "She rode with the band—one of his groupies. Eventually she and my dad became a couple and he put her on tambourine which the other guys hated. Then the fans revolted because nobody wants a tambourine player in a hair metal band. She had to give it up when I came along."

"How did she feel about that?"

"She still hasn't forgiven me for it, which is something I hear about every Mother's Day."

Chapter 30

*L*AST NIGHT'S COMMUNITY BONFIRE WILL FOREVER GO DOWN AS one of the most stressful nights of my life. Dad begged me to sing "Stop Dragging My Heart Around" with him, until I finally gave in. His subliminal message about wanting to take care of me was noted and dismissed—just like in the song.

Nick never said a thing about knowing Dad was a legit rock star. And he didn't blow Dad's cover at the bonfire. Even after the Tom Petty medley when Dad saluted the heavens and said, "Rest in peace, brother."

Donna didn't say another word to me all night. She didn't say anything to anyone as far as I saw. In fact, after she and Kelvin filled their plates, they left the bonfire. I was sad because I liked her and I didn't like anyone being upset with me, but such was life. It was the very reason I stayed away from people. You can't lose a friend you didn't make in the first place.

Still, I'd spent most of the night feeling like a cartoon cat tied to the conveyor belt with a buzz saw inches away from my neck. I noticed the strange looks pass across faces around the potluck table when Dad was singing. And I noted Benny was doing a lot of searching on his cell phone during the event. I doubt he was looking for pickled beet recipes.

My greatest ally for flying under the radar was Clifford with his commentary about Dad being *just okay* on the guitar. He suggested Dad get more practice, which made Dad laugh since he was on *Guitar World*'s list of the best shredders on the planet.

Clifford had crossed his arms and bristled that back in his day it wasn't music unless it had a full orchestra. Clifford was apparently a time traveler from the 1800s. And he may have overestimated the age difference between him and Dad.

The ladies pooh-poohed Clifford and his nonsense until he pouted hard enough that Dad had put the guitar away. Then Dad stole the pan of brownies and made a run for home. The wrong way. Nick stopped him.

I'd gone home and locked myself in my bedroom for the rest of the night thinking about where I could move when this set my life on fire, because . . . baby, it was starting to smoke.

Now I was in the Saturday morning meeting waiting for Miranda to quit yammering on about probate and her ex's—Chuck's—many ex-wives and the fight for who gets to keep the clown suit in the estate. I wanted to ask if the fight was because everyone *wanted* it or because no one wanted to *get stuck* with it, but I didn't want to give Miranda any reason to pontificate longer.

Bree kicked my foot. "We should take my minivan."

"Take it where?"

"The party."

"What party?"

"Shh!" Miranda glared at us from the podium at the front. She went back to her share about being generally put upon and misunderstood by everyone, everywhere, all the time.

Scarlett leaned past me. "That's a good idea. My Porsche is too small for all five of us and so is Layla's Aston."

"It's not mine."

Scarlett adjusted the clasp on her ruby bracelet. "What do you mean it's not yours?"

Charisse leaned past Bree. "Girl, you didn't steal it, did you? I would have thought a former cop would think twice about grand theft auto."

"It's . . . a loaner."

"Shh!" Miranda again. "Really, Layla. One would think you don't want to be here as little as you're paying attention."

"Me?! Varish has killed six hordes of dragons on his cell phone since you took that second lap around how mean the judge was when you tried to make the other ex-wife give you her engagement ring."

Varish glanced up from his game. "I heard all this two days ago. It doesn't sound like there are any updates."

Miranda's face flamed. "It was my diamond first. Chuck stole it from my jewelry box and gave it to that dog groomer." She looked around the room hoping to find an ally. Louise must have looked promising because Miranda gave her a hopeful quiver.

Louise was a timid woman who squeaked like a mouse when she spoke. "Aren't we supposed to be talking about the AA steps in these meetings?" Miranda must have looked menacing because Louise grabbed her purse and fled the room. "I'm sorry. I'm late for choir practice."

Miranda stormed from the platform. "Meeting over. Good luck with your sobriety."

Scarlett checked the time on her phone. "Oh, thank God. Why don't you all follow me home? We'll pick up Ambrose, and Bree can drive us to the birthday party."

Charisse made a face. "Ambrose?"

Scarlett toyed with her silk scarf. "It's a family name. On my husband's side."

Bree pursed her lips. "How'd he convince you to go with that?"

A light coral tinged Scarlett's cheeks. "Because the official name on my son's birth certificate is Demerol and I owed him."

We were silent for a beat.

"Yes, I was high when I filled out the paperwork. I'd stayed off drugs my whole pregnancy and I was celebrating."

The other ladies agreed that that was a perfectly logical explanation, and nothing surprised me after eighteen years on the force, so I just said, "Naturally," and let it go.

A few minutes later we converged our vehicles in the driveway at Scarlett's where she and Ambrose were having a difference of opinions. She wanted Ambrose to get into the minivan to go to the party and his opinion was that Trevor was a doodie head and he didn't want to go to his *stoopid* party for *loooosers* who can do equations.

Scarlett won that round with a reminder that only she knew the Wi-Fi password.

We piled into Bree's minivan, and I asked myself for about the tenth time why am I doing this? I could just go home and let the police handle it. Naps don't take themselves. But something came over me whenever Scarlett started talking about the investigation, and maybe it was morbid curiosity or nosiness, but I just wanted to see what she would do next. I'd never been a part of anything outside of the force. I'd be lying if I said I didn't miss this. And since Castinetto hadn't made an arrest for Chuck's murder yet, it was obvious the official investigation was floundering.

I got stuck with the seat in front of Ambrose, the master of stink eye. "Hey."

Ambrose's frown deepened and he looked away with a sigh.

"Good talk."

Scarlett rolled her eyes. "Don't pay any attention to him. He's just mad he had to turn off Fortnite."

Ambrose kicked the back of my seat. "I don't even like Trevor."

Scarlett sent some eye daggers his way. "I don't care. Just remember our agreement."

She directed Bree down the driveway, through the marble gate, and toward the golf course.

Charisse scooted forward from the seat next to mine and laid her arms on Scarlett's headrest. "So, what's the plan here?"

Scarlett turned around from the passenger seat. "These are the same moms from Chuckles's other parties over the summer. Layla, you'll probably recognize them, won't you?"

"I dunno."

Bree looked at me in the rearview mirror. "You were just there a week ago."

"Yeah, but I was trying not to get shanked for singing 'Baby Shark.'"

From the back seat, Ambrose came alive and started singing. "'Ba-bee shark—doot doo doo doo doo doo.'"

Scarlett snapped her fingers and shot him a look. Ambrose silenced. He crossed his arms over his chest and huffed. Then he kicked my seat.

Bree turned into a tree-lined driveway through a nine-foot-tall wrought iron gate. "Why don't we just try to blend in and ask the moms if any of them knows what happened to Chuckles?"

Charisse snorted. "Blend in? Scarlett's his mom. She would be there. But how exactly do the three of us blend in with one little Chinese kid?"

Scarlett shrugged. "We've got that all figured out, don't we, Ambrose?"

Ambrose was trying to roll his eyeballs back into his scalp. "It's ridiculous."

He was not immediately forthcoming about what he thought was ridiculous. Of course, he was wearing a T-shirt with a snail riding on a turtle riding on a sloth, so he may not have been the best judge on the topic.

I had a bad feeling rising in the pit of my stomach. "I'm not sure you all understand that I don't have any more authority here than you do. I want to go on record as saying that I think we should let the police handle it. I know you all are biased, but most of them are really good at their jobs."

The ladies looked at me like I was one more comment away from being thrown out of the van. Even Ambrose seemed to be casting next-level shade.

Scarlett nodded at me with her eyes nearly squinted shut. "Uh-huh. If you're done covering your butt, can we come up with a plan?"

"Fine. But if you're going to do this, try to find out who saw Chuckles last. Before the party where he . . ." I glanced at Ambrose over my shoulder. "You know . . ."

Ambrose shook his limbs like he was being electrocuted. "Before he died until he was dead?"

"Yes, Ambrose. Thank you."

Bree pulled into the circular roundabout of a tan brick mansion with stone lions on each side of the front door. A valet offered to take her keys and park the van in the back, and a woman who introduced herself as Trevor's Guest Services Escort walked us through the house until we emerged into a rainforest. The air was heavy with mist, and you could hear tree frogs chirping over the sound of a waterfall. I couldn't tell if those things were really happening or if it was coming from an elaborate sound system.

A brunette in a dress made out of actual ferns greeted us next to the table of wrapped packages. "Welcome to the ninth anniversary of Trevor's extraction from the womb. I'm Heather, Trevor's birthing partner."

Charisse and Bree passed a look between them that I interpreted as *What planet is this?*

Scarlett handed Heather a wrapped package. "We brought Trevor a VR headset. Ambrose is very excited to be invited. Aren't you, Ambrose?"

Ambrose gave Heather a practiced fake smile. "Thank you for inviting me, Mrs. Sevenson."

Heather glanced over at the three of us who were obviously not Ambrose's mothers. "And who have you brought with you, Ambrose?"

Scarlett jabbed Bree who was open-mouth gawking at a six-foot-tall statue of a naked man reading a book. Bree's mouth snapped shut.

Ambrose replied in a singsongy voice. "These are my aunties. They are very nice. Thank you for including them."

Heather blinked and gave me a deer-in-the-headlights look. "Your aunties?"

Scarlett grinned much like a shark would. It was more of a challenge. Heather seemed to shrink a couple inches in size.

I threw her a compliment to break the tension before she threw us out. "I like the twigs in your hair."

Heather touched her twigs with a demure grin. "Thank you. I was going for a Mother Earth thing." She swung her arm out and took a step back. "Well, please enjoy the party. All the food is organic and allergy-free. Trevor is in the bouncy castle at the back of the conservatory just before the French doors to the backyard."

Charisse gasped. "Are you telling me we aren't outside right now?"

Heather chuckled. "Heavens, no. Trevor is allergic to grass."

"We'll find it." Scarlett linked her arm with Charisse and practically dragged the woman through the enormous greenhouse.

Orchids draped from a vine twined around a live tree next to a plumeria-patterned chaise. The air was scented with coconut and pineapple. It should have been relaxing but it just made me want a piña colada.

Bree turned her head side to side, trying to take it all in. "Have you ever seen a house like this?"

I had in fact. Lots of times. The only apartment I'd ever seen the inside of during the first ten years of my life was on *Friends*. If Heather's little mansion had a petting zoo I might have been here for a sleepover once.

The party theme appeared to be dirt and leaves. We passed a long buffet table covered in all sorts of raw vegetables. Recycled paper cups full of brown stuff were lined up like soldiers.

Scarlett handed Ambrose a twenty and a cup of dirt. "Go find Trevor and thank him for inviting you."

"Can I be done talking to him after that?"

"Yep."

Ambrose ran to the bouncy house to fulfill his commitment, and we joined the other moms in the meditation room slash cocktail station.

There were a few new faces, but the gang from Chuckles's farewell performance were all here. Janice was at the wet bar. She appeared less drunk this time, but the party was just getting started. Tina was sitting on a chaise frowning at a plate full of celery. The demon in pigtails was here and her Pilates mom was giving her a thorough scolding about biting. Pigtails bit her on the finger.

We decided to split up. None of us wanted to be close to the bar but that decision was made for us the minute Janice called me over.

"Layla? Is that you? I almost didn't recognize you without the red leather and the giant earrings."

"Huh. I would have thought the electric guitar would be at the top of your list."

"Are you playing for Heather's party too?"

Scarlett snickered behind my back. "Looks like you're up. Be strong. If you need an extraction, just say the code word—*spleen-wort.*"

I muttered back, "Yeah, I'll try to work that into the conversation."

She patted me on the shoulder and headed for Tina.

Charisse looked around the room. "I'm gonna circulate and see what I can overhear. Bree, you coming with?"

The blonde nodded, mesmerized by the fountain of three frolicking angels in the middle of the room.

I made my way over to the bar where Janice was picking through a bowl of wood chips. "Today I'm just a guest. How have you been doing since Trilbee's birthday?"

Janice's smile slid into her highball glass. "Don't even talk to me about that nightmare. The police have been all over my house trying to find something that makes me look guilty. I told them I was with the other moms the entire party. I was never alone with the clown."

I told myself to be cool and let the girls do their thing—it was just nice being included for a change. Then cop Layla showed up and told me—I got this. "Guilty for what? I thought it was just a heart attack?" It's always better to make a perp have to over-explain things you already know. It gives them the chance to slip up and say something incriminating.

"Leave it to Chuck McCracken to make me look as bad in death as he did in life. The disgusting little idiot had to get murdered at my house."

"Murdered how? I saw him drop on stage while juggling."

Janice patted a barstool next to her, closer to the bottle of tequila. "Some kind of poison. They won't tell me which, but they've emptied my medicine cabinet, and they keep asking if my husband or I smoke."

I sidled closer to the bar. "Do you?"

She shook her head. "I've never smoked. Disgusting things. My husband quit a few months ago when I told him it was either the cigars or a divorce lawyer."

I tried not to stare at the bottle of Jose Cuervo. "Sounds reasonable. How did he break the habit?"

"Pure willpower." She finished her drink and poured herself another shot of tequila. "We both swear by it."

"Obviously. I heard they suspect the ex-wife."

"I'm not surprised. Chuckles the Clown was a real pig. I don't know what some of these women see in him."

"You say that like it's women plural."

"They all talk about how great this new business of his is. I hear it in whispers at yoga and around the tennis club."

"Really? The concierge life coach massage business is popular?"

She leaned into me. "Apparently, he has magic fingers, and his advice is spot on. These idiots couldn't wait for their next session. Kelly Richardson had worked herself up to a four massage per week habit just to hear Chuck tell her that her hair is pretty."

"The football player's wife? Was getting four massages a week?"

Janice's eyes widened. "Life coaching. That's how it works. You tell Chuck your problems, he oils you up and works on your hamstrings while he tells you what you need to do about them. So I've heard."

"And he was good at that?"

"So good that Kelly trapped him in the coat room at Thomas Deckendorff's party to beg for a last-minute session. Phyllis Veela caught her pleading with Chuck not to tell her husband about the money. And Phyllis is a real gossip, so we all heard about it."

"How much money are we talking about?"

Janice looked around to be sure no one was eavesdropping. "Those sessions cost five hundred dollars for two and a half hours. Kelly tried to tell everyone she was attacked, but Chuck said she lured him in there with a slice of birthday cake. Don't tell anyone you heard this from me, but Kelly has some pretty low self-esteem issues since her husband started touring with the team. She was just begging to be snapped up by the first life coach to come along. Chuck could be a smooth talker and get a woman to tell him intimate details about herself on that massage table—from what I hear. Kelly must have been so embarrassed about something she said that she almost didn't come to Trilbee's party when she found out Chuck would be there."

"Kelly Richardson was at your party?"

Janice shrugged. "Yeah. She's here today too."

"Really. Which one is she?"

She downed her tequila. "Calanthia's mom. Cute little blonde with pigtails. She's talking to that Asian lady now."

I craned my neck to see around the angel fountain and spotted Scarlett in rapt conversation with Pilates mom.

Janice added another shot of tequila to her glass. "Bah. I regret paying that lowlife in advance. He didn't even finish the show."

I watched a drip of tequila run slowly down the square bottle from the rim to the label.

The kids cheered from the other room, and someone started playing an acoustic guitar in the rainforest.

Janice hopped off the stool. "That'll be the entertainment. I want to check it out to see if Trilbee likes him so I can book him for next year. He hated the ones at his party. Oh sorry."

Freakin' Trilbee. I didn't like him either. I followed Janice to the jungle room, away from the booze, where a man wearing a dog costume was performing a song about boogers. An easel set up next to him advertised that he was *Mack and Fleas—Woofertainer Extraordinaire.* The kids were jumping around him yelling like maniacs.

The day this is me, I'm quitting music for good.

Heather sidled up to me nibbling a piece of her tree bark. "He's really good. I'm glad he was available."

"Wasn't he your first choice?"

"I originally booked the clown from Janice's party, but he died so Mack and Fleas was a last-minute substitution."

"I didn't see you at Trilbee's party. Were you there?"

"No. Trevor is allergic to sixteen different things, so we have to be very selective." She held out a wood chip. "Dehydrated carrot?"

"Maybe later."

She nodded and popped it in her mouth.

"How did you come across Chuckles the Clown?"

"I met him a few weeks ago at my husband's company picnic. He was hired to entertain the kids so the adults could relax. He was so sweet. He gave me the funniest business card."

"Why do you say that?"

"It was his job title. I've never heard of a life coach masseuse before."

"Do you still have it?"

She nodded. "In my Fendi bag."

"I don't suppose I could see it could I?"

She disappeared and Scarlett passed me saying, "Kelly Richardson just asked me how much money would buy my silence."

"Wow!"

Scarlett moved into the other room to hit up another mom for gossip.

Heather returned with the same hot pink business card Chuck had shown me in Janice's pool house.

"He told me not to call the number on his website since he had just gotten a new manager, and to use this one instead."

"Did he say why he was changing managers?"

Bree appeared at my side and nudged me.

Heather shook her head. "Uh-uh."

Bree looked at the card and groaned. "Eww. Is that guy giving a massage in the clown suit?"

Heather looked at the card and laughed. "I thought it was a joke."

I snapped a picture of the card with my cell phone. "Did you ever call that number?"

"Yeah. The lady said Chuckles was booked Friday night through Sunday, but he was free today. That's why we're having Trevor's party a week after his actual birthday. Then he died and I had to call Mack and Fleas at the last minute."

Heather was watching the kids' performer and Bree nudged me again. I looked at her and she nodded toward the gift table across the room.

Kelly was in a heated argument with Tina from AA. She had one hand on her hip and with the other she was shaking her bandaged finger in Tina's face. *Now I see the resemblance to Pigtails.*

Charisse sat demurely on a chair behind them taking in every word. She caught my eye and gave me a wink.

Chapter 31

*W*HAT AM *I* DOING?

I turned the Aston Martin into the strip mall. I told them I'm a loner. I said I wouldn't get involved, and yet, here I was, on my way to a post–birthday party debriefing. *What is happening to my life?*

We'd dropped Ambrose at home. Scarlett told him he could order a pizza and have one hour of Fortnite, and he was out of the van and into the house before I had my seatbelt off. Then she said she had a surprise for the rest of us, but we needed to come here to get it. I was having serious concerns about my current state of rationale as I parked the Aston Martin at the far end of the lot.

The coffee shop air was heavy with the smell of burnt toast. The loud shhhkkkweeee of the milk frother just about drowned out Miley Cyrus entirely.

The ladies were hovering over some guy in a beanie cap and Rage Against the Machine hoodie. He was camped out on the sofa with his laptop, and judging from the dishes on the table in front of him, he'd been there all day. I started looking for an empty table, but Scarlett sat right next to the guy and Bree took the chair to his left.

Charisse narrowed her eyes at the guy working and made a face to Scarlett.

Scarlett put her feet up on the surfboard coffee table. "Hey.

How you doing? You working hard? I bet you come here a lot. I'm just gonna hang with my girls and talk some girl talk, okay? You don't mind, do ya?"

Bree called over to Charisse. "Make mine a large since we'll be here talking for hours. I brought some polish to do our nails."

Scarlett took another run at him. "What are you working on? You a writer? I hear a lot of writers work in coffee shops. Do you have any sisters? I bet they like girl talk. Do they paint their nails? Do you mind the smell? Some guys don't like it."

Bree clapped her hands. "I think we should give each other makeovers. I'm thinking about getting one of those unicorn balayage treatments. How do you think I would look with pink, purple, and blue in my hair?"

The young man closed his laptop and looked around. The room was pretty full.

Scarlett looked at me and eyed the chair opposite from Bree then nodded toward the young man.

I took the chair and called over to Bree. "I saw the cutest guy today and he smiled at me. He was so hot. I hope he asks me out. I want to get married. My clock is ticking, and I really want to have a baby soon. Maybe I'll just get a donor. Hey, man, what's your DNA like?"

The kid sighed, inched off the sofa, grabbed his to-go cup, and hustled to the exit.

Scarlett beamed at me. "Ooh. Nice job. You hit like three stereotypes all at once."

Something felt weird inside my chest. It was warm and full. Not entirely unlike heartburn, but not as unpleasant. I shoved it aside. "I take it you're pretty protective of your usual spot."

She snickered. "He was here long enough."

Bree twirled her blond hair around her finger. "So, what's the big surprise?"

Scarlett grinned. "Fingers crossed, you'll see in a few minutes."

Charisse returned with a receipt and placed it on the table. "Nice job, ladies. Drinks are coming out."

I handed Charisse some ones. "So, what were Tina and Kelly Richardson arguing about?"

Charisse joined Scarlett on the sofa. "Girl, you won't believe it. Kelly said Chuckles the Clown forced himself on her and Tina was defending Chuck, saying her ex-husband was a gentleman and would never do anything without a woman's consent."

Scarlett gasped. "She made such a big stink at AA yesterday that she never wanted to hear his name again."

One of the baristas brought over our drinks and Scarlett handed them a ten-dollar bill. I took my fudge whipp with more than a little excitement. *What is happening to me? Do I have a brain tumor?* "What did Kelly say to that?"

Charisse grinned. "She snapped back at Tina to keep her voice down, and said, 'You know how he is. He said I make the best lasagna he's ever had. Before I knew what I was doing, I gave him ten thousand dollars for a mobile spa studio. I need that money back. If my husband finds out, he'll freak. I can't get divorced again.'"

Bree leaned so far forward in her chair that she almost fell out of it. "Wait. She gave him ten thousand dollars for a massage?"

Charisse shook her head. "Not just for one massage. Apparently, Kelly Richardson had invested in Chuck's life coaching masseur business and was having second thoughts."

"Wow."

"And she is so terrified that her husband will leave her that she claimed Chuck attacked her to blackmail Chuck into giving the money back."

Bree frowned. "That's kinda low."

Charisse held up a finger and waved it in front of her face. "That isn't all. You want to know where Kelly got the money to invest?"

"Where?" I asked.

Charisse grinned. "Her dog grooming business."

I choked on my whipp. "Another ex-wife. Haven't these ladies ever heard of moving on?" I Googled Kelly's pro football player husband and showed the others. "He could definitely beat

Chuckles to a pulp if he wanted to." *When did my data get turned back on? Dad.*

Scarlett held up her cell phone showing a photo of Kelly with her husband at a charity event. "I wouldn't want to be divorced from him either. Look at those abs."

Bree shook her head. "I don't get it. What could he possibly be doing to these women in those sessions that they are lining up to hire him to massage them?"

Charisse placed her purple ube drink on the surfboard. "So, I've been thinking about that, and I bet it's not what he's doing, but what he's been saying to them."

I shoved my phone back in my pocket. "What do you mean?"

"Well, you know how a musician can be butt ugly, but all the ladies still fall all over him?"

I had the urge to say, "Not always," but I held my tongue.

Scarlett nodded. "Of course."

"It's because of the songs. They touch your heart with their words of love and stories about how they've had their heart broken and they're looking for the one who can make them whole. Women eat that crap up. Really, he's probably just some creep who comes home late and farts in front of you, leaves his dirty underwear on the floor, and forgets your birthday just like all the others."

Scarlett chuckled. "Yeah, they don't write songs about that."

Charisse snapped her fingers and pointed at Scarlett. "Exactly. Without the music, no woman would look at those guys twice."

I hardly thought that was fair, but memories of my mom and dad arguing about all the above came flooding back to me. They only got along when he was on tour. And Dad was not known for being faithful.

Bree sighed and pulled strands of her hair to the side for inspection. "I've had a lot of therapy. None of it ever involved being rubbed down with scented oil. That's weird, right?"

The rest of us laughed.

Charisse blew out a breath. "Oh honey. Definitely weird."

Scarlett included, "Oh a hundred percent weird."

I set my cup on the surfboard. "What I don't get is, why they would trust that guy to be a life coach. From what I can tell, he was a heavy drinker with a gambling problem and four failed relationships. That's not who you go to for advice."

Charisse chuckled. "Women want to be heard and validated. I bet that's what old Chuckles was doing. I bet he was saying all the right things that these women weren't hearing at home."

Scarlett sipped her latte. "Women can be talked into just about anything if given enough honey. It's later that we come to our senses and regret it."

Charisse shook her head. "And it's a shame too. Because we really need to stand up for ourselves better." She grew quiet for a minute before continuing. "Michael moved out yesterday. I said he could have everything he wanted. Figured he was owed that much for all the years I put him through my addiction. What I didn't expect was for him to take my grandmother's sapphire ring."

Scarlett reached over and touched Charisse on the shoulder. "Oh no. I'm so sorry."

Bree moaned in sympathy. "That's so vindictive."

I wasn't really good at comforting people. My mind always went to the practical side. "Can you get it back?"

She shrugged. "He's probably hocked it by now."

"Well, I can get you information on the pawn shops in our area and you can make some calls. I still have a lot of contacts from my time on the force."

Scarlett added, "You can also get your lawyer to send a letter demanding he return it."

Charisse took a deep breath and let out a sigh. "Those are both good ideas. I prayed that this divorce could remain amicable, but Michael seems to have other plans. I'm just thankful I have my Lord and Savior, Jesus Christ. My sobriety. And my girls. What else do I need?"

We were all quiet for a moment, then what I was really thinking slipped out of my mouth. "I would still want the ring."

Scarlett and Bree immediately agreed with me.

"A hundred percent."

"Don't let him get away with that."

Charisse laughed. "You're absolutely right. That sucker is gonna give me my grandmother's ring back."

Bree grinned. "Too bad Chuck isn't here. He could give you a massage and tell you what to do."

Scarlett nodded very seriously. "How's your lasagna?"

That made us laugh even harder and we failed to notice the woman who was standing over us. "I'm sorry to interrupt. But did you still want to talk to me?"

I wiped my eyes and found myself looking into the face of one of the exes of Mr. Chuckles the Clown.

Scarlett whispered, "Surprise."

Chapter 32

*T*INA FIDGETED WITH THE HEM OF HER SWEATER. "I PROMISED MY-self that I'd never let him break my heart again. Then I walked right back into it and put my marriage at risk."

Scarlett brought a plate of pound cake to the table and set it in the center. Then she handed Tina a coconut water. "How long had you and Chuck been divorced?"

Tina gave her a wan smile. "Three years, six months, thirteen days."

I took a napkin and a piece of cake. I was starving even though I'd had three cookies at AA. There was a good chance I was eating my feelings. "And how long have you been married to your husband now?"

Tina sighed. "Just under two years."

Charisse nodded. "Mm. So, what happened?"

"Chuck came to me and said he was going to be a life coach. People aren't hiring birthday clowns as much as they used to. Too many slasher movies feature evil clowns and people are sud-denly freaked out by them."

Scarlett gave me a skeptical look. "I don't think it's all that sudden."

Tina shook up her coconut water. "He wanted money for a massage table, and ten thousand dollars for a radio spot. He promised me he was good for it because I was still the beneficiary on his life insurance from when we were married. To sweeten the deal, he offered me a preview of services. A complimentary coaching massage. He was offering it to all the moms on the birthday party circuit to help drum up clientele."

Bree bit the end of her hair. "Like—he gives you a massage while he tells you how to fix your life and then he makes you a balloon animal?"

Tina frowned. "Look, I didn't come to be judged. I only came here because she convinced me to get this off my chest so I could move forward."

Bree smoothed her hair back. "Sorry."

Tina huffed. "We talked about all the things I'm going through. Being a stepmom, my issues with my body, my husband's infidelity. I left my career when we got married because I thought we'd have children. But Paul doesn't want more children and that makes me feel like a glorified nanny. Then Chuck set up this old massage table, lit a few candles, and started a weird soundtrack of whales and gongs."

Scarlett nodded. "Oh yeah. I know the one."

"Then he left the room while I disrobed. When he came back and started the coaching massage . . ."

Charisse slid narrowed eyes to mine. "Which isn't a thing."

"He said I needed to take it easy on myself. I was capable of great things. He said I was a beautiful woman with a lot to offer and that I deserved more in life. That I had the skin of a twenty-year-old. Opportunities were knocking, and I should trust myself more and not be afraid to answer them."

My thoughts slipped out of my mouth again. I was really not doing a good job of minding my own business. "Opportunities like investing in a start-up concierge life coach masseur?"

Tina twisted the hem of her cape and nodded. "Apparently. I thought he meant we should get back together. That's why I kissed him."

Bree's head flew back like she'd been slapped.

Scarlett held out both her hands. "But why? His advice wasn't that good. You could get that from any daytime talk show or self-help book."

Tina brushed a tear off her cheek with the back of her hand. "I don't know what came over me, but it's the new low point of my life. Chuck was drawn to broken women. He collected them like baseball cards. He knew just what to say to a lonely woman to make her feel good about herself. It's really easy to get addicted to that feeling."

We passed a dubious look to one another around the circle.

Tina twisted the cap off her water. "I threw myself at him and he turned me down. Do you know how pathetic that makes me? He was a nightmare to be married to. All my towels were ruined by greasepaint. What was I thinking? The horror of what I'd done sent me to a dark place. I put my marriage and my recovery in jeopardy. Why did I let Chuck talk me into investing with him?"

Scarlett muttered. "That must have been some massage."

I checked the calendar on my phone. "Just out of curiosity, when did this bender start, exactly?"

"At my stepson's birthday party. I put out cocktails for the other moms. Cocktails at these birthday parties are expected if you don't want to be ostracized. Then I told myself I'd have just one—to help me through the pain. Then another—just to get me through the party. Then I couldn't stop drinking. I don't even remember parts of last week. Falling into Janice's Jacuzzi in front of everyone and having a stranger take my keys and put me in an Uber was a wake-up call."

Her face was expressionless. I don't think she realized I was the stranger. "Why did you think we were trying to blackmail you earlier?"

"Someone was outside my house taking pictures when I was with Chuck. I saw the flash."

Scarlett's eyebrow shot to attention. "But it was just a massage. Right? Nothing weird?"

Tina's eyes went wide. "No! Just a normal, mediocre quality

massage on a rickety old massage table held together with duct tape. I assumed they were going to Photoshop them to make it look like more and send them to my husband, but nothing's happened yet. Why else would someone be taking pictures of us?"

"Did anyone send incriminating photos to Kelly?" I asked.

She sighed. "No. But she's on the lookout."

We stayed in the coffee shop for a while after Tina left. It's funny how dealing with your own addiction makes you far more sympathetic to other people's addiction, and yet you can still be overly critical about their taste in music or that they made a pass at their chubby, balding ex-husband. "Have you all noticed that Chuck had at least three investors who gave him ten thousand dollars each?"

The girls gave me nods of agreement.

"Paula, Kelly, and Tina—all invested in the business for one thing or another, but did he actually spend the money on what he said it was for? He definitely didn't get the van painted. I saw that myself. And that massage table Tina described sounds like it was bought on Craigslist. Definitely not the mobile spa studio Kelly invested in."

Bree tapped her phone awake, her thumbs flying across the screen. "I've done a few different searches for Chuck Mc-Cracken, Chuckles, and all the words *concierge life coach massage*, and I'm not pulling up any advertising on the radio or social media."

Scarlett had been quietly sipping her latte for a few minutes. "You know, when this started, I just wanted to understand what kind of freaky hold that guy had on Miranda. But now I want to know what exactly he was up to."

Charisse moved over to the couch and laid her head back. "I feel sorry for the women. How low does your self-esteem have to be to hire that guy to be your life coach? I think he knew what he was doing. Manipulating these women with flattery for money. There's no such thing as a life coach masseur."

Bree twirled her hair around her finger. "And someone totally murdered him, you know. I mean, do they think one of those women did it?"

The ladies all looked at me. I had a mouth full of pound cake. "Wha?"

Bree centered her focus on me like I was being interrogated in the perp room. "Layla. What have you heard about the investigation?"

I swallowed. "No one's gonna tell me anything. I'm not just a former cop, I'm a disgraced former cop."

Scarlett rolled her eyes. "Don't you at least have one friend in the police who can give you intel?"

"My friends all died when I was getting drunk instead of having their backs."

She blew me off as only someone over your drama can do. "Uh-huh. But why do they think Chuck was murdered?"

"Because he was poisoned."

Charisse sat up taller. "Now we're getting somewhere. What was the poison?"

"Why? You know someone growing hemlock in their backyard?"

Charisse snapped her fingers. "It was hemlock?"

"No. It wasn't."

She looked disappointed. "Alright. Don't mess with me like that."

Bree set her cell phone on the table. "I mean he totally sounds like a skeevy pig, but he didn't deserve to be killed."

My cell phone buzzed in my pocket, and I fished it out. It was a text from Paula. "Ohsweet."

Scarlett tried to read the screen. "What is it?"

"Paula has a gig for me tomorrow night. A solo act. There's a launch party for a new tech company. They requested me to play background music."

Scarlett gave me some side-eye. "Who requests background electric guitar?"

I held up my phone. "I dunno. Everybody's trying to be edgy these days. Besides, I can't afford to turn anything down. I'm competing with kids half my age who charge pennies to perform because they still live at home. I've got to take the gigs that come my way."

My phone buzzed again with the address.

Charisse didn't look any more convinced than Scarlett. "I don't know, Layla. A launch event on a Sunday night? What kind of business is this?"

I shrugged. "The kind that's paying me two hundred dollars for three hours of instrumental Led Zeppelin. Would you relax? I know this neighborhood."

Bree squeeged her nose up again. "Maybe we should go with you. Just in case."

"I'll be fine. Really."

Another text buzzed through except this one was from Dad.

You need to come home.

Hmm. That's weird. Who taught Dad to text?

Bree grinned. "Don't tell us. This one says the client is the Yakuza or something."

"No, it's my dad."

Another text came in.

It's an emergency.

"I have to go."

Scarlett gave me a concerned look. "Is everything okay?"

"Yeah. I'm sure it's fine. He probably just locked himself in the bathroom or something."

Everything was not fine. I could see the flashing lights from the highway. I pulled into the Lake Pinecrest Mobile Home Park. Two cop cars and a yellow Dodge Charger were sitting in the road in front of my trailer.

I slow rolled past them and caught eyes with Dayton Castinetto. Hands on his hips, his white shirtsleeves rolled up to the elbows, showing off his muscled forearms, his double shoulder holster slung across his back. *This can't be good.*

I had just started the turn into the carport when I spotted the reason for the police presence. Someone had defaced the side of my trailer with bright red spray paint.

MURDERER.

Chapter 33

*D*AD WAS SITTING IN THE SHADOWS OF THE LITTLE SCREENED PORCH with Ringo practically in his lap. Nick sat in the plastic chair next to them.

Ringo looked at me then looked at Dad. He looked back at me and wagged his tail as if to say he needs me more right now.

I read the side of my trailer again and blew out my breath. Anger was rising up from my belly. An irrational amount of anger. The only thing that kept it from boiling over was confusion. *What is this nonsense about?*

Castinetto had come to stand behind me. I could see his smirking face in my mind—the hotshot of the department. All business and steel. Every perp was guilty until their lawyer got them off on a technicality.

"You alright?"

I waved my hand at the destruction of my low-quality private property. "I've been better."

"You have any idea who might have done this?"

"I can't even narrow it down to the top ten. What are you doing here? This isn't your jurisdiction or your department."

"Your neighbor called in the vandalism, and I recognized the address as yours on the dispatch call."

So unofficially then.

The screen door flapped on its hinges and Ringo ran to me. Castinetto reached for his sidearm.

"Don't you dare think about hurting this puppy. He's a good boy, aren't you?"

Ringo licked my face.

Castinetto sighed. "I wasn't going to shoot the dog, Virtue."

"Good. Because I'm pretty sure he can't work the nozzle on the spray paint can."

One of the beat cops strutted over to Castinetto, the highest-ranking officer on site. "No one saw anything, and none of the homes have a Ring camera or security system."

I snickered. "Why would they? This is not the neighborhood where people come to rob you. The only thing here worth stealing is my father's car, and I had that with me."

Castinetto glanced at my mustang covered in pink slips and a couple new red ones. "I don't know. That muscle car's a classic. If the owner took better care of it, it could be worth stealing."

He knew that car was mine. "The thief had better have a tow truck."

The officer handed me a carbon of the report Dad had given and said they'd keep me updated if they found anything, but this seemed like an isolated incident. Code for *You'll never hear from us again.*

The black-and-whites left and Castinetto gave me a cop stare down.

"Did you lie to me about knowing Chuck McCracken?"

"No!"

He nodded toward my trailer. "Someone thinks you killed him."

"Uh . . . I think it's more likely a cop with an axe to grind is leaving me a message about Stratton Park."

Dayton's eyebrow shot up. He took off his mirrored glasses. "You think one of ours did this? That's where your mind goes?" He sucked his teeth and looked away from me. "That's disgusting, Virtue. And it shows how little respect you have for the officers you worked with. That was always your problem."

Ringo leaned hard into my leg and snooted my hand.

I chuckled to cover the fact that I was counting to ten like my former therapist had taught me to do before I refused to go back. "No . . . Castinetto. I think a cop did this because someone left me Melissa's obituary under a six-pack of beer yesterday morning and the neighbors don't know who I am. Someone's obviously been spreading it around the precinct where I live. How did *you* know to find me here, anyway?"

His face was a wall of granite. "From your statement. At the crime scene."

Oh right.

We stared at each other for a beat.

Castinetto smirked. "What'd you do with the beer?"

"Shotgunned it."

His eyes turned to flint. "I heard you've been getting chummy with the victim's ex-wives club."

"Heard from who?"

"Miranda McCracken said you were asking questions of all the ladies."

I snorted. *Miranda McCracken? I'd never heard her last name before. That's hilarious.* "She lied to you."

"You aren't talking to the ex-wives of the victim?"

"No. Well, I've *talked* to them—but not in any official capacity . . ."

He cut me off. "Well, stay out of it. You're not a cop anymore."

Ringo got worried and moved closer to me.

I raised my hands to my chest. "Okay, back off. I am out of it."

He nodded. "Good." Then after a long pause he said, "I don't suppose any of the ex-wives told you about the victim's recent windfall of cash at the track?"

"How much of a windfall?"

"Fifty grand."

"Fifty grand! When did that happen?"

"Three months ago. Apparently, Chuck McCracken didn't owe Sal Polaski a dime. Sal said that one payout made them square. So that guy you saw threatening him wasn't one of Sal's guys. I'm only telling you this because I think you're getting too chummy with the ex-wives and it's looking more and more like one of them is our killer."

"That's hardly a surprise, Castinetto. You think Sal Polaski was in the habit of sending messages to the people who owe him— *Pay up or I'll nicotine you to death?*"

Dayton's eyes slid to half-mast. "Very funny."

"Did you look into his side hustle?"

"What side hustle? Where are you getting this?"

"He'd recently started a concierge life coach massage business."

Castinetto looked at me like I'd sprouted antlers.

"It's true." I held up my cell phone and flashed him the photo. "He had fancy pink business cards made. Maybe someone took offense."

"Everyone should have taken offense. But this is the first I'm hearing about it. We've narrowed the incident window to eighteen hours to account for how long those nicotine patches would take to oxidize."

"Have you tracked his movements? Where was he the day before he died?"

"Clowning at the Herndon Fall Festival until six. No one knows where he was after that, or the morning of the birthday party. His manager claims he had been hiding his schedule from her."

"Did you check his Facebook page? He supposedly put all his parties on there."

Castinetto pulled out his cell phone and started tapping. He glanced at me. "I only have Facebook for work. You wouldn't believe how often I find a perp just by checking social media."

"I didn't say anything. If you want to cyber-spy on your high school girlfriend, it's none of my business."

"I'm not—" He cut himself off. "You have a lot of information for someone who is supposed to be staying out of it."

I left that comment alone.

He stared at his phone screen and shook his head. "Dead end. He only has the birthday party on Sunday listed. Happy Birthday, Trilbee. And he performed at a party for a kid named Baron a week earlier. He's tagged their mothers in the posts.

Geez, he might as well have posted the address with the words *Come get me.*"

"That's weird. Heather said he was booked the night before Janice's and couldn't do her kid's party, so they had to do it a week late."

"Who is Heather?"

"One of the moms on the birthday circuit. Her kid had a party today."

"What were you doing there? Were you playing?"

"No. I was just . . . there. So was Janice Kestle, and Tina Crumm, and Kelly Richardson."

Castinetto's eyes narrowed into steely knives. "Are you kidding me? That's three of our suspects. That's not a coincidence, Virtue. And it's a bad idea for an ex-cop with your reputation to hang around with potential murderers."

"Ah, I had every right. I was invited." *Sort of.*

A deep crimson climbed up Castinetto's neck. "Stay away from my investigation, or the next time I come around you'll need to call your lawyer."

He strutted off to his car, making his big exit. We both knew he was making an empty threat. He could no more tell me where I could go than I could control Dad's movements. I silently hoped he'd run out of gas while his car idled, but no such luck.

The minute he pulled away, every neighbor on my street came out of their trailer and tried to look busy. Donna was watering her plants, Benny was raking leaves, Marguerite was hanging a set of dry sheets on her clothesline as slowly as possible.

"You okay, Keanu?"

Nick nudged Dad, and he answered from the screened porch. "Yeah, doll. I'm fine."

I ran my hands over Ringo's ears. "Let's go check on Dad, buddy."

Ringo started for the screened porch before I did. This dog was smart. Nick stood when I entered. "Are you okay?"

I shrugged. "Yeah. This isn't the first threat I've received, and it won't be the last."

Nick lowered his voice. "But are you okay?"

I smiled. "Yes. I'm not looking forward to cleaning that paint off anytime soon, but I can't afford another infraction with the Lake Pinecrest Private Militia for leaving it there either."

"Do you have a hose?"

I chuckled. "Yes, next to my swimming pool. No! I don't have a hose. I lived in a city condo before I moved here."

Nick rolled his eyes. "I'll go get mine."

He left the trailer and Dad sighed. "I don't like this, baby girl. I don't like people saying things like that about you."

He looked tired. Dark circles had bloomed under his eyes and the lines on his face had settled a little deeper than before. I pulled up a chair across from him and lied through my teeth. "Dad, I'm fine. I'll get through this. Are you feeling okay?"

Dad chuckled. "Yeah."

Ringo whimpered and moved over to Dad's side. He laid his chin in Dad's lap.

"What'd you do today while I was at a meeting?"

Dad's eyes rolled around. "I dunno."

"Like you don't want to talk about it, or you don't remember?"

He shrugged. "One of those."

I pulled out my cell phone and Googled Don Virtue. Sometimes the Internet knew things long before Dad was willing to confess them. I found three ridiculous stories.

One said Dad was in rehab in upstate New York. That was clearly not true; I was looking right at him.

Another said he was living in Greece with a new lover whose name is undisclosed but she's in the new Marvel movie. He wishes.

The third story was concerning. It said Don Virtue collapsed on stage in Stockholm and had to cancel the European portion of the world tour with Society's Castoffs.

He pursed his lips and tried to peer over the edge of my phone. "What are you looking at, baby girl?"

"Nothing."

Ringo barked.

Dad pointed his thumb at the Lab. "Ringo says it's something."

"No one likes a tattletale, Ringo."

Ringo grumbled.

The story went on to say Don Virtue's health had been reportedly in decline lately, and there was concern that he would have to cancel the rest of the world tour.

Dad's face brightened. "Hey, should we go out for lobster tonight?"

I was only half listening to him. I was scanning the article for information on this mystery sickness. "I can't tonight. I have a thing."

"What thing?"

"You wouldn't like it."

"Does it involve Jell-O? 'Cause that stuff gives me the creeps."

"No."

He blew out his cheeks. "Thank God. Nothing should move like that."

"Dad?"

"Yeah?"

"What happened in Stockholm?"

Dad looked away from me. "I don't know what you're talking about."

"Are you alright?"

He breathed out a chuckle. "I'm always alright." Dad shrugged, then he started butchering a Fleetwood Mac song. "Don't stop worrying about your tomorrow. Don't stop. That day'll soon be here."

"Uh-huh."

Ringo barked again and started to wag his tail.

He looked past me and his eyes narrowed. "Baby girl, did you know the side of your trailer says *Murderer*?"

I blinked at him. "I did know that, yeah."

"And your husband is spraying it with a hose."

I didn't even glance behind me. "That's the neighbor, Dad."

"Oh." He nodded to something behind me. "Then who's that old guy?"

"What old guy?" I looked over my shoulder. Nick was holding the hose to the side while Clifford Bagstrodt sprayed Windex on the paint, and Agnes Harcourt scrubbed at it with a tile brush. Myrtle Jean was coming down the street with a sponge mop lifted over her head like a parade grand marshal. "What in the world?"

Ringo was standing sentry at the door, excited that he had company.

Benny and Nick were in deep discussion. Benny cupped his hands around his mouth and yelled, "Layla, do you have any Goo Gone?"

I called back, "Any what?"

He waved me off. "You know what? I think I have some in the shed."

Marguerite came around the side of my screened porch with Steppenwolf strutting behind her. "I have a putty knife if we need to scrape it off, but I am not responsible for what gonna happen after that."

All of my neighbors were in the yard trying to clean the paint off my house. Even Donna was out there helping Foster lay a tarp over the James Bond car to keep the debris off. Pippi cheered them on from her wagon where she was waving a plastic scrub brush in her mouth.

Dad eased up next to me and watched the action. "Oh good, your friends are here to help."

"I don't have any friends, Dad."

Dad snickered. "Somebody needs to tell them that."

Chapter 34

*I*T WAS A STRANGE AFTERNOON. WE GOT RID OF THE RED SPRAY PAINT, but you could still see the shadow of the word *murderer* in the right light. On the plus side, my brown trailer turned out to be closer to beige after being Windexed and power washed.

Donna wouldn't look at me so much as talk to me, but I did see her work up the nerve to corner Dad when the work was done.

I had no idea how that went because I had to shower and change for open mic night. The theme at Dooley's was Classic Rock so I hoped the crowd would be a little more receptive to me than they were the last time I played. Plus, it was Saturday so the place should be hopping. I needed to land some new gigs. The only work I had coming my way at this point was that launch party Paula had set up for tomorrow night, and the money from that wouldn't fund Dad's cookie habit.

Dad whistled when I emerged from the bedroom. "Now that outfit is rock and roll."

I'd dressed in tight black jeans, a faded gray T-shirt, black leather vest, and motorcycle boots. You don't grow up with a headbanger in the house and not know how to dress the part.

Dad stared at my hair. "Nice job on the back-comb. That's the Vavoom Freezing Spray, isn't it? And your eyeliner is righteous. Looking the part is half the battle. You've got a gig!"

"It's not really a gig, Dad. It's an open mic. Sometimes agents attend so . . ."

"Agents will be there?" Dad crossed his arms and nodded appreciatively. "Break a leg, baby girl. I can't wait to hear all about it."

I kissed him on the cheek. "Thanks, Dad. I'll be back soon."

Even though I arrived early, the signup sheet for acts was just about full. I'd underestimated the open mic competition. More groups wanted to play than time would allow so we were each limited to one five-minute slot. I only had one chance to make an impression tonight.

Should I go for something edgy like "Barracuda"? *Or a ballad to show my range? Maybe* "These Dreams" *by Heart.* I decided I'd better wait and see what everyone else played.

The pub was packed and there was a good crackle of energy in the room. I moved back to the bar with the other musicians and ordered a ginger ale.

I looked around. Most of these kids weren't even born back when classic rock was just called rock. I wasn't really either, but I grew up with it. I even thought I recognized some of their faces.

I'm pretty sure I busted a couple of those guys for possession. And isn't that Donny Boyle, the kid who called in the bomb threat at school to get out of a chemistry final a few years ago? Man, I don't belong here. We're not even from the same generation. I'm drowning in a sea of skinny jeans and ironic T-shirts. That guy looks like he came straight from mowing his lawn. How do these kids even know what classic rock is?

I touched my teased-up hair that looked like it was part of a rock and roll musician's costume from the party store. *I look like I'm trying too hard.*

A guy approached the bar and bought a round of shots for all the musicians. "Let's slay tonight!" The musicians cheered.

What does that even mean?

When the shots came my way, I had to turn them down, which brought me more than a little side-eye from the other groups.

The first act was introduced, and they played "Smells Like Teen Spirit."

The next kid played a solo version of "Smells Like Teen Spirit."

Then a girl played "Smells Like Teen Spirit" on her clarinet. That's when I seriously considered going home.

It was a rough two hours waiting for my slot. I changed my mind six different times about what I would play. Most of these kids had researched the top twenty classic rock songs before coming tonight and they'd cycled through them twice. And I couldn't exactly replicate something like "Bohemian Rhapsody" all by myself with just an electric guitar and a loop station. In the end I felt so defeated that I decided to forget the crowd and play something just for me.

I waited in the wings for my turn, and when I was introduced, I turned off my brain, kicked on my loop station, and started the opening chords of "I Hate Myself for Loving You."

I could see on their faces that they were impressed with my playing. Maybe I had underestimated their love for classic rock.

I was barely through the first verse, and they were clapping along. Wow, Joan Jett was really speaking to them.

I was singing my heart out. I knew it was going awesome because the crowd was really into it. A lot of these people must have been stood up before.

I hit the bridge, and they were pumping their fists in the air. They were on their feet now. This might be the best event I've ever played.

And I was playing exceptionally well.

I'd never heard myself play this well.

In fact, I'm not really able to play this well.

I got to the chorus and the crowd went wild.

Something's off.

There was a very complicated riff coming out of the guitar that I knew I wasn't making. I turned to look over my shoulder just as someone screamed, "It's Don Virtue from Society's Castoffs! I can't believe it!"

I could not believe it either.

Dad was six feet behind me playing his pearl Fender. He gave me a huge grin and a nod. This did explain the freestyle harmony that was way out of my league coming through the speakers. I sounded like a first-year student next to Dad, who had come in matching leathers.

It was father/daughter day at the Roxy all over again. That was one of the worst days of my life.

But if there was one thing Dad had taught me in all his years in show business—no matter what happens, you fake it and play through.

So that's what I did. Every cell phone in the building was trained on Dad singing with me. We would be all over social media within minutes. Some of these people were probably broadcasting us live.

I took a step backward to showcase Dad's guitar solo. *It's all part of the act.*

Dad was clearly having the time of his life. Always the professional, he didn't care how small the crowd was as long as they were enthusiastic.

My anger was rising as people began streaming off the street into the bar. The bartender looked slightly terrified at the current state of chaos. People were now climbing on top of the tables to get a better view of the rock legend in action.

The song ended and Dad yelled, "My daughter, Layla Virtue. Isn't she great!"

The crowd roared because it was Don Virtue and he just spoke to them. Meanwhile, *Who is up there with him? Did he say that's his daughter? Didn't she have that nervous breakdown and move to Kathmandu?*

I gave a polite bow to applause, waved my hand out at Dad. He gave a bow to screams of adulation. I grabbed my amp and loop station and left him up there to play the encore that would not be denied.

I made a quick call to Ronnie Voa, an ex-cop I knew who now ran his own security company, and asked him to send some guys to Dooley's ASAP to rescue Dad. He would never get out of there until they'd snatched every ounce of life from him. Ronnie promised me he would see to it personally and I hung up and went to the car to wait.

There was no use trying to leave for home, the parking lot was four layers deep of cars illegally double-parked as people flooded in to see the man who wrote "Sins of a Lover," which had gone double platinum.

I wasn't jealous, mind you. Dad deserved every bit of adoration he got. He worked hard for his career. The entire band had. Dad may have been the front man, but Society's Castoffs was a team effort. That was something he'd forgotten for a while in their early days of fame and their original bassist split on them. He still regrets the way things went down.

He also had a way of forgetting that he and I were a team effort.

What I was right now was furious. Furious he didn't listen to me. Furious he could not let someone else call the shots once in a while. Furious he just didn't respect my wishes no matter how hard I begged.

And as soon as the police broke up the riot Dad had caused, and Ronnie got him out of there, I would give him a piece of my mind and let him know just how furious I was.

Chapter 35

"WHAT DID I DO THAT WAS SO WRONG?"

"Do you see where we are right now, Dad?"

One of Ronnie Voa's guys was in the yellow Lamborghini, two cars in front of us. Another was in a black Mercedes SUV two cars behind. We were playing the shell game with a police escort to throw followers off our scent so I could get us home without a rabid bunch of fans who would never leave my yard once word got out that Don Virtue was there.

Ronnie was in the back seat next to Dad, who was still holding his guitar like a shield. "Now take a right up here at the exotic car dealership. We've precleared the lot so we can blend in and lose a few of these guys."

The SUV moved up to create a screen and cover us while I turned where he directed. The Lamborghini kept moving down the highway with quite a few cars from the bar following. They didn't know Dad had only passed through the sports car before getting into the SUV then moving into the Aston Martin around the block.

"Do a loop around the back to the access road and hold position until they pass by."

Dad leaned forward in his seat. "Don't be mad, honey. Your friend's got it under control."

I flicked my eyes to the mirror.

Dad swallowed hard and inched back in his seat.

We emerged back on the highway, now behind the security detail and most of the fans who had been tailing us. The SUV moved forward while we took an exit ramp and backtrailed some side roads until we lost the rest of the stragglers. Ronnie called one of his guys and told him to do a sweep of the trailer park. Once he got the all-clear we were able to head home. One of his men would stay out front and keep an eye on the trailer overnight to make sure everything stayed calm.

All night, my cell phone was buzzing with job offers from Paula. The bartender gave up her name and number faster than he could dial 911. Everyone wanted to book the father-daughter act.

"Does anyone want just me?"

"Ah . . . No. See if your father will do a short set to get you started then you can take over for the rest of the night. Why didn't you tell me you were Don Virtue's daughter in the first place? Other people have the last name Virtue, Layla. I'm not a mind reader. I can get you into some A-list gigs with that name. The Hundgren wedding is willing to pay double what they were for that Journey cover band, and their lead singer is a very passable Steve Perry."

"No, thanks." I hung up the phone and placed the icepack on the back of my neck.

Dad hovered over me, trying to offer something to make me less mad. He held a cup of tea, a bottle of aspirin, a pillow from my bed, and a chicken wing. Come to think of it, that chicken wing might have been for him. "Honey, please talk to me. I don't know why you're so upset. I was only trying to help. I wish someone had been there to help me when I got started. You know how many dive bars and hick towns we had to play before we were signed by a label? I thought we were going to live in that awful mustard VW bus forever."

I closed my eyes and counted. *Ten, nine, eight* . . . "I asked you not to interfere. I said I needed to do this on my own. This is about boundaries and how you don't have any—or any respect for mine. Why is it so hard for you to get that I've worked very hard to keep people from knowing that I'm the same Layla

Virtue who crashed her birthday Porsche on the way home from a party at Liv Tyler's house?"

He placed the items on the table in front of me and dropped to the couch. "All kids do that."

"No, Dad, they don't. And when they do, it doesn't show up on the cover of *US Weekly*."

He groaned. "Ugh. Why won't you ever accept any help from me? You don't even act like you're happy I'm here."

"Don't do that."

"What?"

"Try to make me feel like the bad guy when you're the one who showed up unannounced and tried to blow my life up."

I heard Dad get off the couch and start pacing. "Baby girl, look around. Your life was already in smithereens when I arrived."

I threw the ice pack on the table. "At least I'm here from my own decisions. My choices. Not from you steamrolling your fame through my life and destroying everything you touch."

Dad flinched like I'd slapped him. The look of hurt on his face pulled the air from my lungs. "How have I done that?"

"Dad, your spotlight is so big, you can't even see the shadow. I know. I've spent my whole life in it. Once people know my father is Don Virtue, I become a tool for them to get something they want. Cathy Semple pretended to be my best friend so she could sneak into bed with you. When you refused her, she sent the nastiest rumors about me around the school. Don't you remember the school psychologist suggesting family therapy because she believed them?"

Dad shook his head and shrugged. That memory was a dime a dozen. Lost in the purple haze.

"Bill Mitchell was my boyfriend for six weeks just so he could slip you the demo tape of his garage band on prom night. He ditched me to smoke pot with his friends as soon as we arrived at the restaurant."

"If it's any consolation, I'm sure I never listened to his tape."

"Coach Hinkley gave me detention every day for a week so

you'd have to meet with him to discuss my 'behavior' because he wanted front-row tickets to the Y2K tour. I wasn't even *on* the volleyball team."

Dad sighed. "That one I remember."

"My whole life I've never known who I could trust or if anyone liked me for just me."

"That's not true. Theodora really likes you for you."

"Theodora's nice to everyone, Dad. She has to be. She's British. Twelve boyfriends I had through high school. Seven of them broke up with me when they found out you were on tour and there'd be no chance meeting. Five of them told everyone they had sex with Don Virtue's daughter, and believe me, they did not. One of them broke up with me on my sixteenth birthday because it got too weird to go out with me with paparazzi following us around."

Dad gave me sad puppy eyes. "Baby girl."

I held up my hand. "That's just the boys. You wanna know how many girls were my *best friend* for a day to get your autograph or steal something from your closet?"

His eyes rolled to the side. "Is that what happened to my gold jacket? Man, that was a custom job."

"Or how many of their moms invited me over to ask some very inappropriate questions about my father?"

His eyes grew wide. "I remember that crazy one with the rabbits who called and said you broke your arm, and when I got there to pick you up, you were fine and she tried to make me eat a pork roast."

"My whole life, people either only like me *after* they find out who my dad is, or they *stop* liking me when they find out who my dad is. I just want one friend who likes me for me. Someone who doesn't believe what they read in the tabloids. I want to carve out a life for myself. Be judged on my own merits. Without you getting me a free pass because I'm rock and roll royalty. Can't you understand that?"

He dropped onto the couch across from me and our knees touched. "I've always supported you. In everything you wanted to do. Like when you got to be the lead in that fancy private school musical. Didn't I come play with the band just so I could be with you?"

I threw my hands up in the air. "Dad! I only got the part because you said you'd play music for the show. The entire cast resented me for it. Sheila Robel was supposed to be the star, but they bumped her down to understudy just to get you."

He shook his head. "I don't remember it that way at all."

"You got top billing in the program over the cast."

Dad crossed his arms and leaned against the back of the couch and gave me a sour look. "What about your job as a cop? Is that my fault too?"

"No, that one is all me. Thanks for the reminder that the first time I did anything by my own merits I was a failure. At least there I'm Layla Virtue, disgraced cop—not disgraced daughter of rock legend. Of course, after that stunt you pulled tonight goes viral, I'll probably be both."

Chapter 36

I WOKE UP UNDER MY BED AGAIN. AT FIRST I THOUGHT, *OH GOOD. I survived another night.* Then it all came back to me, and the heaviness pressed against my chest like a ballistics vest.

I heard the sound of an eighty-five-pound Labrador thumping his tail against my dresser before I actually saw him. "Ringo. To what do I owe the pleasure?"

Ringo licked my face.

I crawled off of the floor and Ringo jumped on the bed. The sky was just turning her lights on for the day. I refused to check the time on my phone—I didn't want to be tempted to see the news alerts. And I wasn't ready to face Dad yet.

I dressed in jeans, boots, and a blue sweater that I'd bought because it matched the ends of my hair. "You have to be quiet, okay?"

Ringo wagged his tail in agreement.

We crept past Dad, still asleep on the couch. I scrawled a hasty note for Nick that I took Ringo to the lake, left it on my door, waved to Ronnie's guy—hunkered down in the gold Thunderbird across the street—and Ringo and I made our way down the path through the woods.

"I don't know why he insists on sleeping on the couch instead of going to a fancy hotel with room service. That can't be good for his back. And it's not like he's banned from all hotels everywhere. Just the ones in Korea and Nebraska. You know what I mean?"

Ringo gave me a little nudge of encouragement.

The lake was enshrouded in mist, like an eighties music video. The birds and bugs were flitting around busy about their morning routine before too many people intruded on their world. Ringo gave a soft growl to a faraway black squirrel who darted into the fallen leaves under the red oak.

I dropped into a weathered Adirondack chair facing the lake and the Lab lay at my feet. "Life was a lot simpler when I was a kid, Ringo. I thought my dad went to work in an office like an accountant. And I believed everyone's mother slept all day and woke them in the middle of the night to eat cookie dough or fly to Disneyland Paris. I had no idea that my life was any different or would get this complicated."

Ringo laid his head on my foot and sighed. He knew exactly what I meant.

"When I was little, I wanted to be a veterinarian. I had it all planned. I'd live in the mansion with my dad, and we'd turn the first floor of our house into an animal hospital. People from all over would bring me animals who'd gotten hurt or sick and I'd make them better. Dad even bought me a toy doctor's kit and a stuffed tiger I could practice on.

"Other people realized who I was before I did and that ruined everything. Just because they loved my dad and his music, somehow that meant I had to share him with the world."

I reached my hand down and ran my fingers through Ringo's soft fur. "At nine years old you just want your dad to take you out for your birthday without having to sign autographs for an hour while your ice cream melts."

Ringo grumbled. I could tell he was offended for me.

"I started drinking when I was thirteen. And I don't have to tell you, the press loves a celebrity crash-and-burn story. They dine for days on DUIs, perp walks, and rehab. The pictures of you at your rock bottom buy their sports cars. They don't want you to die because then the story is over, but a little drug overdose or suicide attempt gives them the chance to report every intimate detail of your life as they *pray for you*, send *healing thoughts*, and repost everything you've ever done wrong in a retrospective—code for new beach house.

"They think they know me because Don Virtue is in the public eye, but I don't even know me. You may not know this about me, Ringo, but I hide from everyone."

Ringo wagged his tail and gave me a smile.

"As soon as you let people in your life, they want to judge you. When they don't know your secrets, they make some up. I'm just so tired of being rejected. I'm also tired of being alone."

Ringo licked my ankle.

"I know you're there, buddy. Thank you. I do deserve to be alone though. I've done awful things, Ringo. I let people down and now they're dead. And it wasn't Dad, or fame, or the paparazzi. This time it was just me. And Dad can't buy my way out of trouble or give a concert to pay for damages. This one I have to live with."

Either the world's fattest squirrel or a human crunching through leaves drew both of our attention behind us. Ringo raised his head and looked toward the woods. His tail started to wag, and Nick's voice floated over. "Here you both are."

"Your dog likes me better."

Nick grunted. "Can you blame him? I let this guy out to pee last night and he went straight to your trailer where your dad let him in. All I could do was shut my door and go to bed."

I laughed and climbed out of the chair. "Sorry about that. I'm pretty sure Dad thinks Ringo is ours. He'll be gone in another week, and we'll stop dognapping him."

Nick gave me a slow smile. "Is that what you want? For Don to leave?"

The ache in my chest was back. "If I could keep him with me without all that goes along with it, I would have him forever."

Nick nodded. He attached a leash to Ringo's collar and handed the end to me. "He needs to practice walking next to people, so hold the leash close. If you stop, he stops."

"Alright. I can do that." We started to trek back home.

"So, what's the story with the guy in front of your house? Is he private security or a reporter?"

"The first one. I'm surprised you didn't hear about it on social media already."

"I'm not on social media."

I stopped and Ringo stopped. "What? None of them?"

Nick raised his eyebrows. "I'm pretty sure social media is
bringing the downfall of our civilization."

I don't know why, but that made him even more attractive. I
started moving again. "You don't want to stay in touch with people you went to high school or served in the Marines with? See
photos of how much happier their lives are than yours and what
they had for breakfast?"

"I'm on the computer for work all day. And if I want to talk to
someone I'll come to your house. You can show me your
donuts."

I giggled. "Oh, you wish I'd show you my donuts."

He laughed. "What does that even mean?"

"I don't know. That's my lame attempt at being cute. I don't
have any experience with it."

He grinned. "I think you're pretty cute. So, what happened
last night?"

I gave him the long version, just so I could talk to him for a
while, stopping every now and then to make Ringo stop with me.

Nick gasped at all the right places. "I'm not gonna lie, I'm
really torn. I'm sorry that Don outed you like that and that people don't know how to behave. But also, I would love to have
seen you two play together on stage. I've heard you sing. You're
really good. Don't let anyone take that away from you just because you inherited it in your DNA."

We were back at his trailer now. Nick reached for the leash
and touched my hand. I didn't pull away and he twined his fingers around mine. "The world is full of trolls who want to steal
your happiness to make up for their own misery. Ignore them
and do what you want. You're amazing just for who you are."

We locked eyes, and before I could stop myself, I was in his
arms. I pushed him up against his door and he reached behind
and turned the handle. Ringo let out a sharp bark thinking this
was some game we were going to play.

Nick backed us into his trailer, and I shut the door with my foot. He was doing that thing with his tongue again. That was gonna make me crazy.

He was leading me down the hall where I knew his bedroom was just on the other side of the door. My body was screaming at me to keep going, but my heart was stabbing me with shame. *Really? This is what you're going to do to Jacob? First you get him killed and then you move on like he was nothing? How are you gonna cut and run from a guy who lives next door?*

I pressed against Nick's shoulders.

Nick pulled back and searched my face. "What's wrong?"

I tried to steady my breath. "I'm sorry. I can't."

Nick quirked an eyebrow. "I'm getting mixed signals here. I'm thrilled to just be your friend if that's what you want because I think you're awesome. But you do know that I'm hugely attracted to you. Are you into me like this or not?"

"It's complicated."

"It's really not." He reached down and unclipped the leash from Ringo's collar. "I like you, Layla, but I don't want to be led on if this isn't going anywhere."

I reached for him but stopped myself. "I like you too, Nick. But I'm not in a place emotionally for this."

"How are you less ready now than when we first met? Did I do something wrong?"

"No, the bar was different. I thought you were just a one-night stand and I'd never have to see you again."

He leaned against the kitchen counter. "Well, that's flattering."

"The truth is, sex is one of the ways I've used people to distract myself from dealing with my problems. And I don't want to do that anymore. It just leaves me feeling empty and ashamed and it ruins the relationships. I want more than that with you. I want you to stay in my life."

"I want that too."

"I don't trust many people. If this thing between us goes bad, I'll lose the best friend I've had in a long time."

"I understand, but my heart isn't something to be toyed with either." Nick reached out and gently ran his hand down the side of my face. "You should go."

A lump caught in my throat, but l refused to cry in front of him. I turned and walked out the door.

All the way across the grass I told myself I was an idiot. *You just ruined another relationship. You don't have any friends because you push people away. Why do I always have to make everything so complicated?*

All I had waiting for me was a sterile trailer that I refused to make into a home, a stack of late notices because I was chasing a pipe dream, and a father who'd only ever been good to me— and I ripped his heart out and stomped on it.

And freakin' Adam Beasley was waiting on my front step.

Chapter 37

"WHAT ARE YOU DOING HERE, BEASLEY?"

"Duuuude! I knew I recognized your father. Why didn't you tell me he was Don Virtue?"

"Keep your voice down! Dad would like to keep some level of privacy."

Adam pressed his hands together in prayer position. "Oh. Oh. Oh. Of course. I understand. Could you get me an autograph?"

I reached for the doorknob. "I'll see what I can do."

"Wait! Layla! That's not the only reason I'm here."

"What else do you want?"

"Don't tell Castinetto I've been here, okay. He's made it clear that everyone is to avoid you at all costs."

"Of course he has. I'm surprised it's taken him this long."

Beasley clenched his teeth. "I'm sorry about that. For the record, I think he's a real jerk."

"Well, on that we agree."

"I wanted to ask you something." He craned his neck, trying to see through the window over my shoulder. "About the case. I know you're officially off the force and all—but you know a couple of the victim's ex-wives and you may have heard things."

"What do you mean, I know them?"

Adam stared at me and blinked. His usual indication that he was clueless. "The birthday parties. I thought you were playing your guitar at them."

"I did that once. And I attended a party with a lot of the same moms as a guest. That's it."

"Oh." He pulled out his cell phone and tapped it awake. "You and Janice Kestle are not friends?"

"We know each other casually."

"What about Tina Crumm?"

I kept my face blank. Something Adam had yet to learn to do. "Same."

His eyebrows dipped as he consulted his notes. "Huh."

"Just out of curiosity, why are you asking?"

"Your name keeps coming up in interviews with the suspects so I thought you might know something."

"Know something like what?"

"The forensics team says that the victim was poisoned less than twenty-four hours before he died. Those nicotine patches are only good for one use. The coroner had to peel them off his feet, so we know they had been freshly applied. If he hadn't been dosed with so many, along with having a heart condition and a crap-ton of alcohol in his system, he might have survived."

"Okay. So, what did you think I might know?"

"Since you've been with a lot of the people who were around him in the hours before he died you might have heard something about who collects the life insurance."

Poker face, Layla. "The life insurance?"

"Yeah, man, the guy forgot to change his beneficiary after he remarried each time."

"Really? Who gets it?"

"Wife number one, Paula Braithwaite. Oh, wait . . . I probably shouldn't have told you that."

Steppenwolf ran into my yard and screamed, *"Erka Erka!"*

Adam grabbed his chest and cursed.

"Paula his manager is also an ex-wife?"

Adam bit his lip. "Please don't tell Castinetto you heard that from me. I just wanted to know if any of the ex-wives have been especially surprised or disappointed that they don't collect. I really need to impress Castinetto, so he'll stop giving me crap assignments."

"Well, this is the first I'm hearing about the insurance going to Paula. But I do have something that might help you get some points."

"Sweet! Lay it on me."

"Tina loaned Chuck a big chunk of money and the life insurance payout was his collateral. She was told she was the beneficiary as the most recent wife."

He pumped his fist in the air. "Yes! Okay, I have one for you."

"Thought I was staying out of it."

Adam made a face and shrugged me off. "Castinetto found out who the guy was who was threatening Chuck at that party where he died."

"Who?"

"His bookie, Butchie Romero. Chuck had been placing a lot of reckless high-dollar bets at the racetrack since he won that big payout, but he hadn't come through with all the payments. He was trying to make another the day he was killed, and Romero had come to collect the cash before he placed the bet."

"How much money in high-dollar bets?"

Adam flashed a wide smile. "Forty grand over two months. Thanks, Virtue. I owe you one!"

He returned to his car, and I went into the house.

Dad was sitting on the couch drinking orange juice, his hair sticking up in all different directions. "What day is it?"

"Sunday."

"Oh. Is it still September?"

"Yeees."

"Good. I haven't missed it."

"You haven't missed what?"

"The Grammys."

"That's in February, Dad. Why?"

He ran his hand over his hair to tame the points. "I'm getting some kind of award or something."

I pulled out my phone and looked it up. "Wow. Dad! The group is getting a lifetime achievement award."

He drained his glass and sighed. "Yeah, that's it. And you're out of juice."

"Why didn't you tell me this sooner?"

"I just finished it."

"No. The award, Dad."

"What award?"

"The Grammy."

"Who's getting a Grammy?"

"You are."

"Oh. That's nice. Don't I already have that?"

"Not this one." I took a long look at him. He seemed more far away than usual. "Are you okay? Have you been taking that medicine the doctor gave you?"

He shook his head. "That's a secret."

"Secret from who?"

"Everybody." He put a finger to his lips. Then he got up and headed for the bathroom. "We need to call Jimmy and tell him we need a new tour bus. This one is garbage."

I rambled around the trailer all day stress cleaning. I'd already scoured the oven twice and in the whole time I'd lived here I'd never once turned it on. I felt twitchy. I wanted a drink. I was at odds with Nick. I was at odds with Dad. My manager might have murdered her last client, and I couldn't shake the feeling like I'd cheated on Jacob. I'd never felt this way after a one-night stand. That just brought my usual shame and self-loathing. But this . . . I hadn't even done anything with Nick and still I felt guilty.

On the force, I was known for my uncanny ability to see through whatever lies a suspect threw at me. It came from a lifetime of having the worst-case scenario turn out to be true.

I'd also learned that the more I trusted someone, the more they could get over on me. I could tell I was starting to have feelings for Nick and that put me in a vulnerable position. As much as it pained me, it was better to have Nick angry with me now before he was able to hurt me.

Dad wandered back into the kitchen looking lost. I cornered him and asked if he felt okay.

"Yeah, honey. I'm fine."

"Are you sure? Maybe you caught something at the open mic last night."

He parted the mini blinds in the living room to peer out into the yard. "Baby girl, I haven't done an open mic in years."

A buzzing vroooom passed the window and I smacked the blinds. "You need to keep the blinds closed, Dad."

Dad's eyes popped wide. "Did you see that? It was like a tiny spaceship."

"Yeah, well, word has gotten around that Don Virtue is in the area, and now we've got drones flying over the neighborhood."

Dad gave me some side-eye. "Like, government drones? Spying on us?"

I poured Dad a glass of iced tea and led him to the couch. "More like people being nosy looking to post a Don Virtue sighting on YouTube. I've already called Ronnie and he's tripled the security outside, but I think its best if you stay inside away from the windows until further notice."

Dad sipped his tea and I could see his wheels turning. "Maybe we should get Jeffrey."

I patted him on the knee. "I think that's a good idea." I called Dad's manager and had him set Operation Doppelgänger in motion for Berlin. Dad's body double, Jeffrey, would be paid to fly on a private jet to Berlin to be "spotted" at the airport and later at an exclusive restaurant or club by the paparazzi. Since Jeffrey was paid more for one of these "missions" than he made in an entire year in his dental practice in Grand Forks, North Dakota, he was always up for the job. Once that story was all over the news, things should quiet down in our neighborhood.

I found my six-month sobriety chip in the pocket of a pair of jeans and clutched it tightly. I needed the reminder right now. If there was ever a day to handcuff myself to the radiator to keep away from a bottle, it was today.

I shut myself in the bedroom, picked up my guitar, and played one of my anti-anxiety songs, "Bridge Over Troubled Water."

By the chorus I realized I was playing in stereo. Dad was on his guitar in the living room singing along. Hearing his voice tell me he was on my side was too much for me, and by the time he was sailing right behind I had tears streaming down my face.

Not the calm I was going for.

We sat in silence for a moment, then I started a tune of my own I'd been working on. I was having trouble with the turn from the chorus back into the next verse. I worked on the notes for nearly twenty minutes when Dad called through the door, "Try it like this." He played a chord progression, and I knew immediately that it was right.

I opened the bedroom door and his face fell. "I'm sorry. Was that intruding?"

My heart clutched in my chest as a wave of remorse washed over me. "No, Dad. That was great. I thought I'd come out here and we could work on it together."

He grinned and it was like he lit up from within.

We worked together for hours until the song was fully formed. It was a haunting ballad about wanting to say you're sorry for a million little things after it was too late. It laid down beautifully for Dad's voice, and I left him working on it to go get ready for the launch party.

Paula had said the event coordinator was interested in background instrumental rock, so I slicked my hair back and dressed in white slacks and a white blazer. Then I added a black lace choker to my neck and a heavy ring of kohl to my eyes. Looking the part was half the battle. I slipped into patent leather red stilettos and grabbed my guitar. I was about to leave the room when I decided to go back for my sobriety chip. I slipped it into my pocket.

Passing Dad on the couch, he looked up from his bowl of Fruit Loops. "What's this for? A vampire party?"

"Instrumental elevator rock."

"That's nonsense."

"It pays the bills."

"So does selling your blood, and it's less embarrassing."

I snickered. "You got me there. Listen, Dad."

He blinked at me. His eyes so innocent while the lines in his face told a thousand wild stories. "Yeah?"

"I'm sorry about last night. I know you were only trying to help."

"I'd do anything for you, baby. I love you."

"I love you too, Dad. I promise to try to do better from now on."

Dad's eyes softened. "Baby girl, I think you're perfect just the way you are."

I had to leave before I started crying again and messed up my eyeliner. On the way to the car, I waved at the new security guard. He waved me over. "Ma'am. There have been some older ladies hanging about. They didn't seem like a threat, but I told them you were quarantined and couldn't take visitors."

"Why didn't I think of that? I could have hung a hazard sign on the front door months ago."

I thanked him and unlocked the Aston Martin. I stowed my guitar and amp in the trunk before taking a quick glance at Nick's trailer. Everything was dark. Maybe they were out. I hope I hadn't caused him to leave for good. My heart ached at the thought of Nick moving away with the dog. I liked Nick, but I was used to people not sticking around. Ringo, however, had wagged his way into my heart. I wouldn't be the same without him.

I backed out of the carport and plugged in the address for the event. It sounded familiar, but after nearly eighteen years on the force, most addresses around here sounded familiar. I got on the highway and tried to quiet my mind. The closer I got to my old precinct the faster my heart was beating. I was passing recognizable landmarks that I'd been avoiding for months. Tonight, they were looming over me with sinister malevolence. Taunting me about the life I'd lost. *Exactly how far away is this gig from Stratton Park?*

I focused on my breathing to avoid a full-blown panic attack. Turn by turn I was dangerously close now. In my mind I could see the smoke rising above the warehouse. I could smell the putrid odor of burning flesh as if it were yesterday.

It's your imagination. Everything is fine. You will be fine.

I pulled the car into a large empty parking lot facing a dark two-story gray warehouse identical to the one where Jacob and Melissa died. Just past the roof's edge was the sooty remains of a burned-out warehouse on the other side of the lot. I was looking at the deserted backside of Stratton Park.

The GPS announced, "You have arrived."

I am not fine.

Chapter 38

I GOT OUT OF THE CAR TO FACE THE BACK OF THE WAREHOUSE PARK. Memories were flying at me in frozen still shots.

A flash of light and the whoosh that sent everything in slow motion.

Jacob being sucked into the warehouse by the force of the blast.

Windows the size of garage doors shattering into billions of speeding daggers.

Everything engulfed in thick black smoke.

Ash falling like dirty snow.

And the smell. The greasy, heavy smell of accelerant and burning flesh will haunt me for the rest of my life.

A flood of memories hit me like a tidal wave. My team was supposed to infiltrate Ricky Hurtado's drug ring as they prepared bricks of heroin for distribution. We'd been collecting evidence for weeks as part of a Narcotics Unit undercover operation. They were supposed to wait for my command to move in. I could see each of their faces in front of me like it happened this morning.

Oscar. He'd joined my team just a few months earlier. Transferred in from the Gang Unit, we put him on the inside, working directly for Hurtado. Oscar was pulled from the building after the fire was out. He'd taken a bullet to the back of the head. He had a new baby at home.

Eddie. He lost a teenaged son to an overdose years ago. He

was one of the first to sign up for the Narcotics task force. He was supposed to cover the fire exit to surround Hurtado's men from the rear. The mission was go-for-broke and we were taking the whole team down. Eddie took three bullets to the chest at close range. His body was found on the main floor of the warehouse, nowhere near the fire exit.

Melissa. The youngest member on my team. She was so passionate about keeping kids safe. She joined the task force instead of taking a school assignment because she said she wanted to learn from me. She was trying to tell me something right before the explosion, but I couldn't understand her. I watched her die in the parking lot, a glass shard the size of a bowie knife in her thigh. She'd never even breached the perimeter.

And Jacob. Posing as the buyer. We'd worked this relationship with Hurtado for months, winning his trust. That day was the big score. Jacob wasn't supposed to begin the operation until I gave the word, but something happened to send him in early, and I wasn't there.

It was a massacre. Hurtado's entire organization got away clean. And I had nothing to show for months of work but a few cuts, a hangover, and four death certificates. Why was I at a bar? And why did they go in early? Why didn't Jacob wait for me? He died in the explosion, his body burned so badly only dental records could identify him.

The tears streamed down my face, and I didn't care. I lost a lot of people I loved. They didn't deserve to die. And I didn't deserve to be sober and get my life on track. Why should I have a life and friends when I'd taken everything from them? All my efforts to launch a career as a musician seemed foolish. They mocked me and made my insides feel hollow. The real reason I wanted to be alone was because I deserved to be alone. I deserved to die with them. I knew just the place to go to destroy myself.

"I'm sorry, Layla, but this is the worst launch party ever."

"I know, like—eww. It's a dirty parking lot and no one is even here."

"And look at you, girl. All dressed up in your fancy blazer, ready to rock."

I used the back of my hand to wipe my face and turned to face the pestyest three women I'd ever met. "What are you all doing here?"

Scarlett crossed her arms over her chest. "Well, we came to hear you play, but now I'm thinking your crack management team fat fingered the address."

"This was not an accident. Someone is sending me a message. And they manipulated Paula to do it."

Charisse looked at her hand. "Well, I wasted a prime quality manicure on this dud tonight, but I don't want to go home. I can zap a Lean Cuisine and binge Netflix anytime. Let's go do something."

Bree grinned shyly. "Scarlett read the address on your text. We wanted to support you."

"Why?"

She chuckled softly. "Because we're friends, silly."

Another tear fell and I could do nothing to stop it. *You gotta trust someone sometime.*

Scarlett tilted her head. "Are you crying because of that blazer? Because that blazer does nothing for your figure."

I nodded yes and sobbed, "It has shoulder pads."

They laughed and pulled me into a hug.

Bree whispered, "What do you need?"

Despite my past with women, my deep-rooted trust issues, and my fear of being rejected yet again, I had nothing left to hold on to, so I took a leap of faith. "Just get me out of here."

Chapter 39

THE DENNY'S WAITER PUT MY BANANA SPLIT WAFFLE AND ROOT beer float in front of me and grinned suggestively. He was about twenty years younger than me, and I had to stifle a giggle like I was still in junior high because it was so ridiculous. The girls waited for him to leave before they hit me with a barrage of questions.

Bree pulled her chocolate malt to her mouth and inhaled the whipped cream. "And just like that—your memories came back?"

"Some of them. I still don't know why I was at a bar. And I don't know how I got so drunk. I mean, I am an alcoholic, but it wasn't like me to get wasted in the middle of the day. And while my team was waiting for me? Maybe I'm giving myself too much credit, but it doesn't sound like me."

Charisse nodded while she chewed her chocolate chip pancakes. "It's not your fault that they all died, Layla. You didn't abandon them. And you didn't pull the trigger. Even if you were off getting drunk, your team should have waited for backup. Was it normal for Jacob to disobey orders?"

I speared a banana slice and dipped it in chocolate sauce. "Not usually. At least not on something this big. He could be a hotshot, but he knew the stakes for this operation were unbelievably high. I can only figure Hurtado's men opened fire from the warehouse. Eddie and Jacob must have gone in to try to stop them."

Scarlett took a bite of her pecan pie. "I don't know. Bombs aren't usually just lying around waiting to go off by accident. It sounds like an ambush. Maybe the only reason you're not dead is because you went to that bar."

"Then that would be the only time in my life that going to a bar has helped anything. We never talked about it, but I'm starting to think Jacob might have been an alcoholic too. He wanted to go out drinking after every shift. It was the main thing we did together. Even when I suggested we go somewhere else, do something else, he was always too tired and too stressed."

Bree dipped a french fry into her malt. "Were you in love with him?"

I nodded. The words got caught in my throat. I'd never admitted it to anyone before and the guilt of our last argument was crushing me. "We had to keep our relationship secret. We'd frequent the places we knew cops didn't hang out. I've spent a lot of time over the past few months thinking about him, and just remembering. Things I said. Things I wish I'd said. The morning of Stratton Park he said he wanted to move in together. I told him I liked the way things were. Our last words were an argument about honesty and commitment. He said he couldn't be with someone who didn't trust him."

Charisse groaned. "Mm! There's no worse feeling in the world than regret. But we don't live in the past, and we can't change anything."

"Here's to moving away from regret." Scarlett held up her fork like we were toasting and for some reason we all held our forks up and clinked them together. I felt ridiculous and wonderful at the same time.

Bree gasped. "We should go to that bar to see if we can jog the rest of your memories back."

I poked at my waffle. "I thought of that months ago. But I'm afraid I'll remember that I'm just a pathetic, careless drunk who got wasted on the job and killed my entire team. Maybe that's really all there is to it."

Scarlett gave me a single nod. "Then you'll know. Step four. And you can move on toward amends."

Bree reached for my arm and squeezed it. "When you're ready, we'll be there for you."

Scarlett covered my hand from the other side. "Just say the word."

If I'm going to commit to this friendship, I need to commit all the way. Even if I'm just handing them the poison to kill me later. "I probably need to tell you all something else."

Three sets of eyes watched me expectantly.

"My father is Don Virtue."

Charisse's eyes grew twice their size. "Are you serious? Is—is this a joke?" She let out a belly laugh, then silenced abruptly. "No, for real. Are you serious?"

Scarlett cocked her head to the side. "Really! I mean I knew you had the same last name . . . So that's where you get your talent from."

Bree held her straw tightly in her mouth like a lifeline. "Who's Don Virtue?"

Charisse gave her a look. "Really? Society's Castoffs? He's only one of the best guitar players in the world. 'End of the Line.' 'Time Bandits.' 'Lanterns and Fireflies.'"

Bree shook her head that she still didn't get it.

Scarlett rattled off more of their hits. "'To Each His Own.' 'Persephone.' 'Sins of a Lover.'"

Bree's eyes finally lit up. "Oh, I like that one. That's your dad?"

I nodded, pride slipping out in the form of a smile.

Bree grinned. "That's so cool. My dad's just an electrician."

I smiled back at her. "That's cool too." I held my breath, waiting for the other shoe to drop.

Scarlett nodded. "I bet he's really proud of you. Following in his footsteps and all."

With shaking hands, I pulled my straw to my mouth and sipped my root beer float. "Yeah. He is. Even if he is single-handedly trying to usher me into rock and roll stardom."

Charisse found her voice again and every thought she'd been

holding on to gushed out at once. "I've always been a huge fan. I have all their records, cassette tapes, CDs. I even went to some of their concerts in the eighties. Have you ever been to a concert?"

"Yes."

"Of course you have. What am I saying? I can't believe I'm friends with his daughter. What was it like to grow up with Don Virtue as a father?"

"Intense."

"I bet it was. I want to know everything, but maybe not when you've just been traumatized by a psycho. I hope we get to meet him one day. How awesome would that be?"

Bree's entire face lit up. "Is it like super easy for you to buy concert tickets? Because I have been trying to buy tickets for Taylor Swift for ages and they sell out so fast."

"I don't really have any special abilities with other bands unless they're fans of my dad."

Charisse gasped. "Oh, sweet Jesus, I just thought of something. Girl, you cannot let Miranda find out. If she was all over Chuckles the Clown, can you just imagine how hard she would throw herself at your father?"

Bree shook her french fry at me. "He'll need a restraining order."

Scarlett snickered. "And she'll want you to start supplying all the refreshments for the meetings. There is no twelve-step program for being crazy."

Charisse laughed. "Don't we know it. That Tina might be back in the program, but that's a woman on the edge if I ever saw one."

Scarlett reached over and took one of Bree's fries. "I still think Chuck McCracken is the key to their behavior. How was he getting all these women to give him stacks of cash? I mean Paula, Kelly, and Tina? Come on."

"They're all ex-wives." I looked at them one by one and scanned their expressions. How were they looking at me? Did they just casually move on from my father being a straight-up legend? No sanctimonious judgment? No requests for memorabilia or cash? Maybe I've been carrying this chip on my shoulder for too long. Or maybe I just hadn't found the right friends before now. *At least I hope I have.*

Bree froze with a fry on the way to her mouth. "What? All of them? Paula too?"

I held up my hand and counted. "Miranda, Kelly, Tina, and Paula. That's four."

Scarlett clicked her tongue. "Well, three of them went on with their lives. Paula has a career and the other two have new husbands. Why are they still supporting this guy? No advice is that good. I mean, I've done some weird drugs, but never anything as disturbing as Chuckles the Clown."

Charisse laughed. "And according to Miranda, he has a string of mistresses."

Scarlett traded a hunk of her pie for some of Bree's fries. "I mean, what was happening in those life coaching massages that pushed one of them to snap and kill him?"

I pushed my plate away. "His murder wasn't a crime of passion. It took planning and forethought to make shoe inserts out of nicotine patches."

Bree's eyes turned sad and pleading. "Do you think they'll ever catch his killer?"

"I hope so. But people get away with murder every day. The file of cold cases is thick."

Charisse cut another wedge into her pancakes. "I hope that doesn't happen. Everyone deserves justice. Even creepy weirdo clowns."

Scarlett reached for my waffle and stabbed a bite. "I think it's obvious that he was killed by one of the women. Not necessarily one of the ones we've met, but probably someone in their circle. And it had to be someone who could get close enough to get into his house and slip something into his shoes without him noticing. What do you think, Layla?"

I shrugged. "Well, Paula said he was living out of his van. It wouldn't be that hard to break in and plant the inserts."

Bree nodded thoughtfully. "It's not like he wore the clown outfit all the time. I mean he had to wear other things, right? Like to go to the doctor, or the grocery store?"

"True. He was working an event in Herndon all afternoon on Saturday, and he would have been wearing the shoes then. So, the inserts had to be planted between Saturday night and Sunday afternoon."

Charisse sipped her coffee. "So, where was he Saturday night?"

I shrugged. "No one knows. Probably at the track."

Bree toyed with her straw. "Don't the police check the GPS on his cell phone? They did with my brother."

"It takes a few days to get that information. Nothing is as fast as it looks on TV."

Scarlett's eyes narrowed. "Maybe he was working for his life coach business. Didn't Tina say he was offering it to all the birthday party moms to build the business? And wasn't Janice a last-minute booking?"

"Well, yeah. That thought did occur to me," I confessed. "Mostly I've been trying not to think about it. That world is full of reminders of my failure."

Bree gave me a soft smile that said she disagreed but wouldn't argue with me. "Don't let one terrible night rob you of who you are."

I swallowed hard to get around the lump of fear that had nestled in my chest all those months ago. "From the moment I met Janice she said he was disgusting. I can't see her letting him oil her up. However, Tina wasn't exactly bragging about having a life coach massage either."

Charisse shook her head. "That's not a thing."

"So, it is very possible," I finished.

Scarlett bit her lip to think. "Kelly was so addicted to his flattery that she was getting a new massage every day. That can't be good for you. She invested all that money in the business. And when she finally came to herself, she tried to extort him into giving her money back."

Charisse nodded along. "Maybe Chuck was at Janice's house Saturday night *and* Sunday afternoon; that would put her in prime position to plant those poisoned inserts."

Bree leaned back in her seat and pulled at her sleeves. "Ooh. That's totally true. But like . . . how can we find that out . . . I don't know . . . for sure."

I pulled up the photo of the business card on my cell phone and flashed it. "We can call the number and see if his new manager will tell us."

Scarlett picked up her cell phone. "Dialing it now. Putting it on speaker."

"Mobile Massage Pros. Kitty speaking."

I waved my hand at Scarlett to go on. She shook her head no and shoved her phone into my hands. "Uh, hi. I was hoping I could hire Chuck McCracken for another session. The first one left me with such warm feelings of self-love." I shrugged, feeling like an idiot.

Bree twirled her hair and mouthed, *"Awesome."* Charisse and Scarlett were silently laughing at me.

After a long pause, Kitty sniffled. "I'm so sorry, but Zen Master Chuck has retired. I can recommend another mobile massage therapist, but Chuck was the only life coach I represented. His was a very specialized service."

"I see. So, you were Zen Master Chuck's . . ."

"Fiancée, yes."

"I was going to say manager."

"Oh yes. That too. Are you a repeat client?"

Scarlett nodded violently and pulled the phone to her mouth. "Yes. This is Janice Kestle."

We waited.

"Yep, I got your file right here."

"I'd like to book a standing appointment for the same time every week. Is that doable?"

There was silence on the line. "It looks like you only had the one session last Saturday at seven. I can send Phillip or Helen to

do an in-home therapeutic massage tomorrow if you're interested, but they don't really want to hear about all your problems. Wait a minute. Janice Kestle? Didn't Chuck die at your
house during the kid with the weird name's birthday party the
next day?"

I pulled the phone back to my mouth. "You know what, Kitty.
I'm gonna have to call you back."

Chapter 40

"*I* NEED TO REPORT THIS. UGH. FRICKIN' CASTINETTO IS GONNA RIP me a new one when he finds out I got involved."

Scarlett blew out a long breath. "I just can't believe it. That chubby little con artist. There's a whole freaky underbelly to Potomac County that I knew nothing about. And I know what prescriptions everyone is on."

Bree twisted her napkin. "Ooohhh, do you think Janice killed him?"

The waiter stood behind her and gave us a weird look. "Can I get you ladies anything else?"

I smiled. "I think we're all good for now. Thanks."

He nodded and backed away from the table. When he disappeared around the corner Charisse snapped her fingers and pointed at me. "We need to question Janice, and girl, you know where she lives."

"No way. I can't just show up at a suspect's house in the middle of an investigation and start asking questions about a crime. It will make me guilty of obstruction."

Charisse's eyebrows dipped together. "Uh—but if she's guilty, wouldn't they thank you for the assist? You know, being a former cop and all? Get you some points."

I snorted. "That's not how that works. There's a proper protocol and procedure. There's an evidence chain of command."

Scarlett pressed. "Yeah, but you're not a cop anymore. You

don't have to follow their rules. You're just a concerned citizen. If we sit idly by while Janice killed the birthday clown, who's next? The housekeeper? The pool boy? The sign spinner in front of Kinko's?"

All three of them were looking at me like I was holding the scales of justice instead of a maraschino cherry. "If you were going to plant toxic nicotine inserts in some clown's shoes . . ."

Scarlett muttered, "Like you do."

". . . Wouldn't you wait until he's finished your kid's birthday party?"

Charisse nodded. "Absolutely. No one wants the clown to die in their backyard. Alibi ruined. You want the sucker to die miles away from your house while you're in the clear. The trick is to know just when to plant the inserts, so he'll be putting them on within a few hours because those nicotine patches don't stay fresh for long. They're not Odor-Eaters."

Scarlett gave Charisse a weird look. "That was extremely well thought out."

Charisse shrugged. "I listen to a lot of true crime podcasts on my commute."

Bree poked her straw around her empty glass while her eyes darted between us. "I don't like getting the police involved. What if Janice is innocent? Once they find out she was using Chuck's life coaching services the night before he died, the cops won't even look at the other women. They'll just pin everything on her. Sorry, Layla."

I sighed. "Most cops really do want to catch the right person."

Scarlett nodded. "See. We don't want to make a big deal about it and be wrong. The cops'll be all over Janice. And how many times have *we* been falsely accused?"

They sat there for a moment cataloging their infractions; then they all kind of agreed that they *were* usually guilty when they had been questioned but they should still probably give Janice the benefit of the doubt.

Charisse checked the time on her phone. "It's only nine o'clock. She's probably still up. Let's just go talk to her."

I could see this was important to them. They'd handed me a lot of trust and I wanted to hand some right back. Preferably enough to cement our relationship without getting anyone busted by my former precinct. It would be nice for me not to sabotage a relationship right at the start for a change. So I closed my eyes, and once again, leapt into the unknown. "Okay. Since I have to report all this to Castinetto anyway, it would be good to know just how involved Janice was before I say anything. And I would like to know if she invested in Chuck's business."

Bree cocked an eyebrow. "Why do you think she invested? She wasn't an ex-wife."

"Because Chuck had blown forty grand at the track in two months, and I'm pretty sure we know where he got the money from."

Charisse gasped. "Chuck was committing investment fraud."

I nodded. "And we've only accounted for three of the investors."

We paid the check and piled into Bree's minivan so we could strategize on the way to Janice's. I was the only one who'd been there before, and I knew we still had to get past the front gate.

We pulled up to the speaker box and Janice's voice came through. "Who is it?"

I leaned across Bree. "It's Layla Virtue. I think I left something in the pool house from the birthday party."

"Can't you come back for it tomorrow? I've had a long day."

"I really need it for a gig in the morning."

She sighed loudly. "Okay. Fine. Come on."

The gate opened and I followed the winding driveway past the duck pond and around the meditation garden. We stepped out of the car and the back lights around the pool lit up like it was daytime. The back door opened, and Janice came out, wrapping a flowered silk kimono around herself. "I don't see why this couldn't wait."

"Janice, I'm so sorry. I'm afraid we've lied our way in here."

She looked nervously from me to the other girls. "What do you mean?"

Scarlett took a step toward the woman who was now shivering gently in the early autumn night. "We know Chuck McCracken had been working his way through your circle of friends, flattering them out of investment money for his so-called life coaching massage business. And we suspect he might have convinced you to invest too."

Her face pinked. "I don't have the slightest idea what you're talking about."

Charisse's tone may have been sassy, but her voice was gentle. "Oh, come on now. Ya do too. Ya been had. It happens to all of us. We know you hired the birthday clown to give you one of his flattery massages where he tells you how wonderful you are and then convinces you to give him a bunch of money."

Scarlett nodded. "All your friends were doing it. And to rave reviews, we hear. Who doesn't like hearing all their problems are because they're underappreciated?"

I gave her a shrug like it was no big deal. "You wanted to see what all the fuss was about. What was the harm?"

"If you're here to blackmail me you've got another thing coming." Janice pulled a cell phone from her pocket. She looked like she was about to call the cops when Bree touched her arm and gave the woman the gentlest of smiles.

"We've all done things we're embarrassed about. We're here to help you, not judge you."

Janice sighed. She looked away from us. "Then you might as well come inside."

She took us into her kitchen, which was the size of my entire trailer, and offered us bottles of Acqua Panna from her glass door beverage fridge. We sat around the granite island while she hammered gingersnaps on a thick cutting board with a meat mallet.

"It was so stupid. Whoever heard of a life coach masseuse anyway? My husband had an affair last year and it ripped my heart out. Then I let those idiots at yoga get into my head about talking to Chuck being better than therapy. The word around the club was that Chuck McCracken would make you feel like a queen and all your problems would melt away. I guess I just wanted to see for myself."

Bree encouraged her to continue. "What did he say to you?"

She looked up at the rack of copper pans hanging over her head. "Oh, he said lovely things. Told me I was amazing. Inside of me lives a spark of greatness and I just need to let it free. I was made for more and I have to go after it. He said he knew my value and my potential and that I could have my best life now."

Charisse snorted. "Those are quotes from Joel Osteen the televangelist."

I took a long drink of my fancy water. I hadn't had one of these in ages. "Did he tell you opportunity was knocking, and you should answer it?"

Janice smashed another gingersnap with her mallet. "He sure did. And then he suggested I get in on the ground floor of his life coaching massage franchise with an investment of ten thousand dollars."

Scarlett snorted. "Oh, it's a franchise now?"

Janice gave her a wry grin. "He even offered to make me the beneficiary on his life insurance for collateral."

Oh no. The life insurance.

Charisse prodded her. "Well? Was it a good massage at least?"

She half shrugged and whacked another gingersnap. "If I had never been to a spa for a real massage and he was Hugh Jackman I would say yes without hesitation. As neither of those things is true, there are certain aspects of the event that will haunt me for the rest of my life."

Bree picked some gingersnap fragments off her sweater. "Wow. That is not a glowing review."

Janice looked up thoughtfully. "You know, even though he told me my hair color looked natural, and the wrinkles around my eyes only made me look sexy, I don't believe Chuck was a trained life coach."

It took everything in me not to roll my eyes. "You don't say."

Scarlett gave me some side-eye and popped a gingersnap half

into her mouth with a grin. "After that night, did Chuck try to blackmail you?"

Janice pulled a tissue from her pocket and blew her nose. "No. But he died the next day. There wasn't time for extortion. But someone *was* in my backyard while Chuck was here. I thought it might have been one of you the way you barged in here."

Bree placed a gingersnap that had gone rogue back on the cutting board. "Why do you think you were being watched?"

"We were up in my sitting room where Chuck had set up his massage table. Someone set off my pool lights. They're motion activated. My husband was away on business and Trilbee and his sister were at their mother's, so I knew it wasn't either of them. Chuck went to check on it for me, but he didn't see anyone out there, so I let it go. We got into the coaching session, and I told him all the things that were bothering me. How my husband doesn't compliment me anymore. How the kids take advantage of me. How Heidi Lucas keeps taking my spot in the yoga room. He listened very attentively, it was all very professional, but I still had this unsettled feeling like I was being watched.

"A little while later when I was on the massage table and he was talking me through a breathing exercise to let go of my stress, I swore I heard a metal thunk under my window. Then the pool lights went on again. I was so rattled that I couldn't finish the session. Chuck stayed for a couple hours just to make sure I was okay. The next morning, he came early for Trilbee's party, and he broached the subject of investing again. But in the harsh light of day, it was so obvious that he was a con artist full of flattering words, telling me what he thought I wanted to hear so he could get something out of me. I called Kelly and found out he had told her all the exact same things and I know that was a lie. That color doesn't even exist in nature. I was so embarrassed. I told him to finish the birthday party and leave. I wasn't going to invest, and I never wanted him to talk to me again. Then I loaded up on the cocktails and kept someone with me at all times so I wouldn't be alone with him. I didn't know he was going to die." She sniffled and pulled another Kleenex from her pocket.

Bree went to her and gave her a hug. "It's okay."

Janice nodded and her lips trembled. She picked up the mallet and smashed another gingersnap.

Charisse looked out the back door. "Where was Chuck's van parked when he was here?"

She stuck her thumb out. "Same place you're parked. Right there at the back of the driveway. I had him pull all the way up to the house because I didn't want the neighbors to see that hideous van."

I looked out her back door with Charisse and took in the yard. "So, you and Tina both heard someone outside when you had your coaching sessions?"

Janice nodded. "Tina saw a flash. She thought someone took a picture of them together."

"Can I see where the table was set up?"

"Sure. The sitting room is at the top of the stairs on the right."

Scarlett and I passed a look that said we were in this together. We took the stairs and walked around Janice's massive master bedroom, an apartment in itself. She put her hands on her hips and considered the row of floor-to-ceiling windows. "It can't be a coincidence that they both heard someone outside. Maybe someone was following Chuckles."

"Yeah. And I don't think Janice had time to sneak off and plant the inserts herself considering she would have been wrapped in a sheet."

"But someone watching them would have had about two hours."

I moved to the bank of windows and peered outside. It would be hard to see anything from the ground, but I had a prime view into the tree house. "If her curtains were open, I bet you could see Zen Master Chuck's entire therapy session from there."

Scarlett gave me a look. "Let's go check it out."

We ran down the stairs and through the kitchen. Janice was telling Charisse all about her newfound love for the cathartic therapy of smashing things. "We'll be right back." The lights around the pool came on as soon as we were outside. We kicked off our heels and ran to the tree house and climbed the ladder.

"Oh yeah. You've got a prime view into Janice's bedroom." I took out my phone and snapped a couple of pictures to give to Castinetto.

"Uh, Layla?"

"Yeah?"

"Look."

Scarlett was pointing at a nail sticking out of the ledge. An infinity scarf patterned in the Serenity Prayer was flapping in the night breeze.

"Ooooh no."

Chapter 41

I PULLED THE ASTON MARTIN INTO THE LAKE PINECREST MOBILE Home Park where I was stopped by a Potomac County policeman. We'd come here to regroup and plan our next step. Clearly, things had escalated while I'd been gone. "What is the nature of your business here today, ma'am?"

"I live here. Layla Virtue. Number one twelve. The minivan behind is with me."

He stepped away and spoke all this into his shoulder walkie. When he stepped back, he waved us forward. "Have a nice evening, ma'am."

I turned by one of Ronnie Voa's men parked at the end of my street and gave them a salute. Then pulled into the carport. I had Bree park behind me.

She emerged from the van and looked around. "No offense, Layla, but isn't that like, a lot of security for this neighborhood?"

"There was an incident. Last night—at Dooley's. Dad surprise-joined me at my open mic set and may have caused a riot."

They stood there, grilling me in silence on my front porch.

Scarlett reached out and poked me on the arm. "I can't believe you went to Dooley's without us."

"Ow! I'm sorry. Did you hear what I said about the riot! Don Virtue is all over the local news now." I waved my hand toward my trailer.

She *tsk*'d. "Next time call."

I tried to act like I was perturbed but I smiled to myself as I gently knocked on the front door. "Dad? Are you decent?"

"Why? If Jack Black's found me again, tell him, no. I still do not want to jam."

"I brought some friends home to meet you."

There was a moment of silence where I thought Dad might have fallen asleep, but the door flew open and he stood there with his hair flowing wildly around his head, his tight black jeans and his tattoos screaming rock star. "You never want me to meet your friends."

Charisse squeaked like a loud little mouse and Bree was trying to show every tooth in her mouth at once. Scarlett threw her hand out to Dad and said, "Nice to meet you, Mr. Virtue."

"Hey, did we do that Jackie Chan movie together?"

"Dad! Noooo."

Scarlett shook his hand casually. "Yes. Yes, we did. Jackie says hello."

I ushered them inside while giving Dad some strong side-eye for which he shrugged and mouthed. "What'd I say?"

After showing them around for the full thirty seconds house tour, I made some popcorn while Charisse fangirled over Dad, and Bree tried to decide if she should fangirl over Dad, having had no idea before tonight who he actually was. Scarlett came into the kitchen to help me with the sodas.

"Hey. Your dad's really nice."

"Thanks. You'll get used to his spaciness. I'm sure he'll ask you another old man racist question before you leave. Or the exact same one again."

Scarlett grinned. "Where's your mom?"

"Hopefully at her house in Malibu. Possibly in one of Southern California's finer rehab establishments. I think her next stay is free."

She nodded sympathetically. "Do you get to see her often?"

"Depends on which step she's on. She comes around a lot when she's making amends, but then she remembers I'm the reason her life went to crap, and I don't hear from her for a while."

"So, she and your dad are no longer together?"

"Not for a long time. Why? You want to be my new step-mother?"

"I don't have the time, what with Jackie's and my busy filming schedule. Charisse might be up for the job."

I looked over at Charisse and chuckled. Thirty years had dropped off her face as she gushed over my father like a teenager. I had all kinds of warning tingles, but I tried to tell them we'd wait and see. I was trying something new. Charisse wasn't a flighty sixteen-year-old. Maybe this time it would be okay.

The microwave dinged and we took the popcorn and drinks to the other room and scrunched around the coffee table.

Dad reached for a Dr. Pepper. "Boy, if I had a dollar for every time a group of gorgeous women sat here in my tour bus."

Bree looked confused, like she thought she'd missed something, but Charisse and Scarlett both giggled.

Dad pointed toward my bedroom. "Layla was born back there on the Kentucky/Tennessee state line."

The girls all laughed and looked at me.

I flipped some popcorn into my mouth and nodded. "Different bus. True story."

Bree twirled her hair around her finger. "What? How?"

"Society's Castoffs were on a schedule. My mom didn't want to leave the tour early, and apparently I wanted to see the next show."

"Which one was she again, baby girl?"

"Yellow bikini in Akron."

"Right."

Bree gasped. "You forgot your wife?"

I snickered. "He gets a little fuzzy on the details of their first meeting because Mom was with a group of girls who showed up half-naked and flashed the band to get on the tour bus."

Dad grinned. "It happens in every city."

We talked for an hour about my life growing up with Don Virtue—only the highlights. I'd keep the harsh details for another day. My dad had done the best he could, given his career and a wife who couldn't get past the summer of love. I determined right there that I would stop blaming him for the way other people treated me.

I would blame them.

We eventually turned the conversation to our problem with Miranda—the main reason we came here in the first place.

Dad was surprisingly invested considering he thought he'd dreamed up the clown murder after watching a rerun of *Brooklyn Nine-Nine.* "Dude. Someone killed a birthday party clown at the party. That's epic."

Scarlett started in with the theories. "I figure Miranda probably saw Chuck with Janice, jumped to conclusions, and killed Chuck in a jealous rage."

Bree shrugged. "Then why not kill Janice?"

Charisse bobbed her head. "Was it jealousy? Or did she kill him because she thought she'd get the life insurance? She's constantly talking about how much alimony he owed her. Did we ever find out where she lands in the marital lines of succession?"

I reached for my grape soda. "Paula was the first, and we know Kelly came after Miranda because Chuck gave her engagement ring to the dog groomer."

Bree twirled her hair around her finger. "Then Tina has to be last. She said they've only been divorced for three years."

Charisse snapped her fingers. "So, Miranda would have assumed Tina would inherit the life insurance."

"Possibly," I said. "But Chuck told each of the ladies who invested that he'd make them the beneficiary of his life insurance for collateral. He could have told Miranda the same thing. And Janice didn't give him any money, which means we're still missing ten thousand dollars."

Scarlett took off her Louboutins and tucked her feet underneath her. "What I can't figure out is how did Miranda know where Chuck would be the night before the party to plant the inserts?"

I leaned my head back onto Dad's arm. "She had to be following him. You heard her in that meeting. She said she always thought they'd get back together one day. Chuck was advertising his life coaching business to all the ladies. And he was hitting up his ex-wives to borrow start-up funds. If Chuck offered Miranda a preview like he did the others, she would have figured out they were all hearing those lovely words from Zen Master Chuck."

I heard Bree whisper to herself, "Eww."

Dad got into the surmising. "Maybe she staked out his van. Didn't you say his picture was on it? That was how those Japanese tourists were able to follow Taylor all over Miami."

"That's a good point, Dad."

"What is?"

"About Chuck's van."

"Who's Chuck?"

"The victim. The clown that died at the birthday party."

Dad looked horrified. "When did that happen?!"

I stared at him for a minute to see if he was punking me. "A week ago. We've been talking about it for an hour."

"That's what we've been talking about? I thought that was a dream I had."

I shook my head to clear it. "I think Miranda followed Chuck to Tina's house and snapped when she saw them together. Maybe she saw Tina kiss Chuck, maybe she saw her give him money—I don't know——but I think that's when she came up with her plan to kill him. She just had to wait for his next party."

Charisse added, "Which he put on Facebook."

"What about the blackmail?" Scarlett asked. "What was Miranda doing taking pictures?"

"I'm not sure there ever was extortion. I think these women imagined that threat between fear of being exposed, and the eerie knowledge that someone had been watching them."

Dad played with the row of silver rings on his fingers. "This is so crazy. Musicians are lovers, not killers, man. There's a reason it's not called *drugs*, *murder*, and rock 'n' roll. What are you gonna do about it, baby girl?"

"I can't do anything. I don't have a gun or a badge anymore."

Bree twirled her fingers through her hair. "Then we just have to get Miranda to confess."

Chapter 42

"HI. MY NAME'S LAYLA, AND I'M AN ALCOHOLIC. UP UNTIL seven months ago I was also a cop. I can see on some of your faces that you're freaked out right now. I know you don't like cops. And you've heard me say that I don't like cops and that I'm triggered to run when I see them. That's all true. And the cops I've worked with don't like me very much either. It's because the last thing I did as a cop, before I hit rock bottom, was run an operation that got my entire team killed."

My voice started to break, and I had to stop talking to settle down. It was hard to hear myself think over the pounding in my ears. I looked across the room and locked onto my three girls sitting next to Dad in disguise. He wanted to come today, and I was done trying to hide him from my little world.

Well, partly. I still made him wear Agnes's leopard print tunic and black leggings, and Scarlett brought him a Dolly Parton wig, so he was over the moon with his choices. They gave me a reassuring wave and I took a breath and soldiered on.

"I led a team in the undercover Narcotics Unit, and we were supposed to take down a local drug ring we'd been working on for months. The day of the operation is a total blur to me. I woke up in the hospital with a guard detail. I'd been brought in with secondary injuries from an explosion. My blood alcohol level was two point one three."

Murmurs of understanding and shock registered around the room. Dad gave me a grin and a thumbs-up.

"I have very little memory of the day past showing up at the Gibson. I don't know why I was at a bar when my team was across town waiting for me. I don't know why I was drinking on duty or how I got to Stratton Park. And I don't know what went so wrong that my partner took the team in prematurely or what they were trying to tell me. But I've been getting vague, hazy flashes of seeing them die. For the intoxication and dereliction of duty, I was suspended pending a formal investigation. I left the force in shame and spiraled—until I came here and admitted that I had a problem and couldn't handle it on my own. I thought just being in the room was enough, but I can see now that to really be successful in the program you have to embrace the community."

I glanced at the girls again. Scarlett grinned. She nudged Bree, who silently clapped her hands while Charisse gave me a huge smile.

"I'm very thankful for the friendships that I've made here, and for those of you who've accepted me for who I really am." I paused to steady myself. "I'm sorry I pushed you away at first, but I'm so glad you didn't give up on me. It's only because of your support that I'm seven months sober today."

The girls and Dad applauded as Miranda presented me with my seven-month sobriety chip. I took my seat and Scarlett whispered, "Are we on?"

"Yep. She's ready to go when we are."

After the meeting, we drove over to Sundrop Roasters. The place was deserted except for those who were working behind the bar, and a couple girls sitting by the door studying for exams. We got our usual seats around the surfboard table. *Aunt Trixie* and I sat on the couch next to Scarlett. Bree and Charisse took the chairs on either end. We brought over a third chair and put it in the middle of them facing the couch. Nancy Sinatra was playing very quietly in the background. Once we'd gotten into position, we waited.

The front door jingled, and Miranda breezed in. She spun around taking in the surroundings. She gave us a smug look like a mom who thinks she's read your diary instead of the decoy you keep in your nightstand. "Oooh, so this is your super-secret place where you all come after the meeting? It's not what I expected, but it's quaint. Have you ordered yet?"

Bree gave her a smile. "No, we waited for you. What'll you have?"

She didn't go check out the menu, but instead pointed to an old poster on the wall from the summer specials. "Hmm. How about a grapefruit soda? That sounds yummy."

Bree went to get our drinks and Miranda eyed Dad distastefully. She smiled broadly at Scarlett then nodded to me. "This is nice. So, this is your aunt?"

Dad grunted, "Hm?"

I nudged him. "Yep. This is my aunt Trixie."

Dad shot his hand out. "Hellooo."

"She came to see me get my chip."

Miranda gave Dad a saccharine grin and limply grasped his hand. "I see. It's nice that you have family to surround you." Then she launched into a repeat performance of her share at AA. "I'm all alone. I've been so stressed waiting for my late husband's life insurance to come through. I need to pay my landlord."

"I understand," I said. "I owe lot fees to my park management and they're looking for any reason to kick me out."

Miranda nodded. "I'm having so much trouble letting Chuck go. I always thought we were soulmates. I'm telling you, that man was harder to quit than cocaine."

Scarlett hummed. "It's not often you hear about a good relationship between divorced people. What was your secret?"

"Well"—Miranda blushed—"in our case I would say it was due to the fact that Chuck never really got over me."

Bree returned with the barista who set the cardboard tray of drinks on the table. "Oh really?" She handed me a purple ube latte. I grimaced at her and took a tentative sip.

It was easy to get Miranda to talk. She'd been dying all week to gain anyone's sympathy, using AA as her personal group therapy. I could see now that she was terribly lonely.

Miranda daintily crossed her legs. "A few weeks before he passed, Chuck and I had a long talk over lunch where he said he wanted us to get back together. He said he couldn't live without me, and he wanted me back no matter what it took. He would even go to meetings with me—just not on Friday or Saturday or when he had to work."

Charisse gave a single nod. "Uh-huh. Is that also when he asked to borrow money to get his new business off the ground?"

Miranda reached for her neck. "How do you know about that?"

Bree took her seat and picked up her latte. "Well, Chuck tried to borrow money from all his ex-wives and Janice, so we figured he worked his way around to you."

I took the Ziploc bag with the serenity scarf out of my boho tote bag that Dad used as part of his Aunt Trixie getup and slid it across the table to the AA leader. "Looking for this? We found it in the tree house at Janice's. Did you know you can see right into her sitting room from that spot? You could probably see Chuck give your friend her massage."

Her lips went tight and thin. "How did you get that?"

"Climbed the tree house ladder."

Her hands shook and she looked around the room. "I really don't think I should be talking about this."

Scarlett gave her a nudge. "It's just us girls."

Charisse pulled out a compact mirror to look at herself and patted at her braids. She kept her voice light and breezy. "I know I feel like I lost a hundred pounds since I told the girls about my husband leaving me for another woman—who turns out to be the return shoe deodorizer at the bowling alley."

We made a big deal over Charisse by pouring on our shock and sympathy over the newest development to her divorce—which was a ploy to get Miranda to talk but also totally sincere.

Miranda eyed Charisse, distrust playing across her brow. She chewed on her lip and looked at me.

"I know I feel much freer after my share this afternoon. It was hard, having to keep my job as a cop hidden from the group. My addiction begins and ends with secrets. If I want to be free and move on with my life, I need to start bringing things out in the light."

Miranda's lip trembled. "You don't know what I've been through. Chuck said he needed a little help to change careers because clowning was a dying art form. He told me he wanted ten thousand dollars to invest in a mobile smoothie bar—not a table where he could rub other women's naked bodies. I emptied my life savings for him. And I checked his van. There is no smoothie bar. You know what I found? A bunch of racing forms."

I nudged the scarf to remind her it was there. "So, you knew he blew your investment money at the track."

Miranda stared at the bag on the table. "He promised he was done with gambling. He said we were getting back together. I trusted him, and he made a fool out of me. Just like when we were married."

Charisse crossed her leg and jiggled her foot. "I know I wouldn't put up with that if my man tried it. Uh-uhh."

Miranda's hands shook. "I didn't! I told him I wouldn't give him another penny unless he was finished with the track for good. He promised me it was over. But I had to know for sure."

Scarlett nodded. "Yeah, but how could you find something like that out?"

"I followed him. I knew Chuck was living in his van parked at the Food Lion, so I waited at the Dunkin' Donuts until I saw him emerge in full clown minus the shoes and the red nose." She turned to Bree to explain since she must have looked like she'd need an explanation. "He can't drive in the shoes, and he adds the nose right before showtime. Anyway, I thought he was heading to the racetrack, but he went to Tina's the night before her stepson's birthday party. I watched him take the massage table inside and I said to myself—bless God, there had better be a smoothie station coming next. When the lights went on in the basement, I lay down on my stomach and watched through the little easement windows—you know the ones . . ."

We all nodded along to encourage her.

"Sure. Sure."

"Naturally."

"Eww. What did you see?"

Miranda grew quiet. "I. Saw. Everything. There were no smoothies! It was just Chuck rubbing Tina's back and telling her she was always the prettiest of his wives. And he kissed her! I took a couple pictures in case I'd need proof later."

Dad lost the Aunt Trixie voice momentarily. "That's totally creepy."

Miranda shook her head sadly. "I just. I don't know. I was so broken. Why would he do that to me? How could he betray me? He'd already left me once before for the dog groomer. Now he was doing it all over again. Am I supposed to just sit back and let that happen?"

Charisse asked, "But why, girl? Why Chuckles? Like did he give you drugs or something?"

Miranda shook her head. "Chuck *was* the drug. He made you feel some kind of way. Like you were the most glamorous woman alive and not some middle-aged, divorced alcoholic. I knew I couldn't live with what he'd done to me."

Scarlett gave her a little nudge. "He needed to be taught a lesson."

Miranda nodded, serious as an Adele song. "Exactly."

Bree twisted her hair around her finger. "Is that when you came up with the plan to poison his shoes?"

"I could never." Miranda looked at the scarf. She shook her head no and her lips rolled in.

I *tsk*'d. "It was a brilliant plan. The cops don't know where to turn."

Her cheeks glowed with excitement. "It was quite genius actually. There's a quit smoking support group that meets at the church on the nights that we're not there, and they have a stockpile of free nicotine patches from the clinic. I took every last one. Then I watched Chuck's Facebook page to see where he'd be next. When I saw Janice was having a birthday party, I knew she'd book one of those stupid life coach massages. She'd been titillated by talk about Chuck at the club for weeks."

Dad giggled. "Oooh. Titillated."

"I didn't even have to follow that stupid fool this time. I just waited in Janice's pool house until his van—that I paid for, by the way—came rolling up the driveway. It was just a matter of time. I almost lost my nerve when I couldn't see anything through the kitchen windows, but when the light came on upstairs, I climbed the ladder into that tree house, and I saw him setting up the massage table. I just don't know what came over me. I was so angry. I'm better than Janice in every way. Why does she get the fancy house and the pool and now my money?"

Bree whispered, "I thought she was gonna say *husband*."

Dad muttered back, "And I'm the crazy one?"

Miranda wasn't listening anymore. Reason had left her, and she didn't have the scarf to pet to calm her down. "I knew I had about an hour to work with, so I climbed out of the tree house and went to Chuck's van. Struggling with all my anger, hurt, and his betrayal, I took his clown shoes out of his go bag and glued the new nicotine inserts in those giant idiot shoes, ripping the adhesive covers off. I knew he'd be putting them on in a few hours for that stupid birthday party. Well . . . he'd get his. And that greasy loan shark who's always hanging around Chuck's events with his hand out for my money would take the blame for it."

"Miranda"—I leaned in—"why would you send me to the birthday party if you knew you had set a plan in motion to kill

Chuck? You knew he would put on the shoes and die before the party was over and I'd be stuck there."

Miranda's smile showed her canine teeth and a little bit of insanity. "You're my alibi. Reena told me you used to be a cop when you joined the program. You'd be able to tell all your cop friends that I was nowhere near Chuck when he took his final bow. And I can finally get my life insurance payout."

She leaned back in her chair and raised her arms. "Whoo!" She picked up her grapefruit soda and laughed. "I've been wanting to talk about this all week but we all know Varish has loose lips."

I admit that I'd heard a lot of confessions in my time. I'd heard even more denials that were bold-faced lies. But I'd never heard a confession that left me with more questions than answers before today. "You're gonna want to buckle up for the news on the life insurance, baby."

The blood drained from Miranda's face. "Why?"

"I think that's something for your lawyer to fill you in on."

"Lawyer? Why do I need a lawyer? I got away with it. You can't tell anyone. What happens in AA stays in AA, right?"

Scarlett rolled her eyes. "We're not in AA, you psycho. We're at a coffeehouse. The only thing sacred here is the No James Patterson rule."

Miranda's grin melted into unsurety. She looked at each of us in turn then looked around the silent room. "What have you done to me?" She reached for the scarf in the bag, but Bree snatched it back.

Miranda bolted from her seat for the door, but the two college girls dropped their books and flashed their badges. "It's over, Miranda. You're under arrest."

Miranda started to hyperventilate. "I didn't kill him. The nicotine did."

Dayton Castinetto emerged from behind the bookshelf and slapped his cuffs on her. He told the barista, Adam Beasley, to read her her Miranda rights.

Dad turned to me. "Are they always called Miranda rights or is it just because her name is Miranda?"

I hugged him. "It's always Miranda rights, Aunt Trixie."

Scarlett and Bree were all aglow over their coffee shop sting to take Miranda down. I remembered my first operation on the force and how I was flying high with excitement over justice being served. *Enjoy it now, girls. In the real world it fades with your next call.* I'd only gotten caught up in this case because I enjoyed hanging around with them. But you'll never catch me telling them that. Scarlett was already smug enough.

The two cops at the front led Miranda out to the waiting cruiser while I removed my wire and handed it to Castinetto. "I hope it was clear."

He wrapped the wire around the battery pack. "I heard every word. You know, all of you will be called in to testify if she denies anything. I suspect a psych eval will happen first."

I nodded and passed him the scarf. "Smart move not putting it in an official evidence bag. I think she would have figured out you were onto her if she'd seen 'Property of Potomac County Police.' "

Dayton's nostrils flared. "This isn't my first undercover operation, Virtue. I only brought you in because the suspect trusted you. You've always had good instincts—about *most* people. I may not be in your fancy Narcotics Unit, but I'm a good officer and I know what I'm doing."

I sighed. "Of course you do, Castinetto. Why do you think I called you from the crime scene instead of calling station dispatch?"

I started to walk away, but he called me back. "Virtue."

"What?"

He nodded toward the door. "So that was your AA leader?"

"Yep."

He considered me for a long moment. "How long you been in AA?"

"Seven months."

His eyebrows shot up. "Since Stratton Park?"

"That's right."

He nodded. "And the beer?"

"Gave it to the neighbor."

He stared at me for a minute. Then his gaze shifted to the three mama bears and the papa bear in drag behind me. "I'm impressed." He shifted his eyes to my entourage again and swallowed. "Just so you know, this was a one-time thing."

"I know."

"Keep working on yourself and let us do our job."

"Of course."

"It will take more than this to earn our trust again and then we'll see."

"You'll see what? What are you talking about, Castinetto?"

"I just don't want to see you get your hopes up, okay."

His face grew pink, and Adam Beasley appeared at his side. "You were amazing, Layla. And your friends did a great job too. I hope we stay in touch. And I really want to meet your father. Don't forget about that autograph."

Dad started to speak, but Scarlett put her hand on his arm. "Shh."

Castinetto glared at the rookie. "Why aren't you at the car?"

"Ryan and McCann have it under control."

"Get out there." Castinetto cast me one more glance. "Catch you later, Virtue."

They left, and the girls and Dad congratulated each other for how well they'd held it together.

Dad nudged me and lowered his voice. "Can we drink the coffee while we're at commercial?"

I smiled. "Yep. I'll let you know when you're back on camera."

I wanted to ask Dad what TV show he thought we were on, but the Sundrop staff were brought back out to reopen the coffee shop, and they distracted him when they started the latest release of Mammoth WVH. "Ooh, I love Wolfie. Maybe we can have him over for dinner."

"Yeah, Dad. Anytime you want." I picked up my ube latte and took another sip.

Charisse joined me on the couch and nodded to the cup in my hand. "Well, what do you think?"

I looked at the purple space juice and grinned. "It's growing on me."

Chapter 43

SOMEWHERE IN BERLIN, OPERATION DOPPELGÄNGER WAS IN FULL swing, and Don Virtue was signing autographs. Things had quieted down at home since there was no chance of running into him in the trailer park. Ronnie Voa had even started several threads under different names throughout the various social media platforms saying it wasn't really Don Virtue who played at Dooley's. That was just an impersonator hired by the pub manager. I was glad to see his team pull out, but we put them on retainer just in case.

Dad and I were in the secret laundry room that Clifford didn't know was in operation at the back side of the lake. We'd just washed and dried all the outfits we'd borrowed over the past week and were preparing to return them to their rightful owners. I caught Dad slipping a hundred-dollar bill into a pocket of each set. "Do you feel better now?"

Dad grinned. "Yeah. What would make me really happy would be if we could go sit by the lake for a while and talk."

"We can do that." We drove around the neighborhood returning Dad's costumes to the various spots where we had snatched them and parked back at the trailer. I grabbed us a couple sodas, and we went across the street and through the woods. It was a warm day and the sun felt delicious on my face as I dropped into an Adirondack chair. Dad settled into the one next to me.

"I still think you should get a medal or your picture in the paper for helping the police, baby girl. You're a hero."

I snickered. "There are heroes no one ever hears about every day, Dad. People who do the right thing without being seen. People who save lives or give to those in need and don't humble brag about it online. Thousands serve their community or their country and pay a price and no one ever knows."

My mind went to Nick. It had been days since I'd seen him and Ringo. I was sad, but I refused to wallow. If he didn't want to be in my life anymore, I got it. I'm not responsible for anyone's choices but my own.

The girls helped me accept that. I didn't set off the bomb that killed my team. I didn't fire the guns. I let them down, yes. But Jacob is the only one responsible for moving the operation forward before backup arrived. I'm not responsible for his death, and I can't take that burden on myself as if I am. I will always love him, and that's the burden I'll carry.

I tipped my face up to the sky and breathed in the crisp autumn air that was scented with dry leaves and apples, and the sage and smoke from Dad's cologne. I hadn't felt this relaxed in years. "I think I could fall asleep right here."

Dad sighed so loudly, I cracked one eye open and looked at him. "Something wrong there, Don?"

He stayed silent.

I pushed myself up in the chair and turned to face him. "What's going on?"

Dad looked at me, bit his lip, and looked away. "You know I leave in a couple of days."

"Yeah. You have to join the rest of the group on tour."

He shook his head, his eyes downcast and pitiful. He reached down and flicked a fallen leaf off his knee. "Tour's over for me, baby girl."

"Why? What happened? I knew you and Simon were fighting again. What does he want this time? A revolving drum platform? A longer solo?"

Dad let out a shaky breath. "I have dementia."

The air was sucked out of my lungs, and for a moment I thought I could see stars. "Oh Dad. You said the doctor gave you those pills for generic memory issues. That it was routine."

"That wasn't entirely true. And I have to throw away all the hocus-pocus pills and get a real prescription when I get home." Dad frowned. "I didn't want to worry you when you seemed to be so sad to begin with. I've wanted to tell you the whole time. It could be Alzheimer's, they don't know. Apparently, they can't diagnose that until I'm dead, which sounds like a load of crap telling someone you have a disease that will kill you and we'll let you know for sure after it does."

I felt like a large pair of invisible hands had circled my heart and were squeezing.

He gave me a sad hint of a smile. "I don't know how long I have, but I wanted to tell you before . . ." He laughed, bitterly. "The eighties were wrong. Partying didn't kill me after all."

I reached out and took his hand and let him talk.

"You know my memory is like Swiss cheese anyway. It's why I call all the gals things like *sugar* and *doll.* It keeps me outta trouble for saying the wrong name." He breathed out a bitter chuckle then his eyes misted over. "It's all gonna go away. The memories I'm the most afraid to lose are the ones with you. Teaching you how to play guitar. Riffing with you in the garage. Playing for you to sing in your high school musical. I know you think you only got the lead in the school play because they wanted me to do the music. But I asked to do the music so I could spend time with you. You were growing up so fast and I missed most of your life while I was on the road. I just hate that all of that is going to slip through my fingers."

"Dad?" I bit the inside of my lip to keep from crying.

"Yeah?"

"Stay with me. You don't have to go home."

"For how long?"

A fat tear rolled down my cheeks. "Forever."

"I would like that."

"Me too."

"We'll need a bigger trailer."

"Definitely."

"And room for the dog."

"It's not my dog, Dad."

"Are you sure? Because I think it is."

"I'm telling you, he lives next door."

"That's no way to treat your husband. They should come with us."

I laughed. "Nick isn't my husband, Dad."

"I think he wants to be."

"We aren't even talking right now."

"You can work that out." Dad started to sing. "Harsh words get spoken. Promises get broken. Old wounds tear open. And love goes out the door."

"Are you trying to sing Grayson Hugh to me?"

"Am I?"

"That's *almost* the words to 'Talk It Over.'"

"How about that."

Someone was crunching through the leaves heading our way. It was Agnes. She was wearing hot pink velour track pants and a leopard print top. A wide pink elastic belt circled her waist. "Hello-o. I tried your trailer, Layla, but you're not home."

I wiped at my cheek. "Yes, I'm aware of that."

Agnes held an envelope out to Dad. "Everything's been notarized."

He took it and glanced at me, trying to judge my mood. It was a tell that started when I was in junior high.

"What's that?"

"We can move into that big house across the lake. The one I showed you on the other side of the park."

"You bought the owner's cottage?"

Dad handed me the envelope. "I bought the park."

Agnes chuckled. "Close your mouth, Layla. You'll catch a fly."

I opened the envelope and pulled out a set of keys and the deed for Lake Pinecrest Mobile Homes. The owners were listed as Don and Layla Virtue.

Dad shrugged. "You said you liked it here."

Agnes put her hand on Dad's shoulder. "I would personally rather live in the mansion in the Hollywood Hills, but then I have good taste."

"Do you know who he is?"

Agnes laughed. "Please. You don't think I recognized Don Virtue from the first moment I laid eyes on him. I followed Society's Castoffs across the country on the Go for Broke tour back in seventy-nine."

"Does everyone know?"

She chuckled. "Nah."

"If you knew who he was, then why have you been calling him Corbin?"

Agnes grinned. "Because it pissed you off." She patted Dad's shoulder. "Don't forget, Don. Book Club at Myrtle Jean's house, seven o'clock. I signed you up to bring your famous corn bread." She gave a little wave and walked back through the woods.

I chuckled to myself. *She's known the entire time who Dad is, and she never let it change the way she treated me. She treats me like crap, but it's the same crap from before so it's almost a compliment.*

I stood and stretched. "Why don't we go home, and you can get Jimmy to send your things over so you're comfortable."

"Yeah? Sweet! Hey, baby girl. Do you know how to make corn bread?"

"Not even a little."

"Do I know how to make corn bread?"

"I don't see how."

We walked through the woods and past Donna's trailer. Ringo was waiting for us on the front step.

"See!" Dad pointed at him. "There's our dog. I told you we had one."

I hugged the Lab and my breath caught in my chest. In my defense, it had been a really sucky few days. "Why don't you go inside while I take this guy home real quick." I was looking for an excuse to talk to Nick. If he was leaving because of me, maybe the news that I'd be relocating across the lake would convince him to stay.

Ringo followed me across the grass to Nick's trailer. I had knots in my stomach. How did I go from fearlessly busting up drug rings to being nervous over a confrontation with my next-door neighbor? My conscience whispered the answer. *It's because you like Nick.* I knocked on the door and he opened it with a smile.

The words *I've got your dog* were on the tip of my tongue, but what came spilling out was, "I'm a hot mess. I've tried to burn it all to the ground several times just in the last week. I have no business being in a relationship, but if I did, I would want it to be with you. I don't want to lose your friendship over this, but if that's the way it has to be I'll understand. Please don't move away and take Ringo." My lungs felt like they were full of butterflies trying to escape while I waited for Nick to answer.

Nick's eyes widened in surprise. He blinked at me a couple times.

Ringo pushed his snout into my palm.

Nick stepped out to the front porch and looked into my eyes like he was searching for sincerity. "I like you too. And I get why it's not a good time for us to be together. It's obvious that you're as broken as I am. When I look at you, I see the same haunted look I see staring back at me every day in the mirror."

A few of the butterflies took off and I could breathe again.

Nick gave me a gentle smile. "But where is this 'I want us to be friends but if not' stuff coming from? Of course, I want us to stay friends. Why wouldn't I?"

I ran my hands over Ringo's fur and felt calm settling around my shoulders. "You kicked me out the other day and you've been avoiding me ever since."

Nick reached for my free hand. "No. No, no, no. I said you should leave because I didn't want you to see me upset. I was hurt and angry with myself for letting things go too far too soon. I don't want to mess things up with us and I did it anyway. You said you were a one-night stand kinda girl, but I'm not a one-night stand kinda guy. I'm looking for something more and I almost let my attraction to you ruin what could be."

A bubble of relief exploded inside me. "So, you're not leaving?"

Nick dropped my hand and pulled me into a hug. "No. And I've been out of town getting some special training."

"I was worried that you hated me."

He pulled back and chuckled, giving me a look that said he thought I was being ridiculous. "Never. But I want us to be real friends. Nothing superficial. I expect you to get me through next month's community meeting and whatever nightmare this Halloween Pumpkin Spice Palooza is that Agnes put on my door today." He reached into his back pocket and pulled out an orange flyer.

I laughed. "I'd like that. I have a lot to tell you."

He folded the flyer up and frowned. Then he let out a sigh. "There is something I need to tell you too. I should have told you when we first met. Now it seems like I was hiding it or something."

"Uh-oh. What is it?"

"The training we went for wasn't for me, it was for Ringo. I train PTSD dogs for vets. That's why I don't name them. Because I don't get to keep them. This guy is a natural with sensing pain and bringing comfort. He graduated yesterday."

Ringo yapped and fanned his tail back and forth.

The shawl of peace rose off my shoulders and flew away with the butterflies. *Ringo was leaving. Man, today really sucks.* My heart had been broken too many times to fall apart now. It was held together by scars and the will to live, but this news carved another little piece of it away. I wondered if Nick could pick up on the tremor in my voice. "So, when does he go to his new assignment?"

Nick reached into the house and pulled out the leash and an orange service vest. He handed them to me. "As soon as you take him home. He wants to be with you. He knows you're hurting. That's why I can't get him to leave you alone."

Nick watched me for a moment then laughed. "Don't just

stand there with tears in your eyes. He chose you. Take him home. I'll bring all his stuff over later."

I dropped to one knee and hugged the Lab's neck. *Of all the things that couldn't break me, this is the one I'm going to cry over.* I *do* need a therapy dog. I sniffled. "Come on, buddy. You're with me now."

Ringo licked my face.

I ran home and threw the door open. "Dad! We got a dog!"

Dad jumped off the couch. "Sweet! He looks just like Ringo."

I snorted to myself. "He does, doesn't he?"

Scarlett, Bree, and Charisse were so determined to be my tribe, even though I came with a lot of baggage, including a smart mouth, a silly Lab who could sense emotions, and Don Virtue—aging rock star, now in the early stages of dementia. It was going to be one heck of a ride.

Well, ladies, buckle up.